# A Dead Man's Ice Cream

# A Dead Man's Ice Cream

Alfredo Herrero de Haro

**C & F Press**

A Dead Man's Ice Cream

# Acknowledgement of country

Part of this book has been written in Dharawal Country. I pay my respects and acknowledge the traditional custodians of Dharawal Country, the land on which I live and work. I also pay my respects to their elders, past, present and those emerging. Sovereignty has never been ceded.

# Acknowledgement

I would like to dedicate this novel to all my friends in Birmingham and to everyone I met during my time there, especially to the Friday Club crew; we had a great time. You all made me feel at home and contributed to a very special chapter in my life. It is in Birmingham where I came of age as an adult and I will never forget the city or its people.

After spending over three years in different parts of England, I spent six and a half years in Birmingham before relocating to Australia for work. Despite the negative connotations some have of the city, I really missed it and struggled with the transition to an Australian way of life. This novel has helped me through the process of distancing myself from the city. Writing it has been cathartic, as I closed this particular chapter in my life. It has been a very long goodbye that has taken me over nine years to write and almost two years to edit. I am particularly grateful to Brian Yecies, Kieran Tapsell, Kimberly Herrero de Haro, Klem James, Poonam Vidyarthi, Shaun Baines, and Looking Glass Editors for comments on earlier versions of the novel.

If you know me personally, remember that I am the same person you know and do not let this novel change the way you think of me. This novel is not a historical account of events, so don't feel cheated if dates or other details don't add up. Names of people and places, businesses, characters, and events are either made up or used in a fictitious manner. Any resemblance to actual people, events, or places is purely coincidental. The comments from the novel do not represent the views of those people on whom characters may have been modelled, nor do they represent my own personal views.

The novel has some controversial content which may cause offence. My advice is to not take it too seriously. I wrote the kind of novel I would have loved someone else to write for me to enjoy. I mixed a bit of symbolism, some experimentation with different literary techniques, some personal experiences, and a great deal of imagination, and this is what I got. There may be some objectionable characters in the book but I want to impress on all readers to be kind to those around you, especially those who are more vulnerable than you, through their own nature or the position they are in. Finally, to my readers: don't spend your whole life waiting. Do something.

Dr. A Herrero de Haro
Wollongong, NSW, Australia
20/04/2022

# Author's note

*A Dead Man's Ice Cream* has 18 chapters, each one written in a different literary style; as the reader, you will have to judge to what degree I succeeded in doing this. The schema at the beginning serves as a tool to navigate the novel. Below, I have provided some additional insights which will hopefully enrich your literary experience as you progress through the chapters.

Several puns appear throughout the book, particularly in the first chapter; these are marked in *italics*. If something looks like a typo and it's in italics, it most likely isn't a typo; if something looks like a typo and it's not in italics, it most likely *is* a typo.

Chapter 1 is written using very simple language. This is intentional.

Chapter 2 is heavily influenced by Lady Gregory's books *Cuchulain of Muirthemne* and *Gods and Fighting Men*. In those books, Lady Gregory uses a style she called *Kiltartanese*, which she described as English with Gaelic syntax, based on the dialect spoken in Kiltartan, Country Galway, Ireland. I have attempted to use this style in parts of the chapter, which might explain some of the (more) awkward sounding sentences and word order; there are also some sentences translated directly from Irish.

Chapter 3, Carl's email, would ordinarily contain more spelling mistakes and other traces of Carl's learning difficulties to better reflect his character. However, representations of Carl's personality and thoughts have been attenuated to make the chapter more accessible.

Chapter 4 is a play in three acts. Although it has a very different tone, this chapter has been influenced by *La casa de Bernarda Alba* (*The House of Bernarda Alba*) by Federico García Lorca. This is a play I wrote a reader's guide for and I have taught it to students most years since 2008. The formatting is not entirely as expected for a play in order to give the feel of a theatrical work without distracting the reader too much with a format they might not be used to.

Chapter 5 follows Charles' train of thoughts. I considered changing his choice of words in some instances (especially his more controversial musings), but I chose to leave them as they are to depict his personality more accurately. In this chapter, it is important to note the disconnect between what Charles says or does and what he actually thinks.

Chapter 7 is a collection of notes from Carl. That explains the draft notes and personal notes, which form the basis of the chapter.

Chapter 11 was originally written as a musical and it had parts of songs embedded in it. I was unable to secure permissions to use all the lyrics I originally had in the chapter, so these have been altered and replaced with fictional songs.

Chapter 12 is written in the style of a linguistic journal, although I have tried to include some explanations to make the content more accessible to non-linguists. Note that this chapter is printed in Times New Roman and it has different formatting to the rest of the novel to align with the style of a linguistic article.

Chapter 14 is written in a similar style to medical notes. There is an intentional use of figures for numbers, rather than writing numbers out.

Chapter 18 comprises a series of monologues. The illogical sentences and lack of punctuation in parts are intended to represent people's thoughts more accurately.

# *A Dead Man's Ice Cream* schema

| Ch. | Title | Scene | Time | No. | Organ |
|---|---|---|---|---|---|
| 1 | Welcome to the *Untied* Kingdom | Five Ways | August 2003 | 8 | - |
| 2 | Meet the genealogical stalker | The school | September 2003 | 10 | - |
| 3 | Mutual *understranding* | The canal | September 2003 | 11 | - |
| 4 | Friday Club diaries | The apartment | October 2003 | 8 | Kidney |
| 5 | The ass is always thinner on the other thigh | The bath | October 2003 | 10 | Genitals |
| 6 | The stress of Birmingham is burning | The graveyard | October 2003 | 11 | Heart |
| 7 | The shadow of the White Elephant | Gibraltar Andalusia | November 2003 | 12 | Lungs |
| 8 | Field report | An online forum | December 2003 | 1 | Oesophagus |
| 9 | Dual citizens: two cultures but no nation | The library | December 2003 | 2 | Brain |
| 10 | Would you like toes with that? | The streets | January 2004 | 3 | Blood |
| 11 | Let's call him Mr Bright Side | The concert room | January 2004 | 4 | Ear |
| 12 | The death of the Cyclops | An apartment above a pub | February 2004 | 5 | Muscle |
| 13 | Closing your eyes opens your ears | At Dr Pope's | March 2004 | 8 | Eye Nose |
| 14 | Medical notes on life | The hospital | April 2004 | 10 | Womb |
| 15 | Circe plays us all | The brothel | April 2004 | 12 | Locomotor apparatus |
| 16 | No shelter for the vulnerable | The shelter | May 2004 | 1 | Nerves |
| 17 | To see it, you need to want to see it | The house | May 2004 | 2 | Skeleton |
| 18 | We spend our whole lives waiting | The nightclub | June 2004 | - | Flesh |

# *A Dead Man's Ice Cream* schema

| Colour | Victim | Symbol | Art | Style | Ch. |
|---|---|---|---|---|---|
| White Gold | Guy in the newspaper | Grandmother Virgin | Religion | Very simple language with play-on-words | 1 |
| Brown | Person in the news | Horse Salmon | Irish mythology | Mythological narrative in Kiltartanese | 2 |
| Green | Philology student | Tide | Philology | Email | 3 |
| Orange | Girl dressed as a nymph | Nymph | Economics | A play in three acts | 4 |
| - | Man at the botanical garden | Flower | Botany Chemistry | Narcissism | 5 |
| White Black | Churchgoer | Caretaker | Religion | Decomposed description | 6 |
| Red | News editor | Wind | Politics | Draft notes | 7 |
| - | An architect | Constable | Architecture | Blogging | 8 |
| - | English literature teacher | Stratford London Dublin | Literature | Dialectic | 9 |
| - | Car mechanic | Citizens | Mechanics | Second person narration | 10 |
| - | A DJ | Barmaids | Music | Musical | 11 |
| - | An ex-army guy | Sound | Linguistics | Academic article | 12 |
| Grey Blue | A painter | Pebbles | Painting | Sensory | 13 |
| White | A mother | Mothers | Medicine | Medical notes | 14 |
| - | A strip dancer | Sex industry | Magic | Hallucination | 15 |
| - | Old sailor | Sailing Abused civilisations | Navigation | Heroic narrative | 16 |
| - | Philosophy student | Comets | Philosophy | Ordered internal dialogue | 17 |
| - | It depends on how you look at it | Ashes | - | Internal monologue | 18 |

# Chapter 1

## Welcome to the *Untied* Kingdom

Awkwardly, skinny Carl stepped off the plane and into his new life, in the city where he would die a few months later. He dragged the mudguard of his right shoe along the metallic floor, as he'd always done since childhood when walking without concentrating. He felt trapped and moved slowly, trying to distance himself from the pushy old woman behind him, while a man in front hit him with his bag. It didn't seem to be on purpose, but he wasn't trying to avoid doing so either. An unusual mixture of politeness, shyness, and clumsiness prevented Carl from complaining. Instead, he stopped briefly in the middle of the stairs as the violent rain hit him before he could take a good look at the control tower.

Carl didn't like change as he didn't cope with it well. Slowly, as was his way with most things, he tried to get used to this new place, but the old lady pushed him until he started to walk again. The weather didn't make him feel particularly welcome in a place that was supposed to be his motherland and he preferred his Mediterranean home. He walked along the tarmac and entered the terminal, loving the feeling of losing the need to decide which way to go, enjoying following his fellow travellers. After a few more minutes of hauling his heavy hand luggage, which was packed with tax free alcohol, he managed to join the queue for passport control, where he read out loud a sign that said, 'Welcome to the *Untied* Kingdom'. The lawyer standing in front of Carl laughed when he heard this. The electrician that had been sitting beside him during the flight found it hilarious that after a week of riots in the UK, psychiatrists, politicians and journalists had failed to describe in all their articles and speeches what this dyslexic Gibraltarian had explained perfectly by just moving a *t* to the left.

The riots had been disturbing in Birmingham. Children just over eight years of age had been prosecuted for vandalising and looting shops. The Asian and Caribbean communities were at war because of murders on Belgrave Middleway. The Sudanese community were demonstrating due to police violence. In Scotland, a nationalist political party had been organising a rally for their independence from England and in Northern Ireland, the families of the victims of Bloody Sunday continued pressing the British government for justice. This was certainly the *Untied* Kingdom, where all ties between the citizens of the country had evaporated in what seemed to be '*Democrazy* at its best'.

Carl stood nervously in the queue as his left hand reached for his pocket. He touched both his passports and continued looking around him while considering which one to use. He felt his Spanish passport would identify him better, as an Iberian citizen, a Mediterranean boy, while his British one would make him more welcome to the motherland and give him a sense of connection with the passport officer; the passport officer wouldn't care less, regardless.

Carl took a few steps when the passport officer asked him to come forward and with his usual indecision, Carl felt unsure about which nationality to represent. He moved his white and golden coat, reached for his pocket, and retrieved the first passport he could grab. It happened to be the one with the picture of the Virgin inside. He showed it to the officer, smiled as if he'd been asked to do so and moved forward when he was given the go ahead. Carl walked to belt number eight when the picture of the Virgin Mary fell from his passport. He gazed at it while picking it up and felt sad that his grandmother, the person who had been like a mother to him, hadn't been there to hand it to him. She would have told him it would protect him on his travels, as she'd always done before. She wasn't there anymore to do the sign of the cross before he set off, but he'd still take the postcard with him wherever he went.

Carl's grandmother had passed away a few weeks ago, the very same day he finally bought his ticket to go to England. He still felt guilty, as if the thought of him leaving had been the cause of her death. He waited for his luggage to arrive on the belt and when he finally saw it, he kissed the picture of the Virgin and placed in his pocket. It was a habit he had inherited from his grandmother. 'For many Christians, the Virgin Mary is their protector, guardian, and guide. In Mediterranean cultures, those are the roles of our grandmothers,' thought Carl.

He reached for his bag, but as he tried to lift it, he remembered just how much he had brought with him. With force, he dragged it off the belt, managing to land it on the floor, feeling guilty for accidently pushing an innocent man in the process; Carl thought he had already made an enemy in Birmingham. It was definitely his suitcase because it had his name on it. Carl had always found his surname interesting. He spelt it *Martín* in Spanish and *Martin* in English. It was hard to explain how a tiny accent mark could represent so much. To him, that accent mark was a huge part of his identity. For others in Gibraltar, that accent mark was the difference between being of Spanish or British descent. It was the difference between coming from a poor immigrant family from Spain or a family of British naval officers. 'Others will always see you as they want to see you,' his grandmother had often said to him throughout his life.

Carl grabbed his hand luggage with his left hand and rolled his suitcase with his right hand, walking towards the exit. He came out of arrivals, finding a large crowd of people waiting for their friends, partners, and relatives. It saddened him that no one was waiting for him. He managed to find the taxi rank without getting lost and approached one of the drivers.

'Any chance you could take me to Edgbaston, near Five Ways?' asked Carl.

'Yes, sure,' said the taxi driver before negotiating a price with him. 'Alright, my friend,' he said with a melodic Asian accent. 'You need help with your luggage?'

'Nah, it's fine. I'll be okay, thanks.'

The taxi moved as soon as Carl had sat down and the driver started his standard polite chatter while entering the postcode on his GPS.

'Where do you come from, my friend?'

'Gibraltar. I'm from there,' answered Carl while trying to take his mobile phone out of his pocket.

'Where's Gibraltar? I've never heard of it.'

'It's a British overseas territory near Cadiz, in the south of Spain.'

'So, it's in Spain then?' The Asian man asked while he passed a sign saying, 'Welcome to Solihull'.

'No. It was part of Spain till 1704, but it's been British since then.'

'What is it then? A little island?' asked the driver, ignorant to the fact that the word *little* might offend his passenger.

'No, it's a peninsula. A neck of land connected to Spain. You just have to cross the street and you're in Spain,' explained Carl.

'How you communicate with them? In Spain, I mean? Do you study Spanish?'

'It depends on your family, really,' Carl went on. 'People in Gibraltar tend to be bilingual English-Spanish, although some families speak more Spanish and others more English.' Carl answered while typing on his phone. 'I've just arrived in Birmingham. I'm sorry I didn't have time to *poo* by Ireland.' Carl pressed *send* before realising his typo, but his friend Myles would find the text funny. Quickly, Carl texted his new housemate. He looked at a sign that said, 'Ice rink' and continued his geography lesson. 'The TV and radio are also in both languages, so you grow up speaking both.'

'And at school? You speak both languages too?'

'We follow the British curriculum and lessons are normally in English, although we also study Spanish at school. It's supposed to be our modern foreign language, but just on paper. For most of us, it's pretty much our first language. We speak English as well. For some people, we have a southern English accent, although others say that our *bowels* are quite different in Gibraltar.'

The taxi driver continued with his interrogation. 'I think I can hear your accent is different from English accents. Is it because you mainly speak Spanish?'

'I do, but it varies a lot from family to family,' explained Carl.

'I have a funny story about accents,' said the driver. 'I picked up a Spanish guy on business a couple of months ago from Birmingham Airport and he was going to *Tanworth High Street*. We got there and he couldn't find his hotel. We were quite confused until I realised that he meant *Tamworth*.

'Spanish doesn't differentiate between *n* and *m* at the end of syllables, plus anyway, phonetically, those consonants are very close to each other,' explained Carl.

'They might be close in Spanish, but in English, they're twenty-five miles apart.'

'Well, something similar happened to me when I was at university,' said Carl. 'My friends organised a short break at a friend's house in Abu Dhabi and I got super excited, but later on I found that it was actually *Aberdovey* in Wales.'

'Oh, yeah, it sounds quite similar,' replied the taxi driver. 'So, what are you doing in England? On holiday?'

Watching the sights out the window, Carl responded distractedly. 'No, not really. Sorry, do you know how long it'll take to get to Edgbaston?'

'Not long. There's not much traffic tonight so it shouldn't take too long.'

Relieved, Carl sat back. 'Ah, okay, thanks. I just moved here,' continued Carl. 'I went to uni in England and I have a friend who is still around so I thought I might as well come back. I only have a few acquaintances in Gibraltar and no family. There wasn't much to keep me there.'

The taxi driver looked in the mirror and saw Carl struggling to write a text message. He paused before continuing with the chat. The taxi was passing through Moseley, where in a few weeks Carl would spend a rather entertaining evening. 'In about five or ten minutes,' Carl muttered while he was finishing his text.

Carl leaned back and he looked thoughtful, unwilling to be disturbed by the driver's chit chat. He stared through the windows and with the exception of a little smile at graffiti with the words, 'When Jesus gives you a new life, make it count', he sat immobile until he arrived at his new house.

The taxi drove away before Carl walked up to the door with his luggage, dragging it to what would be his new house and, quite possibly, his new home too. He studied the facade of the house, examining the white door with a golden line crossing from one left to the other. Carl double-checked the address he had written down to make sure he was in the right place.

A good-looking young man opened the door and shook Carl's hand. 'Hi, nice to meet you. I'm Charles.'

'Oh, hi. Sorry, my feet are a bit wet.'

'Don't worry, it's fine. Hold on, I'll take that. I'll show you to your room and around the house later,' said Charles with a recognisable public school accent. 'These stairs aren't that bad once you get used to them, as long as you have a spare hand to hold the handrail in case you slip, hehe. It's that door there. The room's pretty much what you saw advertised on the internet. The mattress is quite comfortable and it's a size and a half, which is big enough for bringing girls back,' although Charles thought that Carl would struggle to do that. 'The wardrobe's quite big and it has two drawers, which are quite big as well, although you also have that chest of drawers and the bedside table. I think you'll have enough space for your stuff. You could use this table for a TV. I've just bought a new one so you can borrow my old one.'

'That'd be great, yes. Thanks. I'll sort out my stuff first and then I'll go and get it.'

'Don't worry, there's no rush,' assured Charles. 'I'll show you the place quickly and then leave you to it.'

Charles showed Carl the big bathroom upstairs and pointed to the other two rooms. 'That's my room and that's my office.' The office was about the same size as Carl's room but with little furniture. The two new housemates went downstairs and Charles showed Carl the lounge, which he'd already seen when he'd entered the house. The kitchen was next door to it and opposite the dining area. There was a little back garden beyond the kitchen, although the tastefully chosen curtains didn't let him see much of it. The stairs climbed up to the bedrooms and the big bathroom. Under the stairs, there was a small toilet where a girl that Charles had been seeing lately used to go to vomit after every meal; Charles denied his *acuntability*. She had tried to drag him to some boarding school survivor meetings but he always refused and let her go by herself.

'Well, that's it, really,' said Charles. 'This is typical of the houses you get around this area. Lounge, kitchen, dining area, garden, and a little toilet on the ground floor. There are also three rooms and the big bathroom upstairs. The washing machine and dryer are in the garage. You can get there through that door in the kitchen, but as my car's usually in there, you won't be able to go through when I'm parked.'

'That's fine, thanks. Is it okay if I use the loo?'

'Yeah, sure. Go for it. I just got back from work and I've bought about a square *feed* of pizza. You want some?'

'Yes, okay, thank you,' replied Carl. 'I'll try and organise myself for a few minutes and I'll be down in a sec.'

'Cool. I'll put the kettle on.'

Carl went upstairs and after dripping urine on the toilet seat and flushing the toilet, he washed his hands and went to his new room. He kind of liked the house, although he had realised that the unhomely look was not an illusion of the online pictures. The house was a good size and the furniture appropriate but some parts felt sparsely furnished.

Carl started to quietly sing a song or, at least, he tried to. 'En el mar he oído hoy,' he sang as he made sure the bottles in his hand luggage hadn't broken. 'Señor, tu voz que me llamó,' continued Carl, singing something he'd heard from a group of school children at the airport in the afternoon, although he was sure he had heard it before. After checking his bottles had survived the journey, he opened his suitcase, threw some of his trousers on the floor to mark his territory, and went downstairs to have a cup of tea with his new housemate.

'How was your flight?' asked Charles, embarrassed for not having asked before.

'It was alright, thanks, although I thought I was gonna miss it.'

'Oh, why is that? Did you have to travel far?'

'No, not at all, but the airport in Gibraltar only has one runway and it crosses a main road connecting the airport with the town centre. They close the road when there's a plane taking off or landing. A plane was preparing to take off when I was on my way to the airport, so I had to wait until they reopened the road.' Carl shook his head at the memory.

'What if there aren't any flights? Can you walk on the runway?'

'Oh, yeah,' replied Carl. 'There are signs that say things like *runway, please do not litter*, but you just walk across it. Otherwise, they'd have to build a bridge or something.'

'Hm,' is all Charles said. He thought it sounded more like the description of a third-world airport, but he assumed Carl wouldn't like to hear that. 'Have you always lived there?'

'Pretty much. I sound a bit more Spanish than the average Gibraltarian, I think, but that's because we always spoke Spanish at home,' he explained. 'I spent three years in England when I went to uni, but apart from that, I've always lived there. It's a good place to grow up, but everyone knows everyone. After a while, it feels like a very small place. Well, it's less than seven square kilometres, just over two and a half square miles, so it's actually quite a small place.'

'Wow. So, how many people live there, then?'

'Just around 28,000. Quite a lot for its size, really. So, obviously, Birmingham seems massive compared to Gibraltar.'

'Well, Birmingham's a lot bigger than people think. It's the second biggest city in the United Kingdom in terms of population. Had you been here before?'

'No, never. It's my first time. I have a very good friend who lives in the city so that's why I decided to move here.'

'Is he *Llanito* as well?'

'No, he's English but his father is Irish,' Carl answered. 'You know that word?'

'Which word?' asked Charles, looking a bit confused.

'*Llanito*. English people usually don't know that word.'

'Oh, well,' Charles paused for a second, his eyes moving up and to the right. 'You said it before, so I guessed it meant someone from Gibraltar.'

'Yeah, that's the familiar form of it.'

'That's what I thought.' Charles continued sipping his tea, deciding it was a good time to stop with the questions. It was beginning to remind him of work. He'd been on call that night and he was keen to end the conversation.

'Oh, before I forget,' Charles started. 'The water heater's on all the time, cause it's automatic, so the water will start coming out hot after a few minutes if you run the tap.'

'Okay, thanks. Are you going to bed soon?' asked Carl.

'Yeah, sorry. I have a few things to do tomorrow before I go to work.'

'I'll have a shower in the morning, then. I won't keep you awake.'

'Don't worry. Go ahead. It won't bother me,' insisted Charles.

'It's okay. I'll do it tomorrow.'

'Alright, but really, if you feel like having a shower, just go for it,' added Charles, standing up. 'I'm a very heavy sleeper. Don't worry about waking me up.'

'Haha, me too,' said Carl. 'I always set a few alarms because I sleep through them.'

'That sounds like me,' said Charles with a yawn. 'I'm off to bed. I'll see you tomorrow, mate, as I'm not going to work until three-thirty.'

Carl said goodnight in his usual polite manner and stayed in the lounge drinking his tea and taking in his surroundings. The room was tastefully decorated with classy furniture, probably too expensive for what it was. Some fresh-looking letters addressed to the previous tenant were scattered by the phone, on top of the only piece of furniture that didn't quite match the rest. It looked as if it had been inherited from an older relative trying to impress a Victorian visitor. Carl finished his tea while trying to guess what kind of job Charles had. He carried his empty mug to the kitchen to wash it, although he'd forgot why he was there by the time he got to the sink. He went upstairs, brushed his teeth as quietly as he could and went to sleep.

The next morning, Carl woke up neither early nor late. He went to the kitchen wearing his baggy white, golden shirt and found a note Charles had left stating, 'Help yourself to anything you'd like. Mi casa es tu casa'. Carl was pleased after he'd read it as he hadn't bought anything for breakfast. He had a coffee and a couple of slices of toast before returning to his room to finish unpacking.

It was mid-afternoon when Carl heard Charles for the first time. He couldn't hear much noise from Charles' room, but didn't feel confident enough to knock on the door. The door finally opened when Charles went to the bathroom. He stopped to see how the newcomer was progressing with his room.

'All good, thanks,' answered Carl when Charles asked him how he was. 'Thanks a lot for breakfast, I'll go shopping today and replace the bread and coffee I had.'

'No worries, mate. It's all good. Any time. You have any plans for today?'

'No, not really,' said Carl, excited about the prospect of being invited out for a drink. 'I'm going shopping to get some bits and bobs. I might see my friend later. What about you?'

'I'm working from three-thirty until midnight so not much fun for me today. I woke up early to see if I could get some work done, but the day's not being as productive as I'd hoped.'

'What do you do, if you don't mind my asking? You always have to work nights?' asked Carl.

'No, not always. Only some weeks. I'm a doctor. I'm doing my specialty training in psychiatry at the moment. I have to be on call at hospital every now and then.'

Carl felt uncomfortable when Charles had described his job. He asked the first question he could think of to hide his discomfort. 'And how's that going?'

'Work's good. I really enjoy it, but I have to prepare some portfolios as part of my training in addition to my normal work. That's why I had to wake up early today. I have to make sure I update my portfolio this week and I usually have some reading to do. I use the little room as an office to motivate me. This year, my supervisor is quite strict. I have to keep on top of things. His name's Dr Shitty. Well, his surname is actually *Shetty*, but he's from New Zealand and that's how he says it.'

'So, you never rent that room out?' asked Carl.

'No, not really. I like having my own space. To be honest, you're the first tenant I've had. I prefer to live on my own so that I don't have to worry about being noisy or anything, but I thought that it'd be nice to have someone around, as it can be boring at times.'

'Yeah, I know what you mean,' agreed Carl. 'I lived on my own for a few weeks back home after my grandma passed away. It was weird not having anyone around.'

That sounded like the type of phrase Charles' patients might use at the start of a sad story. Charles changed the topic when he noticed the sad look in Carl's eyes. 'Anything I can help you with? How to get to shops or any other directions?'

'Actually, yeah. Do you know where the closest supermarket is? And do you know how to get to the Job Centre in Broad Street?' asked Carl.

'Yep,' Charles said, pointing out of the window. 'You see that road there? The one with the churchy looking house?'

'Yes, I do, thanks,' answered Carl in a more polite and serious tone than was necessary.

'If you follow that road, you'll get to a big roundabout and you'll see a big supermarket just there.'

'Cool, thanks,' replied Carl.

'And that's where Broad Street starts. You'll see loads of pubs and clubs, so if you just walk along there, you'll see the Job Centre on your left. How's the job hunting going?'

'It's not really going at all,' replied Carl. 'I thought I'd wait until I was here before properly looking for jobs. I've applied for a few things, but I've had no luck. I'll pop by the Job Centre and see what they have. I was worried about not finding a job quickly enough, but my grandma left me some money. I could use that if I really needed to.'

'That's good. It's good to have a safety net.'

The two flatmates finished their conversation and returned to their burrows.

It was Carl's first day on the streets of Birmingham and although the city didn't look as good as it did in the postcards he'd received from his friend, somehow, he knew he would enjoy it anyway. The city wasn't as disgustingly clean as some of those pretty market towns he'd visited when he was last in England. The people seemed to prefer newspapers with plastic tits on page three rather than one that discussed politics, but the three locals he'd asked for directions on his way to Telmo Supermarket Five Ways had all been very helpful and polite in their own way. The smell of the third one was not something he was particularly bothered about; Carl had never been the judgemental type.

It was only when Carl entered the supermarket that he realised it would have been better to visit the Job Centre first and do the shopping on the way home. He was supposed to meet his friend, so it wouldn't make sense to walk around Birmingham with his bags of shopping, bags which always contained the same items.

On his way to the Job Centre, he texted his friend to see if they could go for a beer. His friend laughed when he read the text, 'Hello, I hope things are going well. My *jouse* is quite cool and I even have a

*TB* in my room. Let me know if you fancy meeting up for a drink later.' His friend didn't know whether Carl's typos were a product of his accent or his clumsy fingers.

By the time Carl had left the Job Centre, he'd received a text from his friend saying he wasn't available, but that he could meet the following day. This was a good enough answer for Carl.

The experience in the Job Centre was nerve-racking for Carl and awkward for the interviewer, but he was happy to have done it on his own without any help from others. It surprised him how he got a great feeling from being independent. He had always relied on guidance from someone else. Perhaps, it had been his independence his grandmother had been attempting to instil in him for all these years. The lady at the Job Centre had been very helpful. She used one of those machines that, as an unpopular politician of the time had recently said, 'Give chavs an allergic reaction'. The machine showed an endless list of jobs, most of which seemed out of reach for everyone in the waiting room. Carl pressed the bright button and printed out a few jobs that sounded good. He collected his printouts from a slot next to a label that red, 'Made in *Chian*' and took the papers to the lady. She reviewed his CV and appeared confused when she read, 'Gibraltar, UK'. She asked him where it was and Carl went on autopilot, repeating the same information he'd given to the taxi driver on his way from the airport. The woman gave Carl a few pointers on how to improve his CV and showed him some cover letter templates he could use to write his own. He liked the woman. She was pleasant, helpful and positive, making him feel at ease. She gave Carl a bit of a push and the confidence he needed to apply for a few jobs. He saw in her the strength and caring nature of a Mediterranean grandmother. He used the woman's advice and eventually dared to press the submit button on the website a couple of days later, which for him, was the equivalent of shouting out loud 'I can do this STUPID job' at the ears of a prospective boss.

A couple of weeks had passed since Carl's arrival in Birmingham. After several job applications, a few interviews and one successful day, he'd finally found a job. He was still in disbelief, but had to prepare and ensure he was on time for his first day at work.

Carl woke up excited about his new job. He went to have breakfast with Charles, who was on morning shifts for the next few days. Charles had heard Carl getting ready and had put a few extra slices of bread in the toaster, together with an extra cup of coffee. Carl felt good that morning, great actually, the kind of feeling he should have had the morning of his first communion and confirmation.

Waking up early for work and having coffee with his housemate made him feel like a normal, young professional. He was doing what other people, hundreds or thousands of them, were doing across Birmingham at that very same time. He felt completely fulfilled and had a feeling of inner happiness and self-security that he hoped would make him accepted at work, maybe even well-liked, as some character had once said in a play he had read for university. Carl was synchronised with his fellow Brummies. Waking up, having breakfast and rushing out.

The conversation with his flatmate in the morning was good. 'What do you exactly have to do in your job?' asked Charles, although he already knew the answer. But he also knew that Carl enjoyed talking about his administration job at the University of Edgbaston.

Carl walked to Five Ways Station to catch the train to Edgbaston University, which was only one stop away, but a bit too far to walk. He entered the station, showing his monthly pass to the inspector. He'd bought it on the same day he got the job and had been waiting to use it ever since. Carl felt like a real worker, like a real commuter, like a real person.

He even thought that he might be lucky enough to see his friend on the train, as it was the same route he used for work. Instead, he saw someone else; someone he'd heard about. A few days ago, over a drink at a bar, his friend had told Carl there was a guy who travelled on the train from Five Ways. Sweaty, too fat to be called chubby, in his mid-thirties, with a bandana on his head. He smelt like piss and sulphur mixed with juice from dirty socks. The guy waiting for the train had to be him. There simply couldn't be two guys with that kind of smell. Carl only realised this once the man had sat next to him and by that point, he felt too bad about moving to another coach as other passengers were doing. His friend was certainly right about one thing: the guy had a friendly face. He projected a disturbingly positive attitude. You couldn't help but smile when you saw him. It made you want to sit with him on the train journey. Until you got another whiff of his body odour, that is. Carl felt guilty, very guilty, when he concluded it was the same feeling flies experienced when they were attracted to a garbage bin.

Carl almost apologised to himself for thinking this and decided to grab a copy of a newspaper lying next to him to get his mind to focus on something else. It was laced with the smell of expensive perfume from its previous reader. It contrasted sharply with the smell of the guy on his left. A few pages were creased, as newspapers get when you read them in a very confined space and need to turn pages holding both elbows together. He managed to turn a few pages and felt his chest tighten when he reached a page with the headline, 'Panic in Birmingham'.

You never knew how accurate those newspapers were, but there it was, a full-page article with information about a murder in the city. Carl read it carefully, as the other eight people on the carriage were doing, judging by way he saw them doing the sign of the cross. They were possessed by a collective mind. The passengers were reading the same article, every one of them invaded by the same feeling of morbidity while breathing in the odour of the guy with the bandana.

Carl got off at University Station, a convenient stop for those who worked or studied at the University of Edgbaston. The clock struck eight o'clock in the morning and he was eager to show his monthly train pass again. He asked for directions to the School of Languages and felt ready for his first great day at work.

# Chapter 2

## Meet the genealogical stalker

*'I swear by the oath of my people,' said Cuchulain, 'I will make my doings be spoken of among the great doings of heroes in their strength.'*

*As Lady Gregory moved about among her people, she learned to love the beautiful speech of those who think in Irish...*
*...Kiltartanese, English with Gaelic syntax...*

*We should keep these personages much in our hearts, for they live and will have lived in the places where we drive and go marketing, and sometimes they have met one another in the blocks of flats that cast their shadows upon us...*

*...and indeed, if there was more respect for Brummie things among learned men and women from Birmingham, this novel would not have been left to a Spaniard.*

Two teachers who worked together were on their way to work. They talked about their job, the future of their college, and about many more great deeds. They ended up bringing happiness to a vulnerable soul and this is the way it happened.

It was nine o'clock in the morning plus one hour when the horse of m*h*etal stopped at Kings Norton Station. The train had been delayed at New Street because of the almost daily signalling problem. Myles

Joyce walked out of the train and looked both ways, right and left, and left and right, and saw a figure the like of Greg, the son of John. The train made a noise the like of a horse when it stopped, and the train lifted a cloud not smaller nor bigger than that risen by the cattle of the glen on their way to the slaughterhouse. Myles saw the son of John, and they both wished a thousand happy mornings on each other's souls, knowing that two people shorten the road. The one and one of them met outside the barriers and with a strong look in their eyes, without words, they argued which way to go, to the sunny side of the glen of Kings Norton Park, or to the side in the shade, and they decided, mutually, without the sound of words it was, that they were to follow the path the Sun marked for them. Almighty Myles and wise Greg walked along the pavement while they discussed their daily matters. Their issues weren't significant and they weren't original either, but they belonged to their morning ritual. The after-summer sun was leaving its last breaths in the morning of the day, while the dark brown leaves awaited quietly on the trees before they decided to fall. These two warriors of modern-day battles made their way forward through the car park while the godlike m/ietal horse could be heard leaving the station. They carried on their walk, shoulder by shoulder the like of horses o' the Sun, with sounds and words coming out of their mouths that the local flowers had heard many times before.

'May God be with you. It's a good morning we have here,' said the son of John.

'May God and Mary be with you. It is indeed,' said his companion. 'It is mornings like these that make you feel sorry about going into the cave, prisoners of our jobs for almost more than three times three hours a day.'

'It is true words you're speaking, my dearest of friends, although there are worse things that could land upon the spirit of yours and mine,' replied the son of John.

Both their souls agreed on this as they stepped on the very few bright brown leaves that had fallen impatiently on the ground, for the time when the falling of them would be appropriate wasn't quite near yet.

'What were the happenings of you during the holidays?' continued the son of John while continuing his rhythmic walk.

'Ceol agus craic,' replied Myles to his companion. 'Until I had to look after the mother of mine as it is a bad illness she had upon her, although it went off her soul on the *turd* day.'

The son of John nodded, 'It is many a bad illness there is around, and it is with great strength that it afflicts all of us. It is me myself that felt the like of a cold during the very first day of the break. I had taught the lessons, fought the students and their spirits with as much strength as I could and it was with glory I came out of that last term, but on the first day of the break, my soul felt weak as the snow in the spring, but it has recovered since then.'

'It is a pity, I know,' continued Myles. 'But that's how it works with people the like of us. *Hw*en you work with the oldest of the youth, you may find yourself ill in the time of your rest. If you lie down with dogs, you'll rise with fleas,' explained Myles the talkative one. 'It's the same as it is with doctors. There is a lass I have heard about, and a doctor she is, who has fallen ill many a time because of the like of viruses at the hospital. However, it is the norm this is within their early years of medicine, as the body prepares itself later to defeat the like of similar viruses.'

'True words are those that you're speaking, my friend, but it is with resentment and self-pity that I welcomed my illness, as the suffering of it meant that I couldn't obtain the joys of my break, the long-awaited summer break. But it is now, that our break has finished, and it's with strength that we must embark upon the next few weeks, until we obtain the next deserved break for the souls of ours during the next half term,' the son of John added.

'Well, my dearest of friends, Greg the wise one,' said Myles the vision bearer, while checking the shade of the sun on his right palm. 'It is with fear and regret that I approach this new term of ours, for I know that people the like of my Irish grandfather had a mile of what it takes to succeed in the battle of our business, and even he himself found it hard to last until the end of the term. And I know that a long term it is that we have ahead of us, and it is many a few surprises that we will encounter. However, it is beyond afield that the misfortunes will be at their strongest point, and they will be evident to us in three ways. We will suffer in our professional lives, we will suffer in our personal lives, and we will suffer in our social lives, when all the city of

*Bhir mhing na nHam* will feel devastated by the great tragedy to come. That is why it is that I await the month of June with pain in my heart, as some very sad news will be laid upon us then. Some other sad news will meet us on the way to that month, but it will not be until June that we will know the full depth of our misery.'

The son of John, Greg, knew those were true words Myles Joyce had spoken, which is why he changed the topic of the conversation to something more mirthful. 'It is good, at least, that the first day back at work is not a teaching day.'

'That's true, indeed,' said Myles while inspecting the brown car on his left. 'I know these interviews can be tiresome, but they certainly are a good way to start the term and to get back into the shape of things. It is fun some of these interviews can be. I remember, and not a long time ago it was, in the last round of interviews, there was one girl from one of our feeder schools. It is that she was showing me her predicted grades at GCSE and great pride shone upon her face. It is that I was writing down the subjects she wanted to study at college with us, and then she showed me her extracurricular feats; an escort she'd written she was. I was shocked at first and then laughed about it. It was a struggle for her to see what I was laughing about, and when I asked her about that job, she explained she had worked as an escort for a charity that looked after vulnerable elderly people. She wanted to say that she had worked accompanying and helping the elderly, but she'd written using the word, 'escort'. I just told her that I was surprised she'd written that word because I thought she meant a very different kind of occupation. She didn't comprehend her error. So, I finished the interview and offered her a place. It's amusing what youngsters write in their personal statements but a sad time it is when meanings and words get broken in half.'

'A sad time it is,' said Greg the listener, as both their bodies carried on walking through Kings Norton Park sharing a bag of hazelnuts. 'I don't think I will do many interviews today. I might do a few and disappear to get some work done. I have to teach a history module this term and it's mostly ready, but I want to be prepared for tomorrow when the first lesson comes. I harbour deep regret for having accepted the teaching of this module. I should have consulted about this with my head of department first, but she had a few days off ill before the end of the last term and was unreachable.'

'A wise man never commits to a great deed without a woman's advice,' said Myles. 'I myself had a similar problem when I changed exam board last year. You never know how much work is involved until you start planning the lessons. But laziness is a heavy burden, and I am sure you'll get your head around it in a few days. Just make sure you stay one page ahead of the students. It is Travel and Tourism I have to teach now as well, as my timetable was light and I was a few hours under, filling up my schedule was equally a burden, but now I am used to it.'

Their bodies and minds continued walking along Pershore Road, passed the deadliest of roundabouts after Kings Norton Primary School, and then they moved onto Redditch Road. Our heroes carried on with their journey and, after a few minutes, they crossed the road, turning into Downland Close, where they saw the sign that said, *gKings an-Norton* Sixth Form College. At that point, they knew their relaxing morning walk was coming to an end. Myles would meet his dear friend Carl later on in the day for a drink, but that was still some clouds away.

Stately, Myles Joyce and Greg Johnson walked through the entrance of the college, knowing that it would be a grand day. The two of them parted ways and went to their offices to prepare for the day ahead while stopping with their co-workers on their way to enquire with a polite 'How was your break?' which was typically part of the routine of the first day back.

It is busy the canteen was, with a different menu for the day, 'Salmon for all, and knowledge for some'. A member of the support staff stood in the middle of the place, surrounded by a multitude of people, the same way as the crowds used to surround old Oisín when he was telling the stories of his old friends of the Fianna. The member of the support staff would call the names of prospective students, and these would go to the designated table for an interview where teachers would take up the necessary information to process each student's application. Myles Joyce was there, along with Greg the son of John, and Barry Each of the shiny head was there too with his friend Keith Capall, as well as many a friend and co-worker too.

And so it was that Myles was writing down the student's information as he overheard Barry's interview with his student, since it is the case that little pigs have big ears. Myles laughed when he heard Barry's comments and couldn't believe he was actually saying things the like of those, and this below is how it happened.

'Okay,' said Barry to the student, 'this is the address we have for you in our records, is that correct?'

'Yes,' answered the students with a nod.

'And that's the phone number we have should we ever need to contact home, is that correct?' asked Barry.

'Yes, it is, sir.'

'Okay,' continued Barry, and pointing to his notes asked, 'is that your current school, then?'

'Yes, it is,' the student answered again.

'I went to that school once; it's a shithole. And the headmaster, Mr Cookson is a twat. You can't trust a guy who's only a letter away from having *cock* in his surname. You'll be happy to leave that place,' said Barry to comfort the student, who seemed slightly nervous. 'Is that thing on your head for religious reasons or fashion?' said Barry in an uninterested tone.

'For religious reasons,' answered the student.

'I thought so,' replied Barry. 'It couldn't be for fashion. It looks ridiculous.'

Barry continued with his interviewing skills, and when he saw the box the student had ticked to select his ethnicity, he said, 'Really? You're too dark for that, aren't you?'

The student had already become used to Barry's personality and ignored the comment.

'Okay, just a few more details and we'll be done,' said Barry. 'Do you have any learning difficulties?'

'No, no learning difficulties, sir.'

'That's what I like to hear. It makes our job easier, you know,' added Barry. 'And, finally, any physical disabilities?'

'No, no disabilities, sir,' the student answered with a flat tone.

'You sure?' said Barry. 'Can you see okay with that wonky eye?'

'Yes, I can, sir. My eye is totally fine,' explained the student.

It is then that Barry moved on to write down the student's qualifications. 'Wow, mate,' said Barry, 'I've seen dyslexic monkeys with better GCSE grades than yours.'

The student didn't feel brave enough to challenge the comment. 'Some of them are a bit low, but I'm studying hard and I will take a few resits, so I will turn some of those Es into Cs,' he said.

'It's not a salmon until it's on the bank,' said Barry to advise the student not to claim premature success. And so it came to pass that Myles had to go to collect another student, and he felt regretful he couldn't finish hearing the rest of Barry's interview.

It is seldom you meet a person the like of Barry, although Mr Capall was quite similar. Barry, however, was even more eccentric, at every single level. He had a senile dog and a senile cat. He had to make sure his dog didn't leave his house as it always forgot where it lived and roamed the streets howling at streetlamps. Barry's cat had a different set of issues; it used to cry every couple of hours because it had forgotten that it had already eaten and was diabetic, so Barry had to inject him with insulin twice a day, at first and last light of the day.

It is a long working day that was, but Greg succeeded in planning his history lessons for the week and Myles and the son of John departed the college even more triumphantly than when they'd walked in at the beginning of the day.

Redditch Road, and then the tiny and busy roundabout, and then Pershore Road, was the way they took. They continued talking and walking towards Kings Norton Station, while they shared the few brown hazelnuts they had left in the bag from the morning.

'Yep, that sounds good,' answered the son of John when Myles asked him if he'd like to accompany him and Carl for a pint later on. 'How do you know that guy?' asked Greg.

'I met him at uni,' replied Myles. There was a James Joyce society at uni and we both attended its readers' club one semester when they were doing *Ulysses*. We both absolutely love that book, and I was studying Spanish and he was from Gibraltar, so we had the language in common too,' explained Myles. 'Carl didn't know many people at uni but there is no old stocking that doesn't find an old boot.'

'Oh, cool,' said Greg of the curious mind. 'And how come he's moved to Birmingham?'

And this is what Myles said as they were getting on the train: 'Gibraltar's a pretty small place and he didn't have a job, and he really liked England when he came over to go to uni, so his grandma convinced him to move to England. She was the only family he had, and she died recently,' explained Myles. 'He was very close to her, and I also think that coming here will make it a lot easier for him to get over her loss. I don't know much about what happened to his parents or the rest of his family, but I think that coming here was also a way of getting away from any past problems and dodgy memories.'

'But is he OK?' asked the son of John.

'Yeah, he's fine. He's a really nice guy, but you'll realise that there's something a bit different about him. You'll notice straightaway he's on the spectrum, Asperger's of some degree, but some days it's a lot more obvious than others. He's never told me about it, but I think he might have seen psychiatrists and stuff. He can socialise and that, and even has a few friends, so it's not as bad as some other people, but I think he's getting worse. He used to have a bit more of a spark. I remember he wrote a piece on politics once for our uni newspaper and it was good. I only read the draft though, as he never finished it or submitted it to the editor, but he definitely said some stuff there he wouldn't say today. I rang him over the summer and he wasn't in,' Myles went on. 'His grandmother picked up the phone and I talked to her for a bit. She was so grateful that I was helping Carl move to England, so that's why he came to *Bhir mhing na nHam*. She was very sweet and was quite worried about him. She didn't say it, but I think she knew she was quite sick and she wanted to make sure he'd be OK once she wasn't there to help him, like anyone else with a vulnerable child. She put it in a weird way, saying that Carl had been unlucky enough not to be a more obvious case for social services.'

'A sad story it is,' said the son of John. 'I'll go for a pint with you guys and meet him.'

'Yeah, that'd be cool,' said Myles. 'I wanted to meet up with him tomorrow to go for one of those 'two for one' cocktails, but I have a lesson after work and won't be able to make it.'

'What lesson?' asked the son of John.

'Didn't I tell you? I'm taking Irish lessons,' explained Myles.

His brows rose. 'You never said anything.'

'Well, you remember I was using a book to teach myself Irish on the train on the way to work, right? I found a lady that teaches Irish here in *Bhir mhing na nHam* and I'm having two hours of lessons a week, starting tomorrow.'

'Alright,' said the son of John.

'I'm really getting into it. I think it's a great language, and the language of my ancestors, so I thought I had to learn it. And funnily enough, this teacher's family and my family are from the same Irish county.'

'She could be your cousin,' joked the son of John.

'Yeah, I know,' said Myles of the wandering mind. 'You know I really like researching into family trees and that. I found her teaching profile on a website, and I just thought I'd check her family tree to see where she was from in Ireland. She's been in England most of her life, but I managed to trace her family back to fifteenth of December 1882, which is when her great-great-grandfather was born in Maamtrasna, Connemara. So, I can actually turn up to the lesson tomorrow and tell her that, as she might not know much about her great-great-grandfather.'

'I think that might really freak her out,' said Greg shaking his head. 'She'll think you're a stalker and will call the police.'

He chuckled. 'Yeah, you're right, actually. She'll think I'm a genealogical stalker!'

It is then that Myles told the son of John more about his genealogical research, and about what he'd found out about his own family. 'It's interesting what you find out when you just do a bit of research,' explained Myles. 'My dad's Irish, although way down the line, he comes from English military men who went to Ireland when they were battling in Cromwell's army. Eventually, they stayed over and married some of the locals, the typical Anglo-Irish aristocrats, a mixture of Catholics and Protestants. My mum's Austrian Jewish though. My dad moved here in his early twenties but my mum was born here, her mother moved to England when she was ten, and because both her parents were German speakers, she always had a strong German accent, well, Austrian. I still laugh when I think of her not distinguishing between *eating crab* or *eating crap*.

'So, what about your mother's family? Did they come here escaping from the war?' asked the son of John.

'Yeah, they did. My mum's grandfather used to be a lawyer in Austria but they came here when things started getting a bit nasty for the Jews. They thought here they'd be safe but when he came here with his Austrian passport, he was taken to a camp in the Isle of Man because they thought he could be a spy.'

'Who thought that?' asked the son of John.

'The British, either the police, or the army or someone did. But he was let out of that camp after a couple of years I think, and then he started working as a translator for the British army,' explained Myles. 'My mum says that he never really talked about the camp much, but she says that what really got him angry was that they'd taken away a brown jacket he had. He was a prisoner in a camp for a few years and the only thing he complained about is that someone stole his brown jacket almost as soon as he got there... one of the guards of the camp. I did a bit of research on my mum's side of the family, and I managed to contact a distant relative who lives in Vienna. His family used to be horse merchants but now they run a prestige car dealership outside Vienna. They are the stereotypical Jewish family.'

'So, you're like Harrison Ford, aren't you?' asked the son of John with a joke in his head as they were stopping at Selly Oak Station.

'Why? Does he also have a family tree decorating his room at home?'

'I don't know about that,' said Greg the tall one, 'but I think he's also half Irish and half Jewish. I remember an interview when he said he felt Irish as a person and Jewish as an actor, or something along those lines.'

'Hehe, that's a good way of looking at it,' said Myles of the brown eyes. 'I think I feel Irish as a drinker, and Jewish the other two hours of the day.'

'Yeah, I can see that,' said the son of John.

The both of them saw Selly Oak Station disappear in the distance as Myles started to tell the son of John his religious history.

'I was more Catholic than anything else when I was a kid, which is a bit weird for a kid with a Jewish mum,' Myles of the many gods started explaining, 'but I saw my Irish family a lot more, so it was more of an identity thing. I was also a Buddhist for over a year, but then when I was sixteen and ten days, I realised that you couldn't really be a Buddhist coming from a council estate. I had to do a bit of research into Nazi Germany when I was doing my A2 in German, so then I decided to become Jewish. Then, about three years ago I become a Messianic Jew.'

'Wow, mate, you've been around!' said the son of John. 'So, what's the difference between a Jew and a Messianic Jew?'

'Messianic Jews are Jews who believe in Jesus,' explained Myles.

'So, that's a Christian, isn't it?' asked the son of John with confusion in his head.

Myles the religious one continued explaining the difference while our two great heroes continued on their way towards New Street Station carried by the horse o' *mhetal*.

It was ten after *a chlog hwen* Myles and the son of John walked down the ramp on their way out of New Street Station, when everyone else in the city centre was going the opposite direction. The shoal of people walking up the ramp, tired and slow after their three times three hours shifts, reminded Myles of exhausted salmons swimming up a stream. The two friends continued up the street until they got to the corner of Union Street, and then they turned right on their way to *Dhirty* O'Brien's, where Carl, the *turd* member of this Holy Trinity, was waiting for them.

'May God be with you!' said the son of John when he shook Carl's hand.

'May God and Mary be with you!' answered Carl of the distant land.

Carl had just finished his first 'blonde in the long black dress' when Myles offered to buy another round. 'Can I have three pints of the extra cold stout, please?'

'Sorry, son, we only have the real stuff in here,' said a strong Dublin accent behind the bar to let Myles know that they only had Arthur's original draught stout there.

'Yeah, that's fine,' said Myles while he was reaching for his wallet. 'I'll also order some food...'

The three of them sat at a table underneath photos of the river Boyne, they raised their glasses saying *sláinte,* and Carl started to tell Myles about his job after his first sip of stout.

'So, yeah, I went there to the interview, and they were pretty much the questions we'd been practising at yours,' said Carl to Myles the helpful. 'It's a language centre that is inside the School of Languages, and I just do some general admin.'

'So, do you have much work to do?' asked the son of John to enter the conversation.

'I do now, because all the language courses are starting soon and you always have some late enrollers and some people who want to change their courses, but I think that it'll get a lot quieter because they don't allow any more transfers or group changes after the tenth.'

'Well, that's good,' said Myles. 'I'm glad you're enjoying it, and you could maybe progress in there, or even move to another section of the university once you're in.'

'Yeah, I think once you're familiar with the procedures of the university, you might be able to transfer to other departments if you want to, although I really like the language area. Plus, I get a few little perks. I can, obviously, use the university library and get books out, and I can also do language courses for free, so I might enrol in a French course.'

'That should be good, actually,' said the son of John. 'I think those language courses must be quite good to get to know people as well.'

'Yeah, I think so,' replied Carl. 'When I went to university I joined a James Joyce readers' club, although the only person I ended up meeting regularly was this guy,' said Carl pointing at Myles.

'Yeah, but you're happy you met me, man,' said Myles the kind-hearted one, 'I took you to some good parties.'

'Yeah, like the one with the pipe,' said Carl bursting with laughter.

'What happened there?' asked the son of John.

'We were on our way to a house party at a halls of residence called Henry France,' started explaining Myles, 'and we found a ten-foot pipe next to some roadworks, so we grabbed it and ten minutes later we got to the party with a crate of beer and a massive pipe.'

'And did they let you in with that?' asked the son of John curiously.

'Yeah, they did,' answered Myles. 'And it only took a few minutes until people started using it as a giant straw.'

'Yeah, I still have the pictures,' said Carl with a smile on his face.

Myles the happy one continued talking about their deed, and these are the words he said: 'People were sitting down and with the help of two other guys took the massive pipe to their mouth and held it in a bit of an angle so that the booze would fall down slowly, then someone else would pour some drink into it. Then, when that person couldn't drink anymore, we had to use a saucepan as a lid so that the booze wouldn't fall on the floor. It was disgusting. Everyone drinking from the same pipe and mixing all kinds of random drinks in the pipe, the saucepan had leftovers of the bacon and cabbage that someone in the house had been cooking and on top of that, the pipe had a bit of mud and sand inside. It was disgusting.'

'But so much fun!' added Carl.

'What happened to the pipe after the party?' asked the son of John.

'Well, my friends Jordan and Joel Liverpool, who lived in that place, loved the pipe and wanted to keep it for another party, so they just lifted up the false ceiling in the corridor and left it in there. There were all kinds of crap that students had been accumulating there for ages, and…,' Myles stopped to laugh a bit before he continued with the story, 'and we found there in the false ceiling an inflatable sheep with a cheap dildo glued to its ass, so that became the pet of the house. They put it on a chair in the kitchen and stayed there the rest of the year. They used to live with a Welsh guy called Jaz and he took the Welsh flag off his wall and wrapped the sheep in it. Such a great bunch of people,' concluded Myles as he made some space on the table for the salmon the waitress was serving them.

The son of John was laughing and showing his teeth, which seemed the colour of dark brown because of a coating of stout.

'So, what is it that you teach?' Carl asked the son of John when the laughs about the pipe story were dying off.

'I usually teach psychology, although this year I'm also teaching history,' answered the son of John as they were all devouring their salmon.

'That's a bit of a change, isn't it?' asked Carl before having another sip of his stout.

'Yeah, it is,' said the son of John, 'but they do that at times if your timetable's light or if they need to cover some extra groups they've had to open.'

'That's what happened to me,' said Myles of the thirsty mouth. 'The enrolment numbers in my subjects have been a bit low in the last two years, so they've asked me to teach Travel and Tourism.'

'Alright, I didn't know that,' said Carl. 'So, how's that going?'

'It's very hard to sort yourself out when you work in two departments. Saying that, teaching Travel and Tourism is interesting,' said Myles. 'You'll be surprised at the kind of students I get there.'

'Really? Why?' asked Carl.

'Well, there are some special cases,' said Myles. 'The course has a strong coursework component, and what those kids write in their coursework's hilarious. I have a student now that wrote, *the best way to get to Italy, is to get a flight to Geneva and then catch the train*. Then I was like, are you sure? I'm convinced that somewhere in Italy there must be an airport, at least one. He said, *no, there isn't, I've researched it*, so I just left him to it.'

The son of John laughed between sip and sip.

'Another classic one is the kid who wrote, *the bombing in Zurich was a tourist act*. I just said, *well, they had rucksacks, but I don't think there were tourists*. Some of my students can't tell the difference between *terrorist* or *tourist*. They also write things like, *I live in a terrorist house*, instead of, *terrace*.'

Again, the son of John laughed. 'I have a student that always writes, *the pacific problem*. I just say to him, *Pacific is an ocean, not a problem*.'

'Yeah,' said Myles. 'I've had that a couple of times too. I had a few good ones last term, actually. One girl wrote, *Amsterdam is the capital of Germany*, and then a few paragraphs later she wrote, *Berlin is a city east of the German border*. I just asked her if she'd been using a book from the sixties, but she didn't get it.'

'That's like Barry's student,' said the son of John. 'Barry showed me an essay the other day on media from one of his kids in his GCSE resit group and the opening line was, *I like TV yeah, because it gives me a bear joke*.'

Our Holy Trinity laughed. 'I'd heard that one before,' added the son of John. 'That's the same kid whose parole officer came to college at the beginning of the year to tell student services that he was very worried about students knowing about his past and his electronic tag, and then he came in the first day to his P.E. lesson wearing shorts to play basketball shouting, *hey, yo, check out my tag.*'

Carl laughed and was happy, one of his happiest moments in *Bhir mhing na nHam* so far. Feeling part of a group was not a feeling he was used to.

'I know that kid,' said Myles. 'He's the one who calls me, *yo, sir,* and wrote, *fisho* for *fish* in a Spanish exam. His girlfriend does Travel and Tourism with me and she wrote in her coursework, *The Sagrada Familia is Gaudí's church. These historical monuments are very expensive but what really puts the building costs up are the locations, as they always build them in tourist areas near the centre.*'

'That sounds about right,' said the son of John. 'Some of our kids think historic monuments are just being built in tourist spots to entertain tourists, instead of imagining that maybe those historic monuments are what attract people to the area in the first place.'

Carl went to the bar to get another three pints of the real stuff while the other two teachers continued laughing at the table, and by the time he got back to the table, the topic of the conversation had changed.

'So, what did you do if you couldn't find a van to hire?' asked the son of John to Myles while Carl was putting some drinks on the table.

'Well, it all worked out pretty well,' Myles the ingenious one started explaining. 'It was my friend O'Sullivan's stag weekend, and I used the college minibus to go to Edinburgh. I'm in charge of the Duke of Edinburgh awards at college, and quite a few of the countryside routes and camping sites were closed a few months ago because of the spread of the Mad Cow disease, so I thought I had the perfect alibi to take the bus to Scotland, as the Scottish routes were open. So, I got the college minibus, and I went to O'Sullivan's place, where the other four times three lads were meeting. We were all there, and the last guy, a crazy guy I used to live with who now lives in *Bhir mhing na nHam*, turns up with a crate of stout and a bucket. We all asked him what the bucket was for, and he just said that he'd have to piss somewhere. By the time we'd passed Manchester, where we had to pick another guy up, the bucket was already half full of piss. Anyway, we got to Edinburgh on Friday night with the college minibus, went out all weekend and then drove back on Sunday night. On Monday, I got a phone call from the principal asking me if I knew where the minibus was, so I said I'd taken it out on a trip to Scotland to do a bit of fieldwork and investigate if I could take my Duke of Edinburgh group there. He was relieved because he thought that someone had stolen it, but still asked me to go into his office. He obviously didn't believe me and carried on asking me what tracks were opened in Scotland. I'd done my research, so I started talking about a track near Stirling, but that the accommodation wasn't great, but that there was another good track near Bandrum, and that because it was near Edinburgh, we could stay in Edinburgh and drive there to do the walking. He asked me why I hadn't requested authorisation from him before taking the minibus, so I said that I'd signed on the minibus register and since I didn't ask for his permission to go on other Duke of Edinburgh trips, I didn't think I had to ask for permission for this one. I know for a fact that he didn't believe me, but the mileage was correct for a trip to Edinburgh, so he couldn't do anything about it.'

Carl and the son of John laughed together.

'I even claimed the petrol money back and got two days off in lieu because of spending the weekend on college business,' added Myles the witty one.

Our Holy Trinity continued telling stories the like of that, and it was a grand time they had. The three of them seemed happy and smiled between sips and more sips of stout, although the happy times came to an end when Carl lifted his head up and said, 'Wow, another one!'

Myles and the son of John looked at the television and they saw Kathleen Ni Houlihan presenting the evening news. The television was on mute but the three of them recognised the streets of *Bhir mhing na nHam* in the news report and read the headlines that said, *Victim found near Edgbaston school*. They saw a police officer being interviewed and a few images of what seemed to be a street gang, although there wasn't much that they could guess about what had happened.

'It is with sadness that I receive that news,' said Myles the foreteller, 'because I believe that this is the beginning of a dark year, a year in which we will be involved in some sad happenings in one way or another. Bad cess to this year. I am with my living in *Bhir mhing na nHam*, and this place will see its darkest nights within the next year. It is a wedge of itself that splits the oak, and the wedge is now loose.'

It was ten o'clock when Carl made it back to his room from *Dhirty* O'Brien's after three times three pints of stout. He took off his brown trainers and left them underneath his bed. Carl stood up in the middle of his room, shaking like a dying horse, looking through his window at a school. A school soulless at night without any children in it. Without any children copying from their history book.

Carl reached to his desk and grabbed a book, perhaps the best book that had ever come out of Ireland. 'Oh, what a grand night it was,' said Carl. 'With the sweet stories of Myles the great, and the companion of the son of John. Many a laughter I had with these great men, whose equals I have never seen, neither east nor west. There is no strength in my hands tonight, there is no power within me, like a tired horse at the end of the road. It is no wonder I to be sorrowful, being thrown down in the sorrow of drunkenness. Everything is a grief to me beyond any other man on the face of *Bhir mhing na nHam*. Now my strength has run away from me, it is with great tiredness that my whole body feels tonight, my hands, my feet, my arms, my legs, and my head, tired, tired, drunk, and tired, but no matter how long the day, the evening will come. I didn't come from the west on a horse from *Tír na nÓg*, riding the sea; I came from the south inside a flying horse o' m*h*etal, riding the skies, from *Tír bhral nThar*, not from the land of the youth but from the land of the pirates as the children of Breogán call it. It is long the clouds are over me tonight! Tomorrow will be a long day to me! It is long the clouds are over me tonight! With the want of something for my headache tomorrow, it is long the clouds are over me tonight! It is a pity the way I am, it is long the clouds are over me tonight! I am the last one standing of the Fianna of *nDirty* O'Brien's, listening to the voices in my head, it is long the clouds are over me tonight.'

A Dead Man's Ice Cream

# Chapter 3

## Mutual *understranding*

From: Carl
Subject: My Birmingham adventure!!

Hola, everyone!

I received last week an email from one of you guys saying that I haven't sent any emails lately because I'm too busy sleeping with fat sweaty guys, so I decided to email you to prove to you that I'm not doing that. The world of philology is keeping me busy.

I met up with Myles eleven days ago, that friend from university, and a guy that works with him at a local Sixth Form college. We went out for a drink after work and by the time I got back, I'd already thrown up a few times in the street. Also, I did make a discovery and if you mix salmon and stout, your vomit comes out green.

Luckily, I didn't have to go into work till eleven the next morning as ICT services had to finish installing some new computers and stuff, so I managed to sleep a few more hours than usual. I don't really remember waking up, getting dressed, or leaving the house. All I remember is sitting on the train and looking at the canal on the way to work not knowing how I got there. I think I was still drunk and all I could think about was about how dirty the canal water was. It was just green, dirty green, salmon and stout green, and I don't know why the ducks were swimming and trying to go against the mini tide created by the canal boats when they could have walked on it perfectly well. The water looked like it had the consistency of solid jelly. As I was examining the green tide, I got a draft of air on my face that smelt like rotten egg mixed with vinegar, and yep, when I turned around, that smelly guy I've told you about before was sitting a few rows behind me.

I entertained myself a bit more, looking at the water in the canal until I started feeling sick, but then it was time to get off. I managed to get to my office at bang on eleven o'clock, took a look at my diary and felt lucky I didn't have much to do that day. The new language courses had already started, so I didn't have much admin to do. I wish all days could be like that, a few emails here and there, changing some names from one register to another, and then some payment forms. The forms are quite easy. You just need to photocopy a form per tutor, (tutors are language teachers in my department; lecturers are the ones who teach in the School of Languages, formerly known as the School of Philology). Anyway, you just have to photocopy a form per tutor, leave it in their tray, and then send an email with the instructions on how to fill them in before the payment deadline. It doesn't take long but once I'd photocopied all the forms and went to leave them in the trays, I realised that instead of photocopying the forms on double sides, I had photocopied the same side twice on each form, so I had to start again. I then spotted a typo in the email I had sent with the instructions as I had typed, *a shite office* instead of saying what colour the office was. You know I do those kinds of things. By the time I was ready to go, I got an email from a student asking me to switch him to another group, so I did that before I left as I felt it wouldn't be fair to not change his course just because he'd sent me the email just a few minutes after the final deadline. But that was annoying because if I'd finished a few minutes earlier, I would have got to walk to the station with Penelope. She's a very good-looking Spanish lecturer. She's new, I met her last week, and I really like her. She's come into the office a few times to say hi and we've talked about Spain and that, and she's said the usual jokes and comments about Gib, so there's a bit of banter going on. She's very nice and smiles a lot, so I want to see if I manage to walk back to the station with her at some point. I'm usually nervous talking to people. I don't know, but it's different with her.

Anyway, by the time I'd left work, my hangover was coming back, very badly actually. I saw the train coming, but I started feeling sick when I tried to run to catch it, so I just stopped and waited for the next one. It was one of those hangovers where you can still taste the alcohol at the back of your tongue. The headache was getting a lot worse, and at one point it felt like someone was shaking my head, so I just made it back home and looked for some painkillers. I couldn't find any and I felt bad about grabbing any off my housemate, so I went to the little corner shop and paid an extortionate price for them. I had two with a bit of milk and that was the biggest mistake I could have made that day. I felt like the two tablets got stuck in my throat, and all I could taste was the milk that had started to go off and was repeating on me. I was supposed to meet Myles later that evening but there was no way I could have made it outside of the house, so I had to text him and cancel on him. I really felt bad for a few days, as I'd told him I'd go to the pub quiz with him, but I really didn't feel well. I crawled to bed and I suddenly felt freezing, so I just grabbed a green jumper I had by the bed and put it on top of the pyjamas I was already wearing.

The next day I woke up nice and early and, luckily, the hangover was gone. I hadn't seen Charles for a few days as he'd been on nights, but he was there in the kitchen when I went to have breakfast. It was nice to catch up. He's a really cool guy, and I like him, but I know what you'll say, that I like everyone and that for me everyone's nice, but he's been very helpful and quite nice to me, although it's a pity he works so much because we haven't been able to hang out much. We just talked about how work was going and he said he'd been very busy because one of the guys from work was on holidays, so there was extra work for him and his team to do. But he said things should get a bit calmer when the guy comes back and that he'd be able to go for a few drinks then.

The rest of the week was quite easy at work, so I just did the usual admin stuff and talked to Penelope a few times. She's so nice. She's currently doing some research on Andalusian culture in Lorca's plays, so we talked about it for a bit. She said she was planning to go to a conference in Granada, so I recommended a few things for her to do and a few places to visit around the south of Spain. Myles had invited me to go to a party on Saturday and I was so close to asking her if she fancied it, but I really got nervous when I started thinking about it and I didn't say anything to her in the end. I know I've always done this, but with this girl it's different.

That party on Saturday was really cool, but the beginning of it was quite bizarre. Myles has a friend called Barry, who works with him at a local college. Barry teaches English and he's a really interesting guy. He's the stereotypical philologist; he loves reading, writes shorts stories and poetry, and he also writes some articles on literary criticism. He also plays the guitar in some kind of rocky, folk band, and he's a very rare mixture of hippy, bohemian, and party animal. Barry had a very tough upbringing, running away from home when he was a kid, and finally growing up going from foster parents to foster parents. His biological mum was North American, but she moved to England when she was in her early twenties. Her granddad was something like a fourth or an eighth Native American, and Barry was quite interested in learning about the Native American movements. He had read somewhere that the tribe his mum descended from had been eradicated some time ago when the government gave the Indians some blankets to protect themselves during a really cold winter. The blankets were infected with anthrax, and when they died, the government took over their land. They were convinced that they'd find gold on their land, but they never did, all they found were some old carvings on stones telling some ancient stories, so all the government got out of extinguishing that tribe was a short academic article on ancient narrative techniques. Barry also told us that something similar had happened during another war when a guy gave the Indians blankets infected with smallpox. I think the guy opened a college. Anyway, Barry seemed very into his Indian heritage, and into a hippy American master student at Edgbaston Uni. When they first met, Barry told her he pitied Americans because it's really difficult to sound intelligent with that kind of accent, but she found him funny and they became friends. Anyway, she once told him that she knew a guy who lived in Moseley who was an honorary member of some American tribe. Moseley is a pretty bohemian neighbourhood in Birmingham and it attracts those kinds of people. The guy was going to have a little party on that Saturday and invited Barry to pop by beforehand, as Stella, the

American student, had told him that Barry would love to smoke the peace pipe and have some kind of Indian ceremony.

Myles, Barry, Stella, and I got to the little apartment in Moseley and after a few minutes, the honorary Native American finally opened the door. He told us to wait in the lounge as he was boiling some water to prepare for the ceremony, so we just waited there and examined the decoration of the flat. Some landscape pictures on the wall, some flowers made out of colour paper in a vase, and a few slices of old pizza on the coffee table by a book on Medieval Romance literature decorated the room. We all thought that the ceremony thing would be just a bit of a laugh, but the guy took it quite seriously. He came out of the kitchen and brought two bowls with some boiling water and leaves in them, which he said were used as a perfume to purify the air. He really was getting into the whole ceremony thing, and he had a very strong Black Country accent that made it all even funnier (the Black Country is an area next to Birmingham). He went into his room and came out a few minutes later carrying a peace pipe and a bag full of leaves, and wearing some traditional Indian dress with feathers. He told us to sit on the floor on the side and said that he needed all of us to be facing west. He stood up shaking the peace pipe in the air, then started singing some phrases in an Indian language while he was walking in circles, and then sat down after he'd blown a bit of sand to the west. He took some green leaves and put them in the peace pipe and started smoking it. I don't know what it was, but it could well have been just tea or something like that. Barry was quite worried about choking when it was his turn to smoke, and Stella and the Black Country Native American started their hippy talk saying that Barry had been touched by the Indian spirit and that was why he was looking so fazed out. I think he was like that because he had smoked some weed on the way to Moseley.

We finished the ceremony and then the guy told us how he'd become an honorary Native American and started talking about Indian beliefs. He told us about how Native Americans can't believe how people could mine the land, which they interpret as hurting Manitou, the Spirit of the Earth, further explaining how they always sit on the ground to be close to the Spirit of the Earth, which is why they don't understand why people can sit on chairs away from the Earth's touch or live in tall buildings, removing themselves from the Earth's spirit even further. I thought those were interesting points.

A few minutes later, the first guests of the party came over, and that was pretty much the end of the Indian ceremony. I met some cool people and there was a guest who everyone said was a *Germanphobe*; he washed his hands a lot and was always using alcohol gel, but I don't know why he feared Germans so much. I guess he was just racist, because someone was talking about the rights of old people and the terminally ill to end their life and he started saying pretty bad things about *the youth in Asia*. I got drunk very quickly and I was supposed to stay at Myles' that night, but it didn't quite work out. We went to a pub called 'The Aggressive Cockerel' and then to 'The Cow's Skull'. I was quite drunk and I couldn't find Myles anywhere. My phone battery was flat and I didn't have any money left for a taxi, so I had to walk back home, and you won't believe what happened on the way there.

I was still quite drunk, but it was very cold, so I was sobering up quite quickly. I started walking towards Selly Oak, which is the student neighbourhood in Birmingham, and once I saw Edgbaston University campus, I just walked towards it. I had the feeling that I wasn't really taking the shortest route, so I joined the canal as soon as I could because if you follow the canal, it takes you straight into the city centre. So, there I was, walking along the canal, the green water reflecting the bright light from the Moon, and I'd just passed the part of the university where I think there is a rowing club or something like that and, suddenly, I saw some lights and about eleven people just in front of me. It was the police. One guy came running towards me. He didn't know what to say at first as he seemed quite surprised to have seen someone along the canal at that time; it was quite late. The guy told me that I wasn't allowed to continue walking along the canal. I told him I was trying to get back home near Five Ways, so the guy said he'd explain how to get there after getting some of my details down. He said it was a standard procedure and wrote down my name and contact details and asked me quite a few times what I was doing around the canal at that time. He also asked for the contact details of those people who could confirm where I'd been that night. I don't think he liked it when I said that my phone had no battery and that I couldn't give him Myles' phone number, but I gave Myles' other details as best I could, and I also told them where he worked, so that they could talk to him if they wanted. The cop explained to me how to get to Five Ways and, as I was saying thank you and was ready to leave, I saw the cops taking something out of the canal. Some of the other cops pointed their torches at it, and I saw that what they were taking out of the canal was a dead body. The cop I'd been talking to got in the middle to block my view and asked me to leave immediately, so I did and started walking back to mine again.

I couldn't stop thinking about it and I was quite scared. The police must have thought that it was very random to be walking along the canal on my own at that time. I couldn't stop thinking that he'd asked for my contact details, and I got quite scared thinking that they might come to my home or to work one day asking to interrogate me. I finally made it back home, and by the time I got in, I felt quite sober. I went into the kitchen and I saw on the table the journal I'd brought from work the previous day. Penelope had published an article in that journal, and I thought I'd give it a read to see what it was like. The journal had a few tea stains on the cover now and I was sure it'd been Charles, but it was my fault for leaving it on the kitchen table. There were a few used tea bags in a bowl and a used mug in the sink. I took the tea bags out of the bowl to put them in the bin and they were still dripping a bit, so somehow that reminded me of the dead body again, as I could see blood dripping from its face as the cops were pulling it out of the canal.

I made myself a cup of tea and went upstairs on the computer. I hadn't been in Birmingham for that long and I already knew of three murders. Everyone calls Limerick stab city, but I was starting to think that it was much worse down here. I thought about putting the news on, but I thought that if the police had found the body only a few hours ago, there wouldn't be anything on it in the news yet. So, I went to sleep and had a very good lie in.

I woke up at eleven the next morning, and I immediately felt quite happy I didn't have a hangover. Somehow, my phone was charged, so I guess I must have plugged it in at some point. When I checked it, I saw a few missed calls from Myles and a text asking me where I was. I texted him saying that I'd made it back and he called me straight away. He said that he was very worried about me because he'd heard about a body being found in the canal and thought it could have been me. I told him I'd seen it and that the police got my details because I happened to be walking around there when they got the body out. Myles asked me if I'd been fully interrogated. He told me a friend of his works as a security guard at university and that he's the one who called the police when he'd heard some noise near the rowing club. I went on the net looking for some information on the murder, but I couldn't find anything, so I just spent the rest of the day trying to understand Penelope's article on poetic language in Lorca's theatre.

This morning, on my way to work, I couldn't stop looking at the canal from the very moment I got on the train at Five Ways Station. The water still looked green, and the autumn wind created a bit of a tide that was hypnotising. I sat in the middle coach this time trying to avoid the smelly guy and when I looked around to make sure he wasn't anywhere near me, I found a newspaper. There was a long article on Saturday's murder, but it wasn't too informative. The article didn't say much I didn't know already, except that the victim was a philology student. It said that the murder had happened on Saturday night, that the police had been called by the security services of Edgbaston University, and that the victim was a girl in her twenties. In fact, that was the only factual information, as the rest of the long article was just a hypothesis about the crime, and it wasn't clear whether they were the journalist's or the police's hypothesis.

I left the copy of the newspaper on the green seat and started going up the stairs at University Station. I turned left when I came out of the station and I saw again the green canal water and the tide the wind had created. There were eleven ducks swimming towards the city centre and I was just wondering whether those ducks knew anything about the murder on Saturday.

Anyway, I think that's all from me. I had some free time today at work and thought I'd put together an update for you guys. How's everything going down your end? Any news?

Well, guys, I hope you're all doing well and hope you make it to Birmingham for a visit at some point.

A cuidarse
Carl

# Chapter 4

## Friday Club diaries

### Characters

CARL: A Gibraltarian in his mid-twenties who has recently moved to Birmingham.

CHARLES: Carl's housemate. A psychiatrist. Slightly older than the other characters.

MYLES: A friend of Carl whom he met at Loughborough University.

KAZIM: Myles' former flatmate at Loughborough University

ZAIN: Kazim's friend from Moseley. He works for the UK government managing crisis and security cases. They all tease him saying that he works for MI5.

ALESSANDRO: An Italian ICT engineer Zain met at the sauna in his gym. He's a tad boring (sorry, mate).

GEORGE: A lanky ginger car engineer that Zain also met at the sauna. (I know, that's Zain for you). Sometimes they call him *GG*, short for *Ginger George*.

FERNANDO: A Spanish guy from Jerez, in southwestern Spain. He works as an aeroplane engineer and met Kazim on a night out.

JAKE: A doctor they met on a random night out.

PENELOPE: A Spanish lecturer who works with Carl.

WHITE GUY: A guy who sits with his friend next to the Friday Club crew.

BLACK GUY: A guy who sits with his friend next to the Friday Club crew.

COP: A police officer who saw Carl by the canal when they found the victim's body. He doesn't speak in the play. (I know what you're thinking: Why is he mentioned here then?).

# ACT I

*It's eight o'clock and MYLES' central Birmingham apartment is quiet. It's a small apartment with a combined kitchen and lounge area. The lounge door leads to the small hall where the front door and the buzzer are. The bathroom door is to the right of the buzzer. The laptop's playing the same songs as every other Friday. A Spanish and an acoustic guitar are lying on the carpet. Everything in the room is covered by an orange light that comes from an old lightbulb.*

*The buzzer rings and MYLES opens the door without even asking who it is. He leaves the front room open and someone comes through a couple of minutes later.*

KAZIM:    *(Walking into the lounge and taking his coat off.)* I've got a present for you, cunt.

MYLES:    What is it this time?

KAZIM:    *(Smiling while he hands MYLES a little box.)* You're gonna love this shit.

MYLES:    *(Looking at it.)* A box of lamb kidneys reduced to eighty-eight pence? I've always wanted one. Thanks, mate.

KAZIM:    Any time. You deserve that and more. It was a good price. Supply and demand, you know!

*They hug jokingly.*

MYLES:    What d'you wanna have?

KAZIM:    I've brought some vodka and orange mixer. D'you have ice?

MYLES:    *(Grabbing a glass and pouring some ice in it.)* There you go.

KAZIM:    Who's out tonight?

MYLES:    The usual Friday Club crowd. *(Opening a can of lager he's just taken out of the fridge.)* Carl's coming with his flatmate.

KAZIM:    Is she hot?

MYLES:    Don't know, haven't met him. He's a psychiatrist.

KAZIM:    What? He's coming with a bloke. *(Taking a sip of his drink.)* I like Carl, he's a nice guy, but he needs to start surrounding himself with some pussy. Also, I've told you before, Friday Club's becoming a cock fest, and you're not helping by inviting more blokes.

MYLES:     That's because whenever a girl comes here, someone ends up shagging her.

KAZIM:     Damn right. *(The buzzer goes off again, KAZIM presses the button and comes back to the kitchen.)* That's because you only bring tarts here. Did I tell you I had a bit of an argument with that chick Jake brought last time?

MYLES:     No, what happened? *(While looking towards the door to see who it was this time.)*

KAZIM:     I was quite drunk and so was she, I pulled her at Ritzy and then she threw up, not necessarily in that order, as I found out later on. Anyway, I went back to hers and I ended up shagging her. Then someone rang in the morning and I picked it up. I was still drunk, and I thought it was my phone. An older guy asked if this was Clarissa and I just said, 'I only met her yesterday, and I didn't catch her name, but I guess that's her,' and I passed the phone to her. (KAZIM giggles.) It was her dad and she wasn't happy.

*KAZIM and MYLES laugh as the door opens. GEORGE comes in with ALESSANDRO and ZAIN.*

ALESSANDRO:     *(With a slight Italian accent.)* No girls here then, as usual.

ZAIN:     You should be used to it by now. We should change the official time of Friday Club from eight o'clock to eight *o'cock*!

ALESSANDRO:     Yeah, that'd be quite accurate.

*They newcomers put their shopping bags on the kitchen worktop. They take some cans out and put the rest in the fridge. The buzzer rings again and ZAIN goes to open the door.*

MYLES:     How was your week?

ALESSANDRO:     Alright, a bit busy with work but I managed to meet up with the Frenchie in the end.

KAZIM:     You bastard! I love her tits. Perfect half coconuts. She's French. I'm sure she has black hairs around her nipples and everything. *(Licking his lips.)* Hm…

*ALESSANDRO laughs as CARL comes in with CHARLES. KAZIM gives CARL a hug.*

KAZIM:     *(To CARL.)* Bastard! How you doing? I haven't seen you since… since our goodbye party at Loughborough.

CARL:     It's all good, thanks. I went back to Gibraltar for a few years and now I'm back, living here in Birmingham. *(Pointing to CHARLES.)* This is my flatmate.

KAZIM:     *(Facing CHARLES.)* So, you're the shrink? You and Carl have so much in common. You both work with autistic people. You call them patients and Carl calls them academics.

CHARLES: *(With a very posh public school accent.)* That's a bit insensitive.

KAZIM:     But you didn't say it wasn't true! Anyway, nice to meet you. I'm Kazim.

CHARLES: I'm Charles. Nice to meet you too.

MYLES:     Hey, Charles. Nice to see you've made it. I'm Myles. *(They shake hands.)*

CHARLES: Hi, nice to meet you. Carl's been telling me about you. Which one of you is plastic brick man?

MYLES:     It's him! *(Pointing at KAZIM while he looks away pretending to cough.)*

CHARLES: That's a bit of a funny name!

MYLES:     Well-deserved though.

CHARLES: What happened?

KAZIM:     Well, the day didn't start well as I woke up with a boner and I had to wait till the morning glory went down. So, I arrived well pissed off to this interview for an internship with a big plastic brick company and this Viking-looking twat asked me all kinds of shit questions, proper arrogant he and his mate were. Anyway, halfway through the meeting, the older guy opens up a box of plastic bricks, puts them on the table, and says, 'I would like you to use these pieces to clarify what you want from us for this project'. I was lost for words, so I grabbed the plastic bricks, made a willy and gave it to them. The older guy looked a bit puzzled trying to figure it out, and asked what exactly it was that I wanted from them, and then he asked if I'd tried to make the pound symbol to ask for money, because it looked like something else, so I just said, 'no, mate, can't you tell it's a cock? I just want you to go and fuck yourselves'.

ALESSANDRO: Haha, was that the day of the blind guy and the parking fine?

KAZIM: Yeah, it was a fucked-up day, but luckily, there's always a blind person in orange when you need one.

CHARLES: *(Confused.)* What?

KAZIM: I was running late for that interview and I ended up parking taking half of a zebra crossing. I was coming back to the car after the interview and I saw a traffic warden putting a fine on my car just as I was about to cross, bastard! So, *(KAZIM stops to giggle.)* I saw an old blind guy wearing a bright orange top walking towards the zebra crossing, I offered to help him cross, grabbed him by the arm and then I shouted at the traffic warden while I opened my car with the remote key. The warden guy must have felt bad, so he broke the ticket while I was still crossing the street with the blind guy from my arm. When the traffic warden went to the next car, I just said bye to the blind guy, got in the car, and drove away before the traffic warden saw me.

CHARLES: That was a bit harsh on the blind guy.

KAZIM: Nah, he was a grumpy bastard. Oh, man, that really was a fucked-up day. I went to a funeral after that and the priest must have been retarded because the coffin was at the front of the church, with the lid open during the service and he started swinging the incense holder by the body as some sort of infidel ritual and the twat dropped it and got incense all over the dead person's face. The priest and his little helper were trying to clean all the incense off the face, the widow was crying, such a fucking mess.

*They all laugh. MYLES introduces CARL and CHARLES to the others. GEORGE gives them two cans of lager from the fridge.*

GEORGE: Hey! Welcome to the Friday Club.

ALL OF THEM: *(Raising their drinks.)* Cheers!

CHARLES: So, this is Friday Club, then? Carl told me that Friday Club is where the brightest minds of Birmingham meet every Friday.

*The buzzer rings again and ALESSANDRO goes to press the button.*

MYLES:   Yep. To talk about all important current issues in society. We have experts in all spheres of knowledge here. We have Zain, who's the expert in national security and politics. Alessandro, the ICT engineer. George, the automobile engineer. I'm the expert in education.

KAZIM:   And I'm the pussy expert.

CHARLES: So where are the girls then?

KAZIM:   They're waiting for us in the pub. There are clits of women waiting for us.

CHARLES: Clits of women? Is that like a pride of lions? I'd never heard that one before.

KAZIM:   Yes. The flexibility of the English language lets you come up with these magical collective nouns. A clit of women, a twat of public school boys, you know.

CHARLES: Why a twat of public school boys?

KAZIM:   Oh, so you're one of them, right?

CARL:   *(Interrupting shily.)* Thinking about my grandmother, a bravery of women is more accurate. Spanish grandmothers are the engines that keep families going.

CHARLES: *(Ignoring CARL's comment and looking at KAZIM.)* So, how come all those *clits* of women aren't here?

KAZIM:   I thought we could have a boys' night.

MYLES:   Nah, he just scares all the girls away with his filthy jokes!

CHARLES: I can see how he'd be the expert at that.

KAZIM:   *(With a mixture of pride and sarcasm.)* I'm the best at that! I have now learned that a small investment in everyday products can result in huge returns when it comes to comedy value.

CHARLES: *(With a challenging tone.)* It sounds like there's something you want to tell us.

*ALESSANDRO, ZAIN, and GEORGE laugh. KAZIM has a sip of his drink and the door opens. FERNANDO walks in.*

KAZIM: *(Shaking FERNANDO's hand.)* Another Spaniard! As if we didn't have enough with Carl.

*CARL smiles and doesn't feel British enough to say anything about the comment. FERNANDO shakes hands with CARL and CHARLES.*

FERNANDO: *(To CHARLES, with a strong Spanish accent.)* Hi, I'm Fernando. Are you Spanish?

CHARLES: Nice to meet you. No, I'm English.

CARL:       *(To FERNANDO.)* Hola, *encantao*. Soy de *Hibrartá*.

FERNANDO: *Coño, pues somos vecinos. Soy de Jerez.*

CHARLES: *(Addressing FERNANDO a bit confused.)* What's your name again?

FERNANDO: Fernando.

KAZIM:       *(To CHARLES.)* You can call him *Fanny* though, for his initials. His full name is *Fernando Antonio Nieto Yuste*.

CHARLES: Oh, yeah, *Fanny*. Unfortunate initials.

FERNANDO: Yeah, *(points at KAZIM.)* This bastard always loves to introduce me as *Fanny*.

KAZIM:       I keep telling you, the girls love it!

*FERNANDO goes off to say hi to the other Friday Club members and gets a bottle of whiskey outside a cupboard.*

CHARLES: So, what was that story you were gonna tell us?

KAZIM:       Well, Myles was seeing this bird, and in his defence, she was quite hot, but she was a bit of psycho. *(KAZIM has another sip of his vodka and orange.)* He'd given me a spare set of keys to his flat because he was going to be at work all day and he was going to get some furniture delivered, so I said I'd wait for it because I was gonna finish work early. He'd told me that he was going to meet up with the psycho for dinner, so I knew he'd bring her back to his.

FERNANDO: *(Looking down and taking his hand to his forehead.)* Oh, yeah, I remember that. I can't believe you did that!

*ZAIN, ALESSANDRO, and GEORGE start laughing and shaking their heads.*

KAZIM:       I did him a favour. I really did. You guys know these murders they've started calling The Birmingham case, right? *(CARL and CHARLES nod.)* I cut a few articles from the newspapers and blu-tacked them around his bedroom wall. Then I got some condoms and filled them up with milk, tied them up and left them around his room.

CHARLES: *(Taking his hand to his mouth.)* Oh, fuck!

KAZIM: *(Having another sip of his drink before continuing with this story.)* Myles came back from the restaurant with the girl, he sat in the lounge to have a drink and then he took her back to his room. At first, she was grossed out when she saw the condoms on the floor, but then she freaked out when she realised that the articles and photos on the wall were of murders and then...

*ZAIN and ALESSANDRO laugh out loud.*

MYLES: *(Talking over KAZIM.)* She just started shouting, ranting hysterically, immediately grabbed her bag, and ran off. She left an orange umbrella, so I tried to contact her to see if she wanted it back and she'd even blocked my number. When I tried to call her, I heard something like, 'Orange advises you that you are not allowed to contact this number'.

ALESSANDRO: *(To the MYLES.)* I'm surprised she didn't report you to the police. She must have thought you were the murderer.

ZAIN: *(In a joking tone.)* Exactly! That's why I think she didn't report him. Because she thought he was the murderer and was scared he was gonna kill her.

*CARL and CHARLES laugh shyly.*

KAZIM: I did you a favour, mate. You know she was a psycho!

MYLES: Yeah, but now she must be telling everyone about it. It's a pity as we had some chemistry.

KAZIM: Did you have any MUDS?

MYLES: Yes, a couple.

CHARLES: What is a MUDS?

KAZIM: *(To CHARLES.)* You gaylord! You don't have any MUDS?

CHARLES: I might have some if I knew what they were.

KAZIM: That means you have no MUDS.

CHARLES: What is a MUDS?

ZAIN:     Man, every person has at least one MUDS!

CHARLES: *(A bit annoyed.)* What the fuck is a fucking MUDS?

KAZIM:     Mate, don't get so emotional about it. It's not our fault you don't have a MUDS.

ZAIN:     Man, it's quite simple *(he starts explaining as CHARLES is looking a bit angry.)* A *MUDS* is a *movie that remains unfinished due to sex.* It's like you go to a girl's place or she comes to yours to watch a film, you press play, you start messing around a bit as the title comes up, and by the time the initial credits appear on the screen, you pause the film to go for a shag.

ALESSANDRO: Yeah, then your flatmate comes and sees your film paused in the credits and shouts, 'MUDS, MUDS, MUDS' right outside your bedroom as you're shagging the girl.

KAZIM:     Or a donkey, if you're Spanish. *(Talking to CHARLES.)* Sorry you don't have any MUDS, man, those are the best movies. *(KAZIM laughs.)* You're too fucking boring; bet you have loads of MUDWAs.

CHARLES: What's that?

KAZIM:     *Movie that remains unfinished due to wanking.*

CHARLES: *(Laughing.)* Yeah, I think we all have some of those.

KAZIM:     Well, I don't think Myles is ever gonna get another MUDS. *(Looks at MYLES and laughs.)* That psycho bitch is gonna cockblock you for life! *(KAZIM continues giggling as he puts his drink down to go to the toilet.)*

CHARLES: *(To MYLES.)* When was that? The thing about that girl I mean.

MYLES:     About a month ago, since then we haven't had any more girls at Friday Club. Hopefully, it'll be just a coincidence. A dry spell.

CHARLES: I think girls in general are a bit scared of being out and about lately anyway.

ALESSANDRO: It's been two murders with no connection and people get scared.

ZAIN:     No. *(He clears his throat.)* It's been four.

ALESSANDRO: Four?

ZAIN:     Yeah, those two murders that they used to think were score-settling are apparently linked to the one of that girl from the canal. And they found the body of another girl this morning at eight.

GEORGE: Shit, I didn't know that.

ZAIN:     Yeah, that's why a police chief had to hold an emergency meeting. It was on the news earlier. The Black community says the police didn't do anything when they found the bodies of two Black guys, but now that two White girls have been killed, they're actually starting to do something. The spokesperson said that they originally thought the first two crimes were isolated cases of score-settling, but now they have some reasons to think that they're all connected.

GEORGE: Are you serious?

ZAIN:     Yeah, but they haven't said much more than that.

MYLES:     So, are you're not working on that case?

ZAIN:     No, I only deal with bigger security risks. If it's a crime, the police deal with that.

CHARLES: *(To ZAIN.)* So what do you do?

ZAIN:     I'm a civil servant. I work on coordinating security measures.

CARL:     Wow, like James Bond?

ZAIN:     No, that's what people usually think. If something happens, like Foot and Mouth disease, I just meet with some politicians, draft a plan of action and make sure it's carried out, like talking to hospitals and making sure that they have enough vaccinations and things like that.

KAZIM:     *(He comes back from the toilet and grabs his drink.)* I'd give that eight minutes.

ALESSANDRO: *(To KAZIM.)* You dirty bastard! *(To the GROUP.)* Several wanks later he comes out. His cock smells!! I think it's all that curry he eats!

CARL:     *(To ALESSANDRO.)* That's very racist.

KAZIM:     *(Shaking his head.)* Nah, it's okay, Carl. It's just a joke between mates. It's like when Zain walks into a place and I always yell out, 'Has anyone called a taxi?' *(Looking at ALESSANDRO.)* Nah, he is a good one. He's actually just started a movement to get rid of a bunch of statues around Birmingham of people who were involved in the slave trade.

ALESSANDRO: *(To CARL.)* Laughing. I also caused a bit of an uproar at work when I changed the question of ethnicity on the HR system to a Likert scale. Number 1 was Northern Scandinavian, 3 was Mediterranean...

ZAIN:     *(To KAZIM.)* I'd still check your drink for pubes though.

KAZIM:     *(Inspecting his drink.)* Nah, it's clear. Unless there's an orange pube here and I can't see it in this light.

GEORGE: An advantage of being ginger.

ALESSANDRO: Shit, I forgot.

CHARLES: Pubes?

ZAIN:     *(To CHARLES.)* Yeah, if you leave your drink behind, someone can call 'pubes', and all of us need to pull out one of our own pubes and chuck it in the drink.

ALESSANDRO: Yeah. If you leave your drink behind, you're asking for it.

CHARLES: That's disgusting.

KAZIM:     Nah, mate. It's alright. It's a lot better than the tea bag. The tea bag is when you leave your drink behind and they dip their balls in it. The nasty one is when someone properly fully submerges their balls in your drink. You can even get crusty bits of shit and everything. The tea bag takes more skills though, as you need to have more liquid in the glass, and you need to make sure the bouncers don't see you to avoid getting kicked out. You also need more time. It takes a little more finesse. It's an art form.

CHARLES: *(With irony.)* That's a nice touch. I'll remember to never leave my drink unattended around you guys. *(To ZAIN.)* It's good to see that someone with such a serious job like yours still has time to have fun.

ZAIN:     Always.

FERNANDO: *(To ZAIN.)* So, you think that you'll get involved with the Birmingham case if it gets worse?

ZAIN:     Nah, I doubt it. I don't know in what category they will have put the investigation, but if they find more victims, they'll just put together a special team. In that case, the fewer people who know what's going on, the better.

CARL: So, what do they know about the case?

ZAIN: Not much. They haven't even said why they think that the four deaths are related.

KAZIM: Four deaths? I thought there were only three.

ZAIN: No, they found another girl this morning. *(To KAZIM.)* You were walking in the toilet when we were talking about it. A fresher that was on her way back from a fancy-dress party was found between Selly Oak and Harborne. They didn't say much more, just that she had a kidney missing.

GEORGE: Fuck, that's sick.

ZAIN: Yeah, the person who found her was on the radio before, but the police haven't confirmed if the thing about the missing kidney is true.

CHARLES: So, are they going to put a special plan in place?

ZAIN: Don't know. I guess they'll bring someone from London to help with the case.

MYLES: That's quite bad, then.

ZAIN: Yeah, it was quite bad. They showed a picture of the girl on the telly that was taken at the party where she'd last been seen. She was a cute girl dressed up as a nymph.

GEORGE: That's quite sad.

ZAIN: Yeah, I know. *(Taking a sip.)* It's the second victim they've found around that part of Birmingham, so they're planning to increase the police presence in that area.

KAZIM: I'm sure they'll get the bastard. *(KAZIM grabs a guitar and starts playing 'Fairy Tale of New York'.)*

*The Friday Club crew continues having a few drinks while KAZIM and MYLES sing a few songs. GEORGE pours himself a rum and orange and sits in the circle joining the rest to listen to the songs. The eight of them sing whatever lines they know of the songs being played.*

FERNANDO: *(To the GROUP.)* So, what's the plan for tonight?

GEORGE: I'm meeting Fletchie and the Impregnator in Jug and Violin tonight.

ZAIN:     Who's the Impregnator?

GEORGE: A friend from the gym. We call him the Impregnator because he got two girls pregnant the same month.

CHARLES: That's a very stupid mistake to make.

GEORGE: I know. We find it hilarious though, so we call him the Impregnator. He didn't end up with either of those two girls but he started going out with a girl with two kids, so he ended up with four kids in one month. *(To CHARLES.)* Just don't shake his hand or he'll impregnate you as well.

MYLES:    *(Laughing with the other guys.)* He should have done the same as our old flatmate at uni.

KAZIM:    Oh, fucking hell, he was such a fucking retard.

MYLES:    That's one way of putting it… *(Covers his mouth before coughing, has a sip of his drink, and starts with the story.)* We were having a few drinks in the kitchen one night before going out and he went to the toilet. We all assumed he was going to empty the pipes before getting them inspected, so we forgot about him.

FERNANDO: You mean take a shit?

KAZIM:    No, he means having a wank before going out to avoid the sperm going up to his head and not thinking clearly in front of the girls.

MYLES:    Yes, that pipe. Anyway, eight minutes later we heard him scream like a maniac and the whole corridor stank like burnt hair. The fire alarm went off and he ran into the lounge, with his trousers down around his ankles, walking like a penguin, and with this pubes on fire.

ZAIN:     What the fuck did he do?

MYLES:    Well, he had heard somewhere that an increase in temperature can make men infertile for some time, apparently a bit of fever can make your little swimmers not work for a few days. He wanted to shag a girl that night and thought he'd push it to do her without a condom, but he was scared about getting her pregnant, so the clever retard used a lighter to heat up his balls in the toilet in preparation for the night out.

ALESSANDRO: *(Laughing.)* Classic.

KAZIM:    Yeah, a fucking genius he was … his pubes caught fire and he burnt his balls!

ALESSANDRO: Did he shag her in the end?

MYLES:   Nah, he came out with us, but he was walking like John Wayne all night, and you could smell his burnt pubes wherever he went. He went to the toilets to spray some perfume from the toilet attendant and the toilet guy had a massive argument with our mate when he took the aftershave bottle to his balls, so he gave him £8 and the guy was as happy as Larry, but then his balls starting stinging so he got pissed off and went home before he could see the girl. I think they actually really liked each other, our flatmate and the girl, not our flatmate and the toilet guy, because there certainly was some kind of unfinished business tension whenever those two met in economics class.

KAZIM:   *(Leaving the guitar on the floor.)* She was quite a nice girl, actually. But I remember the first time I met her. She told me she was going to start a small business and that she was looking for someone to her get *cunt* sorted. *(Laughing.)* It was her accent. She was from Belfast and meant *account*.

FERNANDO: *(Addressing KAZIM.)* That's funny. Was that the same as the ginger guy and the shit?

KAZIM:   Nah, that was our other flatmate. We lived with some real fuckwits that year. *(Looking at GEORGE.)* You gingers are fucking retarded, I think the orange of your hair burns your brain.

GEORGE: Yeah, man, that's why ginger people smell when it rains; it took me ages to get rid of that smell. But there are more of us out there than you think, and we'll take over the world one day. Before, you could only see us in documentaries about witchcraft and in religious paintings, as Judas has always been portrayed with orange hair, but we're stronger now and we are out. We even have jobs now. I love being ginger though; it was the best choice I ever made. Even my cock was ginger once. One of Fanny's compatriots invited me to her apartment near Brindley Place. She cooked a paella for me and everything and I realised her hands were quite orange, apparently from the paella spice she'd used.

FERNANDO: Oh, yes, I know which one. *(Shaking his head.)* That stuff doesn't go. It's saffron with something else and it stains a lot.

GEORGE: I know. We didn't shag but she gave me a hand job. When I got home my cock was all orange. And, man, that shit doesn't go. I had an orange cock for eight days.

KAZIM: *(Looking at GEORGE.)* GG, that's cos you never wash, dirty bastard. *(THEY ALL laugh.)*

ZAIN: *(Looking at KAZIM while serving himself a rum cola.)* So, what did that other ginger guy do?

KAZIM: Ah, yeah, well, we got bored at uni, so we went through this phase of weighing our shit. So, I'd come out saying something like, 'My shit was 300 grams' or whatever it weighed…

MYLES: *(To KAZIM.)* Nah, yours were more like 800 grams.

GEORGE: *(Laughing quite loud.)* It's all that curry.

KAZIM: *(To GEORGE, laughing.)* Fuck you, orangutan, I'm gonna send you back to Borneo if you don't shut the fuck up!

ZAIN: *(Almost choking on his drink.)* Haha.

KAZIM: *(Sucks his teeth at GEORGE to intimidate him jokingly.)* Yeah, so, hm… yeah so, right. We had had this little competition going on. And one day, this retarded ginger cunt goes into the toilet and comes out eight minutes later. We all thought that he'd gone for a massive one and that he was going to be top of the league, instead, he just said that the scales weren't picking up the weight.

CHARLES: *(Entering the conversation.)* What did he mean it wasn't picking up the weight?

KAZIM: We all thought it was a bit weird, and then we heard our other housemate shout, 'What the fuck!' followed by a, 'Guys, check this out'. We went to the bathroom and there it was, a kitchen plate with a shit on it on the scales.

FERNANDO: No way!

CARL: What?

KAZIM: *(To FERNANDO.)* Yeah, man, we all started crying with laughter, but the ginger twat didn't know what was so funny… fucking hilarious. The ranga twat was so funny! He thought that everyone else had weighed their shit like that, and it wasn't until eight minutes later when we had all calmed down that we explained to him that the way to do it was to weigh yourself before and after going for a shit, and he just followed that with, 'Oh, fuck!'. Of course, we didn't bother cleaning that plate, we just threw it away.

*The eight members of Friday Club laugh in chorus.*

ZAIN:     *(Shaking his head.)* Fucking hell!

KAZIM:     Talking about fucking, are we going to leave Myles' early for once and get some pussy at The Elizabeth?

MYLES:     That's not gonna happen, mate. Every Friday night you and Fanny come here saying that you're definitely gonna get laid and eight drinks later all you do is scare all the girls away.

KAZIM:     They run away after they see you, *(pointing at MYLES, laughing, and shaking his head from side to side.)* You ugly cunt! I'm sure that the psycho girl has left pictures of you around town to warn all the girls in Birmingham about you.

MYLES:     *(After laughing briefly.)* You bastard!

CHARLES: The Elizabeth sounds good. I haven't been there in a while.

GEORGE: Should we have a shot before we go? The initiation ceremony for Carl and Charles!!

KAZIM:     *(Getting the shot glasses out before anyone agrees or disagrees with GEORGE.)* There you go.

*The buzzer goes off and FERNANDO goes to answer while GEORGE starts pouring some orange liquor into the glasses.*

ZAIN:     *(Checking his phone.)* I've just realised I got a text from Jake. He texted eight minutes ago saying he was on his way here.

GEORGE: *(Looking for another glass.)* Okay, I'll get another shot for him.

*A mixture of greetings and insults receive JAKE as he enters the lounge.*

JAKE:     *(Smiling to the GROUP.)* Fucking hell, guys, what a welcome! *(Looking at CARL and CHARLES.)* Hi again.

GEORGE: *(Putting on a Spanish accent.)* Fuck you, man! *(Hands him a shot.)*

All:     *(Lifting their glasses.)* Cheers!

JAKE:     *(Rubbing his hands while everyone's putting their glass on the kitchen benchtop.)* Guys, I'm gonna have to get you some drinks tonight.

I've just checked my phone as I was getting into the lift, and I've just made over 800 quid on the horses.

CARL:       Wow, that's good!

KAZIM:       *(To JAKE.)* Bastard, I didn't know you knew anything about horses.

JAKE:       I don't. I don't even know how many legs they have, but I've been working on geriatrics this week and old people love talking, and there's this old Irish guy there who loves horses, so every time I went to examine him, he'd show me his little cards and magazines with info on horses, so I just talked to him about it to keep him company. He'd been telling me all week about a race that was on today and he showed me his betting plan, told me what horse he thought was going to win and all that stuff, so I talked to him for a bit longer. He's a bit senile but recently diagnosed and he hasn't totally lost it yet. He had been living in a house with his wife and some friends till a bit over a week ago; eight people sharing a house and the youngest one was eighty-eight. Anyway, I kind of realised he knew what he was on about, so I put some money on the same horse as him. I didn't really know how much I could trust him, so I didn't put too much money on that horse, but I'm definitely gonna go to see him on Monday and see what he reckons for next week's races.

ALESSANDRO: *(Jokingly.)* Is it legal to use your patients in that way?

JAKE:       There's nothing written about it.

CARL:       *(With an innocent voice.)* Is it morally okay to do that?

JAKE:       Well, what's morality these days? My day started like shit so I'm glad things are turning out better. *(Shows a bruise on his right forearm to the guys.)* I woke up with a proper hard-on this morning, so I had a wank and I came in the shower. I went to have an actual shower a few minutes later, and I stepped on some cum and slipped.

KAZIM:       Fucking hell. Your jizz tried to commit parricide.

GEORGE: *(Laughing while checking the time.)* Are we going out?

*Everyone nods.*

MYLES:       *(To JAKE.)* Was it very cold outside?

JAKE:     No, it wasn't too bad, actually, just wear a jacket and you'll be fine.

MYLES:     Cool. Nice jacket by the way.

JAKE:     Thanks, man. It's from ash cash.

MYLES:     Is that the brand?

JAKE:     *(Giggling.)* No. When someone's going to be cremated, we have to do a cremation form. We have to check that the person doesn't have a pacemaker, or that it has been taken out, as it can explode. Anyway, we fill in this cremation form and we get eighty-eight quid for it. We call it, *ash cash.*

ZAIN:     That's a bit of a twisted economic transaction.

JAKE:     It gets worse. I work with a junior doctor who uses her ash cash to buy new shoes or handbags, and then she names them after the person she got the ash cash from.

KAZIM:     That's fucked up. *(He smiles and nods.)* I like her.

JAKE:     *(With irony.)* Economics at its best!

MYLES:     *(Looking at JAKE.)* Aah, actually, now that you say it, I'd heard about ash cash before, but I didn't know it was called that. *(MYLES clears his throat.)* My aunt died eight years ago. She had a dodgy blood transfusion in the eighties and ended up with kidney failure years later. They cremated her when she died and I remember my dad complaining about an additional charge on top of the cremation fees. That must have been the ash cash. My auntie always said she wanted her ashes buried next to an orange tree they used to play under in their childhood home, so my dad and his other sister got on the case. *(MYLES takes a sip of his drink and giggles.)* They knew airport security would most likely find the ashes, so they took the ferry to Ireland instead. *(MYLES giggles again.)* So, my dad and his sister drove back to their childhood home one morning and parked outside the house, waiting for the owners to leave for work. Once they'd left, my dad and his sister waited for eight minutes, and then went into the front garden of the house and buried my aunt's ashes under the orange tree.

*Everyone laughs.*

ZAIN:     Probably illegal, but I like it. *(Looking around.)* So, are we going out?

MYLES:      Yeah. Let's move.
ZAIN:       *(To MYLES.)* Could I have a plastic cup?
MYLES:      Yes, they're up there.
ZAIN:       Plastic cup anyone?
CARL:       Yeah, I'll have one for the road.
CHARLES: No, I'll be alright, thank you.
ALESSANDRO: I'll just get a beer.
KAZIM:      Come on, fuckers!

*They grab their coats and their drink and walk to the door. MYLES is the last one to leave, putting his hands in his pockets to make sure he hasn't forgotten anything. He switches the orange lights off and leaves the lounge in complete darkness. He walks out the front door and locks it from the outside.*

*Slow curtain*

# ACT II

*A section in a pub in central Birmingham covered in a gloomy orange light. CARL, MYLES, ALESSANDRO, and ZAIN are sitting at a kidney-shaped table. Behind them, there's an odd painting of what seems to be a weird bug, half worm, half butterfly, surrounded by smiling worms and butterflies coming out of a nymph's right hand.*

ALESSANDRO: Yes, I'm thinking about buying a place because I'm fed up with renting.

ZAIN:     Is it because you're living with that dodgy guy who's going out with a ladyboy?

ALESSANDRO: No, it's not that. They're both cool. It's just that rent money is a waste. I never thought about buying before because I'd always thought I'd go back to Italy, but I can't see that happening now, so I've decided to put that money into a property. Houses always go up, so even if I decide to go back to Italy in a few years, I could sell it or, maybe even better, rent it out.

ZAIN:     So how come you're not thinking about moving back to Italy then?

ALESSANDRO: It's a bit weird to explain, but I've been there a few times recently, and I'm not sure I could actually live there anymore. It just feels... slow. Nothing happens. My childhood friends are still doing the same things they were doing eight years ago. People seem to operate in slow motion.

*FERNANDO, JAKE, and CHARLES come back with drinks. They pass them out to the others and sit down.*

ALESSANDRO: So, yeah. I guess I've become more used to life in England and now it's hard to go back. It also makes sense to stay in terms of business potential. But it's weird, at this point in my life I'm not sure where I belong. I just see myself as a bit too English to fit into life in Italy, and a bit too Italian to feel like I totally fit in into English society.

FERNANDO: I know what you mean. My family asked me a few weeks ago if I was gonna move back to Spain, but I don't think it's gonna happen. I think in terms of work over there, it's all about what contacts you have. People don't care about your experience. It's a really weak foundation for a solid economic system. I really prefer the lifestyle in Spain, and especially the weather, but I don't think that in terms of work it can offer me what I want. Saying that, if I could work in Spain but for an English company getting paid an English salary, I'd go there tomorrow.

JAKE: I'll miss you guys if you went back. Birmingham wouldn't be the same.

CHARLES: *(Looking at FERNANDO.)* So, you know how long you're gonna be in England?

FERNANDO: I don't know, but I'm open to anything. That's why I decided not to buy a place here, so that if I get a good job offer somewhere else, I can just go.

ALESSANDRO: I think it's time to buy now. I'm just starting to look around at the moment and wanna see if I can get anything near the centre.

ZAIN: It's always the time to buy. If the property prices are down, it's the time to buy because you can afford it. If prices are up, it's the time to buy because people think that they'll carry on going up.

*Two guys in their twenties come up to the GROUP.*

BLACK GUY: Sorry, guys, do you mind if we squeeze in those seats there?

CARL: Yes, sure, go for it.

CHARLES: Hm... *(Not in a convincing way.)* Of course.

*They sit down. They're not at the table but they are close enough to talk to the GROUP without having to shout.*

WHITE GUY: It's a cucumber field in here tonight, in it! I *fink* the birds are hiding tonight!

ALESSANDRO: Yeah, it's a lot quieter than other nights.

*CARL stands up, waves at someone at his eight o'clock, and a girl comes over*

CARL:      Hi, I... didn't expect to see you here!

PENELOPE: *(With a noticeable Spanish accent.)* Oh, hi! Yes, I wasn't going to come out, but a friend convinced me to.

CARL:      *(Proudly.)* Hey, guys, this is Penelope. She is a Spanish lecturer from work.

ALL:       Hi there.

FERNANDO: *(To PENELOPE.) ¿Te vas a sentar?*

PENELOPE: *(She looks around.) Ah, no sé, estoy a ver si veo a mi amiga.* *(Looks at everyone else at the table.)* Sorry, it was rude to speak Spanish.

CARL:      *(To PENELOPE.) Siéntate, esta silla está libre.*

PENELOPE: *(Sitting down under the painting of the nymph.)* Yes, I might as well. I wanted to get up early tomorrow, but I came out because a friend of mine wanted to see a guy she likes who was coming here with his friends tonight. So, here I am. The loyal moral supporter. I think she's with him now.

ALESSANDRO: *(With a flat tone in his voice.)* Don't worry. We're more fun.

*GEORGE and KAZIM come to the table laughing.*

MYLES:     Hey, where were you?

KAZIM:     Recruiting! Friday Club numbers have been down lately. So, I went with GG on a recruiting expedition.

GEORGE: Yeah, man. This Aussie guy was arguing with the bouncer cos it's his eighteenth and he was coming out to celebrate, but the bouncer was telling him he is not actually eighteen just yet, and that he couldn't come in. The Aussie guy tried to argue that because Australia is eight hours ahead, he is already eighteen if you travel twenty-four hours that way by plane, so the bouncer just told him that he can go back to Australia then and celebrate his birthday there.

KAZIM:     Kangaroo rapist motherfucker! Cunt. Being upside down for so long is no good for their brains.

JAKE:      *(Laughing.)* Any new talents out there then?

KAZIM:     Nah, just a Black guy and his chavvy boyfriend! *(Addressing the two guys sitting by their table.)* Oh, hello again!

WHITE GUY: Hey, pipe man!

BLACK GUY: *(To the people at the table.)* You know this guy? Can't believe he smokes a pipe! That's bad ass, bro.

GEORGE: Yeah, and whatever he smokes smells like ass too.

*KAZIM and GEORGE sit at the table. KAZIM hits his head on a shelf as he's sitting down.*

KAZIM: *(Taking his hand to this head.)* I'm too clever for you, fuckers. Losing some neurons will only bring me down to your level.

GEORGE: *(To the guys at the table while they're still laughing.)* Oh, guys, you missed it!

MYLES and ZAIN: What?

GEORGE: Kazim and I started talking to some girls on a hen night. Kazim asked who was the one getting married. You should have seen her! A war pig! He went up to her and said, 'So, you're getting married? Who the fuck would marry you?'

*Everyone at the table laughs, except PENELOPE, CARL, and CHARLES.*

ZAIN: Did he get a slap?

KAZIM: Nah, she loved that shit!

GEORGE: Her friends were really angry, but the girl laughed and invited Kazim to a shot!

CHARLES: Can't believe you got away with that!

MYLES: He always does!

KAZIM: *(To MYLES, looking at PENELOPE.)* So, you've been recruiting too?

PENELOPE: No, I recruited myself!

KAZIM: *(To PENELOPE, in a jokey manner.)* Nah, it doesn't work like that. You know it doesn't work like that, although we could start a legal case and call it, *Vagina v Friday Club.* *(CARL looks down, CHARLES doesn't react, and the rest of the table, including PENELOPE, giggle.)*

CARL: *(To PENELOPE.)* Oh, these guys are Kazim and George.

PENELOPE: *(To KAZIM and GEORGE.)* What kind of name is that? It sounds like a cleaning product.

KAZIM: *(To PENELOPE, trying not to laugh.)* George? It's a typical English name, you foreigner.

PENELOPE: *(Giggling.)* No, *Kazim.* That's the name that sounds like a cleaning product.

KAZIM: It is. A fucking great one by the way!

BLACK GUY: *(Addressing KAZIM.)* Nah, it's Asian, in it, bro?

KAZIM: *(Turning to talk to the BLACK GUY.)* It's Australasian, thank you very much. My family is from Fiji.

PENELOPE: So, you're from Fiji then?

KAZIM: No, I'm not. I'm British. *(Rises his glass.)* To the queen!

PENELOPE: So, you were born here?

KAZIM: That's not relevant. *(Shaking his hips from side to side.)* I don't need nobody to tell me where I'm from.

MYLES: *(To PENELOPE.)* He's like that. Don't take it personally.

CHARLES: I thought you'd behave a bit better in front of girls.

KAZIM: You were wrong, mate!

*PENELOPE laughs shortly.*

KAZIM: *(To PENELOPE.)* So, where are your friends then?

PENELOPE: I think my friend is with a guy she likes.

KAZIM: What a tart!

PENELOPE: Hey!

KAZIM: What? You're gonna say it's love?

PENELOPE: Well, actually, she really likes this guy.

KAZIM: *(Pointing at MYLES and mimicking PENELOPE.)* Oh, she likes him.

PENELOPE: *(With irony.)* Very funny.

MYLES: *(To KAZIM.)* Come on, be good!

KAZIM: I'm being good. It's her friend who's behaving like a tart!

*PENELOPE laughs again, ALESSANDRO checks his watch, and JAKE and ZAIN finish their drink.*

CARL:      *(Looking around.)* Drinks anyone?

JAKE:      Nah, I'll get this one, courtesy of Mr MacFadden!

PENELOPE: Not for me, thanks. I'm gonna go in a sec.

GEORGE: You see, Kazim, you always scare them off!

PENELOPE: No, don't worry. I just came out for a bit to give my friend a bit of moral support, although as we say in Spanish, I ended up being the candle holder.

CARL:      *(Laughs.)* Yeah, that happens to me all the time.

FERNANDO: *(To the GROUP.)* That's how we say in Spanish, *to be the third wheel.* You hold the candle for two people to snog.

KAZIM:     So, you just watch and try to get a mental picture for the wank bank?

PENELOPE: Uh! No, not really. You just help your friend get a bit closer to the person she likes.

CARL: That's very nice of you.

*PENELOPE nods and smiles.*

MYLES:     Well, remember, Friday Club's on every Friday. Pop by any week, and if we think you're half decent, we might even invite you another week.

PENELOPE: Hehe, that's very considerate, thanks. And yeah, I'll pop by. *(PENELOPE puts a piece of chewing gum in her mouth and extends her hands to offer some to the guys. CARL, ALESSANDRO and FERNANDO pick one.)*

KAZIM:     Thanks, but I don't take sweets from strangers. It could have drugs in it.

PENELOPE: *(Teasing KAZIM.)* Yeah, I'm that person your parents warned you about when you were a kid. Anyway, nice to meet you, guys, and I might see you at Friday Club soon.

KAZIM:     Sleep tight, and next time bring some of those tarts you know!

PENELOPE: *(Stands up and smiles.)* I will. I'll bring some really filthy ones.

KAZIM:     Ooh, I like her.

CARL:      *(Stands up.)* You live by New Street, don't you?

PENELOPE: *(Surprised.)* Yes, how do you know that?

CARL:     You told me once by the photocopier.

PENELOPE: *(Surprised.)* Ah, Okay. Yes, I live there.

CARL:     I'll walk you back.

PENELOPE: No, don't worry. I can go on my own.

CARL:     No, really. There have been loads of dodgy stuff going on in town lately. I would feel better is you let me walk you back. It'll only take a few minutes.

PENELOPE: Okay. Thank you for that. Bye, everyone.

ZAIN and ALESSANDRO: See you, nice to meet you!

GEORGE: See you soon, mate! And bring girls to Friday Club!

KAZIM:    Yeah, you promised us some filthy tarts! So, none of that bringing respectable boring girls that expect to be taken on dates!

PENELOPE: *(Smiling.)* Don't worry. I'll bring what you're looking for.

MYLES:    Nice to meet you, Penelope. Carl had told me about you, so it was nice to put a face to your name.

CHARLES: *(Looking at CARL getting a bit shy.)* Yes, nice to meet you.

FERNANDO: *(Standing up to give her two kisses on the cheeks.)* Venga, nos vemos pronto.

CARL:     *(Looking at the painting of the butterfly.)* I should be back soon. I'll give you guys a call on my way back to see if you've moved.

GEORGE: I'm gonna go soon to meet up with Fletchie and the Impregnator but I'll catch you next Friday.

MYLES:    Yeah, see you in a bit. Keep us posted.

CHARLES: Okay, mate. See you in a bit.

*Everyone sits at the table again. The conversation continues and it is obvious that the guys are scanning the room looking for girls. JAKE comes back with a tray of drinks and KAZIM, ZAIN, MYLES and ALESSANDRO cheer.*

JAKE:     Fuck, that was awkward!

MYLES:    What? Carl's mate?

JAKE:     No, not her, she's really hot by the way, that was fine. *(To KAZIM and FERNANDO.)* I just saw UV girl.

ZAIN:     Who?

KAZIM:    Fuck, is she here?

FERNANDO: *(Covering his face with both his hands while he laughs out loud.)* Did she say anything to you?

ZAIN: Who the fuck is UV girl?

JAKE: *(Raising his voice to be heard over FERNANDO's laughter.)* I pulled a girl in Ritzy a couple of months back… I didn't even know her name, but we ended up going to the toilet together and she gave me a blow job in the cubicle. Amazing! She was good! She's one of those girls that goes out with toothpaste to freshen up before giving head. Oh, man, I couldn't even walk after that. We went back to the sixties room and the UV lights were on and I just started looking at her and was like… 'Oh, fuck!' I didn't say anything though, I just continued making small talk, sipping my drink, and feeling quite awkward, so I made an excuse to go to the toilet. She then realised that everyone was looking at her and finally checked herself in the wall mirror and saw that she had cum over her lips and along the side of her face and it was quite visible under the UV light, and quite obvious what it was.

ALESSANDRO: *(Laughs.)* Excellent. Oh man, maybe she should use that toothpaste and be freshening up *after*.

KAZIM: You should have seen her. She looked like a Dalmatian with that cum pattern on her face.

JAKE: Yeah, she didn't look great. She got angry, so I didn't say anything to her and walked off. But that wasn't everything. She walked out of Ritzy and I forgot she'd given me her keys, card, and phone to look after cos she had one of those useless little bags.

ZAIN: Shit! Did you go after her?

JAKE: Nah, I thought she'd be gone by then, so I had a few more drinks with Kazim and Fernando.

KAZIM: I kept on telling him we should pay for drinks with her card, but this stupid cunt refused to.

JAKE: Yeah, last thing I needed.

ZAIN: So, what happened then?

JAKE: She caught a taxi and went home, and then she had to wake up her parents to get into the house and borrow money to pay for the taxi.

ZAIN: Well, that's okay then.

JAKE: No, not really. I went back to work on Monday and I was telling my boss about the blow job thing. He's a highly respected doctor and recognised worldwide in his field, but he's a dirty bastard and a really cool consultant, so we really get on well. But... *(JAKE pauses before he laughs.)* What are the fucking chances? I told the guy, he first giggled and then stopped, looked at me seriously, and said, 'How funny, cos my daughter woke my wife and me up on Friday night to let her in and to borrow some money for a cab cos she'd left her purse with a friend'. I thought he was joking, so I laughed, and that really pissed him off, and then he said, 'You didn't know her name, right? I'll show you a photo to see if you remember her'. And it was her, man. It was so fucking awkward!

ALESSANDRO: Fuck, man, that's awkward!

JAKE: Yeah, it was bad.

ZAIN: Did her father say anything else?

JAKE: Yeah, he said that if I ever went anywhere near his daughter again, he'd make sure I wouldn't finish my training in the West Midlands.

KAZIM: That's harsh.

JAKE: Well, is it? I kind of get where he was coming from. I went back to my car and took the girl's stuff and gave it to the consultant. I would have loved to see the conversation when he gives his daughter her stuff back and explains how he got it all.

*THEY ALL laugh, have a sip of their drink, and then start planning the rest of their night.*

*Curtain. Curtain to get stuck 'accidentally' an eighth down*

# ACT III

*KAZIM, MYLES and CHARLES are back at MYLES' apartment. The dimmer lights give the scene an orange colour. CHARLES is sitting on the leather sofa next to a copy of 'Of Mice and Men'. MYLES is boiling some water and KAZIM is playing the acoustic guitar.*

KAZIM:     (*Sipping cider.*) So, do you think Carl got lucky? He's been gone for a few hours now.

MYLES:     Don't know, but it's a bit weird he isn't answering his phone.

CHARLES: I've just texted him again, so let's see if he replies.

KAZIM:     (*Talking about CHARLES to MYLES.*) He's a cockblocker. What a cunt! He'll turn the porter sour in your guts!

*CHARLES laughs but the buzzer rings before he answers back. MYLES opens without asking who it is and goes back to making some tea.*

KAZIM:     Was that him?

MYLES:     Don't know. We'll see. It's either him or the boys with the food. (*To CHARLES.*) Would you like some sugar in your tea?

CHARLES: No, don't worry. Just a bit of milk, please.

*The door opens and GEORGE and FERNANDO walk in.*

GEORGE: *Hola*, fuckers! I found *Fanny* at the chippy, and I thought I'd come and say hi.

KAZIM:     Orange-haired bastard! (*To FERNANDO.*) What did you get in the end?

FERNANDO: Pizza and some chicken with chips. I love Ionian pizzas.

*MYLES gets some plates out and starts putting the food on the plates.*

MYLES:     Where are Alessandro and Zain?

KAZIM:     Bumming each other. (*Nodding his head with energy and looking at CHARLES.*) They really are, don't get jealous.

CHARLES: I think I'll be alright. I don't wanna step on your terrain.

FERNANDO: *(Passing the plates around.)* No news of Carl then?

CHARLES: No. We've been calling him and I texted him again a few minutes ago, but no answer.

MYLES: *(Passing a cup of tea to CHARLES.)* I'll try and call him again in a bit. Knowing him, he'll be sitting down outside of Penelope's place looking at her window and crying.

GEORGE: *(To KAZIM.)* Dude, get some chicken too.

KAZIM: Nah, I'll be alright, I'll just have some pizza.

FERNANDO: Oh, Myles, I've just seen Gary as well.

KAZIM: What? Where was he?

FERNANDO: He was in the chippy.

MYLES: I haven't seen him since the toilet night!

GEORGE: What toilet night?

MYLES: *(Sitting down on a chair next to KAZIM.)* Yeah, didn't I tell you about it?

GEORGE: No, what happened?

*CHARLES puts the copy of 'Of Mice and Men' on the armrest next to him so that GEORGE can sit there.*

MYLES: Sorry, I thought I'd told you. D'you remember when we went to my work social and ended up in Ritzy with Gary?

GEORGE: Yeah, I do. He said he'd invite me to a few beers and then he asked for money to buy the round.

MYLES: Yeah, Gary does that. Anyway, he said he didn't have money for a cab and asked me if he could stay at mine, so I left him stay. *(Pointing to the heater.)* It was cold and that over there wasn't working, so he asked to sleep head-to-toes in my bed with me and I let him. Anyway, I woke up at eight in the morning to go for a wee-wee and Gary wasn't in my bed. I was half asleep and went to the toilet. I walk in and step into a pool. There was over an inch of water on the floor, and some orange underpants in the sink. I couldn't work out what had happened, and Gary was nowhere to be seen, so I went back to sleep. When I woke up a couple of hours later, he was there in bed again.

GEORGE: Shit, that has Gary written all over it!

KAZIM: Oh, yeah. I remember you telling me this.

CHARLES: *(Leaning forward.)* What happened to that guy?

MYLES: Well, Gary told me in the morning. He went to the toilet at night and his underpants accidently dropped into the toilet. He didn't feel brave enough to put his hand in there to grab them and thought he'd flush them down. He flushed but, of course, the toilet got blocked, and all the water came flowing over the bowl. He then just grabbed his underpants, washed them with bleach because I didn't have any soap left, and left them in the sink to dry.

GEORGE: So, why didn't he go back to bed?

MYLES: He says he felt a bit dodgy coming back to bed with no underwear on, so he went to sleep naked on the sofa, and then when his underpants had dried off, he put them on and went back to bed.

GEORGE: How the fuck did he manage to drop his underpants down there?

MYLES: That's not the worse part. The guy, somehow, got bleach on his arse and left the print of it on the leather sofa.

GEORGE: No way!

MYLES: *(To CHARLES, while moving a cushion from the sofa.)* Check it out yourself!

*CHARLES, GEORGE, and KAZIM look at it and laugh.*

GEORGE: Haha, that's hilarious! He is mental. He went to Morocco on holidays once and he ordered an omelette at a restaurant. He got charged a lot for it and got quite pissed off. Anyway, he complained to someone at the hotel, and they told him that the nearest chicken farm was eight hours away and that eggs had to travel a good distance to get there. So, he got this bright idea in his head and came back to England, sold his apartment, and used that money to open a chicken farm in Morocco. He was filling a need, right? So, he finally had everything set, he opened the farm and all that, and within eight days, all the chickens had died of heat strokes.

CHARLES: Shit, that's bad!

GEORGE: I know, man, but lesson learned! He found out why there weren't any chicken farms in that area. I guess it's something to make you think that there is always a reason for everything, even if you can't see it.

CHARLES: Yes, I guess so. *(To GEORGE.)* So what did he do after closing the chicken farm?

GEORGE: He…

*The buzzer rings, GEORGE opens the door and comes back to the lounge.*

GEORGE: It's Carl.

KAZIM:   Let's see if the old boy got some action.

*CARL walks in and goes to the toilet, leaves his shoes there, and gives his coat a good shake. He goes to the lounge. He is completely soaking wet.*

MYLES:   *(To CARL.)* Hey, dude. Fancy a cup of tea?

CARL:   Oh, yes, please. Thanks.

*MYLES puts the kettle on and takes out a mug and a bag of tea.*

KAZIM:   Did you touch her tits?

CARL:   Oh, no, not at all.

CHARLES: It took you ages to get back. I sent you a text to see if you were okay.

CARL:   *(Looking at the floor.)* Yes, I'm OK now, thanks.

GEORGE: What happened, man?

CARL:   I walked her back and saw her getting into her place. The orange light of her room came up and I just stood there.

KAZIM:   You perv! Good lad.

CARL:   No, it wasn't that. I was just looking at her window when a cop came up to me. He said he remembered me from one night when he saw me by the canal at night.

GEORGE: Oh, shit. Was that when you walked into the police getting that body out of the water?

CARL:   Yes, that was it. The cop recognised me and asked me what I was doing looking into the flat. I just froze.

CHARLES: *(Curious.)* What happened then?

CARL:     He asked to see some ID and I just took both my passports out of my pocket.

KAZIM:     Why did you have both your passports with you?

CARL:     I always do when I go out in case something happens.

KAZIM:     You could just take one passport out and leave the other one at home.

CARL:     I know, but I can never decide which one to take and which one to leave at home.

GEORGE: You should take it in turns, man. Depending on what nationality you feel like on the day. If you want to work hard and come across as a professional and respectful person, take your British passport out. If you want to party, have a siesta, and watch donkey porn, then take your Spanish one out. Simples!

CHARLES: *(Curious again.)* Anyway, so what happened?

CARL:     The police guy was confused when I showed him two passports and asked about them, so I just told him that I was from Gibraltar and that I have a British and a Spanish passport.

KAZIM:     Had he ever heard of Gibraltar? Some cops aren't the brightest chickens on the farm.

CARL:     No, he hadn't heard of it. He asked me the usual questions about what I was doing there and where I'd been tonight, and then he got his walkie-talkie out and called the police station. I was far too nervous and shaky to hear what he was saying on the radio and when he stopped talking to his colleague, he asked me to sit down on the pavement saying that I wasn't looking very well.

CHARLES: *(Without the intensity of a real question.)* Why was that?

CARL:     I don't know. I felt really scared. He was so suspicious of me. I thought the guy was gonna take me somewhere and my brain froze. I was just shaky and couldn't talk. I was really nervous and scared. The cop was nice in the end and offered to give me a lift, but I just said I wanted to sit down and get a bit of fresh air.

KAZIM:     And it was then when you got wet?

CARL:     Yes, it started raining but I felt like I couldn't move. I just sat there thinking that the cop thought I'd done something bad and that he was going to be following me.

MYLES:     Nah, come on. It's his job. He just saw a guy looking into a window.

KAZIM:     *(Jokingly.)* And looking like a right perv!

MYLES:     *(To KAZIM.)* Come on, mate. *(Looking sadly at CARL.)* I'm sure the cop just thought he'd better check what was going on. It was quite unfortunate that he was the same guy that saw you that night by the canal, but I wouldn't worry about it.

*CARL walks to the leather sofa and sits on the armrest. He complains when he sits down, puts his hand underneath his bottom, and gets out a creased copy of 'Of Mice and Men'. MYLES walks up to him and gives him a cup of tea.*

CARL:     Thank you.

MYLES:     No worries.

KAZIM:     *(Looking at CARL.)* Hopefully, you'll have learnt not to perv outside girls' houses.

CARL:     *(With a small smile.)* Yes, I have. D'you think that cop will follow me or something?

CHARLES: *(Serious.)* No, not at all. I think the police are quite worried about the murder cases, so I don't think he'll start following you. *(Sipping his tea and looking at CARL.)* He might just write a little report on what happened with you tonight.

CARL:     *(Agitated.)* Are you serious? *(Looking at MYLES.)* Will he do that?

CHARLES: *(Proud of the reaction he had caused in CARL.)* No, come on. It's just a joke. He won't even remember having talked to you tonight. Don't worry about it.

MYLES:     *(Looking CARL in the eyes.)* Charles is right. Don't worry.

CARL:     So d'you think they have a serious investigation going on?

CHARLES: Of course. Especially after the complaints about the police not investigating the first two crimes. It was all over the news.

CARL:     *(Scratching the lower part of his back.)* But they don't seem to know much about it. All they said on TV is that they believe the four crimes are related.

KAZIM:     Yeah, but you have to remember that they always know a lot more than they say they do. I'm sure that they already have an idea of where to look for the guy.

CHARLES: *(To KAZIM.)* Why did you assume it was a guy?

KAZIM: It seems like it's one of those crazy serial killers, and they're always guys.

CHARLES: That's not true. There have also been women convicted as serial killers.

KAZIM: Maybe some random one. But it's always some sick weird bastard that's found guilty of those types of crimes.

GEORGE: Yes, and then they always interview the neighbours, and they all just say how nice the guy was, how he'd always helped old people cross the street and all that crap.

MYLES: I think that's why it takes the police so much time to get them, because no one suspects them.

GEORGE: But you must! There must be something weird about those people. I think from now on, I'm not gonna trust anyone who's nice to me. I'm just gonna trust the bastards!

KAZIM: *(Playing some chords with the guitar.)* Like me?

GEORGE: No, not gay bastards, just bastards!

*MYLES walks up to the kitchen worktop and leaves the plate he's just finished next to the box of kidneys that KAZIM had bought for him. He grabs a box of eight oranges.*

MYLES: Fruit anyone?

GEORGE: Yeah, I'll have some.

*The boys continue drinking their tea and some of them start peeling an orange. KAZIM plays a few chords and CARL sits down and grabs the other guitar.*

KAZIM: *(Playing some chords.)* I forgot you used to play the *autistic* guitar.

CARL: Yeah, It's been a while though. *(CARL sips his tea.)* So, guys, what did you think of Penelope?

CHARLES: She was hot. You have good taste.

MYLES: She seemed cool, and she wasn't put off by Kazim's jokes. Like when he said that he'd heard that she'd been out for *a fellatio* in the morning, and she replied, 'Very funny, a *facial*'.

KAZIM: *(Laughing.)* Yeah, she's good value.

CARL:     I think she's amazing. She's sweet and fun, and always seems so relaxed and calm.

KAZIM:     Maybe she takes drugs.

CARL:     No, I mean. Even at work, when everyone else is stressed, she's always the only one who's calm. It's as if nothing can phase her. She appears relaxed, peaceful, and just…. happy. And that makes me feel safe. *(Trying some chords.)* My grandmother once said to me, 'Don't judge others by what they have or by what they do, but by how they make you feel'.

*The Friday Club members nod and continue drinking. KAZIM and CARL start playing a song together and the boys lean back, listening quietly. Some of them start closing their eyes.*

*Slow curtain*

# Chapter 5

## The ass is always thinner on the other thigh

It was ten o'clock in the morning when Charles was in the bath examining his genitals. *Lalala, the best song to sing when one's touching one's genitals.* Thought Charles. *They seem healthy to me. They seem quite round actually. This bit's fine, that bit's fine too. It seems like I have some round and healthy ones. A perfect piece of craftsmanship. Grand, as they'd say in Ireland. Grand sounds like grande, big in Spanish. And it's big, they are big; everything's big down there. I'm happy with them. Girls are happy with them too. Everyone should be happy with them.*

Charles decided to get a bit more hot water in the bath, so he opened the tap and slid his back down until his chin was about to touch the floating froth. *I should go for it. Movember, the month for testicular cancer awareness is back. I should do as that chick suggested. I might even look hot.* The hot water carried on flowing, and the floating froth was about to hit his mouth when he closed the tap. *Oh, I can't see my little soldier now, now I can. Floating in the water like a lotus leaf.*

Charles began breathing slower each time. *I'm lucky to be on my own. Your own is the best company you can have when you are perfectly content with yourself.* He moved his feet up and down in the water. *Now I see them, now I don't. Now I see them, now I don't. So, what is it then? I need to go to the bank to pay the cheque in. I need to take the trousers and other things to the dry cleaners, sort out my new phone, meet Dr Pope for lunch and do the food shopping for the week. Eggs... I fancy eggs. I should also try to get some veggies for a change.*

*Oh, and the staff social. I need to send the confirmation email today. And wine and bread; everything's about wine and bread.*

Charles pulled up the plug after ten minutes of meditation and stood up in the bath, rubbed himself softly with his towel and stepped outside of the bath onto the mat. He took one last look at his genitals on the mirror in front of him and put his underpants on. *I'd better give the bath a bit of a rinse, I don't want the Spaniard to be touching my pubes.* Wearing just his underpants, Charles went back to his room after cleaning the bath and brushing his teeth, sat at his computer and moved the mouse. *When did she e-mail me? It was on that Thursday, so it should be around here. Staff... staff... staff... here it is. Staff night out; confirmation needed.*

Hi there,

*Just confirming that I'll give you the pleasure of my company on the next staff night out.*

Charles

Charles stood up and started pulling clothes out of his wardrobe. *Jeans, which jeans? Sorted. T-shirt or shirt? Where was it we were going? Oh, yes, I'd better wear a shirt so that he doesn't have anything to complain about. I'll get the passport in case they get arsey in the bank, and the cheque's here. The stuff for the dry cleaners, and the bag that's in the kitchen.* Charles went downstairs to the kitchen and grabbed a bag, where he then put his trousers before leaning over the kitchen table. *Is that chorizo again? This guy is certainly a creature of habits.* Charles pulled his coat from the hanger in the hall area and went outside, scratching his crotch after closing the door.

He went on the under pass at Five Ways and walked along Broad Street, where he helped a blind man cross Bishopsgate St. *This drunk Irish guy must be taking the piss. Blind as a fucking bat he says he is, but he felt that van coming in front of him. Queer idea of Birmingham he must have.* Charles ensured the blind man was okay to be left alone before he moved on, peering at the pubs and clubs on both sides of Broad Street. *Even during the day this place looks chavvy, smells chavvy, you can smell the tan plaid patterns in the air.* He continued walking along the street, holding his breath until he passed Brindley Place on his left. *I don't know why the whole street isn't like this; nice, classy, clean.* He got to Centenary Square and immediately noticed a new display of assorted flowers and the preparations to assemble the Christmas ice rink. *They do it earlier every year and the German market will be here in no time. Great places for dates! If you take a girl to the market, then for a skate in the ice rink, you're in.* He walked along Paradise Forum and came out of the other end, leaving the Central Library on his left. *This place looks quite quiet now. Can't believe how different it'll look in a few weeks with the German market. I'm going to need to start hunting to see what girls I bring here this year. Which girls will be the lucky ones?*

Charles walked down New Street and turned right as soon as he passed Mail Room Bar, carried on until the end of Pinfold Street and walked into Tim Foley Dry Cleaners. *I love it in here. Nice and warm.*

'Morning,' said a shop assistant, wearing a bright smile and a flowery dress.

'Hi there,' replied Charles. 'I'd like to get these ten garments dry cleaned, please.'

'Yes, sure. They'll be ready on Tuesday after ten o'clock in the morning. Is that okay?'

'Yes, that's totally fine,' said Charles.

She punched into a register. 'That'll be £10 per garment, please.'

'That's fine. Also, these trousers have some blood here. It's not as dodgy as it sounds, I'm a doctor. Will it come off?'

She squirmed a bit. 'Yes, I think so,' said the woman grabbing a pen. 'I'll just make a note here to make sure we check that it comes off.'

'Excellent, thank you.'

She refocused on the screen in front of her. 'Now, if you could please check that the amount is correct and then enter your PIN, please.'

'Yes, thank you.' Charles put his card back in his wallet.

'And remember, please, any time after ten o'clock.'

'That's great. Cheers,' replied Charles.

'Thanks, bye.'

Charles turned left as he came out of the dry cleaners and then onto Navigation Street. *Okay, dry cleaners done. I'll get this cheque done and see if I can check the phones before I meet up for that lunch.* He walked up Lower Temple St passing a pub called 'The Playwright' to his left. *The playwright, like Shakespeare, someone said that after God, he has created the most. Not convinced. Some called him the bard, I'm sure it originally was the bastard but the 'a', the 's', and the 't' got blurry in the old document. What a kiddy fiddler he was. Shakespeare, the chap that writes like Synge. A bit of Shakespeare lives in every single English person and thanks to him, paternity is legal fiction. The Playwright, in the heart of the Great City of Birmingham. Great city my beautiful ass. A cool city, but not pretty. The only pretty part of Birmingham is the Jewellery quarter, and that's only because it doesn't look like Birmingham. The bohemians of Moseley, the middle-class people of Harborne, and the ghetto kids from Ladywood, they all form the ten tribes of Birmingham. The Playwright... shit, I think that was the place where we ended up after that crazy work social waiting for the girls to turn up. A few of them wanted to suck my cock so something must have happened for them not to turn up. All of us guys sitting there in a right state, elbow to elbow drinking the last bit of that cheap wine and finishing off that baguette as if we had never eaten, as it if was going to be our last supper. O'Brian, the old Hindu consultant, me, Mohammed, Greek Nicholas, James Williams, and Amanjeet, and then that twatty barman came and asked us why we had sat by the alphabetical order of our religion. Those uneducated people have no clue, or manners. Religion's a funny thing, but not good funny like when that consultant said to a widow in a funeral that he hoped she followed her husband soon and then someone told him that he got the religions mixed up. Religion's not funny like that, but funny like awkward funny.* Charles turned right into New Street when he got to Telmo Supermarket, walking confidently into the bank. *Wow, she's hot!*

The woman looked up at him, 'Good afternoon, sir. What can I do for you?'

'Hi there. I just want to pay this cheque in, please,' answered Charles, noticing the flowers decorating the entrance.

'Yes, of course. We have a new quick deposit system. Would you like to try it?'

*Fuck, yeah, she's hot. Come to daddy, bitch.* 'Yeah, I can give that a go. As long as you explain to me how it works.'

'Of course.' She leaned closer, pointing with her pen. *Jesus, she smells good, like a sexy rose.* 'All you have to do is write the name of the account holder here, the sort code, the account number, and then the amount on the cheque,' she explained.

'I can do that,' Charles nodded with what was probably a cheesy smile on his face.

'Okay, so, now, all you have to do is put that in that quick deposit box. The money will appear on your account by the end of the day, and it'll be available within the next ten hours.'

'That's fine.'

'Anything else I can do for your today, sir?'

'No,' answered Charles. 'That's it. Thank you very much for your time...' he leaned closer to read her name tag. 'Jasmine.'

'You're very welcome.'

With one final glance at her, Charles walked out of the bank and walked down New Street until he found the first phone store. *She was hot. I need to get in there. I'll get in there. She'll love it, how could she not?*

He walked around the shop and stopped by the latest overpriced phones, where he started to read the specifications.

'Hello, sir. Do you need any help?' A young man approached.

'Yes, thanks,' Charles nodded absently, staring at the selection. 'I'd like to get a new phone and I would like it to have a good camera and a good microphone.'

'Okay. And are you happy to go with any network?'

'Yes,' answered Charles. 'But I travel abroad a lot, so I'd just pay for it to have it SIM free and just carry on using my current SIM.'

'That's fine. But phones are usually quite expensive SIM free,' explained the shop assistant.

'Yes, I know. But I'd rather go for that.'

'Okay. Do you prefer any type of phone or brand in particular?'

'No, not really. I've got this one,' he held up his phone, 'but it's time to change it I think,' explained Charles.

'Is the screen cut open?' Asked the shop assistant with a thick Brummy accent.

'Yeah, it is. Still works though, but I didn't have time to change it before, so I just carried on using it.'

'Did you have insurance on that phone?'

'No, not at all.'

'That's a pity then. How did you do that to the phone?'

'Oh, it's a long drunken story.'

'Okay, well, we can start by taking a look at these ones...'

After another ten minutes at the shop, Charles came out and went up New Street until he reached Ethel Street, where he turned left and stood outside Julien's Maison. *I'll see what Dr Pope thinks of it. Great food, price and atmosphere but I'm sure he will find something to complain about.*

A smartly dressed man in a pristine white shirt waved an envelope at Charles as he turned into Ethel Street. *Wow, he seems happy today. Let's see how long this lasts.*

'Good afternoon, Dr Pope, how are you?' asked Charles, walking up to him.

'I'm well, thanks. And you?'

'Great, thanks. I've just been sorting some stuff out,' replied Charles in an automatic way.

'Oh, and by the way, you can call me, *Dad*. Here you go, I have a card for you. Have you bought anything for yourself?'

'Thanks for the card,' said Charles. 'Yes, I've just got a new phone, my old one broke.'

'Do you still have the same number?'

'Yes, of course, that won't change.'

'That's good. Oh, before I forget, Jonesy says hi.'

Dr Pope senior and junior went upstairs into Julien's Maison, where the midday rush didn't let them many seats to choose from.

'So, what do you think of the place? Do you like it?'

'Yes, indeed, Charles.'

A skinny young man with David Byrne etched onto his name tag welcomed them and asked one of the girls to take them to a table. The waitress took them to a table by the window with flowers on the tablecloth and gave them the menu when they sat down. *She's not that bad. A bit chubby and dirty hair. But I think she'd look good on a night out,* thought Charles. *I think she likes me. She must like me.*

'So, how did your meeting go?'

'It went well, thank you,' replied Dr Pope. 'All of us believed that the guy was perfectly fine, so all we had to do was to agree on what to include in the report for the trial.'

'So, he's due to have a normal trial then?' asked Charles.

'Oh, yes, of course. The bastard would suck whisky off a sore leg but there's nothing wrong with him in psychiatric terms.'

'That was quick.'

'Yes, I know,' Dr Pope agreed and went on. 'It's one thing to have the police giving us all the drunken scum and minor criminals, saying that they have mental problems, and another thing to have these kinds of cases. The tricky ones are all those petty criminals, because you talk to the police and tell them that they are okay, and that it's the responsibility of the police to deal with them and the police come back to you again saying that the guys really have mental problems and that it's the psychiatrist unit's responsibility. The police are just plain lazy and try to dump those cases on us to deal with. But this one was a serious one and it was the solicitor who claimed on the grounds of mental health.'

'And those ones are easy to send back to the police? Asked Charles, showing some interest in the topic.

'Oh, yes. You'll learn a lot more about that with time, but if it's a serious crime like this, the psychiatrist team examines the case and the evidence, and then meet up to reach a conclusion. If they decide that the guy's healthy enough mentally to stand trial and to be judged, then the court takes over the accused pretty much the same day. None of that sending the guy back and forward.'

'But the solicitors might actually try and get it reassessed, right?' asked Charles hopefully.

'Yes, sometimes,' explained Dr Pope. 'But the verdicts from the psychiatrist team are usually quite decisive, and once they've been issued, the solicitors know that that path's gone.'

'So, what do you think will happen to him?'

Dr Pope simply shrugged. 'What needs to happen will happen,' he answered while readjusting the buckle of this belt. 'That bastard will get life in prison in a sex offenders' unit. Cases like these are the ones that make you think how lucky Americans are to have the death penalty. In the UK, we should at least cut the guy's balls off.'

'Yes, I know.'

'Anyway, how's your portfolio coming along, Charles?'

Shaking off the topic, Charles ran a hand through his hair and took a breath. 'Good, thanks… it was a bit slow to start with, but it's picking up now. It's just a matter of going through all the standards carefully and making sure I use all the evidence I can gather.'

'Yes. When I work with junior doctors, it's always the same. They usually complain saying that they don't know how to meet a certain standard when they already have plenty of evidence to show for it and…' Dr Pope paused when he saw the waitress approaching their table.

'Excuse me, gentlemen. Do you already know what you'd like to drink?' asked the waitress with a smile.

'I'll have a small glass of Rioja,' said Dr Pope while he grabbed a bit of bread from the basket at the centre of the table.

Charles scanned her up and down before answering. 'I'll just have any bottle of lager, please.'

*Yes, she definitely needs to lose a few kilos. Her accent is a lost cause though. My genitals in her mouth will improve her elocution.*

Nothing else interesting was said until the waitress came along with the main course, coughing as she walked. By this point, Dr Pope already had a wine stain on his shirt.

*Fucking hell, I didn't know they had Typhoid Mary serving the tables here. Her tits are actually good. That's one good thing about chubby chicks.*

Charles got a gorgonzola cheese sandwich with finely diced Spanish onion and salad with olives on the side.

'What the hell is that?' asked Dr Pope.

'The Mediterranean sandwich. It's good.' Charles took a bite.

'It certainly is true what they say,' added Dr Pope. 'God made food, and the devil cooks it. My lamb looks good. Oh, I forgot to tell you, Charles. I was in the Post Central complex on Monday and I buzzed in at your apartment, but you weren't there.'

'Monday? I didn't get back till late. I met up with a few friends after work,' replied Charles. He got distracted and cut the fingertips of two of his fingers. 'Bollocks,' shouted Charles.

'Are you OK?' asked Dr Pope.

'Yes, thanks, just a silly cut,' replied Charles covering his fingers with some tissues and pressing firmly. 'So, how come you came to see me?'

'I just thought it'd be nice to catch up and go for a meal.'

'Well, that's what we're doing today,' Charles stammered, unable to control himself.

'Yes, I know. But it would have been just to do it as a spontaneous thing. Just a bit of an unplanned outing.'

'Is everything okay, Dad?' asked Charles, leaning in.

'Of course, why? Can't a father want to take his son out for a meal and a drink?'

'Yes, of course, but you know what I mean. This just doesn't sound like you.'

'Come on, Charles. That's a bit harsh, I think.'

Charles paused, pressed his teeth together and started speaking angrily. 'Well. You are the one that sent me to that boarding school and then refused to get me out of it when I begged you to.'

'Not that again. You know I did it for you.' Dr pope kept his tone calm.

'No, you did it for yourself,' Charles scowled. 'You just didn't want to have a kid around because you were too busy with work. So… you sent me away to become a part-time dad at Christmas and in the summer.'

'Your mum was ill. I just didn't want you to have to go through it and see your mum in that state.'

'So, you parked me in a boarding school and deprived me from the last years of mum's company.'

'You were a kid. You didn't know, and you still don't know how bad she was. You wouldn't have liked to see what the day-to-day with her was like. You'd have hated having to see it every day.'

Charles felt himself heat up with anger and couldn't seem to stop himself from what was about to come out. 'So, you just decided that I didn't need parents anymore and sent me away. You ignored what I said to you when I came home, just as you ignored what I used to tell you in my letters. I still have ten of those letters I found in the wooden cabinet once I went back home. Any father would have taken his child out of a boarding school after reading those letters. I have never met anyone who actually gives a shit about their kids who has sent them to a boarding school. As a psychiatrist, you should have known that sending your kid to a boarding school is a recipe for a dysfunctional family.' He paused for a breath. 'What did mum think of all of this?'

Both of them sat silently and had a few sips to gather some time to think. Dr Pope looked outside the window and had a small bite of bread and another sip of wine. It wasn't till a few seconds later when both of them felt able and willing to look at each other in the eyes.

Remaining his composure, Dr Pope explained, 'She wasn't in a fit state to make choices. I had to make that choice for her, for me and for you. And I really believe that it was the best thing that could been done given the circumstances.'

'Did you show the letters to mum?'

'I showed her most of them.'

'Most of them? So, it's not bad enough that you ignored what I told you in the letters, but you only showed mum what you thought was good for you to show her.'

'No, Charles. It wasn't about me. It was about you and her. The only things I didn't show her were the bits that I thought would get her upset and wouldn't do her any favours.'

'So, you lied to her then, saying that I loved the place when I didn't. You didn't do that for me or for her. You only did that because you knew she wouldn't forgive you for letting me stay in that place. Horrible food, constantly being beaten up, and crying on a daily basis, wanting nothing more than to just go home.'

'Charles, son. Look at you know. You don't think it did you any good?'

'That's not relevant,' replied Charles in a bitter voice.

'Yes, it is. It was everything about you and your future. You went to a very good school, not perfect, but a very good school. You got great results and went on to do medicine. Now, you're working as a doctor, have a very good salary, and you have a really nice big apartment all for yourself right in the city centre. You've done very well, and you wouldn't have done this well should I have not made the tough decisions I made. You don't want to see that because it's easier to deal with the loss of your mother by channelling your anger and negative feelings towards me.'

'Don't try to analyse me, Dad. You're not at work. And I'd rather have a worse dead-end job and have better memories of a happy childhood… with my family,' he added bitterly.

'I'm not analysing anyone. I'm just telling you how things are and that for you, the grass is always greener on the other side.'

'We all have things in our past that we're not happy about, son, but we can't let those things ruin our present. Don't let the phantoms of the past take away your pleasures of the present,' advised Dr Pope.

'You need to learn to put all that stuff behind you and start enjoying your life.' Dr Pope finished his sentence with a smile. Charles finished his bottle of beer with a long sip and looked at the bottom of the bottle.

*He always does it. He always fucking does it. He can't be right. He cannot be right all the fucking time. This forget-about-the-past-crap-to-enjoy-the-present line, that's the standard phrase you use to talk to victims of abuse. Why do I always feel like he's talking to me as he talks to his patients?*

'Okay, Dad. Don't worry about it. Let's just forget about it.'

'I have forgotten about it,' Dr Pope muttered. 'You're the one that has to forget about it.'

Charles continued thinking to himself. *Why is this fucker now saying this? He knows it's him with all his crap that brings all this back. It's not my problem. He's the one bringing this up all the time.*

'I'll forget about it, Dad. What are you having for pudding?'

'I'll just have a quick coffee. I have to go back to the hospital.'

'I thought you'd be done for the day,' said Charles.

'I wish. The police called me again. They have found another body and they'd like me to meet up with an inspector for some reason. He's coming to my office.'

'Maybe they think you've done it,' Charles chuckled at his own joke.

'It's not funny, Charles. Some sick person's out there out of control, and for all I know, they have no clue about how they're going to get him.'

'Why do you think it's a guy? It could be a girl.'

'I don't know much about it, but it could be more than one person.'

'Have they asked you to help?' asked Charles.

'No, they haven't. And if they do, I'll say no. I've been working all morning on an article that I want to finish soon, I just need to add a few charts,' explained Dr Pope before ordering coffees for both from a waitress nearby. 'I don't really want to talk about the case. I want to meet up with the inspectors with no preconceived ideas and then I'll see what the situation is.'

'They must know something,' said Charles. 'Five victims so far, including the guy they found a couple of days ago, the one they found by the botanical gardens. Actually, six with the latest one. They must know something,' he repeated restlessly.

'I don't know. I'll have to see what they want from me,' said Dr Pope, waving a hand in a dismissive way as the waitress brought the coffees.

Charles had a sip of his coffee and coughed. 'Come on,' uttered Charles. 'They can't be that stupid. The police need to know something. They ought to. I refuse to believe they are that fucking stupid. Six bodies now. They must have found something.' Dr Pope was getting a bit restless, so Charles changed the topic.

'Okay, continued Charles, 'I just hope your meeting goes well. I think I might just go and get a haircut. I was going to do it next week, but I'll just do it today and get it out of the way.'

'It's about time, Charles. You look like that crazy chemist from TV.'

'Thanks, Dad. That's exactly the look I was going for.'

'Excuse me. Could I have the bill please?' called Dr Pope as the waitress was walking by.

'Don't worry, Dad. I'll get this,' offered Charles, reaching into his pocket

'No, it's fine. I'll get it.'

'No, come on. Let me get it. You always pay. I'll get it this time,' insisted Charles.

'Okay, thanks. Is there anything you want?' asked Dr Pope.

'No, of course not.'

'Here you go, sir,' said the waitress to Charles as she handed the bill over.

'Thank you. I'll pay by card if that's alright.'

'Yes, of course.' The waitress handed the terminal over to Charles. 'Just enter your PIN here, please.'

*Yes, she's actually doable. As long as she keeps her mouth shut,* thought Charles while entering his PIN.

'Thank you, gentlemen. I hope you enjoyed your meal.'

'It was fantastic, thanks.' Charles offered politely.

'Of course, we did. The lamb was especially delicious,' said Dr Pope before smiling at the waitress. Dr Pope senior and junior went downstairs.

'Well, Dad. Good luck with your meeting.'

'Thanks. I don't really know what they want, so I hope it'll be a short one.'

They walked up Ethel Street. Dr Pope senior turned left, and Dr Pope junior turned right. *Well, that's it. I've told him straight about the issue with sending me to boarding school. I knew I didn't have to attend any of those boarding school survivor meetings to tackle any trauma about being dumped when I was a kid. I've told him straight.* Charles walked down New Street, passing the saxophone busker who was playing his usual song. *Again! Can't believe he's playing it again! How many times is this guy going to play the same song in one day? That's pathetic busking, mate. Learn at least ten songs before you go busking. Man, if I busked, I'd be pretty good at it. I'd learn to play all kinds of good songs, and I'd make sure I learnt at least one new song a week. I could easily do that. I'm good at that kind of stuff.*

Charles continued walking and saw a girl coming out of New Street Telmo Supermarket with a bottle of wine and bread in her bag. *She's hot. Should I get her number and shag her tonight? Nah, I'll get my hair cut instead.* Charles turned left onto Corporation Street and walked up until he reached the North Western Arcade. He turned left into it, passed a flower shop and walked into Papadopoulou's Hair Saloon.

'Good afternoon, sir. Do you have an appointment?' the girl at the front desk asked.

'No, I don't. I was just wondering if you'd be able to fit me in.'

'Yes, sure. Take a seat and someone will be with you soon.'

The owner's son offered a simple wave to Charles on his way in as he sat down and crossed his leg as manly a manner as he could while looking around the place. *She's hot. Hope she's the one that cuts my hair. I wouldn't like that fat bloke to get anywhere near me. Where are those days with sexy hairdressers? Hairdressing and air stewardship, two professions where hotties have been outnumbered by fatsoes and faggots.* A smiling young lady came up to Charles.

'Hi, sir. Would you like to come with me?'

Charles looked at her with disappointed eyes. *No, I don't want to go anywhere with you, butch bulldog. But I guess I will have to.* 'Yes, of course. Thanks,' he said, hoping his disappointment didn't show.

The girl took his coat and hung it on the coat hanger. She adjusted the seat for him, wrapped a thick towel around his neck and covered his shoulders and upper body with an apron.

'What kind of hair cut would you like today?'

*Anything except what you have. Fat and with bright hair. What colour is that anyway? You really need to sort yourself out, mate.* Charles took his phone out and showed a picture to the hairdresser. 'Something like this, please. Just don't worry too much about the sideburns.'

'Okay. And are you having your hair washed as well?'

'Yes, please.'

The hairdresser started running her comb through Charles' hair. *Why do fat people always have such warm hands? All of them do. It might be because their hearts need to pump more blood, so it could well be a consequence of that. Yeah, they have higher cholesterol levels, their veins can't carry as much blood and their cholesterol-filled hearts need to pump more blood to get the same amount of oxygen to their cells. Fat cells. And they can also drink more than skinny people. They can drink more because they have bigger bodies and more litres of blood, so it takes a higher level of alcohol to reach the same level of alcohol per mg of blood. Pure chemistry. Alcohol is also a depressant, so at the end you end up having a depressed fat person. Then, to top it up, alcohol is highly calorific, so the depressed fat person gets fatter, and fatter, and fatter. And then they just dye their hair with some stupid bright colour and work as a hairdresser.*

'Is this length okay?' she pointed to the portion she planned to cut.

'Yes, pretty much. Just a tiny bit shorter, please,' answered Charles.

She nodded. 'So, how's your day going?'

'Not bad so far, thanks. It's my day off, so I'm just trying to relax a bit,' explained Charles.

'Oh, that's nice. That must be nice. So, what do you for work?'

'I'm a doctor.'

'Wow, that's impressive. You're well clever then? A lot of studying for that, isn't it?'

'Yes, five years at university and then your training years,' explained Charles.

'Yeah, that's long. I couldn't do that. Too long, it is. So, what do you specialise in?'

'I'm currently doing my specialty training in psychiatry.'

'Wow, that sounds difficult. And what do psychics do?' asked the hairdresser.

'Psychics read your mind. Psychiatrists try to cure mental illnesses,' answered Charles with sarcasm.

'Like psychologists do, ain't it?'

'Kind of, but no, not really,' replied Charles. 'Psychologists do a three- or four-year degree at university and that's it. We do five years of medical school and then train for another five years or so, ten years in total. We prescribe medicines and they don't.'

'No, I definitely couldn't do that. I wasn't great at school, you know. I didn't really find it difficult, I just found too much to handle at times.'

'I see,' Charles said with utter disinterest.

'I have a brother, he's the clever one in the family. I always say to him that he should try and do medicine.'

'So, what's he doing at the moment?' asked Charles.

'He's doing some chemistry course at university. It's... I don't really know what it is. It's like chemistry but not chemistry itself, if you know what I mean.'

'Right...,' said Charles.

'He's doing chemistry, and some biology too, and then he examines plants and sees how plants are phonetically modified.'

'You mean genetically?' Charles corrected the girl.

'Yeah, that's it, thanks. Genetically modified it is, plants grow faster and that. Like a doctor for plants. He's the clever one.'

'It sounds like an interesting course.' Charles used his right hand to scratch his nose and started looking in the mirror. *You're dense, mate. I think your brain is phonetically modified, if you actually have one. Fat, with a weird haircut and thick. What a catch you are! He's like a doctor for plants. He must be doing something like agricultural studies, or chemistry engineering applied to agricultural studies or something like that. But how many things can actually go wrong with a plant? Add fertiliser, and water, and that's it. Well, saying that, they must also study what kinds of viruses kill the plants, pest and all that. They must turn up to the farm, see that the plants are dying, get a sample and analyse it to see what's happening. Then, if they find some virus, or pest or something, they'll have to see what products kill it. If they don't have anything, or if it's a new strain, they'll have to start researching what can kill it, and then do the trials to make sure that the product they develop kills the virus but not the plant. That can actually be quite fascinating. Isolate different plants and try different versions of the product to see what works well and what doesn't. But, also, they'll need to make sure that the product they develop isn't harmful to humans. Hm... that's a bit more complicated than I thought. How would they test that? They could give it to people like this fat girl and see what happens. Saying that, there can't be that much variety in the kinds of viruses that attack plants. They must be quite simple, and most likely, they'll mainly have problems with bugs. They'd be easier to kill. Plus, they won't change as much as viruses do, so once you have some chemicals to kill a certain bug, you can use that year after year. They might actually get used to the product and develop resistance towards it, but they'll be nowhere near as tricky as the viruses or bacteria that humans get. And what about the taste? Because they must also make sure that the chemicals don't alter the taste of the products. And what if the fruit isn't sweet enough? I guess they must also add things to modify the taste. And the texture. That's not botany, is it? No, botany is... looking after a garden so that the lotus leaf floating in the water looks nice in pictures.*

'Is this length okay now?'

'Yes, that's good, actually,' Charles nodded.

'Good. If you just come over here, I'll wash your hair.'

Charles followed the hairdresser, sat down, reclined his head back onto the white marble sink and the water started running through this hair.

'Is this temperature okay for you?'

'Yes, sure. It's fine, thanks,' answered Charles.

'Perfect. Just close your eyes to keep from getting shampoo in them.'

Charles closed his eyes and his breathing slowed down. *My balls are itchy. Oh, no, little ones, I can't touch you know. This fat lesbo might think she's getting me horny and try to do me here. I'd better not risk it. I'll leave you guys for now until later when I give you the attention you deserve. Okay, bank done. Phone done. Family lunch. Haircut done. I just need to get some food on the way back and that's it. Bread, wine, and something for dinner today, and then I'll have lunch at work all this week, so just some stuff for dinner for four nights. I'll see what they have.*

'Would you like a bit of product on your hair?' the sweet hairdresser asked.

'Yes, sure, that sounds good, thanks.'

The hairdresser put some wax on Charles' hair and directed him to the till. There, she worked out the total while Charles grabbed his coat. *Come on, let's see if you can work out the total. Actually, I'll check myself in this mirror here. I look very hot. She's done a great job. I guess there's a reason why she was employed here. Birmingham, the second biggest city in the UK, and this is the only place I trust with my beautiful hair.*

Charles paid the bill, offered a polite thank you once again to the hairdresser and walked out on to the North Western Arcade. He saw Bull Street from the left corner of his eye as he turned right onto Corporation Street. *Bull St, the home of the original chocolate factory, the most historic spot in all Birmingham.* Charles walked down Corporation Street and turned right onto New Street. He walked up the street and passed Victoria Square. He went through Paradise Forum and then along Broad Street. *Okay, what else do I need to get? Oh, yes, bath gel and shampoo. And what can the police possibly want from my dad? It's a bit random to meet up with the police. I know he's done some work with them before, but that business of finding a body and calling him? That's a bit random. What's he gonna say to them anyway? Yes, I can confirm that this guy's dead. They don't have enough information, so they surely can't ask him to try and come up with a profile of the murderer. Do they think it's one person or do they think it's more than one? How could one murderer make them think that there's more than one people involved? Obviously, he'd need to make sure there's a common theme or something recurrent to show the link between the murders, but what could one leave there to make them think that there's more than one person involved? I think an easy thing would be to use different hands for the killing. Obviously, if you use a knife, the angle of penetration tells whether the murderer was right-handed or left-handed, so that'd be an easy way to confuse them. Would they actually fall for that? They should. The area of the body where the person was stabbed can also show the height of the murderer, so maybe stabbing someone with both hands at different heights of the body could make them think that there were more than one person involved. There must be more things that could be done to lead the cops through the wrong tracks. They must know all those little tricks. They simply must know them.*

Later, Charles walked into his house with a few shopping bags and went directly into the kitchen. He put the meat in the fridge in order of expiry date to make sure that nothing went off. He put the cold meats on the top shelf. 'Alright. Breakfast stuff here, and lunch stuff here. What's that?' He pulled at a container filled with something he couldn't recognise. 'This Spaniard really eats anything. At least these days he covers his chorizo, so that I don't have to drink milk which smells like paprika and raw pork.'

Charles had finished putting everything away when he heard the front door. 'It's a bit early, he can't be back this early.'

'Hello?' shouted Charles.

'Hi, Charles. Hold on.' Carl walked into the kitchen.

'Hey, mate. I didn't expect you this early today,' said Charles.

'I know, I started getting a really bad headache at work. I only had to do a bit of admin today, so I asked a colleague if she could cover for me, and I left. The headache was starting to get quite bad.'

'Are you coming down with a cold or something?' asked Charles.

'I don't know. I've been feeling a bit weird lately, but it got worse today. I started having a headache in the morning, but it got worse after lunch.'

'Did you take anything for it?'

'I don't like taking pain killers because I already take enough tablets a day, but I took something that someone gave me at work.'

'What was it?' asked Charles.

'Some paracetamol, I think.'

'How strong?'

'I don't know,' Carl shrugged. 'I took two tablets and it got a lot better, although I think it's coming back now.'

'Have you been drinking enough water lately?'

'I haven't drunk anything since breakfast today, but I really don't fancy it.'

Charles grabbed a pint glass and opened the tap. *He's blinking a lot. He's really blinking a lot.*

'Thanks, Charles,' said Carl when he grabbed the glass of water.

'So, apart from the headache, how are you feeling, mate?'

'A bit weird. I haven't been able to sleep very well lately, so I feel very tired and a bit shaky.'

Charles walked up to him, grabbed his eyelid, and examined it. *He's really blinking a lot. His hands are a bit shaky, but he's really blinking a lot.*

'Does my eye look OK?' asked Carl.

'Yep, you have a nice and healthy Iberian eye, mate. Have you eaten enough?'

'Well, I haven't been feeling very hungry lately. I had breakfast and a bit of a sandwich for lunch, but I really didn't feel like finishing it. I don't know. I just feel sleepy and tired, run down, and I don't feel like eating or drinking at all.'

'You have to, Carl. I know sometimes you might not feel like having anything at all, but you're going to have to force yourself to eat and drink something when you are feeling like that. It only makes it worse if you don't.'

Charles put his hand on Carl's forehead. *He doesn't have a temperature, and his nose isn't running.*

'Nah, you don't have a temperature. It might just be stress. How are you feeling these days, Carl?'

'Alright, I guess. I just feel a bit unsettled. I'm finding work a bit hard because I am not able to focus and concentrate on anything. I get my work done, but nowhere near as fast as usual.'

'Are you worried about work? Are you worried that they might sack you for something? Have you seen Penelope lately?' Carl stuttered a bit when he tried to answer the questions and started looking to his left. *He's blinking's getting a lot faster. Does he actually realise he's doing it?* 'Don't worry, Carl. I'm sure everything's fine. Are there any hobbies that you miss? Anything you used to do in Gibraltar that you really enjoyed or gave you a little bit of an escape?'

'I loved sitting in the main square, just sitting on a bench eating sunflower seeds,' replied Carl.

'It must have been good with the sun on your face, not having to worry about anything.'

'Yes, it was great. Just not having to worry about anything,' Carl reminisced.

'That must have been very relaxing, Carl. And I'm sure you loved just having the fresh air touching your face. With nothing to worry about, just relaxed on a bench, munching on your sunflower seeds, looking at the pigeons flying by and trying to get some food left by the tourists. That must have been a very good feeling, Carl. I'm sure that made you feel very relaxed and happy.'

'Yes, it really made me feel good,' replied Carl almost hypnotised.

'I know. I can imagine how peaceful it was. Let's just focus on that.'

Charles smiled and stopped talking. *He's blinking's a lot slower now. It's really a lot slower. What should I do with him?*

A Dead Man's Ice Cream

# Chapter 6

## The stress of Birmingham is burning

The white and black round gadget on the wall marked ten o'clock when a dark-suited figure walked into the room. Another figure, in scrubs, uncovered the body on the stretcher, put his right hand on his forehead, then his stomach, then his heart, then the right part of his chest, and then he looked at the body's heart.

'Here you are,' said the figure in scrubs.

'I see. You're right, the testicles and penis have been cut off. Someone really took her time to do this,' the suited figure said.

'Her time? Why do you think it was a woman?' asked the figure in scrubs.

'There'd be one twisted enough to do it. A mutilation like this is usually very personal and passion-driven. I wouldn't be surprised if it was a woman who had found her husband shagging someone else and cut his genitals off to make a point.'

'She bloody well made a point. He bled to death,' explained the figure in the scrub.

'That must have hurt,' said the suited figure. 'He sure as hell isn't going to be cheating on this woman again. She must have already cooked the balls and cock in a stew by now, so I don't think you'll find them.'

'We have already found them,' said the scrubbed figure.

'Where?' asked the suited figure.

'They were in his mouth, crushed, and seemingly chewed on before he died.'

'What? Chewed on? Someone cut his genitals off and made him eat them? What kind of person would do that?'

'That's your job to tell us, I think. I can show you the body and analyse whatever you want me to, but you're the one who tells us what kind of person did this.'

'Where are his bits then? You haven't put them back,' the suited figure said.

The figure in the scrub finished uncovering the body, 'I put them between his feet, didn't want my boss to think I'd been playing puzzles with the evidence.'

'Do you know what kind of instrument was used to cut them off?' the suited figure asked.

'Something sharp, very sharp.'

'Jonesy, mate. Tell me something I don't know.'

'It could have been different things. A cutter, a very sharp knife...'

'A scalpel?' asked the suited figure.

'Yes, a scalpel is a possibility, of course.'

'So, any signs of fighting?'

'No, not at all,' said Jonesy.

'So, are you saying that someone cut this guy's genitals off, fed them to him, and he didn't even try to show resistance?'

'That's right. He didn't. He was blind drunk, blood-alcohol levels were through the roof. He was so drunk that maybe he hasn't even realised yet that he's dead,' replied Jonesy.

'Where was he found?' the suited figure asked while looking at the body.

'In Edgbaston, behind the Botanical Gardens.'

'Are there any witnesses? Any other clues?'

'I don't know. I'm only the caretaker. I simply put these poor souls into their little fridges. The inspector is the one who chases the sinners. I think he's preparing a report for you, so that should make things a bit clearer. Last I heard, he was just about finished,' said Jonesy.

'Okay, that's fine,' the suited figure said. 'I told the inspector to drop by my office after lunch, so I'll see later what he's prepared for me,' the suited figure said.

'Have you got any idea of what's going on?' enquired Jonesy.

'Well,' the suited figure said. 'I need to see what the report says first, and once I've seen a bit more information on the cases, I'll hopefully be able to come up with a working theory.'

'Well, I need to go and prepare a bit of paperwork for a body they're taking today, but feel free to stay here with the eunuch. Just knock on that door before you leave and I'll put the body back in the fridge.'

'Don't worry,' said the suited figure. 'I need to go and send a couple of emails before I meet Charles for lunch.'

'A proper family lunch then. Say *hi* from me,' Jonesy said while packing away. It was nice to see you.'

'Nice to see you too, Jonesy. If whoever did this is as screwed up as it looks like, we might see each other soon.'

'Well, I'll be here. So just let me know if there's anything I can help you with.'

'Of course, I will,' said the suited figure before making his way out of the room.

The suited figure looked at the body on the stretcher once last time on his way out. While waiting for the lift, he couldn't help but satisfy the impulse to scratch himself between his legs, maybe just making sure it was still there. He absent-mindedly reached for his phone in his jacket's left pocket. He saw the numbers in the lift lighting up during his ascent and said out loud with his hand in his pocket, 'This little organ moving is the only difference between me and the body lying on the stretcher. I don't get why some people complicate matters by adding souls, sins, gods and eternity to the equation.'

The suited figure came out of the vertically moving box, walked along the corridor, and stopped at a door where, 'Dr Pope' could be read on a rectangular metal plate. He opened the door and walked around his office nervously. The man sat down, placed his hands heavily on the keyboard, and started biting his bottom lip. He started tapping the letters in the keyboard for a while and then stopped. He squinted as many of his patients did before verbalising something hard to admit, or as he'd seen Clint Eastwood do in those Spaghetti Westerns filmed in Almeria. Mechanically nervous, he pressed enter. He could breathe normally again.

He grabbed a red envelope from an out tray on his table and started writing something on it equally nervously. He ran his right hand over the part of his pristine white shirt which covered his heart, thought for a minute about what to write on the envelope, and then finally wrote, 'Charles'.

The suited figure went to the office next door, 'Mary, I'm going to go out for lunch with my son. If anyone calls, just take the message, I'll be back in a couple of hours.'

'Yes, I will do that, sir,' replied the woman.

* * *

The suited figure came back to his office with a wine stain on his shirt and had just sat down when his secretary came in.

'Inspector Reilly called again. He said it was urgent. His number's on a note on your desk, and you just received a report. It's by your keyboard.'

'Okay, thanks for that. Did anyone else call?' asked the suited figure while checking the time on his watch.

'Yes, someone from Pharmacy, and he said he'd call later.'

'Thanks, Mary.'

The suited figure grabbed the phone on the table, looked at the note and started dialling the number on it.

'Inspector Reilly,' the suited figure said... 'My secretary said you'd called again and that it was urgent' ... 'When did this happen?' ... 'I see, when will the body be taken to the morgue?' ... 'Okay, I'll do that. Just come up when you finish talking to Jonesy about the other one.'

The suited figure sat back and looked up before going through the report. He then grabbed a bag he had in one of his draws and took out a book. '*Killers*... teach me something, Joseph.'

The suited figure scanned through the contents and read a few pages here and there until he heard a knock on the door. Then, embarrassed, quickly hid the book before asking his visitor to come in. The door opened slowly, and a 'nice to meet you' was heard before the visitor even finished opening the door.

'Nice to meet you too,' said Dr Pope. 'Please, take a seat. I thought there were going to be three of you.'

'My two colleagues are still in the morgue,' explained Inspector Reilly. 'Have you had time to look at the report?'

'Not in detail,' replied Dr Pope. 'I read the information about the victims and a bit of the circumstances of the crimes, but I only got as far as the part describing the missing shoelace of the victim found by the school.'

'Okay,' said Inspector Reilly. 'As I said to you earlier on the phone, we've just found another body, the sixth victim since August. This one was found in the morning.'

'And do you think all those murders are related?' asked Dr Pope while scratching the right side of this chest.

'We don't know what's going on and we are desperate. We aren't sure about all the murders, but one of them had a kidney missing...' Inspector Riley started explaining before being interrupted.

'And the one you found today had an organ missing as well or anything mutilated?' asked Dr Pope.

'No, this one had nothing mutilated,' explained Inspector Riley, 'but it's clear they tried to get the heart out, but we think they ran out of time and just killed the person in the end. The crime scene is still being investigated, so I'm afraid there's not much more I can tell you about this one for now.'

'Don't worry. I'll familiarise myself with the information on the other victims and read the report on the latest one when you have it available.'

'Thank you, Dr Pope. So, do you have any idea of what's going on? Some of my boys think it might be some kind of organ trafficking. There are some gangs that have come to the country lately and those people are sick enough to do this.'

The suited figure felt sad for a moment and then answered, 'Well, as I said, I haven't read the full report yet, so it'd be hard for me to comment on the matter, but out of curiosity, do these crimes seem that well planned?'

'That's hard to say I think,' said the inspector. 'On the one hand, no one has been caught yet for these murders and I'm embarrassed to admit that I don't think we know much about the killer, or killers, but on the other hand, all these victims and crimes seem very random, and they seem to be totally situational.'

'I see what you mean.'

'We don't expect miracles, and we don't expect you to tell us the name of the killer, or killers, but any ideas you may have about the case would be most welcome, and if you could please come up with a psychological profile of the murderer that would be really helpful,' said Inspector Reilly.

'Of course, I'll do my best,' said the suited figure. 'Where was this victim found?'

'In the graveyard outside St. Nicholas Church, in Kings Norton. The caretaker found him just after eleven o'clock. He was a churchgoer who used to help with community events.'

'I see. Thanks for that. I think everything will fall into perspective once I have read the report. Once again, if you could please let me have the latest report as soon as it's ready, that'd be great. I'll ask Jonesy to let me know when would be a good time go down and see the latest victim.'

'Thank you very much. I'll make sure you get the report as soon as possible. I know I don't have to tell you this, but I'd really expect you to keep all this extremely confidential. It'd make things easier for you if no one knows you're involved in the case. The media can really put you in a tough situation.'

'I know, don't worry, I do not want any unnecessary attention either,' said the suited figure while he gave a business card to the inspector. 'This is my mobile number, in case you need to get me outside of office hours.'

'Thank you very much for this, and thank you very much for all your help,' added the inspector as he was leaving the room.

'You are most welcome.'

The suited figure leaned back in his chair and stared at the black and white ceiling as if he was going to get inspiration from it. He coughed three times, leaned forward, and rested his forehead on his two hands before disappearing into his own thoughts.

\* \* \*

'Hi, Carl. How are you feeling today?' asked Penelope.

'I'm okay, thanks. I couldn't get rid of my headache last night, but I went for a walk after dinner and the fresh air really made it better,' replied Carl shaking a bit.

'Well, I'm not teaching till the afternoon. I'll be in my office in case any student turns up, so let me know if you need anything.'

'Thanks, I will. I appreciate that,' said Carl with his usual shy look on his face.

Carl started tapping his fingers on the keyboard and looked outside the window. He saw some girls walking on their way to their lectures, tapped his fingers a few more times, and continued typing. He looked at the black and white round object on the wall and examined the big and the small hands. He then stood up and walked aimlessly around the department. He grabbed some paper, moved to a machine by the door, pressed a button, and the photocopies started to come out.

The caretaker came into the School of Languages office a few hours later and walked up to the window at the end of the office, where he started looking at the big metallic object that kept Carl warm during cold days. He got some thin metallic things out of a metal box and looked behind him when he heard a noise.

'Carl, mate. You scared me,' said the caretaker.

'I'm very sorry. I was just thinking.'

'How are things? You coping okay with the English rain?' asked the caretaker while inspecting the metallic object.

'Yeah, I've actually hardly noticed it recently. I haven't been going out much these days, so it hasn't really bother me. It's all good, but I've been feeling very tired lately.'

'You okay? Have you been to the doctor?'

'Not yet,' replied Carl. 'I haven't been sleeping very well lately, but I will go if things don't get better. It's been really cold in here today, so I hope you can sort the radiator out.'

'I'll do my best, mate. At what time are you going home?'

'My train leaves at eleven past the hour, so I'll have to leave in a bit,' answered Carl.

'Okay, I'll let you get on with things and I'll come back when you're gone to dismantle it and sort it out.'

\* \* \*

Charles was cooking when carl got home that day.

'How was your day?' asked Charles.

'Okay, thanks. I've been sorting things out for next week's exams. What about you?'

'All good, thanks. I've been preparing a presentation I need to finish by Friday. You fancy having some roasted lamb?'

'Are you sure?' asked Carl surprised.

'Yeah, sure. Have some.'

'Oh, thanks,' said Carl while standing awkwardly in the middle of the kitchen.

'It's Okay. It's almost done. Just empty that bowl in two plates for us and take it to the front room. I'll take the rest out, including something to drink.'

Charles and Carl were moving their jaws to crush the bits of lamb, shouting out when they knew the answer to any of the questions on a university quiz show that was about to finish.

'So typical,' said Charles. 'The guys with the common accent representing that shitty polytechnic uni from the north and those posh girls representing that prestigious university from the south coast.' The episode of the university quiz show finished and a new one started.

'That's in Birmingham, right?' asked Carl pointing to the television after chewing a bit of lamb.

'Oh, gosh no. The one in Birmingham is Newman College. Newnham is one of the colleges of Cambridge Uni. I guess both would sound equally Jewish with double *n* at the end.'

'Ah, I had never heard of it.'

'It's a women's only college. My dad went to Cambridge, and he used to go drinking there with his mates when they were on the pull,' explained Charles before taking a sip of his drink.

'Well, I guess a women-only college bar must have been quite an attraction for uni students.'

'Oh, yes, the place to be for all those lusty students looking to sin,' said Charles very surprised about Carl's thoughtful remark.

'So does your dad go to those alumni meetings for former graduates?'

Oh, no, he never does. I don't think he's ever been to any of them.'

There are two young lecturers I know at uni that went to Cambridge and they were talking the other day about the last alumni meet-up they went to. They said they loved it,' explained Carl before taking another mouthful of food.

'Yeah, they're supposed to be very good, but my dad's a bit funny about his Cambridge past. He's not in touch with any of his university friends, and he's the only person I know who went to Cambridge and doesn't have his degree hanging in his office.'

'How come?' asked Carl wiping his mouth with a napkin.

'It's a long story.'

Charles saw that Carl felt embarrassed for asking, so he went on to tell the story to make him feel better.

'My dad's parents are Polish, and they came here after the war. My dad was born here in England, but he didn't start learning English until he went to school, although he sounds totally English now. My grandparents are very traditional, so he had a Polish life at home and an English one outside, and I guess he never felt like he was either English or Polish, just a bit trapped between two countries, I guess,' Charles paused to have a sip of his drink. 'My dad's a bit better about it now, but when he was a kid, he was embarrassed about his parents because they didn't speak English very well, which I think was quite harsh on his part. My grandparents worked very hard to put some money together to send him to university and he was embarrassed about them. You know, that shows you what kind of person he is. He was just fine studying at Cambridge and going out drinking with the money they sent him, but he was still embarrassed about them. He didn't like having a foreign surname, as he didn't feel English enough, so he changed it after graduating. The stupid guy, he had identity problems because he didn't feel British enough and thought that changing his surname would sort it out.'

'So, he changed his surname to *Pope*?' asked Carl.

'Yes,' continued Charles. 'Out of all the English surnames there are, he had to choose fucking *Pope*. I like our Polish surname. It has a few consonants together, so it looks like a WIFI password, but it's our culture and identity. My dad has always been so stubborn. I hate the guy. My grandparents used to recite to me a Polish poem when I was a child, a poem about a very obstinate caretaker of a graveyard who always used to take the soil from one part of the cemetery to another in his black and white sack. His sack had a hole and the soil used to get out through it, so he used to walk around the cemetery collecting the bits of soil from the ground and putting them back in his sack with the hole in it. That's my dad. And he had to choose *Pope* as his surname. It's a very common surname in Birmingham so, as I said to you when you moved here, if you meet anyone with that surname, we're not related. My grandparents are very religious, he wasn't, but he chose *Pope* as a way to reaffirm his Catholicism, even though there are rumours that someone in the family converted to Catholicism during the war.'

'And was he happier after he changed his surname?'

'Not really. People are stupid enough to try to define themselves with external factors instead of with internal ones.'

'What do you mean?' asked Carl.

'Well, who we are, our beliefs, our thoughts, our knowledge of things, they form our personality, and what we do. I mean, the way we act, it's a representation of that personality of ours. The actions we take, and the decisions we make, are a result of our personalities and of our codes of morals and ethics. Our internal personalities, to put it in simple terms, influence external things, like how we react in situations, but my dad is one of those stupid people who tries to do things the other way around. Giving yourself a label or dressing in a certain way doesn't make you anything; your actions define you. That's exactly what ignorant people get wrong and how they operate. They are the ones who are surprised when they find out something about you because they assumed something else by looking at you, the kind of people who would say that they never thought you liked this or that sport because of the clothes you wear, as if people had to wear badges showing their interests.' Charles stopped to have another mouthful of lamb before continuing talking. 'My dad thinks exactly like that. He thinks that with external considerations, such as his accent, his possessions, his surname even, he can alter and influence his internal things, his personality and his feelings, and the way these are projected outside and perceived by others. That's the problem a lot of people have these days. They have issues, and things they don't like about themselves, and instead of working on what matters, their inner selves, they work on what doesn't matter, like their body, or something just to try to change the way they feel about themselves. So, yeah, a lot of people these days try to find themselves using external factors, instead of using internal ones.

'I see,' said Carl a bit confused.

'My granddad's someone to be very proud of, not embarrassed by,' added Charles.

'Do you get on well with him?'

'Oh, yes,' asserted Charles. 'My dad didn't take me much to their place when I was a kid as he was scared that I'd learn Polish from them or something, but I started going there more often as I grew older. My granddad's got the balls that my dad will never have.'

'I'm sure your dad's not that bad,' said Carl in a sweet tone.

'He is,' continued Charles. 'My grandparents are very sweet and great people, and my dad didn't take after them at all. They lived through hell and came out of it happy and ready to help others. One day, the Germans went to my granddad's house and took him and his family away because his dad had some kind of official job or something. They took them to a house where they were being watched by guards and one night, my granddad and his brother escaped. They joined the Polish militia, but they ended up in different places and didn't know where each other was. It must have been so hard. My granddad's brother ended up around Italy, and my granddad went to Egypt, then made it all the way down to South Africa, where he and his group were trained and met a big group of Polish soldiers. From there, they all boarded a ship and went to New York after stopping in Cuba, but they weren't allowed to get off in the US and they ended up going to Scotland in the end, where they joined the British army. If my grandad had left the boat in Cuba, I could be telling you this in Spanish,' joked Charles.

'Haha, yes, true. That's a lot of travelling,' added Carl.

'Yeah, I know, especially in those days when it took ages to cross the Atlantic,' Charles went on with his story. 'Anyway, my granddad joined the RAF and he went back to Poland to fight the Germans. Meanwhile, my grandmother was in a labour camp. The Nazis had been to her town and massacred over half the people there, led by a guy my grandma always referred to as *Carcock,* a sick son of a bitch who apparently escaped to the US after the war. I remember the worst swearing I ever heard from my grandad. When talking about that guy, he said, *and the cunt escaped to America.* Charles looked into space for a second before he went on. 'Anyway, they killed my grandma's younger siblings in front of her, but they left her and her older siblings alive because they were old enough to work in a labour camp. My grandma's cousin was also at the same labour camp; she had been caught while she was on her way to buy a cake to celebrate a birthday. She managed to escape relatively soon but the poor girl was killed eleven days later during an assault on other houses.'

'Oh, no, that's horrible. Such a horrible thing to go through for her whole family,' exclaimed Carl.

'I know,' agreed Charles. 'But the amazing thing is that some people have so much good and kindness in them, even the worst experiences can't change them. My grandma was in a Nazi labour camp for a few years and was forced to dig trenches for a few months. It was cold and raining most days. She only had bread, water, and potatoes for a while and digging was becoming more difficult, but she always talks about a German guard who helped her out a few times. When no other officers were looking, he used to give her his coat and do the digging of the trench for her and one day they were almost caught. My grandma is sweet as she always says, *you see, not all of them were bad. He was very sweet. I think he liked me, hehe.* She has a very kind heart. Even after everything she went through, she says that it's a pity that Germany, a country so rich in the humanities, with an impressive collection of composers, philosophers, and writers, is known by its inhumane actions in its darkest period of history, and by its engineering. You are one of those people too, Carl. Contrary to what happens to most other people, getting older hasn't taken your kindness away. You are one of those people who can find the bright side others can't. You can see what others can't see and you always find the good in others.'

'Oh, thank you very much for the kind words, Charles,' replied Carl in a shy way.

'Nah, it's okay. I mean it. But, yeah, not everything was bad for my grandma. One day, my granddad and his squad got into the labour camp where my grandmother was, killed the German guards and liberated all the women. All the girls hooked up with the soldiers and my grandparents were one of those couples. My grandmother's very cute when she talks about it, she says, *all the good-looking ones were taken, so I was left with this one.'*

'Oh, wow, that's a great story,' said Carl getting some bit of lamb with his fork.

'I think it's amazing,' said Charles. 'And they're so sweet together. They're ninety and eighty-seven and they still hold hands at home. That's what I mean, my granddad's the kind of guy to be proud of.'

'I'm sure your dad really respects all that,' said Carl.

'Nah, he's too much of an ignoramus to do that.'

There was silence and both housemates were moving their jaws to crush the lamb and potatoes watching the silly TV quiz. Suddenly, all the other problems they had talked about lately seemed very trivial and totally unimportant.

\* \* \*

A suited figure with a wine stain on his shirt walked up the front stairs of Post Central. He had a black leather briefcase and a white piece of paper protruding from one of its pockets. He got to the entrance of a block and pressed a few buttons. He pressed again but got no answer.

'Evening, sir!' said a suited old man with a company logo over his heart.

'Oh, hello. I just came to see my son, but he's not here. Have you seen Charles Pope lately? He lives in number eleven.'

'Sorry, sir, but I'm new here. I have only been here for a few days and I'm afraid I don't know many of the residents yet.'

'It's okay, don't worry. I'll call him on his mobile.'

\* \* \*

Some noise was coming out of the black plastic box when one of the two housemates started talking.

'I meant to ask you,' said Charles. 'How are your headaches?'

'They come and go, thanks,' replied Carl. 'It was okay today, but I can't sleep very well these days, so it might just be tiredness.'

'Yes, it could be,' said Charles. 'Have you been to the doctor's yet?'

\* \* \*

A tall figure, in white and black pyjamas, was walking diagonally from one corner to another of the room. He had some papers in one hand that had a stamp on the top saying, 'Confidential', and a glass of wine in the other hand. He took the glass to his mouth and tilted it three times, quickly. His cheeks filled like a balloon and he carried on walking.

*One victim had a kidney missing, another the genitals cut off, and another one the heart almost ripped off. Organ trafficking... organ trafficking... of course it's not organ trafficking. Otherwise, they'd have taken the bodies to a place to take the organs out properly, and they'd have probably taken more things out, and they'd have definitely taken the two kidneys out instead of just one.*

The man stopped, bent his knees until his buttocks hit his armchair, left the glass on the desk, and continued muttering.

*Okay. We have amputations as the ritual, fantasy-based features, which are the links between these three victims, but what about the other three?*

\* \* \*

'No, I haven't,' replied Carl. 'I go to bed and I wake up in the morning as if I hadn't rested at all, so I think once I start sleeping better, the headaches might go.'

'Are you busy at work these days,' asked Charles.

'Yes, quite busy, actually. We have exams coming up so I'm doing quite a lot of admin to get ready for them.'

'I see. And is that stressing you out?'

'A bit, I guess.'

'I think it's stressing you a lot, but you don't realise. You think about work when you're in bed before falling asleep?'

'Yes, quite a few times,' admitted Carl. 'But I think that's normal.'

'That's not normal, Carl. And it's not healthy,' interrupted Charles.

'I just go over a mental to-do list.'

'You don't need that,' affirmed Charles. 'Have you got a planner at work?'

'Yes, I have one. I just write down a few things here and there.'

'Well, what you need to do is, every day before you leave, write down, in order of importance, what you need to do the following day, and cross out the things that you've done. The next day when you get to work, the first thing you need to do is take a look at the to-do list for the day and carry on doing that. Anything that you haven't had time to do in a day, move it to the next. What's very important is to cross out the things you've done, cross out the date as well of the day that's finished and put a big tick on the top of the page, as that will automatically tell your brain to switch off and you won't feel the need to make any mental to-do lists when you're in bed.'

'Does that work?' asked Carl.

'Yes, it does,' answered Charles.

'Okay, I'll do that. Thanks a lot for the advice.'

* * *

*But why mutilate?* thought the man in his pyjamas. *The killer had cut the genitals off but these were found, so this person isn't taking body parts as souvenirs.*

* * *

'Oh, so, did your granddad ever see his brother again?' asked Carl.

'Oh, yes, he did,' replied Charles. 'My granddad's bother lives in Nottingham, like my grandparents. He's a funny guy. There were a lot of Polish people who moved to Nottingham after the war. There's a doctor at work whose granddad was also Polish and lived in Nottingham. This guy told me that his granddad started acting a bit weirdly the last few months before he passed away. One day, this guy from work took his girlfriend to Nottingham to meet his family and they were all having dinner, and his granddad started looking around him, threw the cutlery on the table, and broke out, *Once, I killed a German, during the war, and I buried him in my farm. He* took a deep breath and continued eating. Everyone remained quiet at the table, and no one mentioned anything about it ever again.'

'Wow, that's... that must have been a bit uncomfortable for your friend,' said Carl.

'Yes, I guess, but quite funny I think,' replied Charles. 'My granddad's brother was also very funny. Did I tell you about his visit to Israel?'

'No, you didn't,' said Carl.

'Well, a few years ago, I think it was around eleven years ago, he went to Israel on a religious holiday. At the airport, the immigration officer was checking his passport and said, *Welcome to Israel*, and my granddad's brother said, *Israel, no, this is Palestine!* The immigration officer wasn't too happy about that and told him again, *No, sir, this is Israel,* to which my granddad's brother replied, *What? Last time I was here, this was Palestine!* The immigration officer looked at him seriously, stamped his passport, and said, *Sir, many things have changed since the war.*

'Hehe, did he really say that to the officer?' asked Carl.

'Oh, yes, he did. My great-uncle's the type of guy who says what he thinks. I just can't believe he got away with it.'

* * *

The muttering continued. *What plan did this guy have? It has to be a guy, the killer's too strong to be a woman. But the times of the crimes and the scenes are totally random.*

* * *

'And do you see your great-uncle often?'

'Not that often these days, but I sometimes go to my granddad's and he's there.'

'It must be quite good for them to live near each other,' added Carl.

* * *

The figure in white and black pyjamas continued walking aimlessly around the room, always diagonally from one corner to another. *The victims are so random... and even though the ritual of amputating is constant, the way of killing them is not.*

* * *

Someone knocks on the door. Carl walks to the door, opens it and says, 'Oh, hi, come in.'

'Thanks,' replied Jake as he was walking through the corridor. 'Sorry, buddy, I know it's late. I just came in for a few minutes to borrow a book from Charles. I hope I'm not interrupting anything serious.'

'Oh, yes, the book,' said Charles. 'No, you're not interrupting anything. We were just talking about old people.'

'I love old people,' said Jake. 'It's because they've run out of fucks, and they can't be bothered to follow conventions or try to be polite about other people's opinions or anything. If they want to say something, they just say it.'

'It must be quite nice being like that, although nice is perhaps not the word,' added Carl.

'Liberating,' added Jake.

'Yes, liberating,' said Carl. 'It must be so liberating to be like that. I'm always too worried about what others will think of me,' confessed Carl.

\* \* \*

*And he didn't even bother to get rid of the bodies. He left the bodies in the crime scene, which is far too risky. This guy's really taking risks. But why does he do that? Why leaving the victims at the crime scene?* The man in his pyjamas continued thinking.

\* \* \*

'Yeah, liberating is a good way of putting it,' said Charles.

'Oh, yeah,' agreed Jake. 'It's like the other day at hospital. I was in the ward, and I heard one of the nurses shouting at a patient, telling him to stop. I got there, mind you this was at eleven in the evening, and there was an old guy lying on his bed with his trousers pulled down having a wank. The nurse continued telling him to stop that and the more she said it, the faster the old guy went. The nurse then said that it wasn't appropriate to do that there in the ward and the old guy continued with it and said, *I can't sleep, I'm trying to relax to fall asleep and you're ruining it,*' explained Jake. 'I had to walk off the ward because I was pissing myself laughing.'

'What happened to him?' asked Carl.

'I don't know,' said Jake. 'I guess he fell asleep in the end.'

'That's epic,' said Charles as he stood up. 'I'll go and get that book for you.'

'Hopefully the guy fell asleep,' said Carl.

'Yeah, I'm sure he did,' replied Jake. 'Old guys just don't care. They just do what they want and simply don't give a shit. I think when you get to that age, you give up caring about stuff. You just do whatever you feel like without worrying about what others will say.'

'I wish I could do that,' said Carl with a smile of hope on his face.

'Carl, mate,' said Jake. 'You have to do what you want to do.'

'Well, I always wanted to be a teacher, and teach English literature. I even thought about how good it would be to be a university lecturer, writing articles and teaching your students about the articles you'd just written. I wanted to teach people about Joyce, about *Ulysses.*'

'You should go for it,' said Jake in an encouraging voice. 'Do a PGCE if you want to teach at schools, and go on and do an M.A., and then a PhD if you want to teach at uni. You can totally do that,' continued Jake with a positive tone in his voice.

'I'm not intelligent enough, and I don't have the confidence to stand up in front of people and talk to them. I'm too insecure to teach,' admitted Carl. 'Teachers are confident. They have charisma and they get the respect of their students. I lack all that. I once applied for a teacher training course and I got an interview, but I never went because I was scared.'

'Oh, Carl, don't do that, buddy, don't sell yourself short,' said Jake. 'And definitely don't waste opportunities like that.'

'I know,' said Carl. 'I just wish I was one of those people with a big ego and self-confidence, like those really inspiring teachers and role models many of us have had.'

'Truly inspiring people don't have big egos; they don't need them,' said Jake. 'You just need to evaluate what you want, go for it, and be ready to make mistakes and learn from others. I pity stubborn people who are convinced they know everything, as they are unable to learn anything from anyone. It's also very easy to spot them; they are the ones with an unstoppable urge to correct everyone around them,' added Jake. 'Some of those people manage to come across as very confident people but they are not. Carl, you just have to think about what you want and go for it.' Jake paused before going on. 'Something happened a few weeks ago at work that made me think. I ate a dead man's ice cream and it made me think.'

'What do you mean?' asked Carl a bit confused.

'I was in the doctors' room in the ward and saw an ice cream in the freezer. I'd seen it before, so I asked one of the nurses whose it was and she told me it belonged to the guy in bed number eleven, but that he'd died three days before and they felt bad giving the ice cream back to the family when they came to get his possessions. She said that she was going to clean the fridge the following day and that she'd throw it away, so I asked if I could eat it. She was a bit surprised, but she gave me the go ahead, so I ate it. And as I was eating it, I was just thinking that life's just like a dead man's ice cream. It has a purpose, a reason to exist, a potential to be realised, and that its mission to exist is only accomplished when someone eats it. A dead man's ice cream runs the risk of being thrown away in the rubbish, of melting, and of never fulfilling its function in the world. Many of us are just like that ice cream, we just stay in the freezer waiting to be thrown away and melt down the sink. Don't be like that, Carl. Whatever you want to do, go and do it. Moments and opportunities in life also have an expiry date, and if you don't grab them when you can, you'll be throwing them in the bin and your dreams will melt there. And I'll also tell you what, that ice cream was the best one I've had in fucking ages!'

'What kind of ice cream was it?' asked Carl.

'It was a vanilla and white chocolate one, but that's not relevant,' said Jake. 'You just need to do with your life what you want to do.'

'Yeah, I know,' replied Carl.

'Yes, that's it, buddy. Do with your life what you really want to do with it. And I'll tell you what, aim well high when you set life goals, because once you reach them, you'll have nowhere else to go.'

Carl looked at the floor shyly and said, 'I don't want to be a dead man's ice cream. I don't want my life to be like a dead man's ice cream, melting and going to waste. I want to do things.'

'You are doing things,' replied Jake. 'Some people aren't destined to be happy, no matter how good their lives are, but you are not like that. You like living life and you're here now. You could have stayed in Gibraltar doing nothing, waiting for fate to come to you but, instead, you decided to come here to create your own destiny. That's the difference between passive and active luck, buddy. You're doing things.'

Carl nodded, 'I just don't want to be a dead man's ice cream.'

\* \* \*

*And what about the post-offence behaviour?* The figure in the black and white pyjamas continued going over the cases in his head. He continued taking the glass of wine to his mouth and taking three sips at a time. One of the documents he was reading said, *Kings Norton Cemetery analysis* on the top. He continued reading while scratching the central left part of his chest. He started reading, *The caretaker...* and he stopped to think to himself. *This guy leaves the victims in the murder scene. He doesn't even take them anywhere, or hide them, but then, he hasn't contacted anyone yet. He will, he will contact someone about it. People like this don't enjoy it if they don't see the reaction in others. They need to see that reaction. He'll want to see a reaction,* thought the man in the pyjamas before he closed the file violently.

\* \* \*

'You won't be if you just continue doing things, making moves,' said Jake in a reassuring manner. 'It's like... it's like a chair...,' said Jake before pausing to try to come up with another metaphor that would make some sort of sense. 'A chair is only truly a chair when someone's sitting on it, as it's fulfilling the function it was designed for. When someone's not sitting on it, a chair is nothing. It's the same with people. Many people spend more time being nobody than being themselves. You can only be yourself when you're doing what you're really passionate about. That's how you prevent becoming a dead man's ice cream. Listen to your inner voice, find what you really want to do, and go out and do it.'

Carl nodded again, 'I don't want to be a dead man's ice cream.'

A Dead Man's Ice Cream

# Chapter 7

## The shadow of the White Elephant

Call me Carl. Some months ago —never mind how long precisely— having gathered a bit of money, and with nothing to prevent me from doing it, I thought I would sail inland and see the drier parts of my world. I'd love to say that it's a way I have of driving off the spleen and regulating my circulation, but I had a wedding I couldn't get away from, and an overdue visit to a friend so, in the process, I would write the political article that my editor had been nagging me about for months. *Note to self: Delete this intro if my editor says it is too similar to that book about how much we're willing to sacrifice for our desires and obsessions.*

I was walking along Churchill Avenue as quickly as I could to cross the runway before the twelve o'clock flight from Gatwick got there, (Gibraltar's airport's only runway crosses the only road in and out of Gibraltar, so you need to be familiar with flying times if you don't want to be waiting for twelve minutes to cross the road). A strong wind almost blew away my copy of the Gibraltar News, so I put it inside my red bag before it was too late. I crossed the runway before the plane arrived and I was happy about it, as I'm sure that the kerosene fumes that you inhale from being close to planes aren't good for your lungs. Well, the crossing of the runway was done, I just had to start thinking about what article I'd send my editor back at uni.

I'd been across the border many times, but I knew this time was going to be different. As usual, an old Spanish lady asked me to pass some tobacco through the border for her, but still, I knew this trip would be different. This had happened to me all my life and I still felt bad saying no, but my grandma once told me never to take anything through the border for people who I didn't know, as it could have drugs in it and I could go to jail, and I still believe she was right. These women are called, *matuteras*, in honour of a politician whose dad was a very well-known smuggler when the border between Spain and Gibraltar was closed.

My godfather's son was getting married and, as my grandmother couldn't make it to the wedding, I said I'd go in her place. I thought I could visit some friends on the way. I was almost at the border when I saw Tavares. We smiled and nodded at each other, and he still asked to see my passport before he let me through. This is the British side of us, the anal one. That guy had been my neighbour for over twelve years, and he still had to ask to see my ID to let me cross the border. Everyone knows each other in Gib, so it wouldn't have made a difference if he hadn't been my neighbour. His father was a really funny guy. He lived in Lincolnshire for a few years and used to babysit a former British prime minister when she was a child. He was fifteen and lived next door to her. He never liked her as a politician and used to say to me, 'She really liked it when I threw her up in the air. I should have dropped that bitch'.

At this time of the day, the border's not that busy at all. The Spaniards that work in Gibraltar cross the border before the shops open and go back to Spain after work. The tourists tend to cross late in the morning and early afternoon, and then stay till the evening. The only people crossing back to Spain at that time were the cigarette and alcohol smugglers.

I was now in Spanish territory and, as usual, I started with the ritual of changing the British SIM card for the Spanish one. Two languages, two currencies, two houses, one in Gibraltar and one in Spain, and two SIM cards, to avoid extortionate roaming charges. In Gibraltar, everything comes in twos. Some romantics say that it's part of our heritage, half-British-and-half-Spanish kind of thing, but I prefer to call it *convenience*.

I still had time before my coach journey to Seville, so I decided to go for some food to avoid eating on the bus. I walked along Calle Gibraltar until I saw a place with some unoccupied tables inside and went in to get out of that wind and to have some food on the way. *Note to self: Cut these mundane remarks if I go over the word limit.*

Most Gibraltarians feel quite excited about food when they come to Spain. These are the Gibraltarians whose Spanish origins, if any, go a few generations back, but me, with my recently renewed Spanish heritage, Spanish food was what I'd been brought up with all my life. I ordered a *Campestre*, a good beer from Seville, just to get into the Seville mood, and got the gazpacho and meatballs combination from the set menu. The old lady serving me was nice and didn't bother making any chit-chat about life in *El Peñón*, as they call *The Rock*. I wasn't like other *Llanitos*, the people from Gibraltar, with a twang that gives them away despite speaking very good Spanish. I sounded totally Spanish, something not that normal in the younger generations, but even if one speaks perfect Spanish, they can still know that you're from Gibraltar. It might be the smell, the clothes, or the way we walk, but they still know.

I was glad she didn't bring up anything to do with politics, because just a couple of days ago the last dispute over fishing in the waters had started again, so there was a bit of tension in the air. One of the problems of being such a tiny nation (even if, as I believe, the UN doesn't give us the right to call us so), is that there is no space to vent. It's always the same, there's some scandal in Gibraltar, such as politicians spending public funds on dodgy stuff, they get caught, so they order the Royal Gibraltar Police to get tight on Spanish fishermen. Then, the Spanish authorities react by toughening up the controls on the border and by creating insane queues. In Spain, they bring up the old, *Gibraltar español* and start claiming that Gibraltar is theirs, and the Gibraltarians that cross the border are the ones who get stick from the Spaniards. A few weeks down the line, it all goes back to normal and then it is time for the rotten ones in society, the politicians, to start all over again. I can tell you all, whenever there's tension between Spain and Gibraltar, look a bit deeper and you'll find the issue that is being covered. *Note to self: I could talk about how the same happened to cover up the scandal of the stolen babies and the refusal from the government to investigate many of the cases reported by family members to protect the church, officials, military personnel, doctors and nurses involved. Thousands of babies had been taken by telling mothers that their babies had died at birth and then the babies were sold to rich families. Check the name of the doctor who was found guilty of stealing babies but acquitted because the statute of limitations had elapsed since the crime.*

I had never had any interest in politics or in politicians, but when I learnt about them, I got to despise them. Those cheesy self-centred liars who got promoted in their careers thanks to licking the right person's ass, and tripping up their colleagues as soon as they had nothing to offer to them. However, I must say, I am very thankful that the politicians in Gibraltar aren't as rotten or as corrupt as the Spanish ones, although it's not because our politicians are better people than theirs, they are not, it's because our system doesn't let them take the mickey as much as the Spanish one does. *Note to self: Give an example of one of those politicians who have stolen millions but were never made to return the money.*

Spanish *presidentes del gobierno* (prime ministers) and MPs benefit from the usual extravagant salaries and allowances but they also get ridiculously high pensions for the rest of their lives, meaning having 'worked' for a couple of years, Spanish politicians not just grab the booty and run, as British ones do, they stick their two fingers up at the nation when they start receiving their pension, which, they do as soon as they have left their political post and they can combine with a normal job. Let's just think that we're also lucky because apart from not giving our politicians that pension, at least explicitly, we're not like Spain, where politicians can mix and match pensions from different political posts and still pretend that they care about the unemployed. *Note to self: Maybe tune this down as it sounds very aggressive and it makes me feel uncomfortable.*

Those were the words, more or less, that came to mind when I lifted my face from the bowl of gazpacho after I'd finished with it and saw the long queue at the job centre office of La Línea. They were standing there, some of them weren't smoking, or talking to others, it looked as if some of them weren't even waiting for anything, like they were just there. Unemployment benefits run out in Spain, and the rule is something along the lines of you get unemployment benefits for half the amount of time you've worked. The amount of money they get, and any extra help, varies from government to government, although it's funny to see how the greedy rats, irrespectively of their political party, start cutting back on benefits and public services when a country's going through a tough time, instead of lowering the politicians' salaries, abolishing the stupid idea of having a pension for life, or cutting down on all that money that they get through politics. Money that is illegal in many cases, and immoral in all. *Note to self: Should I delete this paragraph? It looks a bit out of context.*

I was stirring the red sauce of the meatballs when I started wondering if I was really that nasty, if I really had become such a bitter person who thought that there was no one kind-hearted in the world, and I soon realised that wasn't the case. I knew there were many nice people in the world, with their hearts in the right places, with energy and passion to help others, but none of them had chosen politics. I thought of those volunteers that spend their youth in forsaken countries, those teachers and social workers who work in deprived areas because they want to make a difference, ignoring the fact that their work is undervalued and underpaid. I know there are a lot of nice people in the world, it's just that politics isn't designed to attract nice people. Politics attracts the entitled, the kind of arrogant person who thinks that he or she's better than the other forty odd million people in the country.

Politics is designed to attract bastards and evil self centred back stabbers. You really have to be some kind of narcissist to want that sort of job. Some people try to mask the true reality by saying that politics is tough because you need to be very ambitious to succeed in it. That's really not an accurate description. Ambition has a positive connotation to it, ambition is for those people who want to get a promotion because they work hard and have ambitions of beating their own record, to improve at what they do; trying to climb up the ladder by lying and making others look more incompetent than you is not ambition, it's politics. *Note to self: Perhaps use '@' instead of the second 'a' in 'bastards'.*

I had finished my food and I was leaving the bar when I gazed at the people at the queue, thinking that was what made my grandma stay in Gibraltar when the border closed. In one of those rants typical of the Spanish dictator, he decided to close the border between Gibraltar and Spain, separating families until 1982, and planting the seed for future hatred. As it still happens today, Spanish workers went to Gibraltar during the day to work but they found out after their shifts that they couldn't go back to Spain. My grandmother was one of them, although she was lucky enough to have a Gibraltarian boyfriend by then: my granddad. Families were broken, friends separated, and neighbours who had more in common than any politician could explain were divided between two pieces of land; today, with a European Union with no borders, this seems utterly inexplicable. Those parents who went to Gibraltar to work couldn't go back at night to their homes, and the Gibraltarians that were in Spain couldn't go back to their homes either. The story of my birth was told to my relatives in the same ungraceful manner as that of many others. Families on the Gibraltar side would go up to the border, as the Gibraltar side was never closed, while families on the Spanish side had to stay a few hundred meters back, as the Spanish side was heavily guarded. Families gathered at both sides of the border to shout out their news to their relatives, news of deaths of friends and relatives, and news of births, which illustrates how the links between these two towns proved to be stronger than the blockage of an old fart with a moustache, even though many people do everything they can to prove how different and unrelated they are. My grandmother went close to the border and shouted at her family the news of my birth, and then she started crying before she told them the news of my mother's death, who was buried in Gibraltar in a ceremony that was attended by no other relatives because of that stupid border. *Note to self: The border closed in 1969 but my grandma got stuck in Gibraltar when they closed it for a shorter period quite a lot before that. Should I clarify this?*

I walked back down Calle Gibraltar, as the presence of cars from *The Rock* became more 'prominent' the closer I got to the territory, which is another consequence of these long queues. The people from Gibraltar, on their way back from business or holidays, need to leave their cars on the Spanish side to avoid the long queues. They walk through the border and pick up their cars another day.

I was walking towards the bus station as I was trying to get some water off my red bag. I was battling the wind, and when I was shuffling the stuff in my bag, a gust of wind blew away half my newspaper. Luckily, it was just the politics section.

The bus was about to get to Algeciras, and I just started thinking about how easy it was to travel into Spain these days. I know it's just a twenty-minute walk from my house in Gib, but that stupid border made things quite inconvenient for people. People are bemused when I tell them that, until 1982, the only two ways to travel into Spain were getting a ferry into Tangier, and then another one into Spain, either Malaga or Algeciras; the latter is a town just twenty minutes by car from Gibraltar. The other option was to fly to London and then fly back to Spain; for most people that meant Malaga, which is less than a two-hour drive from Gibraltar. Life had definitely got a bit easier these last few years!! *Note to self: Should I move this paragraph after the one about the border?*

We were already in the *término municipal*, municipal district in English that is, of Tarifa. I hadn't seen any sign saying so, but the wind now was shaking the bus furiously. Driving into Tarifa bus station, I saw a traffic sign pointing towards the *ayuntamiento*, which in English means 'town hall', although the best translation for it is 'shithole', where the lying rats piss on the Spanish people's rights and on Spanish laws and get paid extortionate amounts of money for it. That is another reason why we are very lucky in the UK, because we don't have that joke of clown gathering circus that Spanish town halls are. In Spain, every town, however small, has one, with its local mayor, the representative of culture, of festivities, of anything he or she can come up with to bend the rules of morality and get a job. It's not surprising there is such resistance from politicians to reorganise all these towns into district councils and therefore dispense with the costs of running a town hall in every little village. Obviously, it's only surprising to those that aren't familiar with Spanish politics. Mayors of towns who don't even appear on maps can get paid as much as the prime minister, mayors open companies under relatives' names and contract all the maintenance services to their own company, for which they charge up to £2000 to change a light bulb or to lay a tile on the pavement. They tell their relatives or friends which useless piece of land to buy, then they change land registry regulations a few months later to rezone land for commercial purposes and then sell the land to building companies. Other times, if the mayor and minions are too lazy, they'll just force the building company to bride them to give them permission to build on protected land. A politician who doesn't even have GCSEs can end up organising the festivities of a village and get paid more than a teacher or a doctor. It might surprise people, but of course, this is in line with the good old Spanish tradition of not recognising hard work, or efficiency, but to reward the dummy who's better connected. But, saying that, it has its positive side, as it makes journalists' lives much easier. All they have to do when a case of corruption comes up is copy and paste the news from a couple of days earlier. *Note to self: Maybe put all the stuff about Gib first as an introduction to the trip and then follow up with the bits on Spanish politics.*

I didn't start feeling uncomfortable on the bus until we got to Conil, a gorgeous place to visit, classy, and very traditional. I started trying to sleep and something scratched my head when I leaned against the window. I grabbed it with my left hand, and it was red. I must have been half asleep, as it took me some time to realise that it was a pack of tobacco. It had a picture of what looked like the x-ray of not a very healthy person, some rotten lungs, and a note in bold letters that read something along the lines of, 'tobacco rots your insides, it is harmful to you and those around you'. I just started thinking that was what the government should be saying about politics, as far as I know, politics has killed more people throughout history than tobacco ever will. *Note to self: Should I change all this? It makes me sound like a very bitter person.*

I continued sitting on my seat, seat number twelve to be precise, when the bus got into another town, a place that had made the news pretty much every day in the last few weeks. They have a mayor who has recently been accused of slander against a senior royal. He described the senior royal using a list of rather negative adjectives, although he based all his comments on books already published. The interesting thing is that he talked about the senior royal's love affairs and about how, apparently, he had been spending public money on his lover, or lovers. That's pretty obvious, I thought, given that every monarch's money is all public money. *Note to self: Perhaps I could link this bit to the story about that distant relative being grounded at school for not waving to the Spanish dictator when he visited the town.*

I guess all European royal families are pretty much the same: wives who can't stand their husbands, intellectually disabled children from so much inbreeding, alcoholics, thieves, tax dodgers, and kiddy fiddlers. There are quite a few articles about the royal family every month, some defending them, and some telling the truth. One of the most famous things a royal ever did in Spain was to address the nation after a failed coup d'état on 23rd February 1981. The nation had just got rid of a dictator in 1975 and many were afraid they were heading that way again. The result of it was that some people from the military were imprisoned while the royal was beloved by everyone because of his speech to the nation. Other people got very scared, like a second cousin of mine who, as soon as he heard the news, ran to hide in the mountains with a bag of food and a radio with almost flat batteries; after a few hours the batteries went and a couple of days later he ran out of food, so he finally came down after twelve days. He brought with him an intense smell of cow dung and a long-frayed beard, and he left half his weight in the mountains. *Note to self: Following the instructions from my editor, I have to make sure I do not mention any names. Check that I've done this; I don't even say which country the royals are from.*

The royal had achieved enormous levels of popularity thanks to his address to the nation. There were different versions of the story going around in Cadiz. One of the top officers involved had a son living in Cadiz province and was quite well-known because he had a decent rank. The guy called his father a few hours before the coup d'état and said, 'Don't do it, Dad, the royal has betrayed you.' However, his dad went ahead anyway. The military officers carried on saying that the orders came from very high up, and they called the artificer of the plan the *White Elephant*. Some more junior officers had dared to ask about him, but the only answer they got is that it would be revealed in due time. The plan was that the officers and his men would take the *Congreso de los Diputados*, the Spanish equivalent of the Commons, a place where once people of different ideological backgrounds would meet to work with the common goal of getting Spain out of a dictatorship and into a democracy, whereas nowadays it is full of ignorant rats who steal cheese from each other and from the Spanish people. Once in the *Congreso*, they would stop the session and then the White Elephant would come in and address everyone present telling them what new direction Spain was going to follow. The *White Elephant* never turned up, and the coup d'état didn't work out.

Eventually, a royal addressed the nation on TV and the whole of Spain was ecstatic, except those who knew that the only reason why it'd taken him so long to appear on TV was because he got scared of

going ahead with the coup d'état and decided to stop it halfway
through. The officer's son was very angry and made sure he leaked
some information before escaping the country and moving to
Gibraltar. That became a very hot topic of conversation in Gibraltar
back in the day and the topic rapidly filtered back into Spain, although
it never made it into the headlines, proving that freedom of speech
wasn't as free as people claimed it was; the mayor of a certain Spanish
town could say a lot about this. No one knows the full story of what
happened, but people will have a good idea, as secrets always come out
in funny ways. *Note to self: It would answer a lot of questions if I talked about
that other person hiding in Gibraltar, but grandma told me not to tell anyone.*

The bus was now leaving Jerez de la Frontera. The wind had
diminished and there were no more stops until Seville. The whole story
about the White Elephant never made it to the news, although I knew
another one with the words *royal* and *elephant* in the headline was on
the way. One of a senior royal's grandchildren had an accident
involving a gun yesterday and shot himself in the foot, literally literally,
not just literally. Obviously, any family would ordinarily lose custody
of a child for letting him use guns at that age, but that would never
happen to the royal family. All members of the royal family went to
the hospital to see the kid, except a senior royal. He sent a letter to the
media saying that he couldn't face going there as he was quite upset
because it was the 50th anniversary of his sister's death, whom the
senior royal had ironically killed accidentally while playing with guns at
home as a child. Everyone felt sorry for the senior royal, and so did I,
until I heard what had really happened through a friend's friend, a guy
who was doing his gap year in Botswana working in a safari company.
He sent my friend an email saying that he'd seen the senior royal in his
company's hotel. He asked around, and he'd been there before. He
goes there and pays about £70,000 per head for a licence to kill
elephants, and about £40,000 to kill buffalos, which is wrong on so
many levels. The first level is killing animals that are protected, which
is called poaching when the guy shooting the weapon is not a royal.
The second level is paying that obscene amount of money after saying
on the news that he was worried about unemployment and about
families with very low incomes. The third level is to lie in an official
statement, saying that he was too sad to go to the hospital when he was

shooting away like a cowboy in Africa. As far as I know, he's still in Botswana, as my friend's friend saw him there yesterday, so I think the news will filter through by the time he's back. *Note to self: Would it be too much to add other stories from that family friend who studied at that school in Canada?*

Royals are rotten in many ways, all over the world, but there is one that the newspapers are focusing on lately for, as the Spanish expression goes, *being a friend of other people's belongings.* Everyone was quite surprised when this royal moved abroad with his family, but it then turned out that he had opened a charity for disabled children and, as soon as people and governments started donating money, he started stealing from it, until he got a couple of million pounds. Yep, that's it, apparently he didn't already have enough with all the free money provided to him by the state, that he had to steal from disabled children. Other royals knew about it and asked those implicated to flee the country before people found out, but then it was exposed. Obviously, none of them have been, or will ever be prosecuted, as a royal surname is a get-out-of-jail-free card that lets them get away with anything. *Note to self: Should I include here what the art collector who was married to that lady told us about that inheritance?*

On the other hand, those who will be prosecuted are the twelve politicians who stole trolleys full of food from a supermarket to give to families in need and to protest against the lack of social assistance from the government. Yes, stealing should be prosecuted, and having a certain surname might make you different before the law, but not before justice. *Note to self: Check the instructions of my editor again to make sure I am covering the side of politics he wanted me to. I am not very good at interpreting instructions.*

I was only a few minutes away from the bus station and I knew my godparents would be waiting for me. They had done a lot for my family, so I could only return the favour. My grandmother was worried that I'd grow up isolated from our Spanish heritage in Gibraltar, so it was them who paid for the trip from Gibraltar to Tangier, and from there to Algeciras, so I could be christened in Jerez de la Frontera, approximately seventy miles away from Gibraltar.

The wedding was classy. It was in one of those massive Andalusian country houses that aristocrats used to have. The aristocrats had money to run it since all they gave their servants was bread and water, but once things changed and workers expected to receive proper payment, the aristocrats had to resort to renting it out for weddings in order to cover maintenance costs. I met a few interesting people, and this included one of my grandmother's childhood friends. She told me a few stories about their youth, and my favourite one was that once twelve turkeys had eaten some red pebbles the wind had mixed with their grain and my grandmother and some friends had to operate on the turkeys. They created a production line, one used a cloth with some liquid on it to anesthetise the turkeys, another cut the turkeys open, someone else had to get the red pebbles out and the last one had to stich up the turkeys. Over half of them survived!

I had really enjoyed myself but it was time for my long journey from Seville to El Ejido, a small town in southeastern Spain where I had a friend from university. He is actually one of the guys who would proofread this article to make sure my dyslexia doesn't get in the way of people understanding what I meant.

I passed out as soon as the bus started moving but I woke up after we left Osuna's coach station. Not long after that, we were in Malaga province, and we passed a town I'd heard about as a child. My grandmother had two lucky brothers who bought a cow which happened to be pregnant with twin calves, so they started selling milk around La Línea. During the Spanish Civil War, they used to smuggle people who were being prosecuted into Gibraltar by hiding them in big milk barrels. Once, they had to go to that town all the way from La Línea to get an old neighbour's son who was hidden in a farm. The guy spent a few days hidden in a milk barrel, but he finally made it into Gibraltar, where he managed to sail off to a new life.

We had already passed Antequera, and we were close to Malaga when I saw the cliff my granddad had told me about quite a few times. He left Gibraltar for a few years to start an English school in Malaga, the first one in the area, but he had to battle with Spanish bureaucracy for a bit. It all started a couple of years after he'd opened his school, when he got a bill for a couple of thousand pounds in the early seventies. There was an agreement between Spain and the UK that said that foreigners could open businesses in Spain and pay very low level of taxes. My granddad was quite surprised when he got that bill, although he soon found out that schools were exempt from this agreement. He went to London and managed to see the Spanish ambassador to the UK, a very high-up Spanish politician who became vice-president after the Spanish dictator's death. My granddad was nervous to talk to such a well-known politician, although the credentials that some mayors in his school's catchment area had provided made the politician give him an exceptionally warm welcome. A few hours later, my granddad came out of the meeting, with a couple of glasses of wine in his tummy and with an exemption to pay those taxes. He thought it was a great triumph, although the deal would only come into effect if the British government allowed Spain to open a school in London which followed the Spanish curriculum. The school opened not long after in Portobello Road.

Back in Spain, my granddad was very happy with how his school was going. He had even heard about a rich foreign guy who was going to shoot a couple of horses because he was moving back to his home country, so my granddad asked for the horses and used them for extra-curricular activities at the school.

It all went well until his first real inspection from the Spanish Ministry of Education, which was very happy with all the standards of the school except one; my grandfather hadn't followed the law regarding room decoration. Apparently, at the time, in every single classroom, all schools in Spain needed to have on one of the walls a picture of a former Spanish dictator whom some people called *prime minister*, along with a crucifix, and a photo of the Spanish dictator at the time. The law also dictated the distance needed between the ceiling and these items and it was stated in the regulations, in bold, that the Spanish dictator's picture had to be twelve centimetres above the previous dictator's photo and the crucifix.

It was Christmas holidays and my grandad couldn't go back to Gibraltar with my grandmother as the border was still closed, so he thought that hanging up the portraits and the crucifixes on Christmas day would be a good thing to do. The Spanish dictator's wall decoration package couldn't be bought in stationary shops; people had to show endless documents in a special government office proving what they wanted them for. My grandfather had forgotten the hassle he went through to get them, although he soon remembered when he saw the boxes with the label *material oficial* on them.

He hung the Spanish dictator's wall decoration package in every single one of the classrooms of his small school and every twelve minutes or so would shout out, 'Twelve fucking centimetres above the crucifix'. All the school had been decorated according to the Spanish dictator's wishes, so it was time to celebrate this with a few drinks at a friend's party.

His car wouldn't start, so he had to take one of the horses that he'd saved from the rich foreign guy. He thought it would be funny to arrive at his friend's barbecue riding his horse. He'd had a few drinks decorating the school, not enough to make him lose his balance on the horse, but enough to make him go to the wrong house and gatecrash someone else's barbecue riding on his horse. *Note to self: Should I join all these paragraphs together?*

He finally found his friend's house and had a great night there, and then he decided to ride back on his horse. He was in the town main square when he saw the local church and carried on shouting out, 'Twelve fucking centimetres above the crucifix'. He'd read somewhere that, in Spain, the only person allowed to ride a horse into a church is the monarch, during a procession celebrated somewhere in Spain, but the monarch has to carry a red handkerchief in his or her hand. My grandad shouted, 'Twelve fucking centimetres above the crucifix' once again and decided to ride his horse into the church, interrupting the night mass of 1974. The priest stopped, the altar boy hummed some song about Paco's horse, and the people watched, although they were too scared to get the crazy guy on the horse. He rode through, halfway down the aisle, and then turned around and galloped out of the church. The parishioners who wanted to swear, though didn't swear in the church to avoid joining all the politicians in hell, went out to curse at him as he disappeared into the streets.

My granddad woke up the next day with a really bad hangover, so he went to his local bar for breakfast. He ordered a *café con leche* and toast and was halfway through his breakfast when the barman told him that he owed his friend Rodrigo a drink. My granddad asked why, and the barman told him that Rodrigo was at the mass the previous night and that he had talked to the angry people at church and had convinced them not to go after him or call the police. Some of the locals still wanted to go for him but they gave up once Rodrigo explained to them that his friend had drunk a bit too much because he was alone for Christmas and couldn't go back to Gibraltar because of the closure of the border. Rodrigo came in before my granddad had finished his breakfast and my granddad thanked him and bought him a nice bottle of whiskey, as good of a whiskey as you could get in Spain at that time.

The next day, my granddad went back to the bar to have his usual breakfast, just to hear that Rodrigo had had a car accident and fallen off a cliff. My granddad didn't cry in the bar, but he left straight away and went home. My granddad still felt guilty about it the day before he died, saying that Rodrigo had got drunk because he bought him a bottle of whiskey, and that it was his fault that Rodrigo had died. Guilt is a weird feeling. Some people, like politicians, feel none, and nice people perhaps too much. Rodrigo had decided to drink a lot before he started driving, and my granddad didn't make him do it; he just bought him a present. The only way I can explain my granddad's feelings is that the more you love people, the more responsible you feel for their actions. *Note to self: Should I say that the last sentences are from my grandma's?*

My grandad went back to work after that and was just so proud of his school. He couldn't wait to show it to the Spanish politician from London, who was due a visit later on in the year. A few months later, he contacted my granddad to tell him when he'd visit the school. My granddad prepared it all to give him a warm welcome, but two friends told him a few days before that the visit wouldn't happen. He asked why, and a friend said that the politician wasn't going to make it because the Spanish dictator was going to die on Thursday. He couldn't believe it, but he explained that the Spanish dictator had to die on a Thursday. He's dead already, they're just keeping him alive artificially, but they'll disconnect the machines on Thursday. He needs to die on a Thursday to have Friday as the official mourning day, and then the weekend to work on the change of powers. If he dies during the week, the whole country will rise, and no one knows what will happen then.

His friend was right; the Spanish dictator did die on Thursday that week. I guess that's why my grandad always told me that any change of power between royals, especially if it was due to something weird like abdication, would also happen on a Thursday.

As I finished remembering all that, the coach was about an hour away from El Ejido and I started feeling happier. However, I was passing through Castell the Ferro and the trip started becoming unbearable. The coach driver was arguing about politics with a couple of passengers, and they were shouting out loud at each other. The bus stopped a few minutes later, and I thought it would all get quieter as the two passengers stood up, but they continued talking to the driver for a good twelve minutes, holding up the bus, but everyone had to wait until they'd told the driver how much they disliked a Valencian politician who'd built a regional airport to cash in money with commissions.

The bus moved on and we were now in Adra, a small town that was founded by the Phoenicians in the 7th century B.C. I'm quite familiar with the *mañana* culture of Spain, and I agree with it, but I was somewhat speechless when I saw the driver stop the coach in the middle of a street, put the hazard lights on, and start chatting to the old guys that were sitting outside their houses in true Andalusian style.

I had been in El Ejido for a couple of days and it felt as if I'd been there all my life. I was staying with my friend's family and it was quite fun. His lovely mum made me all kinds of traditional Spanish food, including something local called *migas* (my friend described them as couscous on steroids; they are great with a cold Roja beer, from Granada). They eat *migas* in his town whenever it rains. It's a good thing it only rains there a couple of days a year, because if they did that in England, we'd be eating it 24/7. His hippy brother was always out, and I found it funny that he used to take his very cute little mongrel out with him. The dog was called Bruja, *witch*, and it was very well-known in all the bars of the town. Summer was the busiest time for Bruja's social life with all the festivals and beach parties and she used to come in the morning with my friend's brother and pass out in the cold marble floor of the front room, legs up. All that sleep deprivation for the dog couldn't be good; the booze that she drank couldn't be good either, as she used to drink the booze that people would spill in the bars. One day, the poor dog even ate a bit of hash someone dropped in a bar and passed out till twelve o'clock the following day. I think the dog actually worked out a pattern, and it came to the point that the dog would run away and hide behind the curtains when my friend's hippy brother turned up in the front room with the leash on Saturdays.

I started feeling part of the family when I saw his other brother come out of the shower in his boxer shorts, and when I witnessed the first family argument. They obviously felt very comfortable in front of me. My friend's mum had tried to get his hippy brother to cut his hair for a couple of weeks, but he wasn't going to do it. One day, he was whinging to his mum saying that he'd tried to take Bruja out for a walk, but she didn't want to come out, to which his mum answered, 'No wonder, the dog's embarrassed to go out with you because of your hair'.

I already had my little routine in El Ejido. I would go for lunch at Pepe Litros, this town's identical version of Moe's tavern where they served amazing *migas*. My friend's dad used to go to that bar too and it was great. We would then go for a coffee by the beach at Paralelo Playa, then a beer and bingo at Mundo Paralelo, a heavy metal bar owned by a guy who looked too young to be running his own place, but the mojitos he made showed he had some experience in the business. After that, we'd move on to Zona Rock, a rock bar with the floor covered in sunflower seeds' shells and with a very chatty bouncer. Talking to him provided a perfect snapshot of true Andalucian life; having a drink in the street at midnight, some sunflower seeds, talking about anything, and then he'd throw a couple of jokes in the middle of the conversation. Once the bouncer stopped talking, we went to our usual last stop, A-Cero, an alternative mini club where you could watch skateboarding videos on the screens. *Note to self: Think about shortening these paragraphs as maybe they don't cover the points my editor wanted me to cover.*

The kind of nice life I was experiencing made me realise why people in Spain can tolerate those huge levels of corruption. The mayor of the town had founded a company in his wife's name and got all the repairs in the town done by this company, charging something like £1200 for changing the lightbulb of a streetlamp and building an insane number of roundabouts in the town to get commissions from the company. He ended up going to jail but people were still voting for him. *Note to self: Maybe move this paragraph somewhere else?*

We also went to Almería, the capital, a couple of times, where we always ended up in a place called Botijo. Real Spanish music, a litre of beer or kalimotxo (red wine and cola) for one pound, and a lot of communists, which I soon realised was the common denominator in the places I liked in that part of Spain. Everyone in those bars had either a tattoo, a t-shirt, or a cap with a sickle and a hammer on it, they all hated the royal family, and they all sounded as if they'd just escaped from animal farm.

Another thing that struck me was the amount of people who had moved abroad for work and were there just on holidays to visit their families. Doctors, teachers, engineers, all of them repelled by the Spanish job market. It's not only that the salaries are bad, or that many people have to work without a contract so that the employer doesn't have to pay for National Insurance, but that they have a competitive entrance exam system for public workers (*funcionarios*) which was designed by some drunken monkey. I didn't think it was that bad, until I realised that in that system's point scale you get the same points for a PhD as you do for a week's course with your trade union. Apart from that, those who manage to get a full-time position are put on a part-time contract and get paid half their salaries in cash. On top of that, it's the fact that it doesn't matter how much you know or how good you are, because you won't get anywhere if you don't know the right people. Saying that, it's good for the UK, as it gets top quality professionals to work in the UK without having to invest anything for it. If the UK ever leaves the EU, they'll miss that influx of free highly trained workers. Any half-wit ape would realise that Spain is spending billions of pounds training people who go to work abroad as soon as they finish their degrees and to stop that, they'd have to sort out the employment market, but the Spanish rats, the politicians, are too busy with their dodgy swindles to act on it.

In my last night in El Ejido we went out in Almería, to Botijo, where we met one of my friend's mates. He had some administrative role for the Department of Immigration in Almería and was responsible for making sure that the appeals submitted by immigrants were in order. Instead of just putting stamps on the documents, he used to ring banks and estate agents to double-check that the information in the appeals was true; however, his boss didn't like that he was so thorough, so he demoted him and moved him to reception where he gave tickets to the visitors. *Note to self: Merge this with the other bit on Almería.*

The drive back to El Ejido on *Autovía del Mediterráneo* was great: there were no cars on the road and the moon was beautifully red and big. The moonlight lit the sea, so there were no drug smugglers working nor police to help them. The light on the sea scattered in all different directions when the waves moved, and the channel of lights created by the moon looked like the streets of a city. The wind blew as lightly as it could to make a gentle noise.

A few minutes later, I was at my friend's house in Paseo Juan Carlos I. I was leaning out of his window looking at the stately Sierra de Gádor, a beautiful mountain that looked just liked a bigger version of the one in Shanagolden, Co. Limerick; I think it was *Seanghualainn* in Gailic, the *old shoulder*. Sierra de Gádor was standing in front of me, blocking the view of the rest of the country and, shamelessly, blocking the view of all the corruption that inhabits Spain.

C. M. *Note to self: Should I spell my surname with or without the accent mark?*

Back in his Birmingham house, Carl finished reading the draft of his article, which he never finished or sent to the university newspaper, and he therefore put back in his drawer.

Carl grabbed the latest copy of a local newspaper and went back to reading the article he had started twelve minutes ago. The body of a news editor had been found near the newspaper bureau where he worked. He had been stabbed in the lungs and a sheet of newspaper had been stuffed into his mouth. Carl found it hard to believe that it was the same news editor for whom he'd once written an article himself. He felt guilty for not having finished it and, somehow, reading now what he had written a few years back didn't make him feel any better about it. Guilt always comes out in funny ways.

# A Dead Man's Ice Cream

# Chapter 8

## Field report

Date: **Friday 5<sup>th</sup> December 2003**
Location: **Birmingham, UK**
Forum member: **Jake (AKA *Suave*)**
Title: **It feels good to be out again**

What's up!!

I thought it was time to give you guys an update on how things are going in Birmingham. First of all, do you remember I was seeing that girl I liked, and my friends said that she was a bit of a loose one? A friend and I made a bet that he wouldn't be able to sleep with her within a week. I lost the bet. Also, before anyone asks, no, I'm no longer seeing that German girl I told you about in my last post; I'm pretty sure she got back with her ex. The poor guy will be relieved to have his girl back. I can also imagine they'll have a big fight pretty soon though. I was at hers once and the most awkward TV programme that could come on while watching TV with a German person came up: a comedy show. We turned the TV off and started making out. I didn't bring any condoms the last night I went to hers (the day after my last post) and she couldn't find any around her apartment. Things weren't looking good BUT I then remembered that, during a drunken conversation, her ex had told me that he'd duct-taped a small box of condoms to the bottom of her sofa as an emergency stack and yep, this was an emergency. So, I grabbed some condoms from under her sofa when she went to the toilet and game on! I pretty much emptied the whole box with her. I didn't tell her where I'd got them from, but I left one condom in the box cos I'm not a greedy guy. So, who knows, her ex-boyfriend might be pissed off when he realises someone's clearly been using his condoms with his girl, or he might just be thankful I left one in there for him. Oh, and sorry for punctuation errors. I'm not a linguist.

Anyway, I haven't posted anything in the last few weeks because I've been on call a lot and there wasn't anything worth posting but... it all changed after a legendary night out with my wingman, Eros, who also posts on this forum. You may know him from posts such as *I met her online, we went on a date and she was a bloke*, *Why did her dildo have desiccated coconut on it? I like sniffing knickers and that makes me human*, or *Awkward Christmas Day when you stay with a long-lost relative and find out that someone you shagged on holidays is your cousin's daughter*.

It was one o'clock when I got to Mail Room Bar. I didn't know where this new pub was, so I had to ask some cops further down in New Street. I was meeting Eros for lunch and to give back some DVDs I'd borrowed from him. The pub was one of those real ale ones where you're allowed to take your own food, so Eros was already there waiting for me with a big box of take-away from a nearby place. I scratched my neck before going in, looked at the pretty English building around me, and went in into what would be a pretty epic sarging session.

I'd borrowed from him two DVD sets; one was a pick-up course taught by Player and his team and the other one was a course on relationship management by Welder. Both were very different, but I thought I'd take a look at them to get some ideas.

Eros had been away on holidays for a couple of weeks and I'd been busy with work, so we hadn't been out sarging in a month or more, and I realised during lunch that his game had improved a lot in that time. The guy was shining with confidence, very well dressed, inserting the kind of pauses in his speech that keep you hanging on with excitement to hear the rest of the phrase, even if he was just talking about running out of paper in the toilet, and it looked like he'd bought some great new shoes. Smart shoes are very important to pick up girls, as you can find out yourselves by trying that famous conversation opener. Just walk up to a girl and ask her what the first item of clothing is she notices when she meets a new guy. If you don't like playing it safe, you can try the conversation opener practice game.

## Conversation opening practice game

Walk up to some girls with a friend. Remember to start with the false time constraint so that the girls know that you're not going to hang around pestering them all night, 'Hey, girls, very quickly, before we go back to our friends'. Then, instead of doing the expected, and asking a question so that they know the reason why you've approached them, to stop them from feeling anxious about what the hell you want from them, just turn to your friend and say, 'So, what was that question you had for them?' And then you see what your wingman is able to pull off. If you want to step it up a bit, just say something like, 'So, what was that question you had for them about...' and mention anything you can think of. About plastic surgery, about snoring... you choose.

## The good stuff

So, Eros and I had a proper catch up over lunch and he told me about a mess party that was on that night. It was going to be a bit of a pub crawl at Pub Chamber Pub, then Exception Bar and then Jug and Violin, and there were going to be about £2500 on drinks behind the bar. Doctors pay a mess fee every month, and a couple of times a year they have a party where they use some of those funds to put a tab behind the bar. Those nights were messy, so I thought it'd be a great night to go out in the field after a month. All you had to do was to walk up to the bouncers at the door, say the password *constable* and they'd put a stamp on your hand to charge your drinks on the tab. Good times!! Oh, and before I forget, I need to tell you why constable was the password for the night. Most professions have some inside jokes, just to make boring days at work a bit more bearable. Some of my friends are teachers and they've told me about some of the games they play when invigilating exams. Some are more innocent, like drawing a grid of the exam venue, placing some battleships in the rows and columns of the drawn-up grid, and then playing battleships by moving yourself to a spot in the grid, and the other people say yes or no with their heads depending on whether one of their battleships has been hit. If a battleship is sunk, they pinch their nose and make the motion of submerging under water. All this, while they're theoretically making sure no one is cheating in the exam. Other variables of the game involve placing yourself next to the kid most likely to go to jail first, or anything else you choose. Anyway, in my hospital, we play different games. One of them is coming up with the best nickname for patients and I won it a few weeks ago, when I had a drug user patient called M. P. Disney, he was high on methamphetamine and I nicknamed him *Disney on ice*. We also play to see who has the best patient story and a friend of mine won it a week ago. She was working in A & E (Emergency Department for those of you outside the UK), and a couple came in at one in the morning. They were shouting at each other and having a pretty heated argument. He had a really bad bite on his penis (cock for those not in the medical field) and she was bleeding from a lump on her head. Long story short, she was giving him a blow job, trying to get his dick down to her oesophagus by the sounds of it, then she suddenly suffered an epileptic seizure and clenched her jaw. The guy was in agony and thought she was going to chew his willy off, with froth and everything coming out of the girl's mouth, so he grabbed the ashtray from the bedside table and whacked her with it. The guy was a constable, so we chose that as a password.

Anyway, back to the important bits, the time had come to get ready for a serious night out. I was getting ready and did the usual pre-going out ritual. I had a nice shower, got my best clothes on, listened to some music to get me in the mood, put a pencil and a paper in my pocket, wrote down on a piece of paper three good things that had happened to me during the week, and three good qualities of mine that make me an attractive guy. I also wrote down *constable*, to remind me of the magic word I needed to join the party. Who could have thought that such a simple word could open up such a world of opportunity! I put some balloons in my pocket (balloons, not condoms), and I was ready to go. What I saw that night was the best piece of pick up I'd ever seen before.

I went outside Telmo Supermarket Post Central, a landmark building in Birmingham, and I met with five girls that work with Eros. The girls told me they'd got a text from him asking them to meet me because he'd be a few minutes late. I thought it was bit weird but then

I realised that he'd given me a head start. When you walk into a pub with two other guys, people think you're just another bloke, but when a guy walks into a place with a group of girls, people notice him. Guys are jealous, and say that he must be gay, and girls try to find out which one of the girls he's sleeping with, hoping none, so they have a chance, and you are already up on the game. They all want someone who is in demand. I walked into Pub Chamber Pub, happily, thinking that walking in with the girls will give my game a nice little push. But nothing compared with Eros' entrance. We'd just walked to the high up area at the back of the pub and just when I'd been introduced to the other people in the group, I saw Eros. Genius! He walked in, was walking slowly along the bar and as he walked, the girls turned around to look at him, after that, the guys, and after just half a minute, everyone in that section of the bar was looking at him. He came up to us and said hi, and as soon as I got a chance, I asked him about his entrance. Eros had come up with it during his holidays, after he went swimming with his phone in his pocket and the phone started malfunctioning. He now didn't need a broken phone since he had created a special ring tone for it. You walk into a pub, and you play this ring tone he has developed. It's a very intense sound, of a weird frequency, that sounds almost like a human voice saying something. It goes over other ambient noise in bars, but you can only hear it if you're close enough to the phone. So, you play the ring tone and start walking into the pub, walking past some girls, or boys, you know we don't judge on this forum. As you walk past people, they will stop talking and look at you. All you need to do is get the attention of just one person in a couple of groups. As soon as someone in the group hears it and stops talking to look at you and see if you've said something to them, everyone in the group will do the same, following her eyes and wondering why she stopped talking or listening to turn around. People tend to follow each other's eye movements, so in half a minute, you have all the bar looking at you, and most of the girls in there thinking, 'Who the hell is that guy, and why is everyone looking at him, is he famous?' And that's the beginning of a great night of sarging!

Eros offered to battle the crowds and went to get me a drink. That bar's usually very busy on Fridays, but with that mess party, and with all those free drinks, it was super-packed. He positioned himself next to a really hot girl and asked her if she'd already been served, and when she said, 'no', he said, 'I bet you a fiver that I get served before you'. The girl smiled and said, 'I hope not.' Eros started making eye contact with the barmaid as she was walking to serve the girl. His trick wasn't working, so he went for the classic movement of talking over her when she started ordering and saying, 'Don't worry, we're together, I just changed my mind and wanted to order anything else'. The girl was surprised, but she was enjoying the flirting too much to complain about it. Eros then ordered a few drinks for the girl and then said, 'Remember you owe me a fiver, but you can just get me a drink later instead'. The girl smiled and agreed to it, scratching her neck when Eros did the same. That's when I knew that Eros had gone up to a different pick-up league; he wasn't delivering a set of routines like an entertaining monkey, he was just innovating and planting seed after seed for a great night of success. It was like seeing a master playing chess. He was just enjoying meeting people and things were just happening. It's like someone once said to me, 'Innovation is about doing something different, being successful is just a by-product', and this was a clear example. Once he noticed the girl mirroring his moves, he knew it was time to move on to the next piece of the puzzle.

He was glowing! He grabbed me by the hand and said, 'Your mate Ben's got a girlfriend called Kelly, he bought her an exercise bike and now she's upset'. I didn't have time to ask what was going on before we were in set. We went up to two girls and Eros said, 'Hey, girls, very quickly, before I go back to my colleagues over there'. He pointed at the group of girls I came in with and that DHV (demonstration of higher value) for the AFCs (average frustrated chumps) made the girls feel comfortable, although I'd find out later, he didn't even need to do that. 'Just a quick question,' he continued, 'What would you do if your boyfriend bought you an exercise bike?' The girls said that they wouldn't be happy. Eros continued. 'Our friend Ben bought his girlfriend an exercise bike for her birthday and now she's upset. He said she'd put on a bit of weight lately and didn't want to tell her, so he thought he'd buy her a bike'. The girls looked at each other and said that that was awful. 'Yes, I know,' said Eros. 'But the thing is that our friend doesn't see anything wrong with it.' He continued, 'Wouldn't it have been better to get her a gym membership and say something like, 'we don't spend much time together, so I registered us both in a gym so that we can spend some more time together?' The girl Eros was talking to smiled and said that that would be better. 'So,' he said, 'it's not about the present itself, it's about how the present was delivered.' The girl said, 'Kind of. I don't know, I guess that's how women think. I don't have a boyfriend, but I guess I would be quite upset if a guy bought me an exercise bike.'

Bang! IOI (indication of interest) number one: telling him that she was single. I never escalate things with girls until I get three IOIs, but Eros was in a different league now.

He held out his hand and introduced himself, 'Nice to meet you.' The girl introduced herself and after their handshake, Eros looked at her disappointed, tutted at her, and he said, 'Oh, a boring one'. She wasn't sure what he was on about but then he explained it. 'I read a book a few weeks ago on body language, and the book said, and I agree with it, that energetic, fun, and confident people usually have a firm handshake, and that boring people usually have a very weak handshake'. The girl got a bit angry and said, 'Well, screw you and your book. I'm not boring.' 'Okay,' said Eros, 'I'll give you another chance. Hi, nice to meet you.'

'Hi, I'm Kristen.'

Bang! In my book, that was a second IOI! The girl was in his frame! Eros said, 'Oh, no.'

The girl smiled nervously again and said, 'Now what?!' He then said, 'That's overcompensation. People who want to look cooler than they actually are tend to have that kind of handshake'. The girl laughed and punched him teasingly on his shoulder.

Bang! Third IOI, game on!!

I'd been trying to keep the other girl busy while Eros was talking to his target, so it was hard to see what he was doing at all times, but it was art. I was struggling to keep the conversation going with this girl, and she asked me if he was famous because everyone looked at him when he entered the pub. I couldn't come up with anything worth saying, so I just rolled my eyes and said that it was a long story. I really wanted to see how Eros was doing with his girl, so I did the cube routine. I know, back to basics, but I wanted to have my mind on autopilot while I learnt from the master.

I heard him in the middle of his seeding routine. This is pure magic, kids, so give it a go. He was telling the girl how he loved Pub Chamber Pub. 'They do great pizzas in there,' he said, 'and they're buy-one-get-one-free all day on Tuesday.' I now knew that he liked her. Eros puts girls in three categories: the ones he's not that much into and tries to close the deal on the night, the ones he kind of likes but isn't sure about, with whom he seeds the Pub Chamber Pub cocktail night on Thursdays, and the ones he really likes, and tries to get to go on a date on Tuesday over a pizza and a nice chat.

His performance was a textbook example of a solid seeding routine. He told her about the pizzas, and about the great vibe of the place on a Tuesday (you always have to come out with an event in mind to invite girls to). When you're saying all this to the girl, she thinks, 'Shit, he's going to invite me out, oh, not another one,' then, as Eros did, when you have just sold the event, change the subject. 'So, how do you know each other?' he said. At that point, the girl's confused, and her ego hurts. 'What? He didn't invite me out, doesn't he like me?' You continue the conversation as usual and, a few minutes before you leave, you finish just as Eros did, 'By the way, you know about those pizzas, you gotta try them.' Then, he dialled *07* on his phone and passed it on to the girl, 'Put your number in here and I'll call you to organise a meet up.' That works magic! First of all, the girl's ego's restored, as she now thinks, 'Oh, yeah, he likes me!' Also, if you ask a girl, 'Could I have your number?' it's a lot easier for her to say no. If you say it as an order, 'Put your number in here and I'll call you,' you're showing more initiative, you're more assertive, and it takes a very strong frame to say *no* to that.

As the PUA guidelines say, never walk off as soon as you get a girl's number, as they think that you're more interested in their number than in them. He had a nice chat with her and finished his conversation with her. Then, a polite, 'Nice talking to you, girls,' and we were out of set.

Thanks to the free bar, everyone was getting merry, except us, because like every PUA on a sarging night, we were not drinking. It's funny how hard it is to justify yourself to others when you're not drinking on a night out, so, as the drinks were free, we ordered a beer whenever there was someone at the bar that we liked and then nursed the drink until we got bored of carrying it around. Doctors love their job, and they're obsessed with it. Money doesn't pay how much a good doctor sacrifices to help others, but they can be really boring people to be around once they've had a drink and sometimes when they're sober as well. Thankfully, Eros stayed off the topic of medicine. I wasn't interested in that chat, instead, I engaged in random chats, like sharing my acquired bit of information from a statistician who had worked out that, at any one time, there are at least 8001 people shagging in Bangkok. If you do the maths, there is at least one threesome in there.

The tab at Pub Chamber Pub was over and everyone started moving to Brindley Place, which is a location with a very good balance of Victorian and modern buildings, a nice square, a few bars by the canal, and very pretty lighting. The moon was shining as we walked along the metal bridge to the canal side. A few geese were sleeping peacefully by the canal boats. The big and bright letters of 'Post Central' were shining underneath the full moon, casting a shiny white reflection on the canal water, while the little canal boats grouped together in front of that quirky little café whose name I cannot recall. It's exactly the same view I think about whenever anyone says that Birmingham's an ugly city. Someone I know works at the council and she told me that they're going to build a massive building by the canal, close to Post Central, very tall, with glass all around it, with some fancy restaurants and 360-degree views of the city. To top it all off, there's a viewing deck towards the top sticking out like an Adam's apple in a lanky guy. Architecture can really be stupid when taken out of context but not the case here.

Eros and I were discussing our performance in Pub Chamber Pub during our walk while his female co-workers were talking about some patient with an oesophagus problem. Some drunk guys were, as was the case most weekends, trying to jump over the narrow bit of the canal and betting with the passers-by to see if they could jump over the gap. It's still makes me chuckle seeing the drunk guys pulling themselves out of the canal completely wet. It's a funny gap. It's just wide enough for most people not to be able to jump it but narrow enough to look doable. That's a really dangerous combination in life.

We got into Exception Bar and I went to the bar to get drinks for Eros and the girls. I used the *I'll get served before you* routine and it worked, and then I used Eros' handshake routine and it worked as well. She liked me but at one point a friend came over and took her away. I wasn't annoyed that the girl had gone before I dealt with her cock-blocker friend, I was more embarrassed that Eros had seen it. I'm very good friends with him, and we don't judge each other, but I was still embarrassed. He then said, 'Look' and went straight to a girl who was having a drink with a guy, talked to her for a bit, grabbed her by the hand, and went with her to the smoking area. The guy that was talking to her just stood up there on his own, like a muppet. He'd been alpha-maled big time and I couldn't work out how Eros had done it. That was seriously impressive.

When it comes to avoiding being cock-blocked, I'd always followed conventions. When you open a set, start talking to the ugly girls and move on later to your target. If her friends like you, she'll like you too, and her friends won't cock-block you. If there are guys in the set, start talking to the guys first. The most sophisticated thing I've done in terms of group theory was to look at the girl I liked, wait until one of the guys that was with her went to the toilet or to the bar, go there and start befriending the guy, and later on in the night I could go back to the guy, start a conversation, ask the usual way-pointing question of, 'So, how do you guys know each other?' to find out the relationship between everyone in the group and, if the girl wasn't taken, move on to the target once I was in set. The good thing about that method is that it takes no effort to get into the set. Efficient, smooth, and easy to carry out. Still, I couldn't work out what Eros had done.

I laughed when later he told me how he'd done it. He said that Player had taught him this. He saw a girl who didn't seem that much into the guy. He then gave some non-verbal signs to tell her that he liked her shoes and she smiled back. Then, he walked up to her and said, 'Hey, how have you been?' He said that phrase works wonders to stop being cock-blocked, as when you use that when starting a conversation with someone, people in the group automatically think that you know each other. Then, he said to the girl, 'Oh, Steve and Hannah are outside, come and say hi.' The beta guy stood there like an idiot thinking that she'd gone to say hi to some old friends while Eros took her and made out with her in the smoking area. Awesome work! I knew this guy was now at a different level.

Anyway, the night went on. Eros was busy with his girl, so I opened a set. One of the two girls saw my bright green watch and I went on automatic mode again, and I told her the usual, that the watch was a present from my nephew, that I didn't see him very often and that I wore it when I missed him, etc. Then, I end up with the usual, 'I know it's a bit cheesy, but he's a really cute kid,' then, girls do their usual, 'Oh, that's so cute.' And that's one IOI and I start counting. Some guys say that *cute* is not good; personally, I think cute as in 'you're cute' equals 'you're not a sexual man, you're cute,' and that's not good, but *cute* as in 'that shows that you care about others and have some good fatherly qualities,' that is a great IOI.

I should have escalated after the watch routine, but I stalled, so I just ejected saying that I wanted to check on my friends as one of the girls was a bit too drunk. I thought it was better to say that I had to go to look after a friend, in case I stumbled on them again. A bit later I went back to the girls and got them a drink, I should have done the *ordering a drink* routine opener, but I was starting to get approach anxiety, so I didn't. I was with the girls when I saw a three set not far off. I looked at one of the girls and our eyes met, I smiled, and she smiled back. I didn't realise at the time, but that's exactly what Player says. 'Force IOIs with girls. That's a very good way of measuring how receptive they're going to be, and then you start a conversation having already built some rapport.' He also recommends forcing non-verbal IOIs, such as smiling to a girl when you're with a group of girls, as other girls are more likely to respond positively if they see you with other girls. I looked at her again and our eyes met again. Bingo!!

At that point, I couldn't stop thinking about the 1% rule. There's a pseudo PUA who wrote a short book. It's a funny read, and the whole book's about this guy's theory that says, 'Forget about picking up, why invest effort in convincing a girl to sleep with you when there are some girls that are already interested in doing so?' This guy has something called *The 1% rule*, which says that no matter where you are or what time it is, at least 1% of the girls in your environment are willing to sleep with you a few minutes after meeting you. The whole book explains the system you need to follow to find that 1% of girls. One of the things to do is, if you catch someone's eye, look away, and then look back again after a few moments. If you catch her eye again, then she's interested, and it's game on. The guy published the book under a pseudonym, maybe because the theories in his book might be crap, but with the 1% rule in mind, and with Player's forced IOIs, I walked up to her quite confidently, and following Eros' advice, I started the conversation with, 'Hey, how have you been?' She responded positively, her friends thought we knew each other, and after a few minutes of talking they went to the bar to get a drink and left us there. Welder's method involves developing your own personality to develop those traits that women are attracted to, instead of using a bunch of canned routines. The good thing about Welder's method is that you improve yourself and your life, and you attract people without trying. The problem with Magician's method is that it can feel a bit artificial, it can turn you into just a facade of someone who you're not, and you have to connect a lot of routines together to get the girl. That requires more *in field* work, and you run the risk of running out of material and stalling. That's what happened to me when I was talking to that girl, and I just ejected when her friends got there as the pauses in our conversation were getting longer. But hey, trial and error.

I went back to the girls who worked with Eros and, by that point, he was back as well. The girls tried to give him some stick about using a poor girl, and he replied with, 'We were both mature adults who wanted to spend a bit of time together, get to know each other, and see if it was worth meeting again, but I didn't use her any more than she used me.' It was cheesy, but I loved his answer. By that point I'd got a few texts from the rest of the Friday Club crew and the tab had run out, so we crossed the little square that separates Exception Bar from Jug and Violin and met them in there. For these mess parties, what they do is they put money on tabs at different bars, so that way the party continues flowing and doesn't stagnate in the same bar.

I walked into Jug and Violin, head held high, with a smile on my face, as it's good to project a fun and positive personality from the very same moment you walk into a place. I saw a girl outside the disabled toilet and I thought about the three-second rule. I was going to approach but then I started feeling approach anxiety again and didn't talk to her in the end. According to the three-second rule, you must not think when you see a girl you like, you just have to talk to her within the first three seconds, otherwise you'll suffer approach anxiety. But the three-minute rule says not to bother talking to a girl if you don't think that you will have at least three minutes to talk to her. I thought she was waiting to go to the loo, so I decided to follow the three-minute rule over the three-second one. It's like that post from Sexy Constable, in which he described starting a conversation with a girl he saw outside a building with a majestic marble entrance and her friend coming down to meet her just as he was about to exchange numbers. The hard truth though is that if a girl wants you to have her number, she'll give it to you. Don't blame it on the fact that her friend turned up; just admit that maybe she wasn't that much into you.

We saw the rest of the Friday Club crew and the girls went to get some drinks from the bar before the tab ran out. We were catching up talking about the night and Carl's housemate, Charles, another medic, said that our mate Carl was in the toilet. Charles said that Carl seemed better now, but that they'd been to the Parrot Garden Bar and that, at one point, Carl went quiet and stared at his pint, and then, after a minute, he just asked where he was. Charles said that Carl was a bit of a lightweight and that he didn't sleep the previous night because of the noise from a late party in the house next door. The girls came with the drinks, so we changed the topic.

The phrase of the night came up when Carl came back to the group. He said he'd seen two girls who work at his university talking at the bar, and he spent a few minutes looking at them and deciding on whether or not to go and say hi, but when we walked up to them, he overheard one of the girls say, 'Yeah, try not to get semen in your eye, it really stings.' Carl then thought it wasn't appropriate for him to get involved in the conversation and came back to us. We were actually surprised that he didn't join the conversation, as Carl is a lovely guy, but he can be pretty clueless at times when it comes to social interactions. With that kind of conversation, he might have found two 1%ers.

Anyway, Carl was OK now, and the guys asked us how the sarging had gone, as they always take the piss out of us for doing all these pick-up routines, but they start taking it seriously when they see results or when they all pussy out before approaching some girls and it falls to me to open the set. I told the guys about the exercise bike opener, and they found it hilarious, so one of them thought he'd give it a go and tried it with a girl that was close to us. She wasn't the prettiest chicken on the farm, but she was very pleasant to talk to, she was an architect and quite fun, actually.

I then saw Penelope, a smoking hot girl who works with Carl, and he is so in love with her; it's textbook oneitis. Spanish, super-clever and model material. She was talking to two girls by the stairs, so I guessed they were the girls that Carl had overheard talking at the bar. I didn't say anything to Carl as I didn't want him to latch on to the girls all night, but Charles really liked her, so he went to talk to her. This wasn't the first time in the night that I'd seen someone using the classic, *Hey, how have you been?* opener; the girls didn't cock-block him. A couple of minutes later, a girl who had stepped on Charles' foot unintentionally on her way out of the toilets came up to him and got him a beer. I can't really figure Charles out, but he can be quite sneaky, and he must have come up with a really good story about why that girl brought him a drink, because Penelope asked about it and I just noticed her puppy eyes lighting up when Charles answered her question. I knew right then and there I wouldn't see those two in the bar for much longer that night.

Carl zoned out a couple of times more, so we decided that it was time to go home. He asked where Charles was and I didn't have the heart to tell him he'd gone home with Penelope, so I just said that he'd gone for some food.

All of us started walking home and there were quite a few cops out that we had to dodge to avoid walking into them. The buildings looked pretty. The moon was now shining just above Down Under Bar, with the decorative roof of the building covered in a bit of smoke that was coming out of one of the chimneys; it looked like a scene from a musical. I looked at my kiddy watch and realised it was one o'clock already. We turned into Broad Street, and it was even busier there. An elegant Grade II listed building had a few windows smashed in, and someone had graffitied *Fuck* on the facade, which seemed to be the nickname of the busiest street artist in town.

I then got a text from a friend and I understood why there were so many cops out. They had found a guy dead next to the place where we'd had lunch. An architect found dead, next to his smashed bike, between some very pretty buildings in Birmingham city centre. A bit ironic I thought. The guy had been stabbed next to his chest bone and his oesophagus had been perforated, so they had decided to increase the police presence in the streets. Birmingham suddenly felt very unsafe, not just to me, but to everyone else who was worried about what was going on and about how clueless the police seemed to be about all these murders. I simply couldn't comprehend what could make a person do such things.

## Final reflections

I continued thinking about random stuff on my way home and tried to evaluate the night out. When some people find out about me and the PUA world, they treat me as if I was doing something horrible to women and then I always start thinking about Welder. I once met him in a museum in London. He'd come to give a seminar in London and was making time. I just recognised him and went up to him to say *thanks* for all those free videos and tips he's always posting. He had some time to kill so we went for a coffee. It wasn't the usual AFC interviewing the big PUA star, we just had a coffee and talked about all kinds of general stuff. One of the very few things I said about the pick-up world is about how it was a girl that got Eros and me into the game. At the beginning, we were both trying to get good at picking up women to win a girl back, the so-called oneitis. He laughed and told me that was pretty normal. He knows all the big names in the PUA scene, and he said that every single major PUA out there has become who he is because of oneitis. Either an ex-girlfriend or another girl that they really fell for. The interesting thing, he said, is that as people get better at gaming girls, they realise their own worth and they start moving on with life and go on the mission of finding the love of their lives. But, interestingly enough, none of those guys end up hating the women that got them into the game. Guys end up seeing those girls as the people who made them start working hard to improve a part of their lives they'd had no control over before, who motivated them to start their self-improving path. According to Welder, guys end up finding internal peace by realising that there was nothing wrong with them and that the girls had not tried to hurt them intentionally, just that it was one of many millions of relationships which, simply, had not worked out. Contrary to what many girls think, all decent PUAs you meet out there are guys who are working hard to become good with women, and they're not trying to sleep with 100 women before they're 30; they're just looking for the love of their life in their own way. They want to improve their lives, find someone truly special, and they're willing to work hard to get there. Curiously enough, the people who criticise the game the most are those who don't make any effort in finding the love of their life; they're happy cruising and waiting until the magic happens. Still, people forget that you can create attraction, but not love. Many women say they don't like it when guys train to become good at picking girls up, and what Eros always says to them is, 'Would you rather start a relationship with a guy who thinks that he's got nothing to improve, or with a guy who puts all his time and energy to learn about women, to find true love, and to learn how to keep that girl happy once he's met her?'

Hopefully, Charles' story with Penelope will be an example of a guy working hard to keep a great girl happy, but I'm not sure about that one. I'll have to wait and see.

Cheers

Suave

# Chapter 9

## Dual citizens: two cultures but no nation

'So, have you read *Chamber Music* and *Exiles?*' The old man asked Carl in a London accent.

'Yes, I did, a long time ago. *Exiles* was good but I could only find a couple of poems I liked in *Chamber Music*. I don't remember *Exiles* very well, but I seem to remember that it was a bit like that short story, *The Dead*.'

'Yes, everyone says so,' the old man agreed.

'But it's worth reading, I think,' added Carl.

'Okay, I might take it out today then. I came to get a copy of Stuart Gilbert's *James Joyce's Ulysses*, but I think I can take out two books at once.'

'Can you?' asked Carl. 'I can take out quite a few books at once from the library at Edgbaston University because I work there, but I wasn't sure about the Central Library.'

'Yes, I think you can take two out. I have a pensioner's card, so I think they let retired people take out more books to keep us busy. So, are you looking for anything in particular?' asked the London accent.

'Yes, I am, actually. It's a book a friend of mine told me about, called *James Joyce, Occasional, Critical, and Political Writing*. He said it's worth reading as you have some examples of Joyce's essays from when he was at school, some articles he wrote as a journalist, and a whole mixture of things. He said it's good, as you can really see how Joyce's style developed from when he was a kid up to the last few articles that appear in the book, which are supposed to have a similar style to *Finnegans Wake.*'

'Oh, yes, I've read that,' acknowledged the old man. 'It's certainly remarkable to see the evolution of his style. I know that you can see this in *Portrait*, or if you compare *Dubliners* with *Finnegans Wake*, but it's very obvious and easy to see in his *Occasional, Critical, and Political Writing.* 'So, you said you work at Edgbaston University, are you a lecturer there?'

'No, I am not,' replied Carl. 'I work as an administrator in the School of Languages, but I like reading Joyce. That's how I actually met my best friend. We were both at Loughborough University and we used to go to a James Joyce readers' club. I just got a text from him, he's on his way to the centre, stuck on Stratford Road at the moment, so I'm just killing time until he gets here as we're meeting up for a coffee. Meeting up with friends occasionally is important,' said Carl, proud of his observation.

'It is, indeed. That's interesting, as that's how I met my partner. There is a book club I started going to a few years ago. Old people don't like being alone, so we started to meet up for coffees and now we live together. We moved in together after two months, but at our age you don't have the luxury of waiting.'

'Yes, that's true... I guess,' replied Carl, not realising initially how awkward his agreement came along.

'Yes, a good friend of mine was the healthiest person I've known and then, they discovered he had a brain tumour, and with very little warning, he was gone in two weeks,' said the old man while Carl nodded at him. 'I'll tell you what,' said the London voice, 'you could come around to this book club. We started reading *Ulysses* to mark the centenary of Bloomsday, well, you know, of Joyce's first date with Nora, and we're planning to go to Dublin for Bloomsday this year.'

'It sounds good. When is it?' asked Carl.

'We meet every two weeks, with some longer breaks in the middle,' replied the old man. 'We try to discuss two chapters at a time and we'll finish the book the same week as Bloomsday, so we'll leave the last chapter to discuss it when we go to Dublin. You'll enjoy it.'

'It sounds great, when and where do you usually meet up?' asked Carl in an excited voice.

'We usually meet up every second Wednesday at the Birmingham Art Centre. The Birmingham Art Centre has one of those websites and I know the information is there, but I don't know how to use computers, so I don't know how to find the details on it. Just hold on... I have the number written here,' the old man stopped talking while looking through his wallet. He found the number written on the back of his Stratford Library card. 'This is the number,' said the old man while Carl copied it down. 'I have the dates at home, but if you ring them in the morning, they'll be able to tell you how to register and all that. It's free for students and retired people, but you might have to pay a few pounds a day. We meet up in a small room, but there's a tea and a coffee machine outside, so it's quite comfortable.'

'That's great, thank you,' said Carl.

'You're welcome, so, what's your name young man?'

'I'm Carl, sir. Nice to meet you.' He stretched out a hand.

'Pleasure to meet you, Carl, I'm Stephen. Well, I'll go and take these two books and get my shopping done. Take care of yourself and I hope to see you at the book club.'

'Thanks, Stephen. Yes, I'll ring the Birmingham Art Centre and see if I can join the group for the next meeting.'

'Yes, I'm sure you can,' smiled Stephen politely. 'Okay, well, hope to see you soon, Carl.'

'Yes, thanks, me too.'

\* \* \*

'Hey, Carl. Sorry I'm a bit late, but there was a funeral procession along Stratford Road and the bus got stuck,' said Myles apologetically as soon as he saw Carl in Victoria Square.

'It's okay, I was at the Central Library getting Joyce's *Occasional writings* book out. I was talking to a retired man, and he told me there's a readers' club that meets up in the Birmingham Art Centre every two weeks, and that they're reading *Ulysses*. They discuss two chapters per session, and they'll go to Dublin for Bloomsday,' explained Carl.

'Oh, yes, of course. In June, it'll be the centenary of the day on which *Ulysses* is set.'

'Yes, that's right. Fancy joining the club with me?' asked Carl.

167

'It'd be good, but it depends on what time it takes place.'

'I know it's every second Wednesday, but I don't know the time yet. The guy gave me a phone number, so I'll ring and see what they say.'

'Yeah, that's fine. Just let me know as soon as you find anything out and I'll let you know if I'll be able to make it,' said Myles.

'Yes, I'll do that.'

'So, where would you like to go for that coffee? Although it's two o'clock now, so it might be a bit late for it. We could have lunch somewhere if you want,' suggested Myles.

'Yes, we could do that.'

'What do you fancy? Anything in particular?' asked Myles.

'No, I'm easy. Up to you, you know I am very bad at making decisions,' admitted Carl. 'Charles is joining us later. If you choose a place, I can text him.'

'Well, we could just get take-away and have it in Mail Room Bar, as they let you bring your own food.'

*  *  *

'So, what did you get again?' asked Myles. 'My brain isn't working today.'

'Chips with curry,' explained Carl while dropping two chips on the table.

'That's a really strange combination.'

'Yeah, I know, but I used to have this in Gib all the time,' explained Carl while cleaning some curry sauce from the table.

'Well, that's quite British and Indian at the same time. You colonial people really are quite confused,' joked Myles. 'It must be one of those intercultural habits of yours.'

'I suppose,' agreed Carl without understanding the remark. 'There are people from all over the world in Gib, so we just put all their influences together and claim it as our own, you know, just to find a cultural identity I guess.'

'Do you feel you have a cultural identity?' enquired Myles.

'Do you mean…? People in Gibraltar or me specifically?' Carl tried to clarify the nature of the question.

'I don't know, both, I guess.'

'Well…' Carl started to consider the question. 'When we think about Spain and the UK, we feel like we're not from there and we'll never be from here either. As someone once said, Gibraltar is the story of a small nation feeling trapped, in no one's land, between the UK and Spain. It's like a perpetuated collective of first-generation immigrants. But I'd like to think that I have two definite cultural identities. Maybe it's because my Spanish background is quite strong. Sometimes I really feel British, and sometimes I really feel Spanish.'

'Alright, so does it depend on the day?' Myles teased Carl a bit.

'Hm… I think it depends more on what for, really. In terms of day-to-day stuff, I guess I am quite Spanish, just having a coffee with friends and spending the whole day out, but then when it comes to work or to filling in forms or something, I really change, and I become quite British then.'

'That's a nice balance,' admitted Myles. 'I sometimes feel like I'm more Irish than English or the other way round, but I don't think I have as clear a distinction as you.'

Carl thought about what to say for longer than a normal person would, and then started blinking before speaking. 'Honestly, I feel like I belong to two cultures but to no nation.'

'Well,' said Myles, trying to comfort Carl. 'At least, you were born in a place and grew up in a place you can call home. I was born in England, but I really feel like I'm in limbo sometimes. At school, I was the Irish boy, and when I went to Ireland to visit family, I was their English cousin,' he threw his hands up in defeat, 'I can't win. I don't really feel emotionally attached to either of these places. Rather than feeling like I belong to two countries, I feel rejected by both of them. I am a stranger in my own country… It's like what a friend of mine said about growing up in England with French parents, you find yourself between two cultures and two countries, but you don't belong to either of them.'

Charles came to their table with drinks and interrupted the conversation. 'Hey, ladies, surprise! How are you?'

'Culturally diverse,' replied Carl still thinking about the previous conversation.

'Yeah, we're grand,' snapped Myles.

'Wow,' Charles shook his head with a grin on his face. 'It feels so weird hearing a guy with an English accent saying *grand*.'

'Well, he's Irish,' Carl corrected, pointing at Myles, 'so I guess that makes sense.'

'No, he's not Irish. He was born in London, and he sounds English... he's English,' argued Charles.

'Did you just say that because you don't like being Polish?' enquired Myles.

'I'm not Polish,' said Charles. 'My family is, but I'm not. I was born in England.'

'You speak Polish, and your family are Polish. Where people are born is purely circumstantial,' concluded Myles.

'It's not my fault that we have a real language in Poland, mate,' sneered Charles. 'It's not like in Ireland where you just have a couple of potato-munching farmers speaking a language that they can't even write.'

'Oh, no, they can write it perfectly well,' shouted Myles.

'So, why did all the Irish writers write in English then?' Charles sniggered at Myles. 'Polish writers wrote in Polish, but Irish writers wrote in English, not in Irish.'

'Well, after the introduction of English, independence from the UK was the single most damaging event to the Irish language, although it was good to become independent. If it wasn't for that, we'd be speaking it as our day-to-day language to revindicate our national identity. For your information, I have the same name as the biggest victim of Ireland's linguistic mess, a monolingual Irish speaker. The last monolingual Irish speaker is thought to be Seán Ó hEinirí, who died in the late nineties but believe me, we have more written in Irish than you'll ever have in Polish. We have a lot of mythology written in Irish, and novels and poems, like the ones by Raftery. More literary talent has come out of Dublin than from London, Stratford, and the rest of the UK put together. We have a Nobel Prize in Literature per million inhabitants; that's more than any other country,' exclaimed Myles before an awkward silence started.

\* \* \*

'Could you please tell me again how you found the body, sir?' asked the old policeman scratching his head while his partner was taking notes.

'I already told you twice last night and twice today. I couldn't sleep and my dog was a bit restless. I thought he needed a piss, so I took him for a walk,' replied the witness.

'At two o'clock in the morning?' asked the younger policeman while taking notes.

'Yes, at two o'clock in the morning. My dog felt restless, and I couldn't sleep. My wife was out on a work social, and I thought I'd walk the dog,' repeated the angry witness.

'And then, what happened, sir?' enquired the old policeman, making notes on his clipboard.

'The same thing as the other two times I told you the story,' snapped the witness, restlessly.

'So,' the younger policeman started. 'You're saying that you couldn't sleep, so you took your dog out for a walk, and then your dog walked away, and found this English literature teacher with his brains scattered all over the place behind Kings Norton General Library?'

'Yes, that's it. You finally got it,' exclaimed the witness condescendingly.

'We're not joking, sir,' the old policeman said. 'We're investigating a murder here.'

'I know, my dog found the corpse, and I called you. If I'd killed the guy, I'd have left some oriental food take-away menus next to the body and blamed it on the Chinese.'

'I don't think this is the time to joke around,' the younger policeman snapped while writing on his pad.

'Well,' the witness paused for two seconds. 'I guess this is related to the Birmingham case. That guy killed someone a few weeks ago in the cemetery, and now across the road. It sounds like the same guy to me. It just feels like there's a maniac in my neighbourhood and instead of looking for the bastard, you're interrogating the guy who informed you of yet another crime. I just don't think you have a clue of what's going on,' shouted the witness, shaking his head.

'Sir, there is a whole team of policemen and experts studying the case, and we're making progress,' assured the old policeman.

'Progress?' reprimanded the witness. 'It was all over the news. You arrested an Asian guy who barely spoke any English, you did a terrible job translating the witness' statement and then, to avoid making it look racist, you told the media you'd arrested a British man, only because the guy got a British passport two weeks before you arrested him.'

* * *

'Yeah, it's quite late already,' said Carl. 'I just can't sleep, again.'

'You feeling alright? Did you stay in the pub much longer after I left?' asked Charles.

'No, just a bit longer. Myles had to go home early to get some work done, and I went back to the Central Library to do a bit of reading, but I started getting headaches again, so I came home for a nap. I've just been lying in bed until now, so I might not be able to sleep tonight,' complained Carl.

'Do you remember what you told me about?'

'Yes, why?' asked Carl.

'Well, psychiatrists these days aren't what they used to be. It might be a good idea if you go and see one,' suggested Charles. 'We live together, so I wouldn't be able to treat you. These days, everyone's depressed, and sad, and their children all have ADHD or some mental issue. Loads of normal high functioning people go to psychiatrists. It won't be the same as when you went in the past.'

'I don't know,' replied Carl in a very low voice before starting to walk around the kitchen.

'You could go to Dudley Road Hospital,' suggested Charles. 'It has a very good psychiatry department. They might be able to squeeze you in. You're absent-minded a lot of the time and you withdraw very easily from conversations.'

Carl stopped walking before talking again, 'Is that blood?'

'Yes, it is, I broke a glass and I've just finished cleaning it. It's just a small cut,' said Charles while he was looking around his bare feet looking for more pieces of glass. Charles realised then that Carl always had to stop walking before talking, which he identified as an early sign of dementia.

* * *

'Yes, sir,' replied Carl politely. 'Thank you for that.'

'You're welcome. Just take your tablets on time and you'll start feeling better in two days.'

'Yes, I will take all my tablets,' Carl said in agreement.

* * *

'How was that?' asked Charles.

'It was alright. I've just started taking something different to what I've taken before. I have to go back in two weeks and see how I'm doing. I'm seeing…'

'No,' interrupted Charles. 'No names, please. It is better to keep the anonymity of your doctor. There aren't many psychiatrists in the West Midlands and I may know your doctor.'

Carl nodded. 'Yes, my doctor also encourages anonymity.'

* * *

'Hi, Dad, how are things?' asked Charles.

'Good, thanks, just busy,' replied Charles' father while putting away some documents he had on his desk. 'And make sure next time you knock on the door.'

'Murderer profile,' Charles read a label out loud. 'Are you working for the police again? That's the case on the TV, isn't it?'

'Just knock on the door next time, please,' his father muttered irritably.

* * *

'You're looking a lot better, Carl,' said Myles.

'Thanks, you know, I've been sleeping better lately. I think I can sleep better when it gets warmer, probably because it reminds me of home.'

'You see, Carl? You can say *home*, I can't use that word.'

# A Dead Man's Ice Cream

# Chapter 10

## Would you like toes with that?

Hi, Carl,

I hope you're doing better. It's Myles here. I went to visit you in hospital a couple of days ago and it was nice to see you. The doctors told me that you're quite confused and that you might not even realise who you really are. So, you might think that everything you're going to read in the next few paragraphs are part of a novel, but it's not, it's about your own life. You might think that you're someone else, and you might be reading this thinking that you are a commuter on the way to work, or someone reading a novel during the holidays, maybe a fan of James Joyce who wants to read something in the same style, but that's not really you. If you are reading this, it's because you are Carl, and I am writing to you to make sure you remember. Stop reading and look at your hands. Those are the hands that are always there for me. You are Carl, otherwise, why would I be writing to you to tell you who you are? If you still don't believe it, stop reading, and say it out loud, 'I am Carl'.

The doctors said that they've run a few scans on you and that they couldn't find anything, so they think that the headaches you've had lately have just been caused by extreme stress. Also, they found you had a pretty severe blood infection, which created some kind of weird issue with your antidepressants and may be what caused your hallucinations to come back. Jake will be able to explain all that a lot better than me, I guess. I've known you for quite a few years and you have been in such good form lately, so I'm sure you'll be fine in no time!

Anyway, the doctors said that all being well, you'll be out of hospital by the end of the month, so you'll be back at the Friday Club in no time, mate! They also said that it'd be good for you to have some snippets of past stories to activate your memory, so we had a writing session at the Friday Club and all of us wrote some notes.

You probably won't remember what happened, but it was all quite sudden, a bit scary, to be honest, but I know you meant no harm. You'd been complaining of some extreme headaches, and I know that sometimes you came back early from work, but we all thought that you'd either be hungover, dehydrated, or just stressed at work, because you had to get all your documentation ready for February. The twat you live with, who has now decided to call me, *His royal Irishness*, sorted out an appointment with you to go and see a psychiatrist. You'd been on treatment for a few weeks and you were pretty much back to normal, but then a few days later you started complaining about some weird dreams. I honestly thought you were just stressed again, but I think your visions came back, because there were a few times when you were talking to me and you continued looking over your shoulder as if you'd seen something. Anyway, three Saturdays ago, at about three o'clock or so, we were walking by the canals on our way to Brindley Place and I remember you asking very insistently where all that blood came from. I didn't know what you were talking about, but you just continued asking where all that blood came from. You just saw blood on the ground all around you and then you were convinced you could see a dead guy at the bottom of the canal and started panicking and pointing to the area where you said there was a dead guy. You then ripped your watch off and threw it on the ground because you said it was covered in blood, it was quite concerning, so we thought it might be best to walk around for a while like wandering rocks to calm you down. I remember you saying that seeing the citizens of Birmingham wandering aimlessly around the streets had always had a calming effect on you. After that, I rang Charles and he gave you some tablets that seemed to help. I'd never seen you like that before, but I guess it must have been because of the news report we'd seen on TV a few hours before, talking about the latest victim of the Birmingham case, that car mechanic who was found in a street bleeding to death near Nick's house. Looking back at what I've just written, I guess I could have chosen a better topic to prompt your memory but don't worry, the last time I saw you in hospital you were in good form, so you'll be fine. You were a bit out of it but pretty funny and witty with your comments. You're like a machine, mate! You just carry on going!

Apart from that, things here haven't changed much for me. I'm now counting the weeks till the February half term and I'm just planning where to go, but I just might stay here and save up a bit of cash.

Well, that's it for me, hope you're already feeling better! Talk to you soon, mate!

Myles

You bastard! It's Kazim here,

Hope things are going well, dude. I really envy you for getting all that
free shit from the hospital! The fat bird on the bed opposite you had a
really cool walking stick, so hope you steal it for me on your last day!
Also, remember that hospitals are like hotels, you're actually expected
to take the towels home and all that shit! By the way, talking about
stealing, you remember about three months ago or so I shagged a fat
girl and nicked her control remote, I saw her on Saturday on my way
into town. I got off the bus at Colmore Row, and I went to get some
pipe tobacco in a little shop next to St. Philip's Cathedral and she
happened to work there. Oh, man, that was so fucking awkward! She
was working out the change and just said, 'You're the bastard that stole
my remote!' She wasn't happy, man! I'd just stolen the remote for her
own good, so that she'd just have to stand up to change the channels
and lose some weight, but she wasn't having any of it, so I just left my
three quid change with her and said I had to go. I farted as I was leaving
her shop, so I left that bitch a good present there. It was one of those
intense ones that you can actually chew! You could feel the density of
that fart in the air!

A lot of shit has been happening lately. I imagine the other guys will
tell you a lot of the boring stuff to help you with your memory, but I
have something better to talk about. You missed an amazing Friday
Club last week, fucking brilliant! We held it at Myles' place, as usual.
You must remember Myles' apartment. It's by Post Central and it looks
straight onto Telmo Supermarket Post Central. Jake's back from South
Africa now and he's doing some locum shifts at Dudley Road Hospital.
He brought a mate from work. What a cunt! Jake's been doing great
lately; he's pulled some serious pussy and I think he's over that weird
girl who looked like a dog! Oh, and you'll love this shit. The fucking
bastard worked at a diabetes ward last week, he took the sock off an
old guy's foot to examine it and he felt something inside the sock. He
checked it and there were three fucking toes in there! Black like horse
shit! Jake found three fucking toes in the fucking sock! Anyway, he
built up the courage to say, 'Sir, I'm afraid that three of your toes have
just fallen off,' and all the old bastard simply replied ,'Oh, yeah, I was
waiting for that to happen'. His fucking toes fell off, man! That's how

fucking rotten some of those old bastards are! They just don't give a fucking shit about anything! They're just fucking fat, have rotten blood and don't give a shit! I can't believe people let themselves get into that state!! Anyway, you'll never guess where this shit is going! Fucking Jake offered to make me a drink at Friday Club and brought back some vodka and lime with a lot of fucking ice! So much fucking ice it looked like fucking vodka slush! I saw him and his cunt mate giggling, but I didn't know why. Then, when I was about one third through my drink, I noticed something weird between all the fucking ice. I thought it was a cockroach at first because it was so fucking black, but when I got it out of the glass, I saw it was a fucking toe! A fucking rotten toe in my vodka! I almost threw up! What a bastard! He then told us the story, we fucking loved it but then everyone started checking their drinks for the other toes, but he'd only stolen one. Oh, man. We were so fucking proud of him! He said that the old guy who lost it isn't quite with it, so he filled in a report saying that the guy had just lost two toes and pocketed the third one! Fucking genius! I love Jake! A great citizen he is! He'd kept it in ice at home, so when he got it into my drink, it was still pretty much frozen, but after a while, it started defrosting and it fucking stank! Like rotten blood or something, so I wrapped it in a napkin and took it out with me. I know what you're thinking, that my jacket must have fucking stunk, but you know I'm a resourceful man. I put some of Myles' deodorant on it before I wrapped it. It was a roll-on and some bits of flesh stuck to it but he's a nice guy, so I'm sure he didn't mind. It's not like his armpits smell much better with all that fucking stout he drinks; he is a fucking sweat machine! So, anyway, we went to Pub Chamber Pub and I saw that cunt I wanted to batter when he called you a retard, so I slipped the toe in his drink! Fucking hilarious! Karma at its best! We were just by the DJ stand watching over and bang, the fucking cunt found it at last!

It was hilarious! The guy went mental, you know that cunt's always cocky with his tight t-shirts and that shit, but he was shit-scared! He just shouted like a fucking pussy. I watched his cheeks fill with vomit, he made an effort to swallow back some of it to retain it but man, that was a different level! He threw up right there and then. Wham!!!! The guy was shaking his head in disbelief and it was like a fucking sprinkler! Not sure if it was just the sight of the toe or the smell, because it

179

fucking stank but it was well messy. Then Sean, the bouncer, came to kick him out because he thought he'd drunk too much. The cunt told him about the toe but couldn't find it. I think the twat had just puked all over it, so he and his mates got kicked out, and I guess the toe got mopped up with the rest of his puke! Too fucking funny! I've just asked Jake to be on watch next week to see if he can get another couple of toes off that old guy. I'll give him three quid per toe. We even wanted to make a kitty at Friday Club for him to buy something cool for the old guy at hospital.

So, yeah, that's been pretty much it. We missed you at Friday Club, you'd have loved it! So fucking funny! A bit too crude for you maybe but you had to be there. So, anyway, fingers crossed, pun intended, for Jake to get us some more toes!

Well, I think that's it, you bastard! Just remember, get that fucking bitch's walking stick, man! Just take it as you leave on your last day, she won't be able to chase you without her walking stick!

Talk to you soon, dude, and keep enjoying all that free shit at hospital.

Kazim

Hey, mate,

It's your ginger mate here, I hope you're well. I was distraught to hear about your breakdown, but Myles told me you were looking good the other day in hospital and that you'll get out in no time. He also said that the doctors think you'll be back to normal soon, that it was just a combination of stuff that got you, but that you should be fine. It happens to us all, that's just what happens when you work too much!

Things are good with me. I got a car. In the end, I got the one you came to see with me, so I could go and pick you up in it when you get out in the next few days. It drives so well! What a machine! I just need to get used to an automatic now! I went for a spin a few days ago and picked Myles up from work. The little busy roundabout by the Green was packed as usual, so I just put my foot down as soon as I saw a gap and the car responded! It's fucking fast, man! We drove along Bristol Road and passed Edgbaston Uni, so we could have picked you up if you'd been at work, but next time. Then after that we just drove along Digbeth to see if there were any pre–St. Patrick's celebrations but there was nothing. It's still a couple of months away but you never know. We'll throw a good St. Patrick's party for you, man, we'll have Friday Club St. Patrick's edition!! How does that sound?

Work's good, but busy, really busy. We have a couple of deadlines coming up and we need to finish a few things for a German car manufacturer, so just working on that. Harry, AKA the Impregnator, just got another girl pregnant, fucking hell! You remember the guy, right? We saw him at Portuguese Chicken Post Central as we were roaming the streets with your Louis a couple of weeks ago. So yeah, he's the one who got two girls pregnant in one month, and then he started going out with a girl who already had a couple of kids. Proper Pot Noodle family, already made. Anyway, he found out a few days ago that another girl he'd been with between the other two and his current girlfriend also got pregnant!! What a stud! You fucking Catholics have good swimmers! You're lazy bastards when it comes to work but you breed like rabbits. I've already told him not to even shake my mum's hand, in case she gets pregnant too.

Well, mate. That's pretty much it from me. I've been working too much lately. Oh, I've just read that Kazim's told you about the toe story, what a night! The best Friday Club ever, man!

Missing you, bro! Get well soon and will pick you up when you're given the all-clear. I have that little machine you left at mine last time, so I'll bring it with me.

Love
Ginger George

Hey, buddy,

How's it going? It's Jake here. Yep, I'm back from South Africa. It was great there. The social aspect of it was shit because there was no one to go out with and there were no bars anywhere near but working there was such a nice experience. I was a bit worried about hygiene and all that at the beginning, but I soon started to really connect with my patients. Up to the point that I feel guilty for leaving them behind. Such good people, and they were so thankful for having me there. It was heartbreaking to walk away from that. It was weird because there were great doctors there, incredibly knowledgeable, and they could just diagnose what was wrong as soon as the patient walked in, but all the patients just wanted to come to my clinic. I'm not sure if it was because they fancied being touched by the English guy, or because they thought that I'd be a better doctor for being White, but I found it weird.

Another thing I found strange was the treatment I got in the big cities. It was like being white and having an English accent automatically meant that you were rich, intelligent and trustworthy. At restaurants, they'd get out of their way to get an extra table for me, they'd let me park in disabled only spaces at supermarkets and they didn't even ask for IDs at the bank. It's just like an article I once read in a sociology lesson at school, being white is an endless and totally underserved stock of free passes to privileges. It was such an eye-opening experience.

I just felt like those people cured me from more things that I'd cured them from. I got there with a whole lot of preconceptions and beliefs about Africa, and they showed me I was totally wrong. What a humbling experience, I'm just trying to re-adjust to England now. They really taught me what being humble and respectful was, to the extent that I only left the country with the clothes I was wearing. I treated this kid that got hurt working at a White guy's farm, and the White guy just said he was stealing there, so that he wouldn't be prosecuted for having young children working for him and he could avoid having to pay the doctor's fees. My colleagues and I had to perform a couple of interventions to try and save his arm. Then we wrote in our notes that some other procedures had been done on an old white guy that had died in the morning so we could claim the expenses on the dead guy's insurance. Proper 1980s American style! Anyway, on my last day there I went into hospital to say bye to the team. I looked it up on the computer and found the kid's address. I went to his house, and everyone in his neighbourhood was so surprised to see a white person there. I went there with my suitcase full of clothes on my way to the airport and I gave everything to his family. My suitcases, my clothes, my watch, my phone, my laptop, everything. I left with only the clothes I was wearing and with three sheets I had with my ticket printed on it. Man, they were ever so grateful for it! I think after they got so fucked by that white farmer it was good to re-establish their faith in White people! I gave them all my belongings and the money I got in my last pay check. I thought I had already taken enough from their country, and it felt great giving them all that. So yeah, that was my South African adventure. It was good, but I'm happy to be back. I don't think I could have ever felt like I belong there being white. I had some South African mates that had been born there and were white, but I just wonder whether they ever feel like they truly belong there. They're not Africans because they're not White, and they're not European because they were born in Africa. Identity is some funny shit.

Okay, enough of that depressing stuff, now on to happier things… Birmingham's treating me really well. I went out with the guys to Friday Club and it was pretty funny, but I'll let Kazim tell you the story. It serves him right for stealing my sister's knickers when he came to mine with you and Myles that weekend for a Sunday roast. What a bastard! He is just like Josh. You remember Josh, right? An upstanding citizen of the world! That was the day you cut yourself while we were trying to repair my washing machine. You repaired it in the end, but I can still see the stain of your blood on my carpet.

Oh, and, yeah, talking about knickers, the knickers sniffer struck again! I don't think you know but Ben told me that he, Josh, Myles and you went to Atoll Bar about three weeks ago to see Nick play. And yes, Ben told me that later on you got some action in Ritzy with a German girl! You old dog! I knew you loved the *Kunst*! It might not be the Spanish girl you're always talking about, but the boys said you did well! You talked to her for a while, and she gave you her number. Anyway, Josh is travelling around Australia now. And you must remember the story I told you about the time he'd stolen some knickers while we went to view an apartment for rent in the Jewellery Quarter. Well, he's surpassed himself! He was in a backpackers in Sydney feeling frisky and a guy in his dorm pulled a fat Scottish chick. They were shagging on the bunk bed right above Josh and he couldn't sleep with the bed moving, so he got his MP3 player out and started listening to music. A couple of minutes later, the girl's knickers fell right on his face. He says that it was like his Christmas and birthday present in one! And you know Josh! He started sniffing them and got quite horny with the whole thing, especially as the girl was being fucked while he was sniffing her knickers, so he started wanking and the bastard came in her knickers, then he just dropped them on the floor and went to sleep. Three minutes later, he was woken up by the girl whinging that she couldn't find her knickers at first, and then she started whinging that the bloke who had shagged her had come in her knickers. The guy said he hadn't, and the girl said he must have, because that wasn't her semen. Josh was just trying not to burst out laughing! That guy's hilarious! Too bloody funny! He's just a fucking machine! He's told me he's going to the north of Australia to pick up some fruit, so I'm not eating anything that comes from Australia until that guy gets out of the country!

Apart from that, it's all good. I've been working as a locum at Dudley Road Hospital and I have another three weeks of work until I potentially move away again. You know, that's why you always call me *the wandering rock*. I'm not sure what to do though. I really want to stay in Birmingham but I may as well experience some new places now that I can.

Well, you fake Spaniard. I hope you're feeling better! I'll see you in no time. I've talked to Charles about you and what you have isn't serious at all. You'll be back to your normal self in no time.

Take care, buddy!

Jake

Hey, dude,

I hope you're doing well. It was sad to hear about what happened to you but luckily Myles and Kazim were there to look after you and they said that you're making a speedy recovery. I've been quite busy lately, which is why you haven't seen me much at Friday Club.

I've been working on the Birmingham case for three weeks now. Some more news has been shared with the *citizens*, as my boss puts it, so I am allowed to talk about it now. I had already been busy, but they found another body the day before you were admitted to hospital, so that made things worse. I've been working with the media and coordinating some meetings with the police, which is hard work. Not much more to say on the case, really. Just exactly what the media says. All the crimes seem quite random, with no connection between them, but there must be something we're missing. The guy must be a sick citizen, a collector, or a medicine student or something, because every single victim's been murdered in a different way, each time by attacking a different organ. But there's nothing to go off. No blood, no trace of the person at all, not even footprints. The murderer must have made some mistakes at some point but we're failing to see them, and I'm convinced he must know that. Oh, well, that's the only thing they're sure about. It must have been a guy, because of the strength needed to do the kind of harm made to certain organs. The last victim, the mechanic, was found near Nick's house. Nick's the guy that took you home one of the many nights you got too drunk at The Elizabeth, on John Bright Street, and you wanted to walk back to Penelope's house to serenade her at her window. You were asking Jake to roam the streets like wondering rocks on the way to Penelope's and Kazim started calling you guys *the wandering cocks*.

It's quite sad seeing what Birmingham's like these days. People are just so scared to leave their house on their own. Everyone's scared. We try to make sure the media doesn't publish too many fear-mongering stories but, to be fair, they should. This guy's quite dangerous, he acts every day of the week, in all kinds of locations. It'd be a lot easier if his actions followed the same pattern of action, but he just seems to go out and act whenever he finds the opportunity. No citizens will be safe in this city until we catch this bastard!

Apart from that, things are okay. I've been reading that book you told me about and I'm enjoying it. And you were right, it's weird. You have all those Irish guys writing poems and stories about Ireland and saying how much they love their country, but still because they're protestant, they really feel like they don't totally belong there. Even so, it's still a good read. I'm a third into it but I'll have to postpone it for three weeks now. We're preparing for that charity marathon for the Leukemia society, and I need to get all the security checks done in the next three weeks. This year's starting from Northfield and going all the way up along Bristol Road into the centre, so it'll be a pain to organise. It's just so much easier when people just do three laps in a loop!! But well, I hope to finish the book in the next few weeks.

Well, that's it from me. Look after yourself and I'll see you when you're out!

Take it easy

Zain

# A Dead Man's Ice Cream

# Chapter 11

## Let's call him Mr Bright Side

*"To all my mates, living and gone, with our friendship of gold, in particular to the ones who didn't live till they were old.'*
Brotherly Anthem, Sensible Pence[1]

'There's a girl from Mars I met once, but you may not remember I told you this. We used to go to bed late, smoking and playing chess, but I never found out her name...,' said Carl, 'but I think her name is Penelope. I always have the same dream!'

'Oh, come on,' said Myles. 'You need to get over her.'

'I know,' replied Carl. 'I had a puppy love crush when I was ten years old. Her name was Lisa Janine. She lived across the road. I caught her with a cub scout in a little blue hat. They were pushin' each other on the swing out back. I remember how it almost killed me. How could she do me like that? I never thought I'd be the same, but now I look back and I laugh,' Carl paused. 'And then I imagine myself talking to Penelope and I tell her,' Carl paused again. 'If I can get over her, I can get over you. It's just gonna take some time, these things they always do,' Carl swallowed some saliva. 'But I think I will.'

The barmaid was scratching her left ear while picking up the used glasses. She looked at Myles and Carl, and said, 'Sorry, but it's four

---

[1] Everything written in italics in this chapter are lyrics taken from songs. Due to copyright issues, some of the lyrics have had to be modified.

.ock and you need to vacate this area as a band needs the concert
oom to get ready for a function.'

'The concert room,' Myles repeated to Carl once the barmaid had
left. 'That's an old-fashioned way of referring to it, but that's alright. I
guess we can finish our drinks in the beer garden.'

'It's a bit chilly outside, isn't it?' asked Carl.

'Nah, come on,' replied Myles. *'Spring's arrived, you feel it, right? Let's
live under the eager sun!'*

'No, thanks,' replied Carl. *'It's chilly out there but boiling in here. The music
gives girls and boys a happy atmosphere.'*

'You can tell you're used to a warmer climate,' Myles teased Carl.
*'Honey, the winter's been pretty icy and solitary. Honey, it's been so long. The sun's
arriving, the sun's arrived, and let me tell you...'* continued Myles. 'Let's just
finish our drinks outside.'

Carl and Myles finished their drinks in the beer garden waiting for
Charles to arrive.

\* \* \*

'Hi, guys. What are you doing smoking?' asked Charles, looking at
Carl.

'Someone we were talking to offered it to me,' replied Carl.

'I think he is ready for a crazy night,' said Myles.

*'Hit me with it, hit me with nitrous oxide, I'm waiting for what's coming!'* said
Carl.

'Yes, I can see that,' observed Charles. 'I just think that you won't
need any other substances after starting to drink as early as you did.'

'Come on, mate,' replied Myles. *'Give me a big glass of something strong,
any cocktail but don't be long.'* Myles coughed. *'In some other place, it must be
four o'clock already.'* Myles coughed again. 'A couple of mates from Kings
Norton Sixth Form College are playing here tonight.'

'Well, they could have chosen a place with a nicer barmaid,' said
Charles. 'That lesbian is a proper grump. Watch a butch! I think she
used to be a man. I can imagine her having an internal monologue to
herself in front of the mirror,' Charles went on. *'My labia don't get blood
every month, my pussy's brand-new. My pussy's got additional flaps, they carved a
hole where my willy was, I was a barman and now I'm a barmaid. Mission*

*accomplished, and now I wee through a tiny aperture, I have to remember to sit down but I like my new nature, and to clean my bum, now I have to do back-to-front, not cos of an erection, but to avoid an infection.'*

The three of them could hear some of the Kings Norton Sixth Form College people rehearsing inside. Meanwhile, Charles started to stumble around the beer garden like a rolling stone.

'Wow,' exclaimed Myles. 'You're a lightweight!'

'Well, I didn't have lunch and I feel like these pints are hitting me hard. I'll get some dinner when the band starts,' replied Charles. 'My card's scratched and I couldn't get more money out. I'll borrow some cash from Carl when I go back in.'

'Haha,' Myles said with a smirk on his face. 'I remember you laughing at that guy asking for money outside Ritzy a few weekends ago,' Myles cleared his throat before continuing. *'You don't seem to shout anymore, you don't seem so cocky anymore, now that you have to ask for pennies to get some food. How are you coping with it?'*

Charles considered for a brief moment before defending himself. *'The hidden meanings are annoying the crap out of me. Maybe it's not as messy as it could be?'*

'I can see how you operate now,' replied Carl. *'Destroying is what you do in your free time, but you're a reject so it's not a crime.'*

It was tradition in the Singing Spire for the siren to sound before a band started. It told people they had a few minutes before take-off. Myles went to the toilet as soon as they'd ordered some food, and he heard Carl talking to Charles on his way back.

*'I'm not a kid, I'm an adult.'* Myles felt proud to see Carl in one of those extremely rare moments when he stood up for himself. He guessed that Charles must have come out with more of his patronising stuff, so he was sure that the reply would have been appropriate.

*'Chasing rainbows is not the way to go, and you can't trust everyone you meet, I'm telling you so,'* said Charles to Carl.

'You can't say that, Charles, you may as well say…' said Myles before stopping to think of what to say next. *'Hippies can't be trusted, actually, no one can be trusted.'*

'Thanks, Myles, it's always the same,' confessed Carl. *'Every place I go and see, someone's always telling me what to do and how to be.'*

'Alright, guys. The band's here,' Myles said, trying to calm things down.

The first band finally came on to the stage. While the guitarist tuned his guitar, the singer introduced the band. *'We're proper musicians and we don't come from far away, after four years we still love to play, and now we're older, but still have our pubes, and have a guy in the band who blows into that tube.'*

'So, do they have a name? Your mates' band?' asked Charles.

'No, not really. They just do open mics for fun, but we call them *Nick Patterson and the rapists*,' said Myles.

'That's an interesting name. Why do you call them that?'

'Oh, it's because we used to call them *Nick Patterson and the other rapists*, but Nick's girlfriend wasn't a big fan of the name, for obvious reasons,' explained Myles.

'Sounds like quite a descriptive name to me,' joked Charles.

'Yeah, pretty descriptive I'd say. A few months ago, we went to a Kings Norton Sixth Form College social and the music tech guy from the college works part-time as a DJ at a local station. Kazim was trying to persuade him to play one of their songs.' Myles started laughing before imitating Kazim. *'There's this song that we've written, and, mate, we're smitten, and we say yeah, yeah, yeah, and we then shake our hair.'* Myles giggled again. *'Come on, mate, you have to play our song in your show, most of the verses rhyme, and my singing's always in time,'* Myles giggled one more time. 'And Kazim pronounced it *tim* instead of *time*.'

The band was playing their fourth song when Carl started to complain. 'My ear aches because of too much loud music. Sometimes, my ears hurt when it's too noisy, and also on planes. That's why I don't like travelling and why I wouldn't go back to Gib much when I was at uni, but I still love the place, regardless.' Carl took a small sip of his drink. *'I will always remember my town, the place I so nicely loved.'* Carl coughed before continuing. 'And when I get there, everything's the same; nothing changes. That's good for me because I don't cope well with change.'

'That's better than here then,' said Myles. 'Everything is being dug up here in Birmingham. They're always doing roadworks around New Street and it's quite annoying. And then the streets are just full of spoilt brats, and they seem to multiply by the day.' Myles stopped talking and shook his head. *'I'll do as mountains, rivers, and trees, I won't be disturbed by the crazy shit that everybody sees,*' Myles stopped to shake his head again. 'It's always the same, like bloody Groundhog Day, over and over again.' Myles sipped from his beer before speaking again. '*I've read it in journals, adverts and books, and it's everywhere where everyone looks.*'

Myles continued his rant but spoke louder when all he could hear was an old Australian guy from a few tables away talking to his friends. '*Back in the day when I was young, I was wild and I never gave a dung,*' the old man said before clearing his throat. 'I was just a kid and we used to live on a farm not too far from Wollongong and you won't believe this.' The Australian started staring into space as he continued with his story. '*Once a jolly swagman camped by a billabong, under the shade of a coolabah tree. He sang as he watched and waited 'til his billy boiled.*' The old Australian man paused his story to take another swallow from his drink.

The band finished playing and everyone remained in silence while they finished their drinks. Carl heard something, a sweet female melody coming out of the barmaid's mouth. She hummed while collecting glasses, and Carl thought he recognised the song. In his drunkenness, Carl stood up, hypnotised by the girl, and stumbled towards her.

Out of the corner of her eye, the waitress saw that a harmless-looking guy was humming the same song and trying to get in tune. She paid even more attention to him when she saw that he walked into a table. The table shook, as did the four glasses on it before they fell to the floor, covering it in broken glass. Broken glass had always annoyed the barmaid, but she didn't mind it this time. She was proud of her ability to enchant a guy to walk towards her, even though it was someone like Carl. 'Controlling others is an addictive power,' said the barmaid to herself, remembering someone else's words.

Carl slid and ended up on the floor, missing a puddle of beer. Myles helped him stand, returning him to his table.

'Mate,' said Myles. 'We're going to have to fill your ears with wax and tie you to a mast to avoid you walking out like that.' Carl, still in trance, nodded four times.

Nick Patterson and the rapists continued playing. This time they went with some original songs, the first one called, *Our principal's a cunt*, and the second one, *When useless governors let our college go to waste.*

The band members went back to the table when their gig had finished. Everyone was getting louder and louder, except Carl, who was on his way to sobering up.

'That was a great gig, guys,' said Myles.

'Thanks, mate, it was fun,' replied Pedro, one of the members of the band, 'although I was distracted by the barmaid.'

'Yeah, I know. It also happened to Carl,' said Myles.

'This place is a bit like *The Lord of the Rings*,' said Kazim. 'A couple of hot girls around, but most of the bastards in here look like orcs.' The group smiled in agreement with him.

'Charles,' said Kazim. 'I think you should ask which of them is Gothmog.'

'Come on, mate,' said Charles. 'We are all grown-ups here. Act like one.'

'Come on, psychiatrist boy,' replied Kazim. '*No one should be so serious, all adulthood is spent conforming to society, why do you want me to start doing that now?*' Kazim had another sip of his drink before talking again. '*And I no longer worry about where I belong, I won't try to fit in again, it's been too long.*'

'Everyone needs to fit in,' replied Charles.

'I think I know what a psychiatrist would say about people like you, mate,' said Kazim. '*Middle-class white boys trying hard to annoy.*' Kazim took another drink. '*Somewhere in a great country, someone forgot to build...*,' Kazim paused to cough, 'a place for people who don't want to fit in.'

The group had a few more drinks and the beer hit Carl hard. The conversation moved on to the topic of health and Carl spoke of his headaches and other issues. During the deep conversation, Carl mumbled, 'It's a good thing I have you, guys, cos I have no family left.'

They all felt a bit sad for Carl, but in different ways. 'A nation's greatness is measured by how it treats its weakest members,' Nick thought to himself as he squeezed Carl's arm. The bands had stopped playing a while ago, but some songs still played out of the sound system. A familiar tune began, and Carl shook his head to its rhythm before he started singing. '*I'm out of my cave and I'm fine and I just want everything,*' sang Carl while he danced away from the table, dragging his foot on the ground. He continued mumbling until he stopped in the middle of the dance floor and raised both his hands. '*I'm jealous, I'll vomit my excuses and walk all over them, but it has to be done, fate wants me to do it, and I start looking into the light and that is why they call me Mr Bright Side.'* The group looked at Carl in awe. 'This guy had no family,' said someone to himself. 'The poor guy has some social difficulties,' thought someone else. 'And some mental problems to top things up,' thought another person. Kazim shed a tear while everyone was looking at one another and said to himself, 'He fucking is Mr Bright Side.' They smiled, nodding in agreement and stood up to join Carl in the middle of the dancefloor, *'He gives her a cigarette, and she smokes it, and they get into a taxi, now they're in bed, and I can't take it, and I can't get it off my mind …'*

\* \* \*

'Good evening, Inspector Reilly speaking. How can I help?'

'Evening, mate. It's me. Sorry to bother you, but the guy in the morgue has something you might want to see.'

'Okay,' said Inspector Reilly. 'You know what it is?'

'No, sorry, mate,' replied the voice at the end of the line. *'Santeria ain't something I do, a crystal ball ain't something I own.'*

'I get it. I'll be there as soon as I can.'

\* \* \*

'Evening, sir.'

'Evening, Humphrey. What is it?' asked Inspector Reilly.

'Well, as you might know by now, the body had the two ears cut off.'

'Yes, I know that. I haven't seen the body yet, but I've heard.'

'Well, ah, the thing is that, as I was going to inspect the cut, I saw something made of plastic wedged in the ear canal. I removed it and realised it was a memory card. I inspected the other ear and found another one there.'

'Really?' asked Inspector Reilly. 'Have you listened to the audio yet?'

'No, not yet. They are still covered in blood. I will clean them and, hopefully, they should work,' said Humphrey.

\* \* \*

Inspector Reilly was waiting in a meeting room on the following day when another police officer walked in. 'Rod, we'll go through everything when the others get here,' said Inspector Reilly.

'What is it?' asked Rod. '*Let's not wait for them, as we stand up in this building.*'

'It's okay. I can wait and we can all go through it together,' replied Inspector Reilly.

'Nah, they'll be pretty late, you know…,' said Rod while putting his things down. '*Simply put, it's one more Saturday.*'

'Well, I'll give them a couple of minutes more,' replied Inspector Reilly. 'How are you doing anyway, Rod? You look a bit tense.'

'I just got a pretty harsh letter from my girlfriend telling me it's over. Well, I guess I should call her my ex-girlfriend now.'

'The young exotic lady?' asked Inspector Reilly.

'Yes, that one,' replied Rod. '*I met her by the side fence of a building site, standing by the canal, I had a vision, and then I kissed her outside a dirty factory.*' Rod stopped talking to hand over a note to Inspector Reilly. 'And now it's all over. Read this.'

'Oh, ah, I don't think I should read it,' said Inspector Reilly. 'I'm sure it's quite personal.'

'Please, read it. Maybe you'll notice something there that I didn't. Can't make it any worse. I mean, we've had fights before and have always sorted things out, so I wasn't expecting this. I always try to rationalise things,' explained Rod. '*If she says that I'm a pain, I ask myself what to buy her. I should stand up for myself, but things are okay like this. You don't really care if you don't suffer, right?*'

'Well, not really, Rod,' said Inspector Reilly. He started reading the note after being asked again, pausing and coughing four times. '*I hate your repulsive and retarded face, together with your stupid cowboy footwear…*'

'They're called *botas de montar*. They're Spanish,' interrupted Rod. 'Please, go on.'

'I'm not sure I should,' replied Inspector Reilly, uncomfortably.

'Please, go ahead,' insisted Rod.

'*Every time I talk to you, you talk so much shit that I have to use cotton buds to clean my ears,*' read Inspector Reilly in a poetic voice. 'Well, she's foreign, and I think maybe she didn't understand the subtleties of some of these words.'

'Oh, no,' replied Rod. 'I think she sent a very clear message. Read the bit about the water.'

'Hmm…' Inspector Reilly cleared his voice as Rod hurried him along with his hands. '*Why don't you find out how long you can hold your breath under water?*'

There was an awkward silence when Inspector Reilly stopped reading. 'Well… people say a lot of stuff in these kinds of notes that they don't mean, especially if they're angry. It's like a letter I wrote to an old girlfriend a few years back,' said Inspector Reilly. '*20th April 1990, hey, chick, how are you doing?*' Inspector Reilly stopped before confessing what he'd said in that letter. 'Anyway…' said Inspector Reilly, as he tried to change the topic. 'I remember you told me that she had experienced some issues in life before. Those things always come out. There is an eighteenth-century poet that explained it very well.' Inspector Reilly cleared his throat before continuing. '*Things don't ever change, what comes around goes around, and it's not strange, when things go back to what they used to be, and it will happen to you, and it'll happen to me.*'

'So true,' replied Rod, nodding.

'Yeah, it is. I guess that's what's happening with this psycho murderer as well. Whatever issues he's had are coming out now,' said Inspector Reilly. 'I didn't want to disturb you yesterday because I only got it very late in the evening, but Humphrey found something in the latest body.'

'What? What is it?' asked Rod.

'Well, the body had both ears chopped off and they were on the floor, and he found two SD cards inserted into the eardrums.'

'What? That's sick,' said Rod.

'I know, but it's even worse than that,' continued Inspector Reilly. 'Humphrey cleaned the memory cards and gave them to me.'

'And?' asked Rod.

'It was the recording of a murder, but a different one. Not this one,' explained Inspector Reilly.

'What?' asked Rod in utter disbelief.

'This guy was a DJ with a studio in one of his rooms. The murderer used the mixing table to delete his own voice from the recording, leaving the other victim's voice. He was an ex-army guy and, believe me, he shouted and begged for mercy,' explained Inspector Reilly.

'That's seriously sick, and a lot of work.'

Inspector Reilly went on. 'The killer then used the same mixing table to channel the noise from each speaker into two different mono tracks, right and left. He saved them on different cards, which he placed in the DJ's right and left ears.'

'As if the victim had heard the other murder,' said Rod.

'Yes, exactly.'

'Actually, can't we send someone from tech to check the mixing table?' suggested Rod. 'If the killer recorded stuff and then edited it, there might be an older version of the recording, a master one or something, with the killer's voice still not deleted.'

'I've ordered that already. The team's been looking into it, but they haven't found anything. No master recording, no fingerprints.'

'How did he get in?' asked Rod.

'There was no damage on the door or windows, so either the victim left them open, or the killer knocked on the door and the victim opened it,' explained Inspector Reilly.

'Are there any footprints?' asked Rod.

'There was some mud. They are trying to determine how the killer got in and where he came from using the type of footwear, size, etc. There must be a reason why he killed this guy. He left behind more forensics in this crime scene than in all the previous murders put together. I'm just clueless. I'm talking to Dr Pope later on today, so I'll see what he thinks.'

\* \* \*

'Good morning. Is Dr Pope available?'

'Morning, Inspector Reilly,' replied a secretary. 'He was waiting for your call. I'll put you through.'

'Morning,' said Dr Pope.

'Good morning. We found the other victim, the one that was recorded onto the SD cards that the murderer left in the DJ's ears. We are still working on the scene for that one. Did you find anything in the recordings we sent you?'

'I listened to them a few times,' explained Dr Pope, 'and this is going to sound weird, but I don't think he is as much of a psychopath as I previously thought he was.'

'Really, Dr Pope? The guy's killed eleven people already, well, twelve with the one who was recorded. He usually amputates a part of their body, although this twelfth victim just has several cuts on the muscles of the arms and legs. The killer even recorded one murder, mixed the recording, listened to it again and again until he got the final recording and left it in the ears of another victim.'

'I know,' Dr Pope said, 'but I don't think he's enjoying this, at least not anymore.'

'What do you mean?' asked Inspector Reilly.

'I think he wants to get caught. That's why he left the recording.'

'Do you think? Because this has to end. I just can't stop thinking about the victims,' said Inspector Reilly. '*Opportunities wasted, nothing is safe...*' Inspector Reilly paused for a second. '*Yet, it's difficult to assimilate it, broken dreams and delicate lives.*' Inspector Reilly shook his head. 'If he wanted to get caught, he would just turn himself in, right?'

'Not really. I don't think it works like that. Leaving the recordings is a new level to the challenge. He's finding it too easy to get his own way. There's no challenge, so he's just making it more difficult for himself, and easier for us because he's not getting as much of a kick out of it now,' explained Dr Pope.

'Do you really think so?'

'Definitely, it's the thrill of it,' asserted Dr Pope. 'I think he feels frustrated he hasn't been caught yet. In one sense, the issue is he's not getting enough attention. If his goal was just to kill, he wouldn't be making things easier for us. He wouldn't be leaving us messages. He's got other reasons for it. That's why he wants to get caught. He craves the attention.'

'Do you believe that the less attention he gets, the more clues he'll leave for us?'

'Yes, I think so,' replied Dr Pope. 'However, it might also mean he strikes harder and more often. He has an agenda and he'll do everything he can to complete his masterpiece.'

'Should we prevent the media from reporting on the crimes and continue the investigation without informing them?'

'Well, I think you have to balance it out. You give him attention and he continues killing until he finishes his job, or you stop reporting on it, make him nervous and angry, and wait for him to make more mistakes.'

'If we share our investigation with the media, we can ask for co-operation from the public.'

'Inspector Reilly,' said Dr Pope. 'You have asked for that co-operation for a few months now. Have you received any useful information at all?'

Inspector Reilly looked down at the floor. 'No, none at all.'

'There you go. It doesn't sound like you'll be closing many doors if you increase pressure on the media not to report on anything they hear about the case.'

'Yes, I know. I just don't know what to do. We've achieved nothing in these past months,' a frustrated Inspector Reilly confessed. 'I just don't see it.'

'See what?' asked Dr Pope.

'The pattern. There must be a pattern. There must be a theme.'

'I think there is, but we are failing to see it,' admitted Dr Pope. 'The amputation, the organs. It's a different organ every time. Even when it comes to the behaviour of the sickest of people, or the craziest behaviour you can think of, there's always a reason for it. It's not easy to see, but there's always a reason.'

'So, what is it?' enquired Inspector Reilly. 'He's clearly not doing it for money because he's not stealing anything from the victims. Also, it doesn't seem like anyone wanted these people dead, so he's not getting paid to kill them either.'

'It must be an unresolved internal issue, as usual,' explained Dr Pope. '*The gods know, now he's gone away from home, he's stopped being a parent, and comes back to the family and doesn't recognise his child.*'

'Ezekiel 25:17?' asked Inspector Reilly.

'No, a White rapper, in some song I heard the other day.' Dr Pope paused for a few seconds. 'I think he wants attention. He's a frustrated person.'

'So, his reasons have changed since he started?'

'Why do you say that?' asked Dr Pope.

'Just because the first three victims did not have any organs amputated.'

'It could always be the first thing he did to make it easier for us. It seems like every couple of victims, he adds something new to help us catch him.' Dr Pope paused before speaking again. 'The murderer uses a scalpel, which he could have acquired from anywhere, but it might be worth checking the inventories of the local hospitals to see if some of their scalpels have disappeared.'

'Could he work at a hospital, Dr Pope?'

'Yes, I think so. The amputations he performed were surgical. The cuts are very precise. He removes the organs without butchering the rest of the body. Those aren't the skills of your average GP. I think we should start looking at the hospital staff, too,' suggested Dr Pope.

'Are you serious?'

'Of course,' said Dr Pope. 'The person who's doing this knows about human anatomy, and even if he's not a doctor, he might teach at a hospital or something.'

'Okay, I'll get my team to look into it,' said Inspector Reilly.

'What should do with the media?' asked Inspector Reilly.

'Don't report anything. The killer will get frustrated and make some mistakes. It looks like he doesn't need any excuse to kill, but we can give him an excuse to leave some clues behind.'

'This whole case is so frustrating,' complained Inspector Reilly. '*You can't get away, you can't escape, nobody will get out of it alive,*' continued Inspector Reilly. 'We have nothing and no one knows anything. Someone must suspect something of someone somewhere.'

'Well, it's always like this, isn't it? Every time you see the interviews of friends or relatives of these types of serial murderers they all say the same things,' explained Dr Pope. '*Everyone knew he was always a nice guy, then things got sour, and he said bye to the guy he once was.*'

'Yes, true,' admitted Inspector Reilly. '*Now I'm here, trying to do what I can, trying to be myself, as if I was a superman. And now I'm trying to keep standing as the world crumbles by my side.*'

\* \* \*

It was four o'clock when Dr Pope walked down the street past Beer School Music Venue in Dale End. There were police sirens in the background, and he heard young girls busking in the street as the sirens disappeared. Their songs caught his attention and he walked towards them. He scratched his ear, following the music blindly when someone grabbed him by the arm.

'Mate, I know they're hot, but if you don't pay some attention when you cross the road, you're going to get run over.'

Dr Pope was about to say thank you when he realised who it was. 'Oh, Peter, what are you doing here?'

'I came back four days ago.'

'And how was New York?' asked Dr Pope.

'Well, you know, busy and loud,' replied Peter. '*Their cars are far from tiny, all the rivers there are shiny, the wind cuts you tenderly, whether you're young or elderly.*'

'And what about Spain?' asked Dr Pope.

'Oh, that was better. I spent most of the time getting samples for a new study on southern Spanish accents, but I managed to visit a few friends. How have you been?'

'Okay, I guess,' Dr Pope said. 'A bit of teaching, a bit of clinic, just the usual.'

'And how's Charles doing?'

'He's well, thanks. He seems to be enjoying his training in psychiatrics and is doing well. They've had some funding cuts, so he's got a lot of patients to manage now, but luckily for him, he's only on call once every four weeks.'

'*It's late and back home, the job's shit, you know,*' exclaimed Peter, 'but I think this specialty suits him better. I remember he didn't enjoy surgery.'

'No, he didn't,' admitted Dr Pope. 'He enjoyed the work itself, but not the on calls and the crazy hours. That job's not easy, but I think it's just this new generation, quitting is how they solve their problems.'

'I know. That's what I see my students do all of the time. They drop out as soon as they find a subject too difficult. They have no drive to succeed, and they look at us, see people our age and whinge,' said Peter. '*Old Johnny considers us traitors, just traitors,*' complained Peter, 'just because we've earned a comfortable life. These kids quit as soon as they have to put forth an effort for something.'

'Absolutely, Peter. I think all this will mean the triumph of useless people in a new society where stubbornness will be regarded as a substitute for ability,' observed Dr Pope.

'*Whenever I look at myself in the mirror, I see everything crystal clear, the time's passed, and it passed far too quickly,*' said Peter. 'Oh, gosh, we're old.'

'I know the feeling,' said Dr Pope. '*You get older with every day that passes. Things get harder and you ask yourself why. The sixties spirit is long gone.*' Dr Pope paused to find the right words to express his idea. '*Sometimes there's a moment when you just turn old all of a sudden, without wrinkles on your forehead but wishing to be dead.*'

Dr Pope's mind drifted when he heard the girls singing again. Both men looked at them in awe as a police siren grew louder in the background.

'Oh, I was sorry I had to cancel on you very last-minute last time,' apologised Peter. 'I was behind on preparing for my trip and that was the only opportunity I had to sort out my things.'

'That's okay, don't worry about it. We can re-arrange and meet up soon.'

'Well, we could actually…' The loud police sirens grew to a fever pitch.

'Yes, we could do that,' Dr Pope said.

Both men walked away from the girls when their singing grew too loud. By the time they had reached Jorvik café by New Street Station, Dr Pope showed signs of stress. The only table they could find was by the window where they could be seen by the people outside. They ordered their coffee while the manager complained on his phone. 'Bollocks to premium location. I broke my balls to open a café in the corner of Stephenson and Pinfold. Now, I get a letter saying that everything's going to be fenced up for four months while they install some shitty, new metro system.'

'Did you have a productive trip then, Peter?' asked Dr Pope.

'Yes. I collected quite a lot of data. All I need now is to get it edited, transcribed, and analysed using some specialised software, all the usual stuff.'

'How long will it take you?' asked Dr Pope.

'It'd normally take me a good couple of months to get everything done, but I have a research assistant and a PhD student working on the project. I hope to get it done within four weeks.'

'You sound like you have quite a system over there...' Dr Pope paused for a while and looked away.

'How about you? How are things? You look a bit run down?' observed Peter.

Dr Pope smiled awkwardly and looked to his side. 'Psychiatry is the kind of job that gets to you every now and again. I think I'm going through one of those periods. Nothing serious. I just need to get on with it and distance myself from work.'

'Well said. Other people's problems are theirs, not yours.'

'Yes, I know. It's just something I'm working on which is driving me insane,' confessed Dr Pope.

'Can't you say you're going away and pass the patient on to a colleague for a while?'

'I wish I could,' said Dr Pope, 'but this time is different. I don't think that transferring the patient to a colleague will sort anything out.'

'Would you still see the patient even if you weren't treating him?' asked Peter.

'Something like that. Let's just say, it wouldn't be easy to end my relationship with this patient.'

'Are you that close?' asked Peter.

'It's a bit more complicated than that,' confessed Dr Pope.

'You always said to give up on patients as soon as you start worrying about them. Oh, no. You've slept with one of your patients, haven't you? Female, I guess?'

'No, no,' laughed Dr Pope, shaking his head. 'I haven't. That'd be an easy one to get out of. It's a bit of a weird case this one. I haven't actually met the patient. I'm given recordings and work from those. There's no interaction with the patient as such.'

'What? That is weird. So how do you tell her how she's doing?'

'She?' asked Dr Pope.

'Yeah, all women are crazy, so I assume all your patients are women. Deductive reasoning.'

Dr Pope laughed. 'No, this one's a man and I don't actually say anything to him. Well, I think it's a man. I am given reports on his encounters, and I diagnose issues etc. Lately, I was given extracts of a conversation to work from.'

'So, you just have to work with the recordings of the patient?' asked Peter.

'Not really. I didn't hear my patient talk. I am supposed to come up with stuff from the context and the other person's reactions.'

'Well, I know that's done in linguistics, but that must be trickier in Psychiatry,' observed Peter. 'You know, I don't think you can analyse someone's personality, behaviour, or issues through another person.'

'I know. That's what I'm finding out, but what do you do in linguistics?'

'It depends. A typical one is analysing someone's accent to see how it varies from his or her normal accent. If we like someone, or if we are trying to convince someone, our accent is assimilated to that of our interlocutor, but if we don't like the person or we want to show that we're different to them, we'll retain our accent, or deviate from it if our accent is similar to our interlocutor's.'

'That really makes sense!' exclaimed Dr Pope. 'So, if someone were threatening you and you wanted the person to let you go, you'd imitate that person's accent as well as you could, right?'

'Yes, pretty much. Does that explain anything?' asked Peter.

'Actually, yes, it does, although it's pretty difficult to follow the conversation as some of the audio is missing. I guess what they cut is where the other person talks.'

'Well, this person sounds more messed up than your average patient,' added Peter. *'Mummy, I'm sure there's something in the back room, hopefully not one of those critters from another planet.'*

'Yes, although this time's different,' replied Dr Pope. 'He is different.'

'You think it's a man?' enquired Peter.

'I'm pretty sure it is, but I can't talk about it though.'

Dr Pope grew quieter until he eventually left. He did not give a false excuse. He told his friend that there was something about the case he wanted to check. *'I really never expected this to happen, I can no longer change it, but it still doesn't look real.'*

\* \* \*

A few hours later, Dr Pope called Peter to ask for a favour. He had talked to the police and asked if they could have someone else listen to the recording and, after some negotiation, they accepted. Dr Pope told Peter the police had given him a recording that he'd managed to get nothing from. Dr Pope could tell that Peter didn't seem too convinced about how much he could help with the investigation, but he managed to spark enough curiosity for Peter to agree to listen to the recording.

\* \* \*

It was four o'clock in the afternoon and Dr Pope waited for Peter at the Parrot Garden Bar, a pub on Paradise Circus known for its live music. Dr Pope was sitting in the concert room when he saw Peter walk in. Peter gave Dr Pope an envelope and nodded. 'This is the long-winded version of what I told you on the phone.' Dr Pope didn't say thanks. Instead, both of them looked at the barmaid singing while cleaning the cutlery. They scratched their ears as they walked to the bar, attracted by her song. Dr Pope, in the few seconds he could escape the spell of the barmaid's music, was hopeful that the report would answer some questions.

# Chapter 12

## The death of the Cyclops

### A linguistic analysis of a recording found at a murder scene: sociolinguistic and phonetic approaches in forensic linguistics

Peter Davies
*Research Institute in Andalusian Spanish, Edgbaston University*

**Abstract**
This article combines sociolinguistics and phonetics to analyse a voice recording taken during a murder. Even though the sections of audio with the murderer's voice have been deleted, a thorough linguistic analysis is carried out to identify clues to help the police find the culprit. The sociolinguistic analysis of the recording provides clues regarding the relationship between the interlocutors, mainly through theories of converging and diverging speech. A phonetic analysis provides clues about the timing and context of the murder, as well as valuable information regarding the sections of audio which have been deleted. A list of likely characteristics of the murderer, identified though the linguistic analysis of the recording, is presented in the conclusions.

**Keywords:** Andalusian Spanish, sociolinguistics, converging speech, diverging speech, register in appealing speech, phonetic processes, psycho bastard.

# 1. Introduction

Sociolinguistic analyses of conversations identify two patterns of interlocutor behaviours: *convergence* and *divergence* (Tijo 1995). *Converging* denotes that a speaker modifies his/her speech to make it similar to that of the interlocutor(s), while *diverging* describes the process in which a speaker uses features of speech that are dissimilar to those used by the interlocutor(s) (Bauer 1995: 5). There is, however, a vast range of terms used by different academics to refer to these two main types of linguistic behaviour (Rodríguez-Murray 1995).

The complex interactions involved in speech processes mean that the behaviour of each speaker in a conversation is usually made up of a mixture of converging and diverging behaviours. As described in Rodríguez-Murray (1995), different domains in a conversation can present different types of behaviour. For example, a speaker in his twenties and another in his eighties from the same geographical area might present converging features regarding pronunciation (they have the same accent) in a conversation but diverging features regarding vocabulary (they use different expressions), as Rodríguez-Murray (1995) explains.

According to Tijo's (1995) theory of sociolinguistic variation, converging behaviour is displayed, amongst other cases, when the interlocutor identifies with the other person in the conversation, or when the interlocutor is trying to appeal to other person's conscience to achieve a purpose. Diverging patterns, on the other hand, are mainly used to show or mark the (social) distance between both speakers, in terms of, for example, social status or ethnographic or regional origin.

Both types of variation operate at different levels, such as morphosyntactic, lexical, or phonetic-phonological levels. The morphosyntactic level involves word formation, the lexical level encompasses the type of vocabulary used, and the phonetic-phonological level explains how pronunciation varies across the recording. These three approaches are considered in the current analysis; however, the focus will be on phonetic-phonological features.

## 2. Methodology

This analysis is based on a recording provided by the police as evidence for the case commonly known as *the Birmingham Case*. The victim, whose nickname is *The Cyclops*, is a former member of the British forces who retired from the army after losing one eye. The recording is 55:55 minutes long, and it was recorded using a Sebastianmarinferhausen 55 microphone connected to a Pacogar sound studio system. The recording was taken during the murder of The Cyclops in his apartment, above The Cow's Skull, in Moseley. The SD cards containing the recordings were found inside the ear drum of another victim. The murderer used Babik audio software to delete the parts where he speaks, having only examples of the victim's voice in this recording. The recording was shared with the author of this paper in an attempt to find further information using linguistic analyses. The victim presented with several cuts to the muscles of his arms and legs, but this is of no interest for the analysis of the audio.

This recording has been analysed in different ways. It was transcribed in order to observe the morphosyntactic features of the victim's speech and the transcription was used to analyse the choice of lexis. The phonetic-phonological level of the recording was analysed to identify converging or diverging patterns of pronunciation which might explain any possible relationship between the interlocutors. The latter analysis was carried out in two different ways: perceptually (to study the recording as a whole), and acoustically (to study variation in sounds in a precise manner).

## 3. Analysis

The analyses from the recording have been divided into morphosyntactic, lexical, and phonetic-phonological levels. Each of those analyses has been taken into account both individually and globally.

## 3.1. Morphosyntactic analysis

The main purpose of the speaker in this conversation was to convince the murderer not to kill him. This analysis shows several examples of converging speech in an appeal to the murderer's feelings.

One type of structure seen throughout the conversation was the use of question tags to enhance the appealing nature of the language, as in, 'I never did anything to you, did I?', 'Come on, *illo*[1], I entertained that ugly bird while you were talking to her friend, didn't I?' or, 'You remember the good times, don't you?' Another type of structure used to appeal to the murderer's feelings was the use of conditional sentences: 'If you let me go, I promise I won't say anything.'

Finally, the last structure relevant for the present analysis is the use of 'you know' and 'you remember that, right?' These expressions are commonly used in everyday speech with an empty meaning, that is, as gap fillers. However, the context of the conversation suggests that these expressions are used here to evoke positive feelings from the murderer to convince him not to kill the speaker.

## 3.2. Lexical analysis

Regarding the lexis used in the conversation by the victim, there are two main aspects of interest:

> 1) The use of an informal language mixed with various formal nouns to refer to the murderer. The use of informal vocabulary such as 'mate', 'dude' (e.g. second 5:05; 5:55) shows either a high degree of familiarity between these interlocutors or that they both are similar in age or social status. The use of words such as 'sir' could probably mean that these two people met in a context where the murderer was in a higher position (e.g. in a supervisory role).

---

[1] *Illo* means 'mate' in Cadiz province, southwestern Spain. More on the use of this word is explained below.

2) The use of various Spanish words such as *amigo* 'friend'or *vamos* 'come on' seems to indicate that both interlocutors have a strong connection with Spanish culture or with a Spanish speaking country. The use of the word *tío* (literally 'uncle', but used as 'matc' in Spain), suggests that the country they are related to is Spain. Furthermore, the use of *illo* ('mate' in southwestern Spain), suggests that the relationship is to the province of Cadiz, or possibly Seville.

### 3.3. Phonetic analysis

The phonetic level is also of interest for our analysis and gives us useful information to help us form a portrait of the murderer.

Firstly, the victim adopts a Spanish accent within the conversation when using emotive language attempting to convince the killer to release him. This is an example of speech convergence, where the victim tries to show his closeness and alliance with the speaker by using features of his speech. A few examples of this are the pronunciation of the English alveolar phonemes /t/ and /d/ as dental consonants [t̪] and [d̪]. At this point, it is necessary to remember that the consonants /t/ and /d/ are alveolar in English (pronounced in the same place as /n/), but they are dental in Spanish, pronounced just behind the upper teeth (Migué 1995). Lack of velarisation of post-nuclear /l/ is another feature from Spanish accents that the victim uses, pronouncing the phoneme /l/ in words like 'well' in the front of the mouth (as it is done in a southern Irish accent), as opposed to in the back of the mouth, as it would be normal in the victim's Yorkshire accent. Finally, the pronunciation of /w/ as [gu] in word-initial position is also a feature which denotes a Spanish accent, pronouncing the word 'we' as [gwi:] (guee).

There are also cases when the victim displays regional features in his Spanish pronunciation. The Spanish consonant /tʃ/ (as in the English word 'chair') is pronounced as [ʃ] (as in the English word 'share') on various occasions. For example, when the victim uses the Spanish words *ocho* 'eight' or *picha* (literally 'dick', but meaning 'mate' in Cadiz province). The use of [ʃ] (sh) instead of [tʃ] (ch) is documented as being present in various southern Spanish accents; however, it is more frequently found in the province of Cadiz. Taking into account that the victim uses words like *illo* and *picha*, it is reasonable to assume that the murderer is either from Cadiz province, or that the victim and the murderer share a link with Cadiz, which the victim uses to sympathise with the murderer.

Finally, apart from the instances where the killer speaks, there are five instances when the conversation was manipulated during the victim's speech. Detailed analysis of the spectrograms and waveforms show that some sounds are incomplete. This can be seen when sounds stop suddenly rather than fading away slowly, as is the norm in natural speech. Furthermore, the irregular trajectory and abrupt changes of the pitch trace in some phrases seems to indicate that there is about one second of recording missing in each of those five gaps.

There are some extralinguistic cues that support the proposed length of the cut segment. At the beginning of the recording, when the first cut section appears, there is background noise of a car in the street. The recording is cut as the driver changes gears and the length of around one second fits the change of revolutions as the car slips into a higher gear. Another clue is given by an alarm sounding in the street towards the middle of the recording. The interval of noise that the alarm goes on for each time is one second, with one second of silence. One of the instances when the recording is cut is at the beginning of the alarm going off and it comes back just before the end of it, showing that the section of missing audio is under one second. Likewise, around the third manipulated section, there is noise from a plane taking off from Birmingham Airport and the pattern of the soundwaves produced by the plane before and after the deleted section shows a deleted portion of around one second.

An important point should be noted here. The properties of the file say that the recording was made at 5 a.m. However, no planes depart Birmingham Airport at that time as there are flight restrictions between midnight and 6 a.m.

The last phenomenon of interest for our analysis is coarticulation. Coarticulation refers to the way sounds alter adjacent sounds (Pech

1955). For example, if we grab a pen and we write a phrase such as 'Samuel loves lettuce', we can see that the same letter is written slightly differently depending on its context. For example, the letter 'l' might have a slight 'tail' joining the previous 'e' to the 'l' in 'Samuel.' It might be a straight line in 'loves' and it might have a longer 'tail' joining 'l' to the following 'e' in 'lettuce'. We do this to minimise writing effort (joining letters is easier than lifting the pen and putting it down again). The sounds of speech work the same way. We pronounce the same sounds differently depending on where they are in a sentence and depending on what the surrounding sounds are, thus cutting corners, reducing the amount of movement that the tongue is subject to and reducing articulatory effort. With this in mind, the spectrograms show that all the five instances where there is audio missing in the region of one second, the tongue moves backwards in the mouth. This is indicated, amongst other features, by the low F2 formants of the vowels; a low F2 formant indicates that a vowel is pronounced at the back of the mouth. Two of the words that appear before the missing section of the audio are 'can' and 'on'. The last sound in these two words were not pronounced [n] (as in 'sin'), but [ŋ] (as in 'sing'), which indicates that the first sound of the deleted segment was [k] (as in 'kilo') or /g/ (as in 'go'). To understand this, the reader can read out loud the sequences 'I can see' and 'I can cook'. In the latter, the final sound of 'can' is pronounced at the back of the mouth, as in the word 'sang', assimilating it to the first sound of the word 'cook'. Furthermore, the victim is from Yorkshire and his speech contains examples of *Yorkshire assimilation*, which is when a voiced word-final consonant becomes devoiced before a following voiceless word-initial consonant (e.g. 'wide' is pronounced as 'white' before 't-shirt' or 'car'). One of the words that appears before the other deleted sections is 'need'. It is pronounced [niːt] (*neet) by the speaker and this tells us that the first sound of the following word is a /k/. Therefore, all this suggests that the first sound of the five one-second deleted audio sections is /k/.

Given that the five sections which have been cut out are under a second, I suspect that the element of audio cut out of the recording is where the victim addresses the murderer by name. This would fit well regarding the investigators' suspicions that the victim knew the murderer. Based on the phonetic analysis above, I believe that the murderer's name starts with /k/.

## 4. Conclusions

A linguistic analysis of the recording provided by the police shows some valuable information about the profile of the murderer through the victim's speech.

In the morphosyntactic level, we have expressions which try to appeal to the murderer's good nature and more interestingly, there are several examples of question tags referring to past events. Apart from using these expressions to increase rapport with the murderer, the victim shows that they have previous knowledge of each other.

Regarding lexis, there is an obvious use of several Spanish words, which are employed to evoke positive feelings and memories from the murderer. Furthermore, it is important to note the use of these words are typical of southwestern Spain, such as *illo*. These words show that either the murderer is from the Cadiz (possibly Seville) province or that the murderer and victim have some connection to Cadiz.

The victim's pronunciation varies throughout the recording, showing examples of convergence. Out of all the variations found in the victim's speech, the most remarkable one is the use of a Spanish accent and, tellingly, a southwestern Spanish accent. These three levels of analysis show that the murderer and victim knew each other, that they share positive memories and that they have some link with Cadiz. Furthermore, the background noise from a plane in the recording shows that the recording was made during 6 a.m. and midnight, not at 5 a.m. as the properties of the file say. Finally, there is strong evidence to suggest the name of the murderer begins with /k/.

## 5. References

Bauer, L. (1995). *Speech convergence and speech divergence in pub conversations*. Wollongong: Innit Brew Publishing.

Migué, M. (1995). *The majestic Kingdom of Murcia and its linguistic superiority over Andalusia: Manuel's philosophical theories*. Wollongong: Innit Brew Publishing.

Pech, J. (1955). *Same same but different in articulatory phonetics*. El Ejido: Pabellón Publishing.

Rodríguez-Murray, C. J. (1995). *Illo, illo, illo, hijaputa la ardilla. Linguistic behaviour and misbehaviour in southern Spain*. Salamanca: Leg in the Pool Publishing.

Tijo, P. (1995). *¿Dónde vas a acostarte?: Influencing linguistic behaviour*. Granada: Shawarma Publishing.

# A Dead Man's Ice Cream

# Chapter 13

## Closing your eyes opens your ears

Dr Pope heard the clacking of the pebbles on his front drive as a burning sensation consumed his nose and eyes. The sound of the pebbles announced his visitor and it seemed to linger in his ears forever. His visitor was dragging his feet along the drive and the little rocks were being shifted around. It was eight o'clock in the evening. Dr Pope scratched his nose and the side of his left eye. Outside, the night was a grey colour interrupted by the blue shape walking slowly towards his door.

Dr Pope, once a calm and patient person, had changed over the last few months into an overthinking, over-analytical and impatient old man. He felt defeated by life in general and, particularly, by the Birmingham case. The blue figure stood outside of his door for a few seconds, brushing his shoes against the doormat. The noise of this friction penetrated Dr Pope's ears and he opened the door before the blue figure had time to knock, making for an uncomfortable exchange of looks between them.

'Dr Pope,' said the blue figure. 'Thank you very much for the call. I really appreciate your friend analysing the tape.'

'It's okay, Inspector Reilly,' replied Dr Pope. 'I'm glad he was given the chance to do it.'

Dr Pope walked back to his lounge where he poured tea for his visitor without asking if he wanted any.

'We've put together some information summarising what we have so far but, if I'm being honest, it's not that much,' explained Inspector Reilly.

Dr Pope's eyes navigated through the report, especially scanning the large table at the front with the time of each murder, the location, and the type of organ amputated in each case. They sat opposite one another, deep in thought, knowing they had nothing to solve the Birmingham case, and feeling worse for themselves than for the victims or their families. Dr Pope explained he was willing to help, but without any faith he could solve the case. Inspector Reilly nodded, looking at the floor, defeated, 'I don't think I can do much to solve this either, Dr Pope, but if you stay a part of this, I think it'd at least help my sanity.'

They shared a comfortable silence as they sipped their tea and looked at the carpet, knowing it was preferable to sharing their thoughts on the matter, but Dr Pope finally spoke. 'What's next?'

'I don't know. I really don't know,' replied Inspector Reilly, regarding a painting of grey and blue pebbles on the wall. 'I guess we can only wait until he makes a mistake, although he doesn't seem like the kind of person who makes mistakes.'

'Everyone makes mistakes,' Dr Pope said. 'He must have made some mistake somewhere, left something somewhere, or maybe someone's seen him and could recognise him.'

'I've spent some time now looking for mistakes, little leads, anything, and everything I've found is in that miserable report over there.'

'What about Peter's analysis?' asked Dr Pope. 'We now know his name starts with a *K* and that he knew the victim. If he knew the victim, he might have known the other victims. Is there a connection between them?'

'We're working on that. One of the things that we also got from the analysis is that the murderer works at night. Your friend Peter said that the properties in the voice recording had been changed to show that the recording had been made during the night instead of the day. We believe the murderer was working that night and needed an alibi.'

'Well, that'll be useful once we catch the person, but we can't just look for everyone who was due to be at work that night,' replied Dr Pope.

'I know. I was just trying to fill you in in what we have so far.'

'Yes. Sorry,' Dr Pope said. 'I think this case is getting to us.'

The two men looked at each other. They complained about the complexity of the case while commenting on the deadly skills of the murderer. Inspector Reilly's tea had gone cold a long time ago and the pauses between their chat grew longer. Their noses detected the acidity of the cold tea and both parties agreed it was time to call it a night. Dr Pope thought about the case for a while, but he didn't come up with anything useful until a few days later.

* * *

Dr Pope visited his friend Peter for dinner, and they were both happy, especially Dr Pope, who did not think about the Birmingham case all evening. It felt as if life had returned to normal and he didn't feel like someone who had failed at catching a killer. With dinner over, it was time to enjoy a drink in the lounge. However, death seemed predestined to be a part of their conversations. That week had been the eighth anniversary of the death of Peter's wife and that was something that got him down every year. Dr Pope, on the other hand, was better at dealing with the loss of his wife; a dark commonality they shared.

Dr Pope's eyes wandered around the room looking for inspiration to start a conversation. His eyes moved nervously, like pebbles in the falling tide, when he saw something that hit him like a rock on the nose. He saw a document that looked familiar. 'Peter, I didn't know you had been asked to collaborate in the investigation of the murders again.'

'What do you mean?' asked Peter.

'That document. I have the same print-out at home. Inspector Reilly gave it to me a couple of days ago, but he didn't tell me you were working on the case,' explained Dr Pope.

'I'm not,' Peter said. He stood up, grabbing the document and passing it to his friend. 'Look,' he said. 'It's a scheme that explains *Ulysses*, that novel I like by James Joyce.'

Dr Pope paused, scanning the document incredulously, 'That can't be right! This looks a lot like the report summary that Inspector Reilly gave me a couple of days ago. Place, time, and organ amputated.'

'Are you sure?' asked Peter.

'I've been reading it for the last few days and it's extremely similar. The place where each murder happened, the organ amputated, the time. How many chapters does it have?'

'Eighteen,' answered Peter.

Dr Pope felt like someone was throwing pebbles at his nose. A sharp pain consumed him. 'That means we can expect six more victims. This changes everything. It's not as random as we thought. He has a plan. He has a plan!' repeated Dr Pope. 'Maybe, he doesn't want to be caught after all. It might just be a personal challenge to see if he can get away with it. He might continue like this until he gets his eighteen victims.'

Peter tried to assimilate all the information as quickly as he could. 'Actually, I don't think so,' Peter pondered, 'I'm sure he'll want this over on Bloomsday, on the sixteenth of June.'

'Why?' asked Dr Pope.

'*Ulysses* is set on the sixteenth of June 1904, and the whole action of the novel happens during that day, when Joyce first went out with his lifelong partner, and that day is referred to as Bloomsday, based on the surname of the main character. Every year in Dublin, they celebrate that day with people dressing up like characters from the novel, and there are performances. They've also started having similar celebrations in other cities. This year will be a big event as it's the hundredth anniversary of Joyce and Nora's first date, a hundred years of Bloomsday.'

'According to this schema, this guy has three months to kill six people. I assume the information in the last six chapters of the novel will give us an indication of what kind of victim he'll be looking for. Maybe even where and how the person will be killed,' hypothesised Dr Pope.

'Yes, kind of,' replied Peter. 'Although the fleeting details in the scheme of the novel won't give us much specific information. Also, it'll be pretty much impossible to guess which specific location or victim the murderer will choose, especially in such a big place like Birmingham.'

'Can I take a copy of this, Peter?' asked Dr Pope. 'I'll show it to Inspector Reilly and see where we take it from there.'

'Yes, sure, take it. You can also look for it on Google. You'll find it under the keywords of *Ulysses, schema, Gilbert*,' explained Peter.

Dr Pope said his goodbyes to Peter and walked towards his car. He was excited for the first time in weeks. His stomach and shoulders tickled as he thought about what this could mean for the case. Rejuvenated, he called Inspector Reilly and organised a meeting for the following day. He had some time before seeing Carl again to escalate his treatment from casual to closer monitoring.

The following day, Dr Pope met with Inspector Reilly and they discussed future lines of action. Dr Pope suggested involving an expert on the book so they could predict the future moves of the murderer. It was all pointing to Peter as the perfect match, who offered a great balance between being knowledgeable about the book and being level headed. It took a short phone call from Dr Pope to get him to accept, as Peter was already expecting the call and had already done some research in the meantime. Peter accepted and said that there was a *Ulysses* book club planning a trip to Dublin for Bloomsday. Peter said he would join the group that week and keep them posted if he discovered anything useful. Dr Pope and Inspector Reilly thanked Peter and concluded the meeting before rushing to other appointments.

Dr Pope found himself walking around his office in the hospital. He had a couple of minutes until his next patient arrived and was nervous. It didn't even matter if they got the best experts on *Ulysses*, the city was too big to patrol and having seen the murderer's previous crimes, it felt like the guy was capable of doing anything he wanted. Dr Pope's secretary rang to inform him that Mr Martin had arrived.

Carl was going to explain to her that the stress was on the *in*, as it's a Spanish surname, but he just moved towards the consultation room when he heard Dr Pope's invitation to do so. Carl stood in the middle of the office, a sheepish look on his face. He could hear his own breathing, still whizzing from a cold he had just recovered from. A blue and grey book cover caught his attention. As he fixated on it, he was unable to notice anything else in the room. He shook Dr Pope's hand and sat down, breathing heavily and feeling more nervous as he listened to his own heartbeat.

Dr Pope wasn't surprised to see that Carl needed more intense treatment, but he was surprised to see how quickly he had worsened. Dr Pope tried to calm him down, asking him what he might have seen on television lately. He noticed Carl was starting to breathe normally.

'Well, lately I have been watching a bit more TV than I normally do. Just the usual, a couple of films, some documentaries,' replied Carl. Dr Pope asked him about the documentaries, avoiding talk of any films with aggressive or sad scenes that might influence Carl's mood.

'I really enjoyed one about serial killers that have never been caught.'

*Well,* Dr Pope thought to himself, *that didn't work, did it?!*

Dr Pope said that it sounded interesting and asked Carl to explain what he had liked about the documentary.

'Everything,' said Carl, full of excitement. 'They presented each case and put it into context, and then they talked about different scenarios and what could have happened. The best thing is they also talked to people who were in prison for similar things and asked them how they would have carried out those crimes. It was very good to get an insight into other people's perspectives. It really helped me understand that people kill others not because they need money, or because they're looking for revenge, but simply because they can.' Dr Pope became uncomfortable when Carl said that.

'It was weird,' Carl went on, 'but they also talked about something called *the blindfolded advantage.* Some of those murderers were related to cops, investigators, the victims, etc. and they knew that they'd have the advantage of doing whatever they wanted without being considered a suspect. The last thing you're going to see is a cop investigating their children from day one. People refuse to see the truth about those close to them when it comes to those cases, so it's pretty difficult for them to be caught.'

Dr Pope froze. His hands were sweaty and a muscle on the right side of his neck spasmed, as it usually did when he was under stress. He didn't know how to overcome it or how to change the topic. 'But…,' Dr Pope started with a long pause, 'if he is friends or is related to the investigators, I'm sure that person wouldn't want to place them in a tricky situation.'

'Not at all,' replied Carl. 'They said, they usually do that because there is some kind of unresolved issue between those people, like a way of getting revenge without hurting your relative.'

'Well, Carl, you have to remember, even though it was a documentary, it's nothing more than a simple television show at the end of the day. You have to be careful with the stuff you believe,' explained Dr Pope with a stern voice.

'Yes, sir,' replied Carl in the manner of a child chastened by a parent.

'What other things do you do in your free time?'

'I work for eight hours and then I go back home. I cook something and then usually read and surf the net. Other days I meet friends for a drink.'

'Okay, what kind of books do you read?' asked Dr Pope.

'Anything, as long as it is good literature. I really like the classics. That way you know the books are worth reading. They have stood the test of time. I don't read anything modern. I don't usually read things published after the nineteen fifties or so.'

'What's your favourite book, Carl?'

'*Ulysses*,' Carl responded without hesitation.

Dr Pope was astonished. He had never heard of that book until the previous day.

'What is the book about and why do you like it that much?' asked Dr Pope.

'The book's about a normal day in Dublin in 1904. It tells the story of some people who live there and who share a relationship with each other. It talks about a young guy teaching in a school, his dad, a couple of his dad's friends, etc. I think it's a way of portraying a whole city in a very intelligent way.'

'I'm going to have to read it,' said Dr Pope. 'And why do you like it so much?'

Carl thought before giving an answer. 'I like the fact that the book's set in just one day, and it tells what's happening in a certain part of the town at a certain time. It's a good way of capturing a normal feel of the town, a slice of life. I also like that every chapter's written in a different literary technique and uses different symbols such as colours or parts of the body.'

'It sounds like it's very well written,' Dr Pope noted. 'What's the main message of the book? What story does it tell in your opinion?'

'It just represents life in a society with certain tensions. At the same time, the author shows anger towards his country,' replied Carl in a surprisingly articulate summation.

'Is it a violent book?' Dr Pope asked, genuinely interested.

'No, there are no assaults, or murders, but there is certainly a lot of anger in some parts of the book. It's a bit like those documentaries about ill feelings between family members triggering a series of murders. It is a violent response towards society, but a non-violent response towards the person the conflict originated with.'

Dr Pope was intrigued by the concept: a purely psychological revenge, restoring the ego, damaging the psyche of the other person without being noticed. He remained quiet for a few seconds, looking to his top left. It was enough time for a socially adjusted person to notice something was wrong, but Carl remained ignorant.

'So, tell me, Carl, how's work going?' Dr Pope asked.

'It's going very well, I think. I have been doing that job for a few months now and I feel like I know what I am doing. I am a secretary in the School of Languages. I help out with things like updating the website, managing information, distributing policy information, etc. It's getting busier now because exams are coming up, but I'm very happy with how it's going.'

'How do you get on with your workmates? Have you made friends?' asked Dr Pope.

'I get on with them, but I haven't made any really close relationships. My housemate said that it's not me, that academics have the same social skills as blue cheese, so I wonder whether he's right or whether I have a problem. But I've made friends with a young lecturer called Penelope. She's Spanish and she lectures in Spanish literature. We bonded over the language.'

'Let's try to not use any names, remember? Just keep things as objective as we can. But that's good,' said Dr Pope, 'because you speak Spanish as well, don't you?'

'Yes, I do. I grew up in Gibraltar with my grandmother and she was Spanish, so I reckon I spoke Spanish as a child a bit more than the average Gibraltarian kid.'

'It's good that you speak a second language,' said Dr Pope. 'Tell me a bit more about your life in Birmingham. Do you live by yourself?'

'I live with a housemate called…'

Dr Pope shook his head. 'We don't mention names in this clinic in case they wish to remain anonymous. This also helps us focus and we can avoid being distracted by trivial facts.'

'I have a housemate,' said Carl.

Dr Pope praised Carl for not saying any names and went on with his questions. 'And how do you get on with your housemate, Carl?'

'We get on well. I found him a bit reserved at first, but once we got to know each other, we started hanging out. It's good, but he works weird hours, so I don't see him for days at a time.'

'Okay, I see.'

'He's a doctor,' said Carl. 'He works as a psychiatrist at Bordesley Green Hospital.'

Dr Pope wondered whether his son would know Carl's housemate. 'It's good to hear things are going well. Apart from all of that, how do you feel these days?'

'I feel a lot better, thank you, Dr Pope. I have been taking my medication on time, and I haven't been feeling as anxious. I haven't had to take any time off work since my last anxiety attack. My housemate has been making sure I take the medication. He's also been very good at helping me control my anxiety.'

Dr Pope remained quiet, looking to the floor in surprise. He rose his chin enough to say, 'That's very nice of him. Are you sure he works at Bordesley Green Hospital?'

'Yes, I'm pretty sure,' replied Carl. 'I have also met some people at a book club I go to every second week. We're reading *Ulysses*.'

Dr Pope grew increasingly nervous. 'What do you do there?'

'We read an episode every two weeks and then we meet up to talk about it. The book has eighteen episodes.'

'Do many people go there?'

'There are about eight of us. It depends on the week, but it's really nice because it's at the Birmingham Art Centre, and sometimes we stay for a drink at the café after the meeting.'

'What kind of people go there?' asked Dr Pope.

'All sorts. Some people are professionals, while some people have unskilled jobs. It's just people who like the book. It's really relaxed, and no one tries to pretend they know everything. People don't usually like book clubs because they find them a bit pretentious and rigid, but this is good. I used to attend another book club at university, and this is a lot better.'

'It sounds like the place to go,' said Dr Pope.

'Yes, it is. Not your usual book club. I discovered another copy of *Ulysses* in my house, and it happened to be my housemate's. He's reading the book as well but doesn't want to come to those meetings because he thinks it'll be boring. Also, he does some night shifts, quite often actually, so even if he wanted to, he wouldn't be able to attend much.'

'Really? I would have imagined psychiatrists to have a nice eight till four shift.' said Dr Pope.

'Yes, he usually does, but sometimes he gets called in at night or has to do night shifts.'

'How often?' asked Dr Pope.

'Maybe once every couple of weeks or so,' answered Carl. 'Sometimes more often.'

Dr Pope looked at the ceiling, shifting his eyes from top right to top left. 'Tell me a bit more about your housemate, please. What kind of hours does he do when he's on call, and does he wake you up when he comes back home?'

'It depends, as some of his shifts seem much shorter than others. Sometimes, they're just a couple of hours here and there, but I guess that is when the hospital calls him to see patients. I never hear him come in, or eat or anything, but what usually wakes me up is when he has a shower on his return. He usually has very long showers, so the noise of the water really wakes me up, although I always manage to fall asleep again.'

'It's good you can go back to bed without any problems,' said Dr Pope. 'Does he ever wash his clothes when he comes home from his night shifts?'

'Yes, sometimes… quite frequently, actually. I asked him about it once and he said that when he gets blood on him from patients who have hurt themselves, it is easier to remove if he washes the clothes straight away.'

Dr Pope breathed out heavily, shrugging his shoulders while he studied the floor. He breathed in again and corrected his posture. 'That's good, Carl. Now tell me, how are you sleeping these days? Is your breathing still rapid when you go to bed?'

'No, not lately, I feel a lot more relaxed during the day and at night. I don't feel as anxious, vulnerable, or worried about things. I guess it's from feeling happier during the day,' explained Carl.

'That's perfect,' said Dr Pope. 'Have you been taking your grey and blue tablets regularly?'

'Yes, at eight in the morning and eight at night, sir.'

Dr Pope nodded in approval while taking notes. His right hand shook. He bit his bottom lip. Air shot through his nose, and he struggled to breathe.

Carl didn't note anything special. He stayed in his seat, quietly waiting to be addressed again. After a few more bites of his bottom lip, Dr Pope's breathing got heavier and noisier, and he only addressed Carl sometime later to say, 'I can see you're doing much better, young gentleman. We can finish for today.'

\* \* \*

It was eight in the evening when Dr Pope received a phone call. He had a feeling he already knew what it was going to be about. He picked up a piece of paper and walked towards his mobile phone. As expected, it was Inspector Reilly, and he gazed at the paper, as if waiting for the inspector to confirm what he had written. Dr Pope didn't say much during the conversation. He nodded uselessly on the phone and, after getting the information he needed, he confirmed he'd look into it. Dr Pope hung up, grabbed a pen, and started ticking things from his list. It was a copy of Gilbert's schema for *Ulysses*, and he looked at chapter thirteen, reading the contents out loud: 'Nausicaa, The Rocks, 8 p.m., eye, nose, grey, blue, Virgin, painting, tumescence, detumescence.' Dr Pope ticked the words *rocks*, *8 p.m.*, *eye* and *nose*. 'What a way to go. He must have seen something blacker than the dark.' He sat down and rested his head on his hands. 'So, this painter is victim number thirteen.'

# Chapter 14

## Medical notes on life

01/04/04

10:00 p.m.: The nurses in white push a stretcher with a pregnant woman on it. Like oxen in the sun, they make a slow progress while the patient clutches her stomach with both hands. The woman continues to shout as they advance towards the delivery suite. More shouting, a bit of sweat, and a lot of swearwords, and the baby is delivered at 10:10 p.m. Mother to remain on intravenous fluids. Small but healthy baby: Tenth percentile for height, weight, and head circumference. Mother and baby doing well. All notes forwarded to Dr Pope, the patient's psychiatrist.

01/04/04

10:10 p.m.: Charles presents to hospital with intense twatiness, general cockiness and feelings of superiority. Hated by some, disliked by many. No drugs have proven to be successful in changing this. He is in hospital performing his one on call in the past three months. He is not busy. Most of his patients are asleep. He sees a white note pop up on his screen concerning a patient who has just delivered a baby. The patient presents with the same psychotic issues as her mother. Charles wonders if his mother's issues are haunting him. His patient showed no signs of anything worrying. He minimises the screen and opens up a browser in search of a new belt.

01/04/04

10:10 p.m.: Carl is at home. He tries to go to bed early, but he is tossing and turning. He cannot sleep and he realises it is because he did not take his medication. Carl finds it weird that his new medication makes him sleep a lot, but that he wakes up tired. His sleep is of poor quality. A possible reason could be the general stiffness of his body. Other side effects of his medication include excessive salivation and moderate weight gain.

02/04/04

10:00 p.m.: Dr Pope has been attempting to meet with Charles, but Charles always claims he is busy. Eventually, Dr Pope rings him to ask how things are. According to Charles, he has been very busy with work, but everything is fine. Dr Pope is not convinced. Dr Pope says that he has gone to his apartment a few times and that he has never answered. Charles' reply is that he may have been either asleep or not at home. Dr Pope asks Charles if he has moved out of his apartment and Charles says, 'No', but that he has spent a lot of time at a friend's house as he needed help. Dr Pope hopes to find some explanation for Charles' behaviour and is trying everything he can to do so. Dr Pope moves onto a more trivial topic before ending the conversation.

02/04/04

10:10 p.m.: Dr Pope rings Peter for help, asking him to attend the James Joyce book club Carl had told him about. They talk about it, but Peter does not think it would be of any benefit. Dr Pope encourages him to attend. Peter finally agrees. Action to arise from the interaction: Peter to liaise with Dr Pope after the meeting.

03/04/04

10:00 p.m.: Charles is working in the hospital and another one of his psychiatric patients goes into labour. It seems like all of his patients are pregnant, and one of the few who is not, recently tied a white doll to his stomach claiming his womb was big with child. Charles had tried to explain that men could not get pregnant, but his patient's answer was always, 'The ox is slow but the earth is patient; it can be done'. A couple of years ago, Charles would have described his patient as a nutcase, although he now knows the technical word for it. Charles' patient had been taken to the delivery suite (the woman, not the guy) and Charles sat down in the corridor. It was difficult to believe the hospital was this busy at night. Charles stared at his white hands.

04/04/04
10:00 p.m.: Dr Pope is tired of going around in circles. He grabs his phone and dials Charles' landline. No answer. It is Sunday night and he expects Charles to be at home resting for the following day. He is starting to believe what Carl told him, but a part of him thinks young men do not always prepare for their following day at work. They meet up with friends and socialise, and do those things that Dr Pope never let Charles do during his childhood in an attempt to groom, as he used to put it, *a disciplined young man with no time for trivial entertainment*. Dr Pope repeats Carl's words regarding the reason behind a serial killer murdering people, 'Because there is some kind of unresolved issue between those people, like a way of getting revenge without hurting your relative.'

05/04/04
10:00 p.m.: Dr Pope reads out loud the parts of the police report that concern him the most. 'Thirteen victims to date, most of them with an organ cut out.' He looks through the pages. 'The team in the lab have concluded that the utensil used in the murder is not always the same. However, they all seem to be extremely small and sharp. Judging by the cuts, they look to be created using specialised surgical instruments. The organs were all removed in an extremely precise fashion, which suggests that the murderer might be medically trained.' Dr Pope shakes his head and adds, 'Or a butcher.' 'Each murder committed in a different location,' 'the victims seem unrelated to one another.' Dr Pope continues reading. 'An analysis of the footprints indicates that the murderer is male, between 170 cm - 190 cm (5.6 ft - 6.2 ft).' Dr Pope sucks his right thumb, shaking his head again until he realises what he is doing. He takes out his thumb and rests his hands on his belly, presses into it and looks to the ground. 250 ml of water taken with 25 g of biscuits. Double dose of biscuits administered to reduce negative feelings. 'No clothes, saliva or skin left at the crime scenes.'

Dr Pope stops reading and looks to the top right, imagining the different crime scenes. He continues to read the document in silence while his eyes widen every couple of lines. 'Unbelievable.' He bites his bottom lip while moving his hands to his belly again. No inspiration found. Repeat procedure in ten minutes to reach desired outcome.

06/04/04

10:00 p.m.: Peter attends the James Joyce book club the following day and calls Dr Pope to revisit his notes from the previous book club and to receive any general pointers for the next meeting the following day. Peter met ten people: a guy who works in administration at the Language Centre of Edgbaston University. Three teachers from a Sixth Form college, a plumber, two housewives and three guys who did not say what they did for a living. They looked at one chapter and a couple of good points were raised, but a lot of crap was also spoken. There was nothing that Peter could vaguely relate to the recent murders. Dr Pope asks a few questions about the administration guy from Edgbaston Uni, asks Peter to find out more things about him and then Dr Pope finishes the conversation while thanking Peter for his help.

07/04/04

10:00 p.m.: Peter has been to the book club. Most of the usuals were there, but the plumber was not present. There were two people he did not recognise. One was a middle-aged man, looked well-educated and was wearing a white shirt and a jacket. The second one was about ten years younger, a bit stocky with a prominent belly which he rubbed several times, like a pregnant woman, and was constantly admiring the females of the group. This week, they talked about chapter fourteen of *Ulysses*, *The Oxen of the Sun*. Set in a Dublin hospital at ten at night, it was 'medicine' as the art dealt with in the chapter, the colour 'white' as the colour of the chapter, 'womb' as the symbol and 'embryonic development', whatever that means, as the literary technique of the chapter. After the meeting, Peter approached the men and asked if anyone was up for a beer. They discussed it for a few minutes until they decided there was nowhere close enough. The younger man asked about the Pistol Kegs, just outside of the University of Edgbaston, only about ten minutes by car. Peter found it awkward visiting a pub full of his students, especially with a seedy looking man. The older man excused himself and Mr Seedy got into Peter's car. All in all, a dull meeting. No one had any in-depth analysis of the chapter and more importantly, no one showed the kind of weird psycho personality trait that Peter was hoping to find. Antidote to feeling like shit for not catching a psycho: not found. Diagnosis: Carl is as autistic as a box of frogs. General tiredness could have influenced Peter's judgement and Carl's autistic traits.

08/04/04
10:00 p.m.: Carl is at home tired, like every day for the last ten days or so. 200 ml of tea with a 1:10 ratio of milk and 50 g of cheap biscuits, self-administered. Carl is in the process of watching television when Charles walks in wearing a white shirt. Charles looks surprised to see Carl still awake. Charles goes to the toilet without saying anything; only after he has washed his hands and had a shower, does he talk to Carl. Carl asks Charles if everything is okay and Charles says he has had a very tough day at work. Charles sits down opposite Carl and starts talking about a totally unrelated topic. Carl finds it weird, but he is happy to have someone to talk to.

08/04/04
10:10 p.m.: Dr Pope walks nervously around his house. He has work to do, but feels unable to complete it. He has rung the hospital where Charles works to talk to some friends and he has received confirmation that his son is the only male trainee psychiatrist there. Dr Pope opens Carl's patient folder and checks his landline number. He dials the number and after two rings, Charles picks up the phone. Dr Pope does not say anything. He does not even breathe. He just hangs up, scared. Dr Pope has used private information from his patient's file for his own purposes. Misuse of confidential information not reported.

09/04/04
10:00 p.m.: Charles and Carl are at home watching television. It is the first time they have relaxed together in the same room for some time, apart from some recent short chats. No issue with their personal relationship has been reported. They have not fallen out, but each of

them has been preoccupied with their own issues. Charles asks Carl how everything is going and Carl explains that he has been feeling a bit better lately. Carl explains that his sleep has improved and he does not feel as tired. Carl swallows a big gulp of saliva while he passes a box of medicines to Charles. Carl also explains that he feels much happier and not as negative as he used to. Carl talks about work and mentions Penelope, at which point Charles displays signs of feeling uncomfortable. In line with the characteristics of Carl's reported syndrome, he does not pick up on the cues and he continues talking about Penelope. Carl reports high levels of satisfaction at having had lunch with her this week. Carl's pupils dilate as he mentions her name. Charles warns Carl against letting Penelope manipulate him. Charles explains this can be quite normal in relationships with very unbalanced social powers. He admits this is the case with his own relationship with this father. Charles says that people who take advantage of the disadvantaged should be heavily punished. Carl is trying to process this while Charles congratulates him on his improvement, adding that it is good that he is sleeping better, as sleep problems can be a side effect of that drug. Charles says that he can see that Carl is improving and that the medication is helping. Carl agrees and compliments his psychiatrist, whom he describes as 'serious but gentle'.

10/04/04
10:00 p.m.: Carl's hand is shaky. He sits down, has 10 cl of water and opens a box of medication. He reads the information pamphlet in detail before taking a dose. He washes down the pills with another 10 cl of water and stops shaking before the medication takes effect. This does not worry Carl, who does not register the fact. Charles has noted this before. Carl fills up his glass again with water and sips it carefully while taking a book out of his pocket.

11/04/04
10:00 p.m.: Carl is in the kitchen. He has consumed 10 cl of water and is shaking, so he sits down. His head moves back and forth, only stopping when he holds it with both hands. Charles observes from the other end of the corridor and creeps closer when Carl starts muttering something. Charles attempts to hear what Carl is saying. It sounds like,

'It's not my fault' and 'Penelope'. Charles walks away and looks at the calendar on the wall. It is that time of the month when the news typically reports on another murder in Birmingham.

11/04/04
10:10 p.m.: Penelope walks home after a long day at work when her phone rings. She grabs it with her left hand while balancing her books and folders with her right. She leaves her stuff at the entrance and answers the phone after checking who it is. She says *hi* in a tired voice before explaining how marking exams has left her exhausted. She listens for a bit before saying that she is also happy with how things are going, but that she has had a couple of busy weeks at work. She smiles at the voice on the other end of the phone, explaining that she cannot meet over the weekend because she has some assessments to mark and return within the next few days. She listens to the caller again. Smiling, she scratches the back of her left ear before covering it with a strand of hair. She says they should make plans once she finishes her marking.

11/04/04
10:10 p.m.: After some thinking, Peter rings Dr Pope and following the usual greetings and pleasantries, Peter says he does not think there is any relevant information to be taken from that book club. He says that no one talks much and, apart from some middle-class women, a few younger guys and a creepy guy looking to score with a bored housewife, there is nothing there. He admits that the analysis is good, at least. Dr Pope is disappointed that nothing has come from it, but is not surprised. He asks Peter to keep going, as he might get some good ideas about how to foresee the next attack through the analysis of the novel. Management plan: continue with prophylactic investigation at the book club.

12/04/04
10:00 p.m.: The phone rings and Peter picks it up. After a long pause, he hears Dr Pope's voice. Dr Pope explains that they have found another body. A woman with a white top was found dead outside the Children's Hospital with cuts to her stomach. She defended herself, as

there were signs of a struggle, but she died. She leaves behind a son who is cognitively impaired. This time, however, the forensic team believes that the knife was used with the left hand, so it could have been a different person. Peter suggests that maybe the murderer injured his right arm and this forced him to use his left hand. Dr Pope accepts this as a possible reason. Dr Pope adds this might explain why the cuts are not as deep or made with as much strength as in the other cases. The murderer may have used his non-dominant hand.

21/04/04
10:00 p.m.: The book club was on today. Myles talked about the importance of colour in *Ulysses*, saying that colours are very rarely present in *Ulysses*, and one must make full use of them when they are given in a description. The others agreed. The seedy guy, self-absorbed as usual, left the room and hit Carl with this rucksack. Carl complained and took off his coat, revealing a big bandage around his right bicep. Peter asked him if he was okay and he said that he was, but that he got cut around ten nights ago and it was a bit painful. Peter asked casually if it had been a crazy Gibraltarian monkey with a razorblade and Carl found that quite funny. Carl answered that he must have been quite drunk because he did not remember it properly, saying that he remembered being on the bus driving around the city centre and a guy stumbling across the aisle of the bus with a broken bike rim, cutting him as he walked past. He only realised when he woke up at night after leaning on his wound. Myles explained that Carl is clumsy and prone to accidents, as he had another bad cut on the arm from walking by the Children's Hospital also around ten days ago. Peter laughed it off. Carl smiled and admitted that he had been worse in the last few weeks. Lastly, Peter asked if it was infected, as an old and broken bike rim would have most likely been dirty. Carl looked confused and explained that it was a very clean cut and that it was not infected. Carl believes it could be due to the fact that his flatmate is a doctor and he bandaged it shortly after. Diagnosis: The book club has been interesting tonight.

21/04/04
10:10 p.m.: Dr Pope's phone rings. He picks it up and is happy to hear his friend's voice. Peter reports on the book club to Dr Pope. Peter

has found out that Carl met Myles at another James Joyce book club at Loughborough University. Peter has met other teachers who know Carl. One of them is an English teacher, who has repeatedly stated that he has Native American blood in him.

22/04/04
10:00 p.m.: Dr Pope answers the phone. Peter skips the formalities and talks about Carl. He has been thinking about him. Peter tells Dr Pope about the cut on the bicep. Peter admits it does not mean he is guilty of a crime for having sustained an injury to his arm around the time of the last murder but he says it is the only connection he has found so far between the James Joyce book club and the murders. Peter also explains Carl's previous cut by the Children's Hospital. Dr Pope asks for further details. Actions arising from the conversation: Dr Pope to check reports on the last two murders.

22/04/04
10:00 p.m.: Carl comes out of the shower. His right arm is wrapped in clingfilm and he walks to his room, leaving 10 ml water splashes on the carpet. He is curious to see how his wound is healing and removes the white bandage. He is thinking about Peter's question. His wound is clean, considering the bike rim may have had bacteria on it. It seems to be healing well, so he covers it again and proceeds to brush his teeth.

22/04/04
10:00 p.m.: Penelope walks into her apartment. She leans against the door and drops her bag on the floor, running her hands through her hair. She takes off her shoes and enters the kitchen, where she sits down after filling a white mug with water. She gulps it down, some of the water spills over the side and lands on her white shirt, just above her belt. She finishes the water and looks through her window for a few seconds, thinking that he is not a bad guy. At the same time, she admits that the whole thing is getting a bit too intense and she is not sure if she can see herself with him long term.
23/04/04
10:00 p.m.: Carl is changing his bandage. He unwraps it and removes the white plaster that is covering the wound. It is looking much better

and there are no signs of infection. Carl is relieved. He dabs 10 ml of alcohol onto it to ensure it is clean and examines it for a second, thinking he has been quite lucky after all. That guy's bike rim could have made a much messier cut. He is also happy that Charles bandaged it straight away. He remembers Charles waking him, explaining he had been shouting in his sleep. It was then that Carl felt the pain in his arm. Charles took a look at it and bandaged it straight away. However, Carl did not remember which shirt he had worn that day. He had gone through his clothes a few times looking for a shirt with a cut in the upper right sleeve, but he did not find it.

23/04/04

10:10 p.m.: It has been another long day at work and Penelope is leaving her office when her phone rings. She looks at the screen to see who is calling and returns her phone to her pocket. She continues walking towards University Station and sees Monarch Hospital standing behind it. The reflection of the moonlight gives the hospital a ghostly white colour, similar to the one of those white Andalusian villages where every person has at least a son or daughter living away and the only noise that can be heard occurs when their grandchildren are begrudgingly brought to the village during the holidays. Penelope's phone rings again. She looks at the screen, breathes in deeply and answers the phone. She starts the conversation saying that she really wanted to meet up, but that it has been a long day. After hanging up, she thinks about how she really should break up with him at some point.

24/04/04

10:00 p.m.: Carl's wound is looking better, but he wants to keep it covered for a few more days. He opens his drawer and realises he has run out of bandages. He searches the bathroom and finds the box where they keep paracetamol and other medical equipment, but there are no bandages. He looks through different drawers and in other parts of the house, but comes up empty handed. Carl thinks this is weird. The night he got cut, they had bandages and the one Charles used on him that night was the perfect size. Carl continues his search, but with no luck. He uses plasters instead and covers them with a white scarf that an Argentinian lady had given his grandmother. That lady had worn it for years during demonstrations as part of the 'Mothers of the Plaza de Mayo'. Carl thinks that in southern Europe, the difference between mothers and grandmothers is a blurry one. Carl sits down and waits for Charles to come home. Charles arrives and finds Carl agitated in the lounge pressing a cloth against his wound. Carl is rocking slightly, looking away from his wound and Charles attempts to calm him down. Carl says that he could not find anything to dress his wound and Charles looks for something better. The bandage does not look great, but Carl is happy enough with it. Carl asks for the same bandage as last time, but Charles explains there are none left. Carl asks where Charles had found the first one and Charles changes the topic.

### 25/04/04

10:00 p.m.: Charles' phone goes off. He recognises the caller and slides the phone back into his pocket. His father has called a few times already and he cannot ignore him much longer, so he takes a deep breath and answers the call before it goes to voicemail. Dr Pope is angry when Charles picks up and he threatens to hang up. Dr Pope calms down after that. Dr Pope asks how everything is going and Charles says that everything is fine. After a few seconds of silence, Dr Pope asks his son when he'd vacated his apartment. Charles denies it at first and then admits to having moved out a few weeks ago. Charles says that the interest rates have gone up and his mortgage repayments have increased substantially, so he rented his apartment out and moved into a cheaper house. Charles explains that he did not want his father to feel like he had to pay his mortgage. Dr Pope laughs and assures his son that wouldn't happen. Dr Pope explains a doctor's salary is enough to cover the mortgage. Dr Pope accuses Charles of having expensive tastes. Dr Pope says that is why Charles cannot afford his mortgage and his lifestyle. Charles feels angry, but does not say anything as he knows that his father is right. Dr Pope is not sure whether he is surprised, shocked or angry. Dr Pope admonishes Charles for not living within his means. Dr Pope is about to hang up when he asks if there is anything else that he should know. Charles remains quiet for a few seconds and simply says, 'no'. Dr Pope knows that Charles has been lying to his housemate about having to work long shifts, but he cannot say he knows he is living with Carl because of confidentiality issues. Dr Pope sighs and wishes his son good night.

26/04/04
10:00 p.m.: Penelope picks up the phone, dials a number and takes a deep breath, waiting for an answer. A patronising, arrogant and intense voice replies at the other end. Penelope asks the voice to stop and very confidently, says she does not wish to continue seeing him. The voice starts talking very fast before Penelope repeats her words, repeating that she wants to end the relationship. Penelope explains how she finds him too arrogant and condescending, and that she cannot continue seeing someone who thinks he is always right. The voice continues talking, at which point Penelope asks him to stop, saying that he is doing it again and that he always tells her what she is supposed to want in her life. With a firm voice, she says there is something else about him, that he can be a very distant person who seems to have a hidden agenda. She does not like that either. Calmly now, she says she really does not want to continue seeing him. She hangs up the phone, drinks 10 cl of water and sits down happily.

26/04/04
10:10 p.m.: Charles' phone goes off. It is his father. Charles does not want a second argument in one night. Charles tells his father he has just been dumped by his flatmate's colleague. He explains that his flatmate also likes the girl. He has had to lie to him on various occasions, telling him he was at work when he was with her. Dr Pope is too confused to say anything because Charles never opens up to him. Dr Pope tells his son not to worry, that a man of his position will not struggle to attract other worthy females. This sounds to Charles more like a phrase from a documentary than fatherly advice, but he takes it. Charles thanks his dad and continues making small talk until the conversation dies off. Treatment: a cup of tea and a few biscuits for Charles.

27/04/04
10:00 p.m.: Carl walks into his room without turning the lights on. As usual, he leaves his tablets in a white hospital tray 10 cm from the left

edge of the desk. The tray, shiny and curvy like a woman's hips, is one of the few things Carl owns that belonged to his mother. Carl lies on his bed in the foetal position and puts his left thumb into his mouth. He scratches the lower part of his stomach with this right hand and breathes heavily, like an ox working in the sun. He takes a white tub out of his pocket and throws a pill into his mouth. Carl starts stretching his legs. Ten minutes later, he hears a mother shouting at her kids next door and he scratches the lower part of his belly once more. He turns on the bedside lamp and a pale white light illuminates the room. He stretches his legs fully, kicking the bedside table and spilling 10 cl of water from a glass. He takes his thumb from his mouth. He takes another of his medicines and the mother next door shouts at her kids again. He scratches the lower part of his stomach and turns on the main light. A bright light floods the bedroom, looking like a white room in a hospital. Carl looks at the white tray and starts walking around his room, clumsily at first, like oxen defeated by the sun. After ten steps, Carl feels more stable and straightens. He feels like he has just been born again. He is ready to tackle life.

# A Dead Man's Ice Cream

# Chapter 15

## Circe plays us all

Carl was walking home when he saw a sign outside of the Jellyfish Strip Club, *£12 entry only tonight*. Carl continued along Suffolk Street Queensway, striding through the cold night. The weird tasting cheese and wine from dinner, combined with his medication, made his vision blurry. He walked with an extended arm to avoid bumping into anything. Carl bent his knees, forcing pressure through his thighs to climb the stairs leading into Post Central. His vision grew increasingly blurry as he went up the escalators. Someone, maybe the security guy patrolling Post Central at night, said something and Carl replied with a mumble. He stumbled past the Post Central restaurants until he came out of the building onto the canal side. He walked in a zigzag pattern, his ankles and Achilles tendons working overtime to maintain his balance. As if pulled by a magical force, he moved slowly towards the metal bridge connecting Post Central with the canal side parallel to Gas Street. His knees started to shake, and he stopped on the bridge, his ankles quivering and his feet pointing inwards. He turned his head, saw lights, and heard some noise, guessing it was Broad Street. 'It was all full of prostitutes, the Birmingham canals, Broad Street, all full of prostitutes, and their potential suitors were pushed along these streets by their locomotor apparatus on cruise control,' Carl said to himself with a slur. That's what he had always heard, that the pretty area of Post Central and Broad Street, where all those bars and clubs stand, used to be a safe haven for prostitutes. 'And the Bull Ring,' he shouted.

It didn't matter who you asked, everyone said the same thing about any pretty or trendy place in the city, 'It used to be full of prostitutes around here. They've done well cleaning this up. You still see some lost suitors every now and then looking for them around these streets.' Carl could suddenly hear the magical voice of his grandmother repeating what she had once said to him when he had asked her what prostitutes were, 'Unlucky women who have had a very tough life and who take up a really bad job to make things better.'

Carl dragged his feet along the metal bridge and passed a strip club called, 'Limb 12'. After repeated glances at it, Carl realised that both numbers were ones. He saw some shades moving in front of him and, because of the smell and the noise, he assumed they were workers from the club who had finished their night. One of the girls said something to him, but Carl couldn't speak. He looked at his knees and when he looked up, he found himself in his own room, muttering, 'Reality is a hallucination caused by a lack of alcohol in the blood.'

That night, Carl didn't sleep very well. He shook and rolled endlessly in his bed. He was jolted and sat up immediately when he thought he heard a noise. He was convinced one of the prostitutes he'd seen was standing in his room, talking to him about magic. Outside, he heard a bunch of her suitors cursing him in jealousy. With slurred speech, Carl explained a trick he'd seen once on television, but he fell asleep after the twelfth word. His dream was blurry, just like his most recent memories of life. He dreamt he was managing a brothel in Madrid, a very successful and up-market establishment frequented by Spanish politicians. All the money they stole from public accounts ended up being spent at his place. Carl couldn't see clearly in his dream. It was like the edges of his eyesight were of a colourless tone and people started getting blurrier by the minute. Suddenly, their bones moved their clumsy bodies around and they spoke in slow motion until the world stopped moving in his dream.

Carl's knees were shaking when he woke up the following morning. He sat on the side of his bed and tried to scratch his head but missed. He stood up, yawning, and dragged his feet along the carpet until he reached the bathroom. He washed his face and continued downstairs towards the kitchen. A thin film of liquid slid down his eyes, covering his vision with a curtain of cold water. It gave Carl an excuse to act like his usual, clumsy self. In the kitchen, his shaky hands attempted to make some simple breakfast, but he stopped when he heard a buzz in his ears. Wherever he turned his head, he saw a bright light at the top right side of his field of vision. He closed his eyes, counted for twelve seconds, and opened them again, but the bright light remained. He gave up, sat down, and ate his breakfast, rubbing toast against his cheek whenever he missed his mouth.

Carl's knees were a bit squeaky as he walked to Five Ways Station. It was twelve minutes past the hour when he stepped into the station. It was busy, like a brothel at full moon. Carl's vision was still blurry. He saw meaty lumps brushing past him as the soles of his shoes scratched the floor towards the platform. As he waited for the train to Edgbaston University, a woman offered him some company in exchange for coins. Carl didn't even register the offer. He was focusing on the goth standing on the opposite platform. With his long hair and the light make-up under his eyes, the man looked like a medieval sorcerer. Carl imagined the tall figure playing with fire and blood in centuries gone by, most likely surrounded by prostitutes to spice things up. Carl heard a noise over his right shoulder. His eyes were watery and assumed it was the train. He bent his elbow and moved his hand to clear his tears, saying to himself, 'I'm dreaming a dream.'

The metallic cage started to move and Carl waddled until he found a seat, using his hands to check that it was empty. The canal water to his right was of a bright unspecific colour and the current seemed to be transporting debris along its surface. Some feathery animals, which Carl guessed to be a raft of ducks, swam around the floating dirt. The birds moved their lower limbs to advance in the water and their upper ones to keep the balance, in a coordinated fashion that Carl was unable to understand. The floating debris reminded Carl of the most supernatural event in Gibraltar, back in the late 1970s, which would come to be known in Gibraltar as *el milagro argentino*.

> It was midnight of a summer's night in the late 1970s when twelve teenagers were having a swim at Eastern beach in Gibraltar after a few drinks. It was dark and something touched one of the kids' legs. He was scared because he thought it was a *Leopold* bloom of jellyfish, but then he thought it might be a

kind of fish. It touched another kid's leg seconds later. Suddenly, a shooting star soared above them, illuminating the water and revealing a human body floating in the water. The kids screamed and started to swim back to the shore when one of them got his arm wrapped around the body's shirt, forcing him to drag the body to shore. It was dark and the adrenaline made the kids walk more steadily. One of the kids ran home to tell his father, who was a policeman, and soon enough the authorities arrived.

The police examined the body and found a tattoo on the right arm. The tattoo was of the person's name and address, together with details of his closest family members. A line at the bottom said, *Por si me desaparecen, como a muchos otros.* The official report translated the tattoo into, 'In case they *disappear* me, as they've done with many others.'

The police took the body to the main police station in Gibraltar. In Argentina, the dictatorship had been accused of *disappearing* people who were against the regime. Rumours circulated concerning the throwing of bodies weighted down with stones into the Atlantic Ocean in an effort to save money in disposal, and to make it more difficult for people to be discovered. The investigation of the man's body discovered by the kids revealed that the corpse had drifted with the currents 12,000 km northeast to the Gibraltar shoreline. That alone was enough to deem this a miracle, but what made this an Argentinian miracle was what happened twelve days later.

An Argentinian lady was transported to the United Kingdom as a refugee. She was fleeing Argentina as she was being prosecuted for her involvement in the movement of the Mothers of Plaza de Mayo, a group of women pressing the government for information on their *disappeared* children. The ship on which she was being transported docked in Gibraltar and a Gibraltarian officer noticed the lady's name. He had a vague memory of having heard it before, and then he remembered. His neighbour, who was dating the son of a policeman, had told him about the body from the beach. The officer told his supervisor, who was somewhat sceptical. He did not believe the story and the officer didn't think much more of it.

A few hours later, the Argentinian lady found a piece of paper on her way to the toilet. The paper was outside an office next to where she had been staying and when she read it, she saw they had all of her details and her son's details. The lady grew angry, enquiring as to why they were pursuing her son, telling the officers that they were wasting their time as her son had been taken by the dictatorship. Suddenly, a gust of wind blew and a folder with her son's file flew to a desk opposite her. The wind moved the first few pages, and the lady shouted when she caught a glimpse of the photo of the tattoo. The officers in the room told her about the body and the lady cried, knowing her son's body had been returned to her.

A bubble of surrealism tinted that night. The mother's desire to be reunited with her son unchained a series of magical coincidences. Since then, the expression *Argentinian miracle* had been used in Gibraltar to describe something truly amazing made possible. The Argentinian lady stayed in Gibraltar, where she buried her son. She became good friends with Carl's grandmother, and she gave her a white scarf she'd worn during her protests at Plaza de Mayo in Buenos Aires. It became a symbol of hope for the Argentinian lady, but she no longer needed it. Somehow, she thought her friend might need it more when she thought of what would happen to her friend's grandson once she was gone. Still to this day, Carl feels that the white scarf has magical, protective powers.

'Something like this has happened before at least once,' said Carl to himself. 'It happened when Columbus was in Madeira and some locals told him that a magical tide had brought a dead man with a wide face to the shores, together with some canes and tree branches never seen before. Another local made Columbus think there was an island across the sea. But the Argentinian miracle was different.' Carl mumbled 'Argentinian miracle,' noting the English translation didn't accurately reflect the magic of the Spanish expression, like many other untranslatable expressions in the world. The metal cage stopped moving at University Station and Carl dragged himself from it. He was pushed by lumps of meat trying to escape. He bent his knees and his thighs contracted to propel him up the stairs. He felt like the mass of meat below his waist carried him, moving him like cattle on the way to a slaughterhouse. He came out of the station, turned left, and walked into a metallic fence in a haze, realising that his walk to the office would be a struggle. He dragged his feet on the tarmac when a brisk noise on his right grabbed his attention. There was a metallic rectangle stopped on the road, standing on four circles. The guy inside shouted something at him. Carl just continued until he reached the other side of the road.

Carl felt nervous and looked at his shaky feet. He lifted his head and found he was no longer in Birmingham, but in a town 12,000 miles southeast from there. A big metallic rectangle came up the street and stopped outside the train station. Carl bent his unsteady knees and got in it. The person sitting behind the wheel said something to him and told him to come in quickly. Carl stepped inside without paying, just like everyone else. The vehicle started moving up Crown Street, turning right after Wollongong Hospital, and then took the first exit at the roundabout into Mercury St. There, Carl saw some bright-coloured flowers outside of a bowling court. The vehicle passed a dry cleaners on the left and meandered over a few roundabouts. Carl dragged his body down the vehicle outside an Australian university with an Aboriginal name. He blinked a few times and found himself outside of the Ashley building at the University of Edgbaston.

Carl stumbled across the cylindric building and turned right into the Language Office. Someone was putting some paper on top of a large plastic box, and the lights it emitted hurt Carl's eyes. He mumbled a greeting and went to his corner. Someone put their hand on his shoulder. Carl didn't notice which one and he didn't hear a question. On autopilot, he said, 'Okay.' He opened his emails and all he could see were lights shooting from the screen, a whole mixture of colours. A piece of paper landed on his desk. He could read that a bit better, so he printed his emails using a large font, and did his work sheepishly in a corner trying not to be seen. The day dragged on, but before he knew it, he was dragging his feet out of work again. Something in his pocket started vibrating. He grabbed it and saw a name on the screen;

however, it was blurry and he couldn't read it very well. He answered the phone and the caller identified herself. It was Dr Pope's secretary reminding Carl of his appointment after work. Carl said thanks and hung up. His day was far from over.

\* \* \*

Carl dumped his own body on the couch at Dr Pope's office and leaned against the backrest. He extended himself fully, as he usually did, and started to answer Dr Pope's questions.

'Yes, sir, I have been much sleepier than usual,' replied Carl, 'to the point where I feel sleepy during the day, as if I have no control of my body. I feel very weak, and I find myself confused all the time. Simple tasks like walking or going upstairs have become very hard. Also, I've felt like I've had loads of out of body experiences. I feel like when I'm doing stuff, I can see myself from outside of my body. I'm really not sleeping well at night, and I feel like that could be why I've been so tired during the day. I go to bed early most nights, but I've been having sinister dreams lately. I wake up as if I hadn't slept at all.'

Dr Pope made sure his voice recorder was capturing the conversation. 'Thanks for that, Carl,' said Dr Pope in a calming voice. 'Tell me a bit more about those dreams, Carl.'

'They're quite sinister dreams as I said, and someone always dies in them, but the weird thing is I always dream them as if I was having an out of body experience.'

'Carl, please, go on,' said Dr Pope.

'It is weird,' explained Carl, 'because I dream of these faces I think I have seen before. The dreams are so disturbing. In one of them, I was walking around a school in Edgbaston. I found a person, killed him and left the body by a school, and I went back to the main road. The person had brown, thick shoelaces and I liked them, so I took one with me.'

Dr Pope froze for a few seconds, remembering what he had read in a police report a few months earlier. 'Yes, Carl, that does sound like a scary dream,' replied Dr Pope, while writing in his notebook. He calmed himself down and swallowed some saliva before continuing with his questions. 'Any other dreams like this?'

'Yeah,' continued Carl. 'I've also dreamt that I was walking around Edgbaston University and a girl started talking to me about some literary analysis she had been doing in class. I continue to have flashes of her green dress. Anyway, she followed me and next thing I know I've killed her, so I ran away.'

'Yes, that's a weird dream, Carl. Have you had any more dreams like those?' asked Dr Pope.

'I've been having one of those a night for the last couple of weeks. It's hard to remember all of them.'

'Of course it is, just do what you can,' said Dr Pope in an encouraging voice.

'There is a dream I've had twice. I am walking to Selly Oak Station and a girl painted in orange and dressed up like a nymph comes out of a house. She starts talking to me about economics. She says her kidney hurts and gives it to me as she faints.'

Dr Pope paused again. He adjusted his posture as he scribbled down his thoughts and focused on his breathing. 'Okay. What did you do with the kidney, Carl?'

'I actually can't remember, but I remember feeling very bad when I woke up because she had asked me to look after it and I couldn't remember where I'd left it.'

'Well, Carl, I can tell you that I'd also feel bad if a girl gave me her kidney and I lost it. Let me take a few notes before we continue.' Dr Pope jotted something down in his pad and stopped the voice recorder for a second to make sure everything had been recorded. He started a new track, just in case something happened to the voice recorder later on. 'Any other dreams, Carl?'

'Yes, a few more. Some are a bit blurrier than others. This one was particularly weird,' explained Carl. 'I was walking around the Botanical Gardens in Edgbaston when I felt the urge to urinate. I walked around the streets but couldn't find anywhere to go. Every single spot was too exposed. Anyway, I found the main door of the Botanical Gardens, but it was closed, so I tried to open it a few times, but I couldn't manage to, so in the end, I decided to go to the back of the building behind the carpark. I started urinating on some plants when this very drunk guy positions himself next to me. He mumbles something that I can't understand. Then I realise that some urine is hitting my shoes.

I look at him, but the urine is coming from the floor. His penis had fallen off and it was pissing on me from the ground. I told him about it, but he was too drunk to care. He just said he had a flying penis and that it did that at times, and that it sometimes went flying by itself at twelve o'clock, moving its pubes in the air like gentle wings to fly to different brothels. He said that this put him at an advantage over other potential suitors. He went on to say his penis had magical connections with some of the Birmingham prostitutes and that was why they spent some time apart every now and then. So, I gave up. I just left him there standing with his penis peeing from the floor.'

Dr Pope ran his left hand over his forehead, making notes and recording the session. 'Thanks for that, Carl. Could you please tell me about more of those dreams?'

'Yes, sure, just give me a bit more of time to think.'

'Would you like a short break?' asked Dr Pope.

'No, it's okay, thank you. I'm trying to think of more, as I'm sure there are a few dreams I haven't told you about yet.'

Carl thought for twelve seconds, his eyes moving in different directions and then, after a short cough, he went on. 'There was another dream that stuck with me mainly because I was using my left hand throughout. I was having lunch using my left hand, and texting with my left hand later on as well, and I remember finding that a bit awkward. Then, I remember wandering around the streets when a woman approached me and talked to me about her son. Unexpectedly, and quite startlingly, I find I've stolen a knife from the place where I'd had lunch. It was covered in blood from my lunch. She said something else, and I pushed the knife right into her. The blood started gushing like a fountain. She moved away from me with a slight rotation. She looked like a sprinkler and then I left.'

'It's okay, Carl,' said Dr Pope said. 'It is normal to have some violent dreams every now and again. They're a natural way of coping with stress and a way of letting bad feelings out. Could you please tell me about any other dreams like those, please?'

'Yes, there's a last one. I was walking around a concert place in one of my dreams and I saw a barmaid come out crying and a guy shouting at her. She ran away and the guy walked off. For some reason, I felt as if I was tied to this guy, and I could only follow him. At first, I was embarrassed, and I didn't want him to see me, although he did see me in the end. Suddenly, I saw myself in his house. I sat in one corner as he recorded music in his home studio. The guy then turned around and gave me abuse. I didn't even apologise for following him into his house. Instead, I asked him to play some songs for me. He got more and more aggressive, and I discovered two letter openers in my pocket. I took them out, one in each hand, and I chopped his ears off. I felt a bit bad for what I had done, and I heard a familiar voice say to me something like, *Now you get the SD cards from the other guy and put them in his eardrums. He'll be fine with that.* I remember asking the voice who it was and then I woke up because my flatmate had broken a shelf in the bathroom.'

'Thanks for that.' Dr Pope saved the recorded conversation and pressed record once again to make sure that, if something happened, the previous conversation was safe. 'And what about that voice? Have you heard it before?'

'Yes,' answered Carl. 'I have heard it in other dreams. I am sure I know that voice from somewhere, but I can never identify it.'

'Hmm… and do you recall any other dreams where that voice talks to you?' asked Dr Pope.

'Yes, I do. I remember I had a dream that I was walking in circles, and I saw a guy next to me doing the same. The guy looked at me and talked to me with the same voice I had heard in my other dreams, and then the voice seemed to come from my head. I suddenly had a big stone in my hand and his eyes were glued to it. I heard the voice again and then I woke up as a door slammed in my house.'

'It seems like we have a pattern here, Carl. Do you remember waking up in many of those dreams? I mean, with hearing the voice you recognise and then with a noise in the house?'

'In a couple of them, yes,' replied Carl. 'I know I have heard that voice somewhere and I just can't remember where. It's a very familiar voice.'

'Is it a male or a female voice?' asked Dr Pope.

'I don't know. It's a bit weird because I hear the voice, I hear the instructions, and I feel relieved when I hear it as I know it's a friendly voice, but I can't pinpoint any details about it,' explained Carl.

'So, you hear the voice, but you can't tell whether it's a male or a female one?'

'Yes,' replied Carl. 'I know it must sound very weird, but it's a bit like when I dream. I know what happened and I remember what some people say to me, but I can't remember whether the people were talking to me in Spanish or in English. The same as when I remember a story or a fact that I was told, but I can't remember if they told me in Spanish or in English. It's like my brain just processes the information, not the form.'

'Thank you very much for that, Carl. I'll tell you what. We'll be done soon, just relax here for another couple of minutes while I look through my previous notes and come up with a plan to tackle these dreams.'

Dr Pope's feet were stuck to the floor. Lifting them, then bending the knee, and moving them forward before repeating the action was a great effort. His steps were much shorter than usual. He felt like life was shaking in a very slow motion. His back crouched, following the rhythm of his confused feet. His ankles weren't rigid enough to keep his feet from quivering while his feet were mid-air. His knees clattered, as they hit each other. His hips shook while his body stood on one leg. His physical clumsiness was being matched by his mental one. After twelve little magical steps, he was at the other end of his office. He took a piece of paper from his desk, but it was so bright he couldn't look at it. His neck twisted and his cheeks pulled at the sides of his mouth to create an awkward smile for Carl. Dr Pope's confusion made him shake, rocking his upper body from side to side like a pendulum. And then, like a magical intervention, Carl asked for the toilet, giving Dr Pope the time he needed to think.

Dr Pope grabbed his phone and moved his thumbs, pressing keys before reading a text he had received from Inspector Reilly informing him of a new victim. It was a strip dancer found by a brothel. Dr Pope put his phone down as his breathing rate increased. His knees shook as he walked to his desk. He pulled open the top drawer, feeling safer when he found an envelope containing a scalpel. He retrieved the memory card from his voice recorder and put it in the drawer before replacing it with a new card. His index finger pressed record again and he placed the recorder underneath his desk. Dr Pope sat, with this locomotor apparatus resting, and waited for Carl to return.

To Carl, Dudley Road Hospital was just like Circe's mansion in the middle of a clear patch of busy Birmingham. Slowly, Carl walked back into the room, with an expressionless face which worried Dr Pope. There were bright lights hitting Carl's eyes from every angle. He heard steps around him where twelve prostitutes in bright dresses were walking in circles.

By pure coincidence, a person walking in the corridor made enough noise dragging their feet that Carl didn't hear Dr Pope's phone vibrate. Dr Pope didn't want to do anything to worry Carl, but he needed to extend his arm and straighten his elbow to reach the phone. Suddenly, Carl asked for a tissue, lending Dr Pope the perfect chance to check his phone's screen while looking for tissues. Dr Pope dropped his phone, which fell screen up. It was reflected on his metallic bin and the message calmed him. He grabbed a package of tissues and handed them to Carl, who was still confused after his session and was awkwardly quiet. Dr Pope said that everything was going to be okay and told Carl he was free to go if he wanted. Carl thanked Dr Pope and used his forearms to get up.

The light through the window guided Carl out and he dragged his feet. He continued along the corridor to the Accident and Emergency Department. Twelve prostitutes discussed their eventful night and stared at Carl's ghostly presence. Carl felt lost and his locomotor apparatus was stuck with no direction to go. He turned in circles believing a fairy was manipulating him with her magic wand. One of the lights in a room in the Accident and Emergency Department flickered. The shadows it projected pointed Carl towards the exit, and he dragged his feet in that direction, confused. That night seemed like more of a dream than the dreams he had been sharing with Dr Pope. He continued down the street, passing a brothel on his right. Outside, there was dancing in the streets, and he saw the spirits of twelve women who had betrayed their lady with her suitors. Circe herself was standing behind the spirits, holding a block of cheese and a bottle of wine that looked familiar. She blew kisses at Carl and laughed about his inability to control his own life.

# Chapter 16

## No shelter for the vulnerable

Once upon a time, and a good time it was, two old Greek washerwomen were walking in the streets of Birmingham after their night shift at the hospital laundry. 'You may not know this, Pythia, but once there were some snails on the road,' started explaining Delphi. 'They were agitated and scared until they saw a gentle shadow walking towards them. The snails told him their problem and the man suggested they live safely inside of him. They jumped and slid under his skin. Those snails are living there still, tickling his skin from the inside, which is why Carl is nervous to this day.'

'I didn't know that, Delphi,' said Pythia. 'But I know that's proof that fate and the gods always have plans for us, although it's up to us to deviate from them. I also know that when society turns its back on someone, it's very difficult, even for the greatest heroes, to succeed in their deeds. The stars that guide sailors have told me this, and the gods have confirmed it.'

\* \* \*

At one o'clock in the morning, a man's shadow emerged from the dark night to follow the stars and spirits that inhabited our land before humans looked as they do today. The owner of the shadow sat inside of a bus shelter and listened to the silence, breathing to calm his nerves, as he tried to forget the turmoil created by Penelope's suitors in the pub, a crew of drunken sailors who had been arguing with his Friday Club friends. Carl, the shadow's owner, had been dragging his heavy feet along the streets, his track on the road leaving some deep marks, and that was how the first road of Birmingham was created.

Carl felt something on his thigh and heard a hiss
Maybe a snake with a sound you cannot miss
It wasn't that
It wasn't a cat
It was just a bit of piss

The flow of warm piss made Carl remember an old legend about how humans learned to use metal. A young warrior had been an outcast from his tribe. He had been walking for one day when he saw a huge animal with a splinter in its foot. The warrior's first instinct was to run, but after having had many people in his village laughing at him, he decided to face the animal. The animal didn't attack him. Instead, it showed the young warrior his foot with the splinter inside. The young warrior used his wooden spear to get the splinter out, but his spear broke. The warrior felt sad and said to the animal, 'Before I met you, I was a useless warrior with a spear I didn't know how to use, and now I am a useless warrior with no weapon at all. I can't call myself a warrior anymore.' The animal asked the warrior to start a fire. The animal gave him a few rocks and asked him to put them on the fire. One hot stone had a thin line inside of it. The rocks started to melt, creating a spear of an unknown material. He used the spear to take the splinter out of the animal's foot and ran back to the village, taking with him his new weapon made of metal and his new knowledge, which made the people in the village choose him as their new leader.

A time in the past when everything was grey
A man came out, during his busy day
He used his hammer
And in a cool manner
Built the shelter where Carl is today

Carl sat inside the shelter, his nerves overreacting to all kinds of insignificant stimuli, and he did not feel safe. A flickering star appears as if it might fall from the sky. It was weak. It was losing intensity and it looked powerless out there, so far from the other stars. This could have been one of those stars that old civilisations used to navigate in new waters, but its time was over. Carl had once heard someone say that souls fly up to the sky and become stars. If people go to the sky and become stars when they die, where do stars go when their time ends? What do they become when they die? Carl was still shaky, and the bus shelter shook with the wind. Winds from every direction except west had taken Carl to the shelter, and now this flimsy construction could not offer him any protection. Looking at the star, he thought that both the Mayans and the Aztecs must have seen something similar when they had predicted their end, their apocalypse. Carl was scared, but he didn't know what of. In an attempt to lift his own spirits, Carl mumbled a limerick his grandmother had created about a navy officer's daughter Carl used to like at school.

> Little miss Yeo played with sweet Carl today
> She made him happy, and he forgot his dismay
> He never sheds tears
> When he hears her cheers
> And she'll make him smile until the sea takes her away

Bright lights pointed at Carl from different angles and they grew more intense as Carl became more nervous. He covered his eyes to protect them. A police car approached and a policeman shouted at Carl. 'Stay where you are. Could you identify yourself, sir?' asked the voice from the car.

'My name's Carl.'

The police officer stepped from his car and asked Carl to present some ID. Carl looked down while he was reaching in his pocket and did not process anything until he found himself handcuffed in the back of the car and on his way to the police station.

The police car moved graciously through the streets of Birmingham as it was rocked by the mild wind. The policemen navigated the sea of roads as proud as the ancient sailors after they'd left their people to discover new lands, determined to advance their civilisation, as uncivilised as this one might have been. The wind, the bumps on the roads, and the swerving of the captain in the car continued to rock the four-wheeled vessel. The prow rose and fell with the wavy road. At the poop of the car, Carl remained gripped by his nerves. After Hurst Street, the car turned to the port with the poop of the ship rocking heavily. The first mate rang his official and informed him that they would drop anchor outside of the station in one minute.

> Carl calmed down with the rocking of the poop of the car
> He kind of knew they hadn't travelled far
> But an officer called Tim
> Was quick to suggest him
> To start praying hard to his lucky star

The car rocked to a stop outside of the police station. Its shock absorbers made the car sway from side to side, like a ship anchored in a harbour before a storm. The officers took Carl from the cabin and dragged him inside. Unaware of what was about to happen, Carl looked at the lights in the corridors, flickering like dying stars. The car crew entered a big room, full of police standing in a circle, looking proud in their uniforms and viewing Carl as a different type of human to them. Certainly, one of a lower evolutionary branch. A savage. Carl positioned himself under the lowest light in the middle of the room. It seemed to lose intensity second by second, flickering out of nervousness. Carl looked around him, feeling judged for a reason he did not understand. He was observed as if he was a rare specimen they had been desperate to see. This was how he had always pictured the moment when Columbus brought the first American Indians to Seville and showed them to the crowds, who judged those defenceless people for uncommitted crimes. They were brought from the New World as a display, or for whatever the Spanish monarchs saw fit. The crowd's job was to ensure the American Indians were seen as inferior so that the crimes to be committed in the years to come could be justified. People have always feared differences and, throughout human history, highlighting differences has always proved to be the most effective way to justify injustice. Any act of cruelty can be executed without remorse if it can be justified. It is a very dangerous weapon. Looking around at the circle, Carl understood he needed to be worried. Across the room, an officer called Bartholomew Houses looked at him pitifully.

The crowd of policemen gathered around Carl. They had heard a lot about him. All that expectation, together with the fact his crimes showed he was soulless, made them look at him as if he was an exotic animal. The cops in their hats looked like a group of domesticated sailors. Their leader, in a bigger hat than the rest, grabbed Carl by his arm and dragged him along one of the corridors.

Carl followed while the man with the big hat pulled him by the arm, grabbing his arm tighter as they passed several closed doors. Carl wanted to ask him to stop but surprisingly, Carl understood it wasn't the best thing to say. Carl was taken to a room with no windows and no decorations. He was left alone. He didn't know what he was doing there. Carl was shaky, his hands rubbing against the desk and his elbows rocked back and forth. As he was sitting on the chair, he thought about the concept of a chair itself. 'In Western culture, we designed chairs to be comfortable, and then stools to go to bars, and all of this elevates us and disconnects us from Mother Earth. I like how some tribes can't understand why people would choose to create an object that would separate them from Manitou.'

The door opened a minute after Carl started to feel awkward. One person came in. Carl continued feeling nervous. This man stood there, grinding his top teeth against his bottom ones. The man navigated around the room, using the lights to guide him to the best place to sit. The man sat to Carl's one o'clock and when he put his arms on the table, Carl read his name badge, *Eumaneus*. Carl thought he looked like a Greek sailor, but he was sure that this name meant *four dogs as savage as wild beasts* in an African language. Suddenly, it all hit Carl. Being unaware of social rules with an unrefined ability to read other people's moods, Carl finally realised something was incredibly wrong. Looking into those lightbulbs flickering in the ceiling made him feel like an ancient civilisation waiting for the apocalypse to happen.

Carl rocked his head back and forth, forth and back, and mumbled something. The man in the big hat bent towards him as he thought he was hearing a confession. Instead, he heard Carl utter, 'If my voice died inland, take her to sea level. Take her to sea level, and make her captain.

Make her captain, of and old... currach, galleon, battleship…, just make her captain of something.'

> Carl looks at his hands as they both shake
> Like when Kazim pissed on Charles's cake
> Silence broke out
> He had no doubt
> This had to be a mistake

The policeman removed his sailor-like looking hat and left it by his side. He stopped grinding his teeth and remained quiet. It was tense. No one said anything. Their breathing was quiet and even the chairs had stopped squeaking. No coughing, no tapping, no nothing, just silence. The moment came for one of those two men to break the silence. The policeman coughed to clear his throat, breathed heavily before speaking.

'All patients have the right to confidentiality. However, doctors have a duty to disclose certain information if deemed appropriate in the interest of public safety,' explained the officer. 'In your last session with your psychiatrist, Dr Pope, you talked to him about what you called a series of dreams you've had lately. Now, the problem is that those dreams, and the details you've given about them, match a number of murders we've had in different parts of Birmingham lately. You are currently under arrest as the main suspect of the Birmingham case.'

Carl was silent. He was shocked, scared of talking. He finally gathered the courage to speak. 'I haven't hurt anyone,' said Carl in a childish voice. 'I have had some bad dreams, but I haven't done anything.' If Carl had been born a few years later, his mental condition would have been diagnosed properly. He would have had support throughout his schooling, and he would be testifying now with a forensic psychologist by his side.

'The details of your dreams not only match secret information we have on file about these murders, but they also contain aspects we had not realised. Some of our staff inspected the evidence as soon as Dr Pope rang us and they found a perfect match with what you had revealed during your session with him,' said the policeman. 'You can deny it and we'll find out with a simple blood and DNA analysis, or you can collaborate. Tell us all about it and if there were any other victims we haven't found yet.'

> In none of the scenes had they found DNA
> That's why the officer simply couldn't say
> That it was a bluff
> And that there wasn't enough
> Evidence for Carl to go to jail that day

Carl looked down at his hands wondering if they could have hurt anyone. To his head came memories of his youth trying to play with schoolmates in the playground. His uncoordinated hands and feet weren't the most popular ones in the playground when being chosen for the teams. He was always picked second last, just before Saul, an intelligent kid with glasses, but with a weak left side of his body due to cerebral palsy. Saul was always picked first when it came to choosing a partner for a school project. He was always described as *un tío mu listo, illo*. Carl always thought it was fair that Saul was chosen first for schoolwork and last for sport. It was a display of his strengths and weaknesses. Carl, on the other hand, was chosen second from last in sport and last for schoolwork, unless a new foreign kid with no English had recently joined their class. Carl looked at his hands again, lifting them into the air and said to the policeman, 'My hands lack the coordination needed to kill people.'

The policeman got angry. He stood up and ran his right hand over his face. 'I'm going to ask you straight and I want a straight answer. How many people have you killed?' asked the policeman.

'None,' replied Carl after thinking about it.

'I'm going to ask you again. How many people have you killed?' repeated the policeman.

'None,' replied Carl again. 'I haven't killed anyone. I had some really awful dreams about killing people and I told Dr Pope about them, but that's it.'

'So how do you explain that some of the details in your dreams match the details of some murders with such precision?'

'I don't know. Maybe it's just pure chance,' said Carl naively.

'Pure chance, you say!' shouted the policeman. 'How do you explain this coincidence then?'

'A coincidence can't be explained. It just happens. That's what makes it a coincidence,' replied Carl.

'It's not the time to be clever,' shouted the policeman, punching the table.

'I'm not being clever, sir. I'm just being myself. I have Asperger's with a touch of autism, or so I've been told,' said Carl. 'But it's not all bad. My grandmother told me it was only a matter of time until a global pandemic breaks out and people stop shaking hands. They'll just tap elbows or something instead. They'll introduce social distancing protocols and people will feel awkward interacting with people they don't know. I'll have a head start and start feeling more normal then.'

The policeman examined Carl through narrow eyes and shook his head slowly from port side to starboard. He walked in circles around the interrogation room before sitting opposite Carl and asking him again, 'How many people have you killed?'

'I haven't killed anyone,' replied Carl.

'I have listened to the recording of your session with Dr Pope. Could you please describe any of the victims in your dream?'

Carl describes one of the men he had seen
He was wearing black and green
and had a small willy.
His voice made him sound silly
and had brown boots which were clean

'Okay, Carl. Could you also describe how you left the man lying on the floor in your dream?'

The policeman retrieved an envelope from his pocket. He opened it and flicked through the photos. He selected one and threw it in front of Carl, as a sailor might throw a card during a game in a tavern. Carl looked at the photo. He was shocked. He stared into the photo for one second and put it down.

'How could that be?' asked Carl. 'That photo. It looks just like the guy in my dream.'

'So, what happened?' asked the policeman as Carl started crying. 'Tell us what you've done, Carl. We want to help you.'

'I haven't done anything,' replied Carl, 'but I've just remembered two more dreams I didn't reveal to Dr Pope. I wasn't trying to hide anything. They've just come to my mind.'

'Okay, Carl. Tell me about them.'

'One of them was a young girl who looked like a prostitute. I have images of her having hallucinations and dragging her feet away from a brothel. The other one was an old guy, with one of those sailor jumpers with the bulky collars. He smoked a pipe. He just looked like Hemingway. He was shivering before crumbling next to his boat by the canal, near Brindley Place bus shelter. I don't know how I didn't remember these two cruel images before when I was talking to Dr Pope. I'm Sorry.'

\* \* \*

Eumaneus left and met with Dr Pope and Inspector Reilly outside of the interrogation room for a handover. Inspector Reilly believed Carl was behind the murders, but that he didn't want to admit to himself what he had done. However, Inspector Reilly had had the cameras of the Botanical Garden checked and there was no trace of Carl. It made him think something else was going on. Dr Pope wasn't sure about the case. Carl was clumsy and not particularly strong, and all of the murders had been thoroughly planned. Dr Pope wasn't convinced Carl was capable unless he had an accomplice.

Dr Pope wandered around the corridor, agitated, swirling like a ship in the middle of the storm. He opened his mouth a few times but failed to utter a word until he finally burst, 'He just lacks the social skills to pull all this out. He just does not have the mental acuity and social wherewithal to plan and commit the murders and then act normally the following day at work.'

'Well, Dr Pope, judging by his reports, it doesn't look like he was the most normal guy at work. I'll tell you what, let's sit together and see what we have on this case,' suggested Inspector Reilly.

Dr Pope and Inspector Reilly walked into an office with a bunch of documents and some watered-down coffee. Dr Pope sat in silence for a few minutes and then stood up. He had a piece of paper in his hand and started shaking it, bringing it to his face to scratch it. He looked thoughtful, agitated, and defeated. He finally threw it in front of Inspector Reilly. 'Read this. Look at the conclusions,' said Dr Pope. 'My friend Peter summarised the main findings in his report very well. The words and accent used by the victim to connect with the murderer are from southwestern Spain and Carl's from Gibraltar where they have that accent,' added Dr Pope. 'I'm not a linguist, but Charles spent a year there when he was in the army, and my wife and I went to visit him. I clearly remember that strong singsong intonation to their voices. For me, however, the most important bit of the report is that the victim seemed to know the murderer. Judging by the gaps in the audio and due to some linguistic phenomena, Peter is sure the murderer's name starts with a *k* sound.'

'So, that's it. We have him,' said Inspector Reilly. Dr Pope nodded as he looked through a window. Eumaneus knocked on the door and entered without waiting for permission. He said that another body had been found. It was an old sailor with Parkinson's who lived in a narrow boat in a Birmingham canal, not far from Brindley Place. 'This matches one of the last two dreams Carl described earlier,' said Eumaneus.

Dr Pope had all he needed to be convinced that Carl was the murderer, but he still had to move past his own reservations and gut feeling. Dr Pope continued to dwell on the case, about how weird it was that everything had developed so quickly, but if Carl was the killer, why was he telling them this now? He considered it and studied the photos from the file while listening to Carl's recordings. Everything fit. Every detail was exactly as shown in the photos. Details that only someone who had been there would know. Dr Pope continued thinking about the photos, about the victims and how the victims had been found.

'What's wrong, Dr Pope?' asked Inspector Reilly.

'Nothing,' said Dr Pope as he got to his feet. 'I am happy that you have finally arrested the murderer.'

'Me too. Don't forget the folders,' said Inspector Reilly as Dr Pope walked off. Dr Pope grabbed the folders and left the room slowly.

Dr Pope returned home an hour later and went straight into his office. He sat down and listened to the recording of his last session with Carl again. He forwarded it until he got to the section when Carl talked about one of the victims. Dr Pope rewound it and played it again a few times, slowly repeating Carl's words.

# A Dead Man's Ice Cream

# Chapter 17

## To see it, you need to want to see it

It was two o'clock in the morning when Dr Pope saw a comet through the window. He was pacing nervously around his house, his skeleton moving from room to room in an aimless fashion. *What's wrong? What's wrong? What's wrong?* Echoed the voice inside his head. *Repeating things to oneself is the most effective way of convincing yourself of anything you put your mind to. Convincing oneself of something is a very good start to ignoring that something's wrong.*

Dr Pope took two steps to his right, and then two more, and then two more. *Doing stupid things bit by bit makes them look less stupid*, he thought. He realised that it was going to be a long night. He couldn't stop thinking about the latest victim. Victim seventeen was a philosophy student who had been found with a few crushed bones in his skeleton. They were still trying to establish if the murder had happened before Carl had been arrested. Dr Pope was agitated and continued moving around the house. He had to think about something, but he couldn't bring himself to do it. *It's one of those times when you're anxious because you have something to do, and anxiety keeps you from doing it. Worrying about something is the first step to doing it wrong.* He stopped walking and gathered his thoughts.

Dr Pope thought this could be one of those cases where obsessions or dreams aren't meant to be fulfilled, as the idea of getting them is a lot more satisfying than getting them. He didn't feel as happy as he had expected. He had obsessed over the Birmingham case for months, but he was not happy. He didn't like how it had ended. *Carl!* he thought to himself. *Why?* He began walking again, but this time, in the opposite direction. *Why, Carl?* Dr Pope felt confused, unhappily confused, puzzled. *The real confusion is when you don't know what's confusing you!*

Something was off. Dr Pope could accept that Carl was involved in the murders, but then if he was, there must have been someone else involved. He thought the chances of catching the other people involved had diminished in catching Carl. It would be difficult, but he believed the best way of catching the others was to allow Carl contact with those people. That would be complicated to arrange, but Carl was quite ill anyway. They could let him out and give him something that meant he couldn't go far. *Strong diarrhoea had never sounded so useful,* he thought.

Dr Pope remained quiet for two minutes, looking into the sky, moving his neck from right to left, always right to left. The rest of his skeleton didn't move. The house was quiet, although a great deal of philosophical phrases seemed to be running around the corridors. He finally breathed heavily, smiled to himself and had a glass of whisky. It was a celebration designed to convince himself that the Birmingham case had finally been solved.

\* \* \*

A few days later, Charles walked into Pub Chamber Pub at Post Central, where Penelope was waiting for him. He greeted her with a smile and a kiss, which she accepted awkwardly.

'What's wrong?' asked Charles.

'You're late,' replied Penelope.

'It was the traffic,' replied Charles.

'An excuse is not an apology,' shouted Penelope.

'What's wrong?' asked Charles again.

'I'm hungry.'

They sat across the table from each other and looked at the lunch menu in silence.

'I know what you're going to have. You're going for the cheese platter.'

'No, I'm not,' said Penelope.

'You're not going to get the cheese? It'd go well with wine,' said Charles.

'I won't have either of those.'

'It's a really nice afternoon for a cold glass of white wine,' said Charles after an awkward silence. 'Or you could have the Spanish beer on the menu. It's from your area, isn't it?

'I'm driving,' explained Penelope.

'Why aren't you ordering the cheese platter? You love cheese.'

'I can't eat soft cheeses right now,' said Penelope looking into Charles' eyes.

'Shit,' shouted Charles. 'How did it happen?'

'You're the doctor. Why don't you tell me how it happened?' asked Penelope sarcastically.

'I know, but… we were careful.'

'Well,' added Penelope, 'I guess we weren't careful enough.'

'So, what do you want to do?'

'What do you think?' asked Penelope.

'I don't know,' replied Charles.

'No, really. What do you think I want to do?' asked Penelope again.

'I…' Charles paused. 'I really don't know.'

'Guess then. You always act as if you know everything and everyone so well… so guess. What am I going to do with this child, Charles?'

The waitress jumped into the conversation unheedful of the heated discussion. She picked out their order in between the awkward silences and left.

'So…,' said Charles.

'So what?' replied Penelope.

'What are we going to do about the baby?'

'I need to think about some stuff. Actually, I should have thought about it before meeting up with you,' admitted Penelope.

They were silent until the waitress returned with their food.

'Your burger looks good,' said Penelope.

'Yes, it does. I usually only get pizzas when I come here,' replied Charles.

They continued eating, exchanging the odd opinion about the food to avoid any further confrontation.

'I'm sorry, Charles, but I really should have thought about it more before meeting up. I think it's better if I go,' said Penelope after a long uncomfortable silence.

'We haven't seen each other since you asked for more space. I thought it'd be a good opportunity to catch up.'

'Yes,' said Penelope, 'but it turns out I need more space.'

'It's okay. I'll cover the bill. Just let me know when you want to talk. Oh, and remember, just in case, the legal limit to abort in the UK is twenty-four weeks.'

'You're a bastard,' shouted Penelope before leaving the table.

\* \* \*

Penelope recalled her grandmother's words as she walked down Commercial Street. *Not many things in life are ideal. It is our responsibility to make them as ideal as possible.* She continued walking. *This is definitely not ideal*, thought Penelope. There were quite a few of Charles' traits she didn't like at all. She couldn't see them having a relationship. As a woman, she felt confronted by opposing ideas. Having a baby and raising it by herself or having an abortion and maybe a baby later in life with someone she was sure she wanted to be with. The first option conflicted with her traditional values. *Being a single mother was never part of my plan*, she thought, *but I guess most things in life are never part of a plan, especially the big things in life.* The second option conflicted with her loose religious views. *Is abortion right? Is this a reasonable excuse? What would the other lecturers from the feminist research group say if they knew I want a man to raise a family? It's like everything in life, saying you're a feminist doesn't make you one, your actions do. It's not anti-feminist to want to have a family, right? Actions define us, and the definitions we and others place on ourselves do not. They just make things blurry.*

Penelope walked towards her car. Her skeleton trembled every time she put her foot down on the tarmac. Something moved in the sky. A younger, naiver version of her would have thought it was a comet. She was older now and thought it was a plane. *What a letdown. Age and bitterness are great at transforming sweet observations, hopes, and transcendentalist thought into shitty realities*, she thought. She got into her car and drove away.

\* \* \*

Dr Pope met with Inspector Reilly to return the files he had at home regarding the Birmingham case. 'Obsessions and dreams. It's always so disappointing when you realise them!' said Dr Pope as he handed the folder back to Inspector Reilly.

Inspector Reilly opened the folder and examined the notes. 'I can't believe it's taken seventeen victims to get this guy.'

Dr Pope nodded. There was an awkward silence. *Any pause over two seconds long gets uncomfortable for Westerners. That's interesting especially considering that two seconds is nothing in life,* thought Dr Pope.

Inspector Reilly selected a photo and presented it to Dr Pope. 'Do you know the story behind this photo?'

'No, I don't think I do,' replied Dr Pope.

Inspector Reilly laughed and began to explain. 'Well, there was this guy called Ronald in the department. He was quite scatty and disorganised. The kind of cop who would go to the toilet and leave his gun by the loo. Luckily, most English cops don't carry guns. Anyway, he was the first person to arrive at the murder scene. He took a few photos and the person in charge gave him permission to start searching for clues, pick up the body etc. After a few minutes, Ronald realised he had forgotten to put a memory card in the camera.'

'Wow,' said Dr Pope. 'So, what did he do?'

'You won't believe it, and this is why he got fired in the end,' continued Inspector Reilly. 'When everyone was having a break, he took the body out of the van and grabbed some of the evidence from the crime scene. He put it back the best way he remembered and took a few photos. He put everything away before anyone noticed it.'

'That's pretty clever. How did he get caught then?' asked Dr Pope.

'Well, because the photos didn't match the description of the crime scene. Someone who was inspecting the photos realised when he saw the victim's watch displayed two o'clock. The photos were supposed to have been taken hours earlier. There was also a book in the scene. The written report said it was between the victim's legs, but this cop had placed it next to his head. The final bit concerned a baseball cap. The written report said that the body had the cap in his right hand but the photo showed the victim wearing it. Ronald got fired, but we had to use a bit of a sleight of hand to avoid other cops and the press finding out about it.'

Dr Pope's face suddenly changed, and he fixed Inspector Reilly with a stare. 'I don't think we can close the case just yet,' said Dr Pope. I have to check something. I'll be in touch as soon as I can.'

Dr Pope's skeleton ran towards his car. He muttered to himself as he drove and he went straight to his office when he got home. Dr Pope picked up his voice recorder and listened to the recording of Carl's last visit to his clinic. He stopped when Carl spoke about that murder. Dr Pope listened to Carl talking about how he had left the crime scene and then paused the recording. He listened to it again and then twice more. 'Yes. I left him there, wearing his cap and with a book lying next to his head,' said Carl in the recording. Dr Pope sat down, moved his head from side to side and grabbed the phone. He almost called Inspector Reilly before changing his mind.

Dr Pope called someone else instead. 'Hello,' said Dr Pope. 'I need you to check something for me.' Two hours later, someone knocked on Dr Pope's door. The person came in with a briefcase and Dr Pope led him to his office. 'I would like you to look for fingerprints in this room, mainly around this desk and around my filing cabinet.'

'Yes, sir,' replied the other man, who did as he was asked. 'I found some prints, sir,' the man said when he had finished. 'I'll look into these and get back to you as soon as I can.'

'Thank you,' replied Dr Pope, showing the man out.

* * *

Dr Pope couldn't sleep that night. He stared through this window, watching the comet in the sky. His skeleton shook while he waited for an email, hoping to discover whose fingerprints they had found in his office. *I really hope I am wrong*, thought Dr Pope. *I can't bring myself to tell anyone else.*

Dr Pope received a text stating the results had been emailed to him. He opened his email and saw the comets flying on the screen as the background image of his computer loaded its content. The report had arrived.

Dr Pope talked to himself in his head as he read the report. *Okay, he found three sets of fingerprints. Number one is mine. Well done, Sherlock!* The second set of fingerprints belonged to Charles. *Yes, of course, he's been around my office in the past.* He continued reading. His eyes grew watery when he came to the next paragraph. He tried to control himself, but the tears came anyway. Fingerprints can last on surfaces for years, but that didn't prepare him to see his wife's prints appear on the report. Dr Pope composed himself. *Okay, there were traces of a fourth person, but they had been wearing gloves and couldn't be identified. These are the only fingerprints found.* Dr Pope paused and noticed a footnote. *Oh, this is interesting. Two of the fingerprints from the right hand had cuts through the middle of them. Initially, it looked like they belonged to another person, but it is now confirmed they belong to Charles.*

Dr Pope knew the person wearing the gloves was the same person who had got hold of the photos. *The person could have scanned them or taken a photo with his mobile and then shown them to Carl. That is the only way in which Carl could have had everything right except the details in that photograph.* Dr Pope continued talking to himself as his skeleton moved around the office. *It doesn't matter how much we try to ignore them. The simplest explanations are usually the correct ones. This psycho murderer has avoided being caught for months. If you want something done right, do it yourself. He is the one who grabbed my bloody photos.*

Dr Pope continued pacing around and talking to himself. *So, the report states the prints with the gloves are only detected on the bottom draw. The person must have known where to look for the photos because the cabinet's lock wasn't forced.* Horrified, a strong suspicion came to Dr Pope. He went to retrieve a hidden spare key for the bottom draw, feeling nervous as he did so. His whole skeleton vibrated. His eyes were watery as he kneeled down and slid his hand between the back of the wardrobe and the wall. He moved his hand down, slowly, and pulled at a thread tied to the little box where he kept his spare keys. The cabinet key was there, but the key wasn't covered by dust, as it should have been. Dr Pope realised someone had taken it. The person had known where it would be. He read the report again and everything made sense. He started talking himself through the epiphany. Charles' fingerprints were in the room as he had been there before. However, the fingerprints with the cuts on the fingers were only around the area where the box was hidden. 'So, that's it,' said Dr Pope out oud. 'He came in wearing gloves and went for the key. He couldn't feel the thread while wearing gloves, so he took them off. He wasn't worried about leaving his fingerprints as he knew that his fingerprints were already there. I would expect to find them, but he forgot about the cut on his fingertips and that this would show me he had been here more recently. He then put on the gloves after getting the key and went straight for the photos from the bottom drawer.' With the realisation, Dr Pope started crying and muttered, 'Bastard.' He sat on his floor and continued to cry for a while, feeling more guilt than if he had killed those victims himself.

Dr Pope considered the whole case. *So, someone takes some photos, shows them to someone, and then that person remembers the images as if it was a vivid dream. How does that work?* thought Dr Pope. He placed his hands on his head again while he remembered his second trip to Gibraltar while visiting Charles. One day, he met one of the psychiatrist consultants at the army base and he told him about a new drug they were testing in a conflict zone. 'Many of our troops need a lot of psychological help when they come back from the battlefield as they bring a lot of disturbing memories with them,' explained the army psychiatrist. 'This new drug is better than any treatment they can get when they return. This drug simply disposes of those memories.'

Those words floated around Dr Pope's head. He remembered how it worked and went through the process out loud. 'You give it to the patient for a couple of weeks. After an initial period of confusion and sleep disruption, the patient returns to an almost normal baseline and the sleep improves once the drug is assimilated into the body. When the sleep gets better, the drug induces a semiconscious state during long sleeping periods, almost like hypnotism. You can tell patients what you want, and everything will be stored as memories in their brains. A typical use was telling a fabricated story to soldiers who had seen civilians killed to replace traumatic memories with more pleasant but fake ones. Initially, the traumatic experiences seem like distant nightmares and the fake stories are processed like vivid dreams. In time, the traumatic experiences disappear, and the alternative story is stored as a memory. In some cases, you can even show photos of things you want the patient to believe. If a soldier felt guilty over a friend's death, they could show him photos of a car accident during his semiconscious sleep to convince him the friend had died in a car accident. The drug has generic side effects, stiffness, salivation, weight gain… pretty much the same side effects as any antidepressant, so it is difficult to detect through a routine medical check-up.'

Dr Pope's skeleton trembled, and he called Inspector Reilly. 'It ain't over until the fat lady sings! I got it.'

'You got what?' asked Inspector Reilly, confused. Dr Pope talked for two minutes. 'So, someone committed the murders and framed Carl by inducing him to unknowingly confess to them?' asked Inspector Reilly following Dr Pope's explanation.

'Yes, that's it,' answered Dr Pope. 'All the images that Carl described match the murder scenes perfectly, except the description that matched the altered photo from Ronald, not the actual crime scene.'

Inspector Reilly paused for two seconds and went on. 'Do you know how they could have shown Carl the photos?'

'No,' replied Dr Pope after a very long pause. 'The analysis report of my desk says the person who took the photos wore gloves, so we don't know who it was.' Dr Pope suggested releasing Carl as soon as they could as this would be the best way to catch the killer, given that the killer would try and get in touch with Carl. Dr Pope finished the conversation with Inspector Reilly and sat down, worried, angry, agitated, but somewhat content. He grabbed his handkerchief and rubbed it over the wardrobe and the wall. He felt guilty about not being honest with Inspector Reilly and not turning Charles in, but Dr Pope was now convinced he'd be the eighteenth victim. He took comfort in knowing it wasn't someone else's life at risk and that by having him as the last murder victim, it would put an end to his misery.

* * *

Carl was released later, and he left the police station where he'd been held. Carl didn't like asking for favours and he was embarrassed about what had happened, so there was no one waiting for him outside. If Dr Pope's theory was right, Carl's body would now be clear of that army drug, as he hadn't had any for some time. It would explain why Carl was feeling more normal now. He didn't want to get a taxi, so he just walked to his house and went directly to sleep. As his grandmother used to say, 'Sleeping is the best cure for all kinds of ailments.'

* * *

Dr Pope listened to Carl's recordings a few times and then to the recording from the Cyclops' murder with the gaps. He was convinced it wasn't Carl, although the analysis of the recordings that Peter had completed made him think something wasn't right. Dr Pope started talking out loud, 'The victim asked to be forgiven and it sounded as if he knew his murderer. The first sound of the murderer's name was *k*, given Peter's analysis.' Dr Pope was puzzled by this, as it meant the murderer wasn't his son. He felt happier for two seconds until he decided to check further details on the Cyclops. He had been based in Gibraltar at the same time as Charles. Dr Pope's skeleton trembled as he lowered his head and cried out loud. '*Captain*. The army guy wasn't saying the murderer's name, but his rank. That's how he was used to addressing him.'

* * *

Carl woke up late the following morning. Charles was walking in circles around the room. He attempted to relax when he saw Carl, but he couldn't.

'Hey, man, are you okay? I haven't seen you in a couple of days,' asked Charles.

Carl stopped before answering. He knew that part of his Asperger's package meant he lacked the ability to lie. He didn't think he could come up with a solid story regarding his previous whereabouts, so he gave a simple reply. 'Yes, thanks, I'm okay.' Carl didn't volunteer any further information and Charles did not ask for it.

'How's everything?' asked Charles.

'It's okay, thanks,' replied Carl.

'Cool. I was worried as I hadn't seen you in a few days. I was even thinking about ringing the police… to notify them you were missing, I mean,' added Charles.

'That would have been quite messy,' said Carl.

'Why? What happened?'

Carl started to speak slowly. He simply could not hold back. 'To be fair, I don't know. I really don't know. I've been seeing a psychiatrist for some issues lately. This was all very weird, but I've been sleeping really badly. I told him I'd been having some bad nightmares and I was arrested on my way home a few nights ago. Apparently, the descriptions of my dreams matched the information they have about those Birmingham murders. They thought I was involved.'

'So, what happened then?' asked Charles.

'They took me into a room to interrogate me for a few hours. They showed me some photos and asked me to explain how my dreams matched those descriptions so closely. They released me last night, but they didn't say anything else.'

'And what did you tell the police? I mean, I don't know how I'd react if I was interrogated,' said Charles.

'I just said the same thing I'd said to my psychiatrist. I went through my dreams a few more times. They showed me some photos and shouted at me. Finally, they let me go.'

'And they didn't say why they had changed their minds?'

'No, they didn't,' replied Carl. 'The same guy who interrogated me told me that I could go. I'm quite scared, though. Maybe they were not allowed to keep me any longer and they're thinking about how to get me into custody again.' Carl was growing increasingly nervous, and Charles wasn't helping the situation.

'So, what's your plan, Carl?'

'Plan for what?'

'For whatever you're going to do now?'

'Nothing. I have to work tomorrow,' replied Carl. 'I'll just do some washing and get ready for that. I also have to make my sandwiches for tomorrow.'

'Are you really going to work tomorrow?' asked Charles.

'Yes, of course. Why?' asked Carl.

'Well,' said Charles, swallowing saliva. 'I wouldn't go to work if I'd gone through that.'

Carl stopped for two seconds and then asked Charles, 'What would you do then?'

'I guess I'd just get my stuff and disappear. If they took you once, who knows if they'll take you again. Clearly, they've already messed up whatever evidence they have and blamed you for it, so it could happen again. And next time, they might not release you.'

Carl thought about it and added, 'I already told my head of department that I was going back to work tomorrow. What I need to do now is decide what to put in my sandwich.'

'Carl!' shouted Charles. 'If you go to work tomorrow, it'll be your life you'll be putting in that sandwich.' Charles calmed down before asking again. 'You're actually going to work?'

'Yes. I told my boss I would. I don't like changing plans,' said Carl. 'There is no point in making plans if you're going to change them. It's like… it's like making a ham sandwich and then taking out the ham and putting in cheese instead… It's not a good way to make a sandwich.'

The sandwich-life analogy caught Charles by surprise. *Surprises are funny*, thought Charles, *as you usually don't expect them. What kind of stupid remark is this, I think hanging out with Carl is making me retarded.* Charles turned back to Carl again. 'So, what are you going to put in your sandwich then?'

'I've never been very good at deciding stuff so I'm gonna have ham and cheese, as usual,' replied Carl, happy with this choice.

That night, Carl had the best sleep in a very long time, finding tranquillity he had not experienced before. In the morning, he kept to the routine he had when things were going well. He woke up, had breakfast, got ready, and walked to Five Ways Station. Carl felt happy going to work, although he felt like something had changed. Things were not the same anymore. His beloved routine had been forced to change. A sour stench hit him, and even though the smell was strong and not pleasant, he smiled when he recognised it. Carl looked to his side and there was a fat smelly guy with a bandana around his head. He looked to be a pleasant man, but he stank of rancid sweat. Everyone in the Five Ways to Bournville journey knew him. The trick was to wait for him to sit and then choose a seat far away from him to avoid the strong smell. That day, however, Carl waited for the man to sit down and then sat next to him. The disgusting smell brought pleasant memories to Carl. Sitting by the man comforted Carl, because it was routine and made him think nothing had changed. *Routine, no matter how boring or disgusting it can be, can definitely bring a calming feeling to us in the most distressing of times*, thought Carl.

Carl felt sad to leave the train when it stopped at University Station. He took a final big whiff of that dry sweat smell and stood from his seat. He left the train to find the station was much busier than usual. *With a crowd like this, it is difficult to imagine I would ever be missed if I never returned*, thought Carl to himself. On his way from the station, the barriers closed on Carl, as if unable to detect he was there. 'Your skeleton is see-through and hollow. That's why you're so light!' Carl remembered his grandmother saying this to him at Teatros Street in Gibraltar.

Carl turned left outside of University Station and continued downhill towards Ashley building. In some respect, his university building was more of a home to him than his actual home in Birmingham. He felt safe at work, protected, although more ignored than before. *Maybe that is because I'm no longer new*, thought Carl. A floating cloud cast a shadow, which made it look like the tower clock was marking two o'clock. He walked through the Arts Building, his usual shortcut, and came to the familiar cylinder shape of his beloved Ashley building. A communist looking grey structure which, despite being ugly, made him feel happy. His skeleton was pushed towards his desk, which had recently been moved out of sight. He liked the privacy but it made him feel invisible. Inconspicuously, Carl moved towards his isolated desk. *Routine is a great cure for many ailments*, repeated Carl twice to himself.

Carl enjoyed his day at work. There were no questions about where he had been or about what had happened to him. It was an easy but rewarding time. Nothing was special about that day, except for the fact nothing had gone wrong. It reminded him of his early days at school. *Doing nothing wrong is much better than doing something right*, Carl had always said to himself.

Carl had been feeling increasingly ignored day by day. One morning, he woke up and he felt very cold. It was one of those days where you wake up with the chill of the night in your body. He had a warm shower, but it did not help. Carl walked to Five Ways Station and arrived earlier than usual. The smelly guy wasn't there, and Carl missed his vinegary smell, so he let two trains go. Eventually, a heavy smelly skeleton came down the stairs to the platform. In a very strange way, Carl was excited to see him. *Routine can bring comfort even in the most distressful of times.* Once again, the smell reminded him of the happy days he had spent at work. He waited until the man sat down and Carl sat next to him. The carriage was emptier than usual, and Carl worried it'd be too obvious, but, in a very unusual way for Carl, he did what he wanted without worrying about what others might say. He sat next to the man and could not smell anything. Carl thought that he might have a bad cold.

The automated gate failed to open when Carl approached it, but unlike the previous occasion, the gate failed to open on his second attempt. Carl was forced to wait until the gate opened for the person behind him. Carl turned left out of University Station and headed towards his office. The day appeared different to him. He walked into his building, unnoticed once again. He sat at his desk but no one said hello. Everyone wore black and kept their eyes to the floor. Carl concentrated on his autistic abilities, realising that maybe he shouldn't ask what had happened to avoid making people upset. Two hours after Carl arrived, everyone left quietly. Carl followed them and climbed into a colleague's car without uttering a word. They reached Lodge Hill cemetery and crematorium in Selly Oak. *A sad space within a happy student neighbourhood*, thought Carl. He got out of the car as a young altar boy handed out some leaflets. The boy didn't give one to Carl, but he looked at the leaflet of the person next to him. Carl discovered he was at his own funeral.

Carl was speechless. He walked around the room, looking at the people there. He walked to the open coffin and saw himself lying there. He could not believe it. He didn't even remember dying. The Friday Club crew were at his funeral, but he could not face looking at them. He approached them and stayed by their side. He heard that he had apparently died of a heart attack. What! Carl could not believe it. He had never had a problem with his heart. He didn't take drugs or anything. Carl had seen movies in which spirits attempted to alert people of their presence, and that they hadn't passed over yet. Carl was concerned he would scare others if he made any usual noises, so he observed the whole ceremony in silence. Carl looked around the room.

There was no one in the room to say sorry to. There was usually a partner or a relative to console at funerals, but there was no relative or significant other in that room to accept any condolences, cards or flowers. *Perhaps that is why I am here. There is no one to take cards or flowers on my behalf. That is disappointing*, thought Carl, smiling as he remembered Kazim's words. 'Carl, mate, disappointing people is what I do best. My vegetarian friends are disappointed I'm not vegetarian, my vegan friends are disappointed I'm not vegan, and my meat-eating friends are disappointed I don't eat pork. Non-smokers are disappointed because I smoke. My friends who are into politics are disappointed in me because I don't vote for the same party as them, and my gay friends think I'm a sell-out because I'm straight.'

Carl observed the whole scene, and he controlled his emotions pretty well. However, that changed when he saw the Friday Club crew waiting for the urn containing his ashes.

# A Dead Man's Ice Cream

# <u>Chapter 18</u>

## We spend our whole lives waiting

### Kazim

'Can't believe this, but I should. I really should. We haven't had any Friday Club outings since you died and it's happened. Can't fucking believe this, but it's happened and now you're gone. And we let it happen, but we should have been better than that. You deserved better than that, and we failed to protect you and to look after you. And if the system fails people like you, we shouldn't have failed you, and we all now feel like shit for it, and the reason is because you deserved more than that, and I haven't talked to the others about it, but I just know that we all feel like shit and it was our fucking fault, and how do we move on from that? We don't move on from that, and we don't move. And the movement's gone. And all those Fridays out socialising have been swapped by early Fridays in bed, and you're gone and it still doesn't feel right and you're no longer here and we can't cope with it. None of us have met up, and can't cope with it and we can't and we just don't meet up. Well, we meet up for our routine ritual of passing on the urn with your flesh in it, in the form of ashes, your flesh is ash, and your ash is flesh. And I know we all do. I know we all have this sense of sadness and of care towards you. Poor guy. All of us feel it. We feel the guilt because of that something extra we all feel we could have done for you, whatever that might have been, when you were still here with us. I'm not sure taking turns to look after the urn will change much. But we try, oh, man, we try. Mr Bright Side, what a fucking great name for the urn. And we all look after you, man. We all do, all of us do this taking care of you except for that cunt Charles. I never liked him. I sometimes don't like many people, but I really especially never fucking liked that cunt and we won't let him look after you, look after the urn, look after Mr Bright Side. And so it's happened, man. It's my turn to look after you. Lying here in bed and I don't quite know what to do with it. Waiting, waiting, we spend our whole lives waiting and I'm just waiting in bed for an idea. The ingenious cunty spirit of Friday Club should come to me here, waiting in bed. Okay, that's enough. Come on, mate, I'll put you into this rucksack lying next to us on this bed. Shit, man. How weird it is that your flesh is in here. All your burnt self fits into this fucking urn. Also, for a guy with such a big face, you fit into quite a small urn. It was weird, it was, yeah, it was weird, your head was not big, but your face was. Come on, mate, we'll do something. I'll get out of bed. Just can't believe it. You were such a nice guy. Fucking nice. Just too nice. What's this, oh, shit, yeah, I need to stir the soil in this plant pot. Okay, fuck, shit, what's next? Carl, we're going out, man. Fuck this shit. We're going out like in the old days. Do you see, mate? Almost there. We'll get to Warwick Road at the end of this road and we can get the bus into town from there. Good old Tyseley, industrial capital of the world! Actually, screw that. Now, let's get a taxi, a tenner to go to the city centre, a tenner, I'll pay a tenner to the first person who takes me there for a tenner, done. You see, mate? You and I out on the piss like in the good old times. Can't believe it, mate, what the fuck happened to you? So, you go to bed and have a heart attack while you're asleep? That's it? It doesn't sound right. It just doesn't sound right. I'm sure that cunt Charles put his willy in your ear or something while you were asleep and you died of a shock at how small it was. Charles, what kind of twat says that? *I don't make mistakes, I'm not that kind of person*, what a cunt. He's a cunt, you should have avoided that bastard! I can't believe he shagged that Penelope bird. She's hot, man. Shit, I hadn't seen that before, a petrol station with a twenty-four-hour booze shop. That is asking for trouble! Look, Carl, that's my primary school. Good school, man, I had so much fun there. So, shit, where should we go to then? It's okay, we're still in Stratford Road, we have time to think. Carl, I'm gonna take you to the good old Pub Chamber Pub and we're gonna see some good pussy in there, man! Almost there. You see? Almost there. A bit further up Bristol Street and that's it and this is it, I told you. There you go, man, we can sit out here and look at the flange walking, like in the old days. Me, smoking out here and you keeping me company, all we need here is that boring shithead Shitalian to bore the shit out of us and then I'm sure you'll be glad you're dead. He's fucking boring but can be funny, like when he stayed at mine after a night out, and almost didn't stay at mine, and got the house wrong or the wrong house and tried to break into my neighbour's house cos he thought it was mine and I came out of my house when the police came to arrest him and I said he was staying with me and it was a mistake but I shouldn't have, and I should have said nothing and that'd have been funny but not funny for him maybe but funny for me though.'

* * *

'Bastard, I can't believe you're dead, man. I'm just gonna order a cider and one of those shitty beers you used to drink. I don't think I ever told you, but I was always embarrassed to ask for one of your beers at the bar. It wasn't a manly beer. It was the beer that all the inbreds drink, like that cunt over there with no neck. Okay, you see, I've just ordered one of those shitty beers of yours and I'm gonna drink it while I smoke outside, like it's a normal Friday Club, like a normal Friday Club night out. … Alright, what next, big boy? Jug and Violin or The Elizabeth. I'd rather go to The Elizabeth cos the birds are hotter there.'

* * *

'Look at this, Carl, those people outside The Elizabeth are a right mess. What a disgrace! That's how you know a place in Birmingham is worth going to, cos there are pissheads outside having a great time. Now, the usual, get some drinks and then go to that tiny dance floor at the back. The one upstairs is far too messy. I can't believe this is the same place where we used to come to play poker on Wednesdays. That was fun, we never won anything, but that was fun. …

Let's go out for a drink and a smoke, you remember? That's when we used to talk to randoms, and that's how we ended up putting together all of the Friday Club crew. Just a group of randoms who were free on Fridays. The greatest minds of Birmingham someone said, and then your cunty housemate Charles saying that we were all the rejects of the Birmingham pubs. He wasn't wrong, but he's still a fucking twat. Oh, Carl, that bird there would be all over you. I talked to her a couple of weeks ago. She did Spanish at uni and she loves all that Spanish-related crap, the lingo, and that stuff. You'd be so in there, mate. And I'll tell you what, she has massive tits as well, and I know you Mediterraneans love big tits. You bunch of perverts. I think it's cos they remind you of cows and you love cows, yogurts, cheese, and all that shit. I'll tell you what, I'll talk to her for you. You see, man. I told you she was cool, she's loving this conversation, man, and I'd love to see you with her. It's a pity you couldn't get inside of her when you were alive, but you'll do so now that you're dead. You'd be proud, man. I went to the toilet and I put a tiny bit of your ashes in my hand. And now... oh, man, this is too good, can't believe you're not here to enjoy the moment. I've just put some of your ashes in her drink while she was talking to that ugly cunt. Now, a bit of stirring, and there you go, mate. You're in! You've pulled from the grave. How much do I miss you, man!'

\* \* \*

'That was good. I saw her drinking your ashes while I was talking to her and it felt like watching you shag her, a proper *I'm just watching* moment. Alright, Carl, time to move somewhere else as they're closing down. I know what, for old time's sake, we're going to Underworld, man. Hill Street, I always hated this street. All the way up, up, up and you walk up, and you get to this place and all you see is a statue of Queen Victoria, waiting there. Waiting. She is always waiting for who knows what and no, but I'll just, no, just one, just one entry for me, mate. I have some dirty clothes from work in the bag, if you wanna take a look go ahead... cheers.'

\* \* \*

'This is the place for just drinking without being distracted by girls. Finding a hot girl in this place is pretty rare, but at least they serve till late, and they have a wicked outside area, and a pool upstairs. Before that, time for a drink. I'll get a pint of that shitty beer you like and some cider for me. Sorted, mate, and now we're talking. Oh, mate, so many good nights here. This place is full of such an amalgamation of random people. Hairy people full of tattoos and losers who have nowhere else to go for their last drink. But I'll tell you what, if you don't have a tattoo and something hanging from your ears, you're nobody in this place. Come on, I'll take your ashes for a walk upstairs. This section is funny. A couple of mirrors on the wall making it look like a strip club with some random pool tables. It's funny looking at the people playing pool when they're off their tits. Okay, let's go to the smoking area, we might see some flange. Come on, mate, we're gonna go on pussy patrol. Look man, those birds are clearly lost. They're too posh for this place. She's hot. Fuck, she's really hot, man! You see Carl, this is why we always wanted to end the night here. Come on, you say you have some badass tattoos, show them… show them, show them to me. Okay, she does. Man, they're hot. I don't even know what she's saying, I stopped listening when I saw that bit of flesh: her left boob on its way to the cleavage. Actually, it's on my left, so it's not her left tit, well, it's the tit on the other left. Shit, man, I'm gonna have to start listening if I want to continue with this conversation. No way, no fucking way, she's an escort? Is she offering? Oh, no, she's not, she's an escort at that posh place in Summer Row and comes here after that shitty pretentious place closes. They're pretentious and racist, unless you're a black footballer and then they let you in. Bastards. Is she joking? Wow, an escort, well, a job's a job. Really nice to meet you, yes, it's been great, you too, etc. Nah, she must be joking, yeah, shit, sure, maybe I'm too pissed to be taken seriously. I won't try to get her number because, I think it's obvious why, Carl.'

\* \* \*

'Alright, big boy, time to go fuck off, disappear from this place and go somewhere else. If you leave a place you need to go somewhere else as you have to be somewhere all the time and you can't be nowhere, because nowhere is a non-place where you just can't be. So, you can't go to a place where you can't be. Nothingness is the maybeness of perhaps. And then you find yourself waiting, waiting, we're always fucking waiting for something, and we spend our whole lives waiting. Waiting is the new thing. Alright, a taxi, a taxi, we need a taxi, Tyseley, off to Tyseley we are, mate. Fuck, fuck, I've lost the urn, fuck, I've left it in the bog, no, oh, no, it's okay. It's in my bag. That'd have been bad, mate. It's bad enough leaving a friend behind when they're alive, but it's even worse leaving them when they're dead. Actually, that's it! Death is a nowhere place where everyone goes at some point. You, everyone can go nowhere, actually, no, you're still somewhere, I mean, their body's somewhere. Well, unless they're incinerated. What a posh sounding word for such a shitty thing. Okay, so death can be a nowhere place for some people. And death awaits, that's it, it's all about the waiting. You wait for something that's not waiting for you. Kinda like doing a no show kinda thing. Death awaits like a, like a, something that is waiting for something else, or fucking waiting for itself. Shitty thing. It's all about the waiting. It's like when people say that they don't mind waiting for someone as long as they know that the other person's coming. What a retarded way of thinking. If you don't think they're coming, hopefully, you won't be as retarded to wait for them. Waiting is so seventies! … come on, I need a cab, Tyseley, a tenner, a tenner to Tyseley, a tenner to Tyseley? Tyseley, a tenner? A tenner? A tenner to Tyseley? Deal! Tyseley, a tenner!'

# Penelope

'And it had to happen to me, to me, and it had to happen to me. With all the girls out there, and all the guys out there, I had to like a guy who then turned out to be a creep. He's a creep, a cute creep, but a creep. Cute's not the word, hot is. Once a creep, always a creep, and I can't believe I fell for it, and on top of that, this, and that and this, and this crappy pill had to fail, and then it had to fail on my stupid fertile window crap, like in that show with the girls checking their fertile window timing stuff, and all this had to happen and his little creepy crawlers had to find this *puto* fucking egg that survived that crappy pill, or whatever the technical explanation is. And his creepy crawlers had to crawl and settle into my innocent egg, chilling out there. So, it's true, it's true, of course it's true that people get pregnant. Stuff gets broken and women get pregnant, shit happens, sure thing it does, fuck, *joder*, and then it had to happen to me, to me, to me it had to happen that his crappy creepy sperm had to crawl and camp in my stupid egg. And what do I do now? What do I do? With what? With my life? With the other life? What other life? And that fucking bastard then says that I took advantage of Carl to make myself feel good, and that it's no good to take advantage of weaker people, and the shithead says that to me, and me waiting to think of options, options… option one's abort, or is that option two? And option whatever is having the kid and having to continue seeing this creepy guy. I should have trusted my first instinct. So now I know why I didn't like him the first time I saw him. Cos he's un *estúpido*, not stupid, *estúpido*, close enough, but totally different meaning. A creepy *estúpido* and I can't trust him. I just can't put my finger on it, but I can't trust him. And I can't have the kid of someone I don't trust. I don't trust him, and I'd find it creepy having to share the kid with him or something. Although he's so self-absorbed that he might not even want to see the kid. Who knows? He's quite hot at times, but it's true what they say, that thing that he's not, not that he's not, that looks don't matter kinda thing. Fuck. I'm pregnant.'

# Zain

'I wait, and I wait, and I can wait more but, wow, this is weird, waiting for a mate to bring an urn with another mate's ashes in it so that I can then wait longer and come up with a, fucking hell, what am I gonna do with the urn? It's Carl, but it's not him. They're his ashes, but that's not him, it's not the guy that, he was a good man. A nice guy, very nice guy. Just, I just can't bring myself to say it and then someone comes up with this idea of sharing the urn. Our time with Carl's come to an end. Everything ends, everything ends, but some things start again, after they have ended, and they end, and start again, and we wait and wait and await and then they end once more, like, like, some things end more than once, I'm sure of that. Okay, so I wait, and I wait more, and get the urn, and then I wait more to do something with it, and I'll take Carl out tonight, well, I'll take him out after going to the gym. I'm not going to do any exercise, but the usual sauna stuff. I hope that naked German bloke's not around today. German people love being naked, and saunas, and that, but I can't expose Carl to a naked German bloke. Actually, I can't take his ashes into the sauna in case they get wet, that wouldn't be cool. In my locker, that's right, in my locker. Carl will be okay in my locker, no one will take an urn. I'll leave him in my locker. Wait, wait, wait, I wait for Kazim to bring the urn, but then Carl will have to wait for me, in my locker, in my locker, while I go into the sauna for a bit. Bloody naked German guy. But wait, wait, Carl will wait, he'll have to wait, as I have to wait for him now. He's dead, he's gone, and I still wait for him. I miss that guy. Oh, the buzz, the buzz, Kazim's here. The urn's here. The ashes are here, but Carl's gone.'

* * *

'That was weird, well, of course it was weird, giving someone the ashes of someone else for a few days is weird, I mean, it's not normal, or it's not tradition, kinda thing. It was good to see Kazim, though, and very kind of him to give me a lift to the gym. Ashes, ashes, hold on tight in there, I'll put you in the locker before I go to the sauna. All you have to do is wait. Just wait there. Waiting is all we do in life. And we wait for the future, but the future's already here and yet, here we are all waiting, still waiting. Carl just wait here, mate.'

\* \* \*

'Well, at least the naked German guy wasn't around the changing room. Fucking Germans, they're perverts, but quiet perverts, not like the Dutch, who are proper loud and evident perverts. But cool perverts. Dutch people are fun. You never get bored hanging out with Dutch people, but Germans, and Germany, Germany's weird. Germany doesn't look like Germany. Some parts of it look like Poland and other parts look like England, but Germany doesn't look like Germany. Anyway, no naked German today is good news. Wow, seems like I've been in this sauna now for a bit too long. Swim or no swim? Nah, no swim, cocktail time at Pub Chamber Pub with Carl, I think. Or with the ashes I should say. The ashes are Carl, but Carl is not the ashes. If that makes sense. Anyway, mate, cocktail time for you.'

\* \* \*

'Carl, I hope you're getting excited, mate. Here we are, in your beloved Pub Chamber Pub. It's two-for one pizzas on Tuesdays and two-for-one cocktails on Thursdays, we spent so much time here. Waiting. We waited for friends, we waited for girls, we waited for drinks. A lot, yes, quite a lot of waiting went down here. A lot of time, actually, and money. I'm sorry I can't have a big one tonight, not a big one tonight, just a cocktail and off we go. I have to go to London tomorrow, some meeting, yeah, one of those meetings, some meeting which will be the same as all the other meetings I've had this week, this month, or this year. The problem with meetings is that people talk too much, they all talk too much. People like you are a dying breed, Carl. Sorry, I didn't mean to say dying, you know what I mean, they're just... not as common these days. You were well-balanced. You didn't say crap when you had nothing to say. Talking should be reserved for people like you, people who talk cos they have something to say, not for people who talk cos they love the sound of their own voices. Actually, thinking about it, maybe you didn't even talk when you had something to say. You were just happy observing others. But not people watching like other people do, just listening to others. Wow, mate, this cocktail is strong. Rum punch, punch, punch, punch rum, mate, that's where it's at. What was that thing you used to say when you saw me drink rum at Myles' place, *ron, ron, ron, la botella de ron*. Well, cocktail one gone, I'll have this second one for you, mate. Then we'll go, or, I'll go, sadly, you're already gone.'

# Myles

'Waiting, waiting, it's all about waiting. We spend our whole lives waiting, waiting for nothing, well, not really, waiting for Carl, or more accurately, waiting for his ashes, which is not the same. Weird, weird, it's weird waiting for your friend's ashes. Saying that, it's even weird for Kazim, and it was his idea. Brilliant. Quite weird, and it's disgusting to be passing some ashes around Birmingham like that, but it's good. It's quite a cool send-off and Carl deserves it. Carl loved Birmingham, he loved this place, and it might not be fair to say that this place didn't love him as much, but hey, he made some friends, he had a good time going out with us, and he had a pretty independent life, the most independent he's ever been, I think. Oh, his grandma, his poor grandma, she was always worried about him, what's gonna happen to my Carl when I am no longer here, the usual cry of people who have a disabled person depending on them or with any dependent in that respect. But hats off to him, he did well, so much better than some other people, yeah, he did pretty well. So proud of him. He got himself a job and he was independent. And he had a pretty normal life, normal, normal, what is normal, I know *normal* people who have less normal lives than Carl did. Normality is not really normality, normality is the more standard of abnormalities rationalised and made normal by society. Normality can be as abnormal as the abnormal members of the group who are observed. Waiting for someone's ashes to take them out on a walk around Birmingham is weird, but it's become normal in our group of friends. Normalisation can happen with the strangest of things, but shit, Carl's still dead. Dead, dead, dead, *la botella de ron…* good things come to those who wait, yeah, right. A weird guy called Kazim is coming with my friend's ashes in an urn that most likely will be wet with drops of Kazim's piss. Dirty bastard, I bet he doesn't even wash his hands when he goes to the toilet. Funny guy though, 'Who the fuck would marry you?' Lad! Only guy I know who can get away with saying that to a bride at a pub! Legend, legend, waiting for the legend, and waiting for Carl, cos Carl's the legend. Can't believe he's a legend now, a story told and gone, and gone, but I'm still waiting for him. Waiting for Carl to be delivered. In an urn. Waiting for Carl, that could be a play, a guy waiting for an urn with ashes in it. It's all about waiting, oh, I think Kazim's here. Carl's ashes are here, but Carl's no longer here and he's here no longer and he's gone, but he's still with us.'

\* \* \*

'The urn's here, the urn's here, the waiting is over, the waiting is over but Carl's not here, still not here and no longer here and never will be, can't believe he's gone but not forgotten, and hopefully forgiven by anyone who ever had an issue with him. I don't think anyone did though, he was such a nice guy. What a loss. And I knew him for years and in his last months, he wasn't how he used to be. He'd changed, his wit and spark had withered somehow, and yet he was still the special guy I once knew. What a great loss. I loved that guy, so many years together, from Loughborough Uni to Birmingham, oh, man, that was tough, a tough move for him it was, but I'm glad I helped him move here, it's the least I could do for someone like him. Glad not for me, but for him and I'm glad I could do something for him. For someone. For him. Someone like him, oh, man, the modern Rain Man, is what that twat called him when we were at uni. It's interesting to see how the people who are bullied the most are the least hateful of guys. He just didn't care. Of course, he didn't. He had no bit of malice in him. He didn't have it in him to dislike people, let alone hate or not love, he was what we should all aspire to be and yet are not and will never be no matter how much we wait for it to happen. Live and forgive, sometimes much more forgiving than living, but still doing things and living in his own way and pretty important though, letting others live. He didn't resent people or hate people. Carl just got on with life the best way he could and that was it. And he didn't want to and Jake told me that he didn't want to, that Carl not Jake is the one who didn't want to and the way he said it to Jake that he didn't want to be a dead man's ice cream, that he wanted to do things and enjoy life and live life and that's pretty epic for someone like that with limitations, with some issues but still doing everything he could to do things, and a dead man's ice cream, he didn't want to be a dead man's ice cream and that's genius. He was like that pure raw genius, full of surprises and you came to us, you could have stayed in Gibraltar, but instead, you came here to us and tried to do something with your life and it was so brave of you. And you would shake when talking to a stranger, but you built the courage to come to us to do something with your life and you taught us a lot of things and no need to have any external factors to find your own identity and your personality and your behaviour is really what defined you, it wasn't your label or external circumstances and I tried. I and I tried. I, well, pretty much I did, yeah, well, I tried to be nice to you, as much as I could, and I hope I never failed you. And not cos I had to, but cos it was the natural thing to do around cos it's all you every, not every but ever showed everyone and society doesn't realise that, and societies ignore the weak and many people do and who was it? It was a woman, or a guy, too clever to be a guy's words, but it made so much sense, what was it, oh yeah, that societies are measured by the way they treat their weakest and most helpless citizens or something along those lines and you were one, mate, but we all tried our best and you deserved it. Someone's got to be a waste of a human to be nasty to anyone like you, mate, or to anyone just half as nice as you were and no longer with us you are, man. Anyway, a special treat, this is a special treat the same as your time with us was a special treat for all of us, and I'm going to take you to a special book club meeting today, one from the James Joyce book club and it's coming and Bloomsday's coming, of course you know, it's your birthday two days later, the Gibraltarian who was almost born on Bloomsday, a good claim to fame, but you never told anyone and your birthday is on Friday this year and that's quite cool, and yeah, pretty cool, but anyway, they're talking about the last episode of *Ulysses*. Just the usual people in the book club. And it's all about waiting, mate. Waiting, waiting, waiting... we spend our whole lives waiting and one chapter where people wait, and more stuff happens in that chapter than in that *Waiting for Godo* play, as its author said, *a play where nothing happens, twice*. And we all wait, like Ulysses' wife and Bloom's wife, we all wait. Life's about the waiting that happens in between and about realising that the waiting is the living and not that the living will happen after the waiting.'

\* \* \*

'Oh, man, so many years together and now you're gone. I have very happy memories here in Birmingham with you, memories and memories, and memoir is a different word, but related in origin, and kinda in meaning as well, one could say. See, walking now down Commercial Street, then turn left through that little side entrance and we're in Post Central. Walk down by these shops that never have anyone in them, and then take the escalators, wave hello to the security guy, shit, what was his name, you used to talk to him all the time. And, then under Suffolk Street Queensway, look up there, that's Ritzy, and then you have Underworld after it, some crazy nights there, man, some good times there. So, we continue walking along Navigation Street, and then left. Oh, look, Peter, the Irish guy selling the Big Issue, crazy, but a nice guy. Victoria Square is here, remember, the emo kids with the skateboards and black make-up, and there you go, the library. It's a weird library, but I kinda like it. I just need to check where the meeting is. You stay tight in that urn, mate, we'll be there in no time. Different location this time, but closer to the pubs. A few of us couldn't make the trip to Dublin so we thought we'd have one last meeting here.'

\* \* \*

'Reading and meetings, reading and meetings, then, listen, listen, listen to people and wait, it's all about the waiting, Carl. Funnily enough, that's chapter eighteen in *Ulysses* is about, isn't it? Waiting for waiting, it's not even about waiting for Godo, it's about waiting for waiting's sake. Oh, Carl, listen, this bearded guy's talking as he always does, twisting his bearded beard and pushing up his glasses with his other hand. This guy could say all kinds of crap and everyone would believe it. He has that look, he has the bohemian look, so he has the credibility look that people appreciate in these bohemian book clubs. Does he do that when he waits, hey? Do you think he twists his beard when he waits? I'm getting visions, bad visions, visions of Molly Bloom waiting in bed, going over her immortal inner monologue and suddenly Molly doesn't look like Molly anymore. She's been waiting for so long that now she looks like this bearded guy. But, in my head Molly has this guy's face and beard, but she's taken off her glasses, of course, why would she wear glasses while waiting in bed in the dark. That'd be silly. Things happen to us while we wait. We think of crap, we think of the past, we think of the future, but rarely of the present. That's true, isn't it, Carl? You certainly were Mr Bright Side, crappy times in the crappy present never prevented you from thinking about a happy present. Some say that the problem with people today is that we live in the past, or in the future, but not in the present. That's what that twatty Charles mate of yours says, that the only people he's met who live in the present are the crazy patients he treats at work. We're all waiting for something, and living in our projection of the future, and worrying about the problems that the future's going to bring to us. And when someone lives in the present it's cos they're crazy. I guess that's why they always say that you need to have big plans for the future, so that you have something to wait for. Who was it that said it, something like *have big plans and goals, as you'll feel lost when you accomplish them and you'll have nowhere else to run.* Well, Carl, I think the way to interpret that is, *have big goals in life, aspirational targets, because once you reach them, you'll have nothing to wait for and you'll be forced to live in the present.* The present is a verb tense, not anything that you can enter willingly. I should have said that stuff out loud. It sounds more interesting that the stuff that guy and his beard are on about.'

* * *

'Waiting, waiting, that's what chapter eighteen is all about. We spend our whole lives waiting. Waiting. Molly waits for Leopold. She waits and thinks, and sometimes talks to herself. Women talk a lot, so are they always talking to themselves? Guys don't talk as much as women and they don't talk to themselves as much but they actually do cos I know so many guys that talk so much but maybe it's all a perception guys talk a lot more rubbish than girls do cos we don't pay attention and you don't realise that guys talk as much, but just a theory there. A theory here is that Molly's not as Molly as some people think, less of Bloom of more of… what was her maiden name? What was it? Well, anyway, erm… she's not that Molly anyway. Eight phrases, right? Or wrong, cos someone told me you can't start a sentence with a number but I did, I did that, no, not, didn't I, but yes, eight phrases, episode eighteen's formed of eight long phrases that she says to herself, she talks about her husband, her affairs, his affairs, and remembers stuff. And remembers how much guys liked her and how much everyone liked her and she said *no* to a lot of lovers and *yes, I will, yes* to Leopold, like Ulysses, Leopold beat his opponents, enemies, or whatever you wanna call them, the suitors was the term I think, not sure if that was the right term, but all the guys wanted to penetrate his wife. But jealousy, that's something that not many people talk about and no one in this book club's mentioning it, no, they don't say anything about it. Well, let's talk about it. What about jealousy? Molly's jealous of her daughter, cos she looks now like Molly used to when she was hot in her youth, and she's jealous of her husband cos he got a letter from their daughter while all she got was a miserable crappy card. Jealousy, that's the engine that moves today's world. And I guess it did in the nineteen hundreds. People are jealous of others with bigger cars, with hotter girlfriends, with better jobs, aspiring to do well in life is aspiring to get others jealous of your life. *If you can get a girl to be jealous of you, you can shag her!* Where did I read that? Jealousy, oh, mate, Carl, in that urn, chilling out, you were never jealous of anyone, you just got on with your life and did what you could with it, but you were never jealous. Jealousy is the beginning of unhappiness, and you were free from jealousy, that's it, that's why you were like that, you were free of unhappiness and that's why you were Mr Bright Side. I miss you.'

\* \* \*

'Can't believe that, it looked like a few minutes ago I was waiting for Kazim to bring Carl's ashes and now I already have to give them away. Oh, Jake, mate, I hope you look after them. In a funny way, I should have put a camera or a microphone inside the urn, oh, man, that'd have been funny. The kind of crazy stuff Carl's ashes must have been up to. Knowing Kazim, he'd have paid strippers to give the ashes a lap dance. Oh, Jake, what are you gonna do with our Carl? Take him out as a wingman? I can't believe Keith, bloody Keith. I thought it was a good idea to take the urn to Kings Norton Sixth Form College. Carl had met my colleagues, and it's almost the end of the term so the staff room is nice and vibrant, and people have time to talk. That day will go down in the history of the college, classically funny in the new sense of the word, I guess. I walked past the entrance like any other day. Neil and Jack doing their thing, Neil and Brack, can't believe that's what the kids call the security guys. Neil and Brack, haha, for Neil's brother, or bro! And who, who was it? Some student told me last week that they call them Neil and Weil, cos Neil's black and Jack's white, so Jack's white Neil, shortened to Weil, genius! Especially for a student who can't differentiate between *a terraced house* and *a terrorist house*. Dyslexia is not just for Christmas, as Jeff says. I love that English department, and yeah, I saw Neil and Jack, and Brack and Weil were there as well, the four of them in two bodies, and Maryam at reception, and then turning left to the North corridor. Foreign languages and English, cool departments, but putting those two together is asking for trouble. Trouble, it's all trouble in the English department, with that leader they have, Susan Maddington, Ms Mad for the kids. And she is funny, and she is cool, and she came up with it, or she suggested it to him, or Keith took the challenge, or someone else might have done it for him, but you know what, and he fucking did it, he just did it, and someone took a photo of him with Carl's urn on a table in the middle of the class, and Keith talking about death and mortality and immortality and the kids writing poems sitting in a circle around Carl's ashes. And that kid who said his religion didn't allow him to be in the same room as a dead person and Keith shouting *don't say that about my mate Carl, he is more alive now that you ever will be.* Funny how kids forget about reporting you to the principal once you bump up their marks. But they really wrote poems sitting around the ashes. Carl was the one to do this, to illuminate, that's why he was Mr Bright Side and he will always be. Looking at the bright side of life and that's him, he was like a proper bright lighthouse, illuminating those around him once again without having to wait for it. And what is all about this waiting? And *no, I don't want to end up like him,* someone wrote in a poem, I don't want to end up like, him? Mate, dead, you mean? *Bad news, son, you will end up like him*, said Keith. Hmm… maybe he was referring to being cremated, or in an urn, or in an urn in a college in a poetry class. No one wants to end up like anyone else. Carl didn't want to end up like that dead man's ice cream, melting without reaching its purpose. Although maybe he did. No, that he didn't reach his purpose, yeah, that's the thing. He did it. He reached his purpose, his purpose was to illuminate all of us around him. Give us hope and show us how to live and to embrace all you have. The good and the not so good, but not in a religious kind of way, in a way of just illuminating and being nice to others. And we felt it. Lucky to have him with us. I don't know what Carl's purpose was, no, I can't say that anymore cos I think that was it, illuminating us, he was Mr Bright Side and he did it. Oh, yes, he did it and I'm sure he met his purpose, but I'm not sure he ever knew, he did it that day in the poetry class and many times before to those who shared a bit of life with him. He illuminated people, he changed people's lives, who's going to forget they once wrote a poem about death to a person they had never met, but who was in an urn next to them? Who's going to forget that? I know I never will. The cleaner who had to clean ashes mixed with coffee from the teacher's desk won't forget either. We will not forget, but you were not a dead man's ice cream, Carl. You did what you had to do, somehow. It's anyone's own fault if they fail to see that. Failing to fail, and waiting to wait, where's Jake? I have something for you, actually, I have someone for you.'

# Jake

'Myles, a nice guy. What a pity to have to see him like this, handing out this urn, these ashes, his friend. Couldn't see it coming, I just couldn't. Carl, man, how did it happen? And you're not here now, mate, that's not right. This city loved you, and I remember, you used to live around there, with that twat Charles, who I haven't seen, but he's just a twat. And this is the road, man, this is where it all begins, after the Five Ways roundabout you hit good old Ladywood, with its working man's club, dodgy people walking around, oh, look, look mate, did you see that, two cops running after a white guy over there. This is the place, man, this is the place. And it sounds weird but there's a really good pub there, kinda fun, it's next to Paolo's laundry, you can see it in the corner, the Tall Sisters, a random Irish-Jamaican pub, but, hey, nice people in there and they serve good stout, great place, but that's the end of civilisation cos you turn here, and that's it, Spring Hill, road, road, and then you drive and wait for the hospital, and in no time, or now time, here you go, now time is now and we park here and that's it. Dudley Road Hospital, a simple name to it, but a good place to work. Interesting cases too. I was doing an A&E shift the other day and a guy walked in with a machete in his chest. Couldn't believe it, what a right mess it was. He survived, though. He was lucky. Lucky people are lucky and they don't always wait for luck. Waiting is about waiting for something to wait for and waiting is… waiting, waiting, waiting, it's all about waiting. Actually, I have to do a catheter for this old man, here, Carl, just wait for a sec. You see? Asking politely is the best way. I was polite, I said please, and now this guy's holding your urn with your ashes while I do his catheter. Sometimes it's all about being polite. And the circle of life. He's on his last legs and holding someone else's ashes. No, no, no, mate, don't drink it, there you go, just hold it, fucking hell, that could have been very messy.'

\* \* \*

'Walking and waiting, that's all one does at a hospital, walking and waiting, it's all about the waiting and less about the walking. And waiting, waiting, waiting, we spend our whole lives waiting. Waiting to be seen by a doctor, and waiting to see a patient, waiting to get better or waiting to die. That's a funny one. We're all waiting to die, but it's weird that people come to this place to do that, not all of them, just the fragile ones, the crumbly ones, you weren't crumbly, mate, you just died. Can't believe it. You were young, you didn't even have time to start waiting to die. And then you left. Well, you're still with us, or your ashes are, but man, that's about it. It's not the same, it's, it's different. Different kinda waiting. Waiting for what? What are your ashes waiting for? Now, I only have one more patient to see and then I'll return you to Kazim. And then we'll see, and the patient's waiting to be seen. And I knew it, and I told you, life's about waiting, even at the end of it, it's all about waiting. But waiting is such a modern society concept, I think. We wait for a better time to do stuff. We wait for a better time to get married, to get children, to get engaged, to break up with someone, to get divorced, there's always a better time than now. The grass will always be greener tomorrow than it is today. Well, mate, unless you forget to water it, in that case, it's just gonna get worse, and you'll be waiting for a worse time to do what you should be doing now. But that's waiting for you, Carl. Waiting kills more people than cancer and it's still not considered a disease. It's all about waiting, but waiting is about nothing, just about projections of a better present in a fake future.'

## Kazim

'Jake, a bit weird, but not a bad guy. He's a dirty fucker. I wouldn't be surprised if he'd stuck his cock in Carl's ashes. He's like that. It's not about the sex drive, it's about being dirty. Fucking hell. But fair fucks, he returned the urn, and whatever kinky shit he did while he had it well, only he, his cock, and Carl know about that. Well, Carl, you've been waiting for something, but not sure what for, but hold on, maybe I can sort that out, why not? Of course, I can, fuck it, we're going out, we're all going out, fuck it. And Myles said it's your birthday and some kind of literary shit day of Bloom's something this week and that the date's perfect but I just don't know what Myles was on about, but we're gonna do some crazy shit, and you're coming with us. A text to this guy, and to the other, and that's it, and that's pretty much it, and then wait, and it's happening, and everything you've been waiting for is gonna happen, mate, well, something is gonna happen. We're going out and celebrating your birthday this Friday, proper Friday Club, that's almost here. We're always waiting, waiting is what people do when they're alive and waste their time. We spend our whole lives waiting. They just wait for something, for better times, for better weather, for happier days, whatever it is, but they're just waiting. And then, you can wait as long as you want, but that's not the answer, is it? Just imagine, that poor bastard at Jake's hospital, waiting for a sunny day to eat his ice cream, he kept it in the fridge, and the family brought it to the hospital for him, but he wouldn't have it that day, he wanted to wait for a sunny day to eat his fucking ice cream, and his days were over before that sunny day arrived. It's England, mate! It's life, for fuck's sake, mate! And he never ate his ice cream. What good is an ice cream if you're not gonna eat it? Luckily, good old Jake was there to eat it, greedy fucker! But he did eat it, and that's not bad, actually, not a bad concept! And I remember you saying this, mate, I remember you, Carl, I remember when Jake told us, I remember it, you said that you didn't want to be a dead man's ice cream. A dead man's fucking ice cream. What a sad thought and we didn't let you and wouldn't have cos you did things! And we won't let you, Carl, we won't let you be that. You know what? We're going out, we're fucking all going out this Friday and it will be fucking perfect and we'll have the time of our lives, and you will be remembered. Fuck it you will be remembered!'

303

# Penelope

'And wait, and wait, and more waiting to do till I decide what to do with this mess, all this messy crappy thing that had to happen to me. And it's Bloomsday today and I am in bed thinking about all this. And it's that day, what a messy magical day of the sixteenth of June. Out of all the uteri and vaginas in Birmingham, it had to be me, and I always repeat to me the same, and his creepy spermy crawlies had to crawl up mine and install themselves there. Shit. And waiting to see what I do. And I'm so jealous of my lesbian friends. Not having to deal with guys in a relationship. Fucking men. Little girls grow into women and little boys grow into big boys, with a willy as a brain, ingrown misogyny, and thoughts of superiority and it's true what that woman said in the training session to all of us women, to go for it, and to believe in ourselves, and go ahead and apply for that promotion, and when thinking about it, and having self-doubts about our abilities, to ask ourselves what would a guy do, and we know, and we are used to it, and we've seen a guy apply for promotion believing he's the best thing since sliced bread, like this fucking Charles. He's a self-centred creep with no desire to do anything for others. Bastard, and I had to get pregnant. And pregnant, fucking hell, I didn't see that one coming. And I don't sleep around. I've slept with a handful of guys in my whole life. And my slutty friends who go on shagging patrol on weekends, and that tart at the bar that snogged that guy I used to like, and none of them got pregnant. But it was a kiss, just a kiss, and I ended up… pregnant. And still waiting, it's all about waiting, waiting for something, waiting for some idea, and we spend our whole lives waiting, waiting for courage, waiting for fuck's sake, what am I gonna do with this? And this apartment is not bad, but not big enough for me and a kid. And it was nice for Myles to let me move in here now that he's moved into Carl's and Charles' former house with Kazim. And poor Carl. He was here a few times. And Charles used to tell me off and he said it a few times, that I knew about Carl and that I knew he was in love with me and that I led him on to make myself feel better, and I did. And I'm guilty of it, and something should happen to me as I am guilty of taking advantage of his feelings, and they were the feelings of someone with a mental disability and I took advantage of him by playing with his feelings, and I'm guilty of it and I deserve to pay for it and what if my baby is disabled? I will have the same worries as other parents of vulnerable people. What will happen to my baby when I'm no longer here? As Carl's grandmother used to think. And it could happen again. Social welfare could miss my child. And it could happen to me as it happened to Carl's grandmother and it well could, cos everything's a circular circle that comes back and of course huh, circles are always circular and it was Amelia, or Adela, or Magdalena that put it so well when she said it's all a terrible repetition and this apartment's not that big. *Viva* this block of apartments, long live these apartments and this one is too small and not big enough for me and a baby and I feel all that Friday Club vibe is still here. I can smell the sperm from those guys in the air having their pre-hunting meetings here. Good apartment though, but fit for a kid? Not sure about that. I'm not sure about a lot of stuff, but I just need to... What was that? Someone's out. I can hear something. Someone's out. What's that noise? Someone's fucking out there? Not fucking as having sex. Someone's out there. I can hear something. Someone's out there. And there's someone outside my door. Who is it? Why is there someone outside my door?

# Dr Pope

'I should have known. I should have known this, well, I should have admitted it. I knew deep down, I kind of knew deep down that Charles was behind this. I supposed it was pretty much just towards the end when I saw it clearly, but I didn't want to admit it and it doesn't take much for a person to cling to any excuse to avoid believing something they don't want to believe, and I lied to myself and it all made sense quite early on. He moved out of his apartment and didn't tell anyone, and he did this to move in with a guy. Not any guy, a guy Charles knew about from his time in Gibraltar. He knew his condition, he knew Carl was moving to Birmingham, and I still don't know how, but he did, perhaps a former colleague from Gibraltar told Charles, and he arranged something somehow and then he planned it and he planned to become his flatmate and he did it somehow. And then Charles did it, and I never knew he was this twisted. He was weird as a kid, but kiddy kind of weird, not this kind of weird, and he committed some crimes, and used some drugs on Carl to make him internalise whatever Charles told him at night, turning them into some kind of memories. Of course, he did that. I could have seen this earlier. He'd left the army, but he had contacts and not cos he has good friends, cos he's not the kind of guy to have friends, just because making contacts and having a plan is what he does and then, the other guy got sick and his dreams became more real. I should have noticed that. Of course, I should have. I just refused to believe that my son had done that. As a parent, you tend to feel responsible for whatever your kids do, but we just can't be, and I've told patients they can't do that. The only behaviour you can control is your own, nobody else's. I should have faced the truth and I still haven't. And I lied. I told Inspector Reilly I didn't know who it was, but I lied cos I did know. I knew it was Charles because no one knew where I kept the key and no one else knew where I kept the photos and he used gloves, but I knew it was him and the report had the fingerprints of three people and yeah, Charles is my son and of course, he's been in my house and in my office and fingerprints can remain for years on surfaces, but it was him and I knew it was him as soon as I read the report and it said it as a very small side note that initially, they thought there was another set of fingerprints, but they belonged to Charles, and they only got confused because there were some cuts on the fingertips and they got confused, but they confirmed they were Charles' fingerprints and I chose to ignore that little detail and I told Inspector Reilly I didn't know anything and I didn't say that they were Charles' and that I knew because he cut himself during our lunch together and I ignored that I didn't tell Inspector Reilly and I said *no, I won't, no*. But I knew, I knew it was him and I couldn't bring myself to accuse my own son, but I knew it was him and I knew I had time, he'd killed seventeen people and had one victim left and I knew the victim would be safe until today because it was going to be today and it had to be today, Bloomsday, the sixteenth of June 2004, one hundred years since the original Bloomsday, Charles would kill his last victim and because of this, I knew I had time. I should have reported him to Inspector Reilly. I knew it was him, but I answered, *no, I won't, no* or at least that's how it sounded in my head. I knew it then, but I failed to face the truth. So, here I am. With the evidence from the case in one hand, a confession in the other, and, and I can't believe it. How could I let it go on for so long? How could I do this? Waiting, waiting, was I waiting? Waiting for something and waiting for nothing. We spend our whole lives waiting. And I was right. I was right, but I could have been wrong, and Charles could have killed someone before, but I knew he hadn't, I knew he'd wait and I know why, because of all the victims. It's a dark and weird way of acting, but things were clear when I found out about one victim, and then the other, and they all had a connection, a connection to someone with mental disabilities and they all had that same connection and they all had been reported for it, for abusing people with mental conditions and it was so weird that Charles was this kind of vigilante, killing those who had abused the mentally ill, the weak in our society, and he knew it, and he made them pay for it. It's a low thing to abuse those kinds of people, but there are other ways of dealing with it, and the next one will be me. And I've read some reports, and they'd done bad stuff, but it wasn't known, none of that was known, oh well, actually, it was known, but it was not acted upon, but Charles knew it from sessions with the abuse victims. And he didn't report it because he had a plan, and his plan was what he's done, and they'd done some bad stuff to those poor psychiatric patients, but killing them is still not right, or it was right? And I don't know, and well, I know I don't know if it's right or wrong, but I know and I think I know why waiting was okay because I know one hundred percent or I think or I'm sure I kinda think that I think I do know that I'm the last one. I'm number eighteen because Charles always blamed me for his mental state, and he always said I made him suffer by putting him in a boarding school, away from me and his mum. He didn't want to be there, and he blamed me for his detachment issues and for all his anxieties in life, and in his eyes, I was to blame for all the bad things that happened to him. He sees me as disturbing his development and causing never-ending grief and detaching him from the emotions of human interaction for the rest of his life. And I could say that I'm as guilty of those murders as my son is. Well, not sure whether to call him my son, anymore. He stopped being my son a long time ago. Maybe it was my fault. Sending him to boarding school was a mistake. He really didn't like it there and it messed him up. Boarding school survivors, they call themselves. I thought it'd be good for him, it also gave me time to dedicate to my career, but that was it. I lost my son the day I enrolled him in that school. He never forgave me for that. He never forgot that I left him there, like dogs in kennels don't forget either. I just left him there, that was when I lost my son. Time to own up to it. And time to own up to what he's done. But still, no excuse, why would he do this? As revenge on me? Just cos he can? He's not right in the head, but maybe, I'm not either for letting it go on this long. I should have stopped it. Bollocks, I should have stopped this. My dad broke into a Nazi prisoner camp with a gun and liberated his future wife, and I can't handle my own son. Waiting, it's all about waiting, about waiting to do the right thing, can't believe I'm even thinking about this, but I'm waiting to be killed today. Wednesday the sixteenth of June 2004, and he's coming for me. I know he is. Time to do the right thing. If I ring Inspector Reilly and tell him to come over, and have a confession ready on my desk, he'll be able to catch Charles before it's too late. Waiting to confess or confessing to wait, but no, it's here and it's being written as my flesh gets covered with ink in all this mess, and it's happening. Confession time it is as it's never too late they say, but it is, sometimes it is too late, but it's happening now. And it's okay, not okay, but it's done, and it's got to be okay. It's done, it's done, it's bloody done. One thing is done and Inspector Reilly is on his way here. He still doesn't know why, but he'll be here cos I've just told him, and

I have everything here. All this is here. All that is here. Waiting, waiting for Inspector Reilly to get here and people aren't the only ones to wait, things wait for us too. Waiting, waiting, life is all about waiting and we spend our whole lives waiting. Things wait for us to do them, to improve them, to break them, and to write them. I have to get on with the writing and writing and no more waiting for this confession letter. And then time, enough time, I guess, for Charles to come and kill me here, or maybe, I should do it myself and shorten his sentence. Maybe, I guess seventeen murders look better than eighteen and I can at least do something for him in my whole life. I can save him the trouble of killing his own dad if that's what he's going to do. Maybe not, but maybe he will. I can't live like this and be processed for it, not having owned up to it earlier, but there's time for a cup of tea. Tea, tea, and where's the milk? There's no milk in this fridge! But there's a box, a box here. Okay, what is it? An ice cream. Bloody secretary. Damn this, almost there. Confession letter. What a weird genre. Actually, I'll take the ice cream. I'll finish the letter. One last little pleasure before killing myself after writing the letter. The ice cream later. I'll wait to have the ice cream. I'll write the letter before finishing myself. Will I do it? I guess it's better that it's me and not Charles. Yep, I'll do it. I'll finish the letter, then the ice cream, and I'll do it. I'll write the letter first. And almost there, breathe, breathe, breathe. What! My heart, my ice cream, can't reach my ice cream. Ouch that hurt, my chest hurts, irony's the name. Too much stress, ah, a fucking joke. I have an aspirin. An aspirin stops all of this. Aspirin can save you from a heart attack they say. It's true, but only true if you have one which I have. I have one here, here, there, here it is, okay, ouch, it hurts, okay, I'll open it but not, it's true, an aspirin can save you from a heart attack, but only if you have one, and if you have an aspirin, only if you want to take it, but I won't take it. I'll wait, I'll wait, and have the ice cream after I die, and I can and cannot. I'll close my eyes, and this will happen, faster, and reduce the wait. Life's all about the waiting. Death is all about the waited for.'

## Penelope

Ah, okay, and now the person's gone. It was someone waiting for the lift. Waiting, it's about waiting, isn't it? But yeah, Charles, hah, he's out of the picture, a lot more out than previously, I just can't bring myself to share a kid with him, that can't be done. He is the kid's dad, and I can't do that, but is that even possible? It is possible cos I just don't know. And then, well, ah, he's out. And now what? Wait, just wait, and I'll be waiting till, I won't be doing that, that thing, can't get rid of the baby, but need to cut ties with that weirdo. And now what? Tomorrow, tomorrow will be another day, and the answer will wait for me then, or I'm waiting for the answer, or the answer is waiting for me? Time, time will wait to show me what to do, but tomorrow will be another day, and everything will be clearer. I'll wait till tomorrow, tomorrow wait for me!'

## Inspector Reilly

'What a way to go. What a way, and what a mess. And this note explains it all. And he was ready to sacrifice himself for his guilty son. What would a father do for a son? Anything, or most of them anyway, and he got lucky. Dr Pope, you were lucky, and you were lucky, but you never knew it. I can see what you were planning, going like that, it's not a nice way to go, but then that's the irony of life, and you were waiting for the courage to do it, and courage got fed up with waiting and did it for you, and you have to laugh about it, or laugh about it is not the right way of putting it, but yeah, it just happened. A timely heart attack before killing yourself and everything is done and sorted. And all this is a mess, not the body, the body is nice and easy, and I'll wait for the team to get here, but I can't read the whole note on the table. You spent your last minutes drafting a note, and you draft the note and you leave your ice cream next to it and it melts and it covers most of the note, and it wastes your last efforts in life, and your life's first efforts in death. You waited for too long to eat that bloody ice cream and now it has ruined your last efforts, but I could have saved you that grief. I should have told you, but I only got permission to do it a few hours ago. And I wanted to do it in person. We found victim eighteen. And it was on bloody Bloomsday. And it was in bed, and the body had soil on it, and everything fitted that bloody Gilbert's schema, but it wasn't a murder. It was a suicide. And a note. And Charles was his own victim number eighteen, and he admitted to everything and explained the things and none of this makes things right, but he was far too ill in the head to know that. And Charles found himself guilty of having abused his powers and having abused, in some ways or another, those weaker than him, and especially of having taken advantage of Carl, not treating him the way he deserved, as it is everyone's responsibility to be nice to the mentally ill and the weak ones around us and Charles found himself guilty. And he was. And Carl's heart attack was caused by the drugs Charles had given him. And still, Charles found himself guilty. Dr Pope found himself guilty as well. And they waited for the guilt to subside, but guilt is a very impatient thing. Guilt will come and get you, and waiting, it's all about the waiting. Life's all about the waiting but guilt doesn't wait.'

## Kazim

'Can't believe we're all out here. It's like a proper Friday Club. Ginger
George, Zain, Jake, Fanny, Myles, and even Alessandro's here. Boring
cunt, what can you expect from a Shitalian? Shitaly, what a mess of a
country. Pizza eating motherfuckers! Well, it's time to move on to
another place. Come on, mate, okay, sorted. We're all here. They're
closing Pub Chamber Pub, but Ritzy it is. It's fucking raining, but Ritzy
it is. Raining is rebirth as some shitty hippy once said, so Ritzy it is.
Carl, mate, you loved Ritzy! You see, we're all going there for a proper
Friday Club. Friday eighteenth of June 2004, two days after the one-
hundredth anniversary of your shitty Bloomsday, celebrating it like
fucking champions, and celebrating your birthday, of course. Happy
birthday, mate. Can't believe how much action your ashes have seen.
Granted, we might have lost a tiny bit here and there, but you're mainly
still here with us. How many memories, man! Walking through the
galleries of the Post Central complex, the BBC to our right, and that
small art gallery with blatantly overpriced crap. Not art, crap. I can shit
stuff with more artistic credibility than that. Art, *kunst* as the Germans
call it. I love that word, I love kunst, there's gonna be so much kunst
in Ritzy. Friday eighteenth of June, it's gonna be full of *kuntst* as the
uni's just finished so all the tarts will be looking for some cock before
they go home for the summer. Last wild night before going back to
their goody-goody roles with mummy and daddy, and then back here
in September. A couple of months of quiet nightclubs then. September
will come, it's just a matter of waiting for it, waiting, it's all about
waiting. September will come, with a new academic cycle and plenty of
pussy. September will come and we'll wait for it. And almost there,
mate. The usual queue to get into Ritzy at this time of night, but almost
there. We're almost there. Oh, man, your ashes are so excited I can feel
them vibrating with the music cos of the bass. I can get you in. Shit, I
need to get you in. This fucking urn's a pain to get into places, mate.
I'll get you in. I've duct-taped the lid and wrapped it in my blazer and
I have you under my arm close to my flesh, so you're sorted, mate.
You're in, you see, I told you, those are the faces on the wall that scared
the shit out of you. You're in, we're all in, except that stupid ginger
cunt. Fucking hell, he loves talking, it looks like he wants to snog the
bouncer. Dirty fucker. Drinks, drinks, we need drinks. Let's see if

Alessandro offers to buy some drinks. Tight bastard, proper Shitalian he is. I told you, I knew he wouldn't. It's a good thing Zain and Myles are into it. Yeah, man, it's gonna be good. So full of pussy in here. Talking about pussy, Jake told me he is here somewhere, but can't see him yet. But he must be around somewhere. Yeah, he's there, talking to those Chinese birds. Let's go over. Random conversation, but they look fun, can't believe that, did you hear that, Carl? Legend, the girls said they were from Korea, George asked North or South, they said they are from the South cos people in the North aren't allowed out of the country, and George responded, *Bullshit, we've just been having a beer with some North Korean guys in the smoking area. They were sound as.* And then that phrase, *By the way, they said the whole thing about the nukes is a misunderstanding. They said they'll sort that out after their holidays* and off they went, the Korean chicks are on their way to the smoking area looking for the North Korean guys. Only George can come up with that shit. Fucking brilliant, and funny though, for a lanky ginger bastard. We need to do something big, man, it's your night, Carl, and we need to do something big. Let's get the group into the mosh pit to show these kids how it's done. You taught us so much, but we waited too long to thank you for it. Fucking waiting. And now you're no longer here and your waiting is over.'

## Myles

'I guess I can't say no to Kazim, after all, he's done a lot for Carl. And he got him in here in the urn somehow. Can't believe it, after knowing Carl for so many years, I end up going out with his ashes in Birmingham. But here we are, so that's everyone in this mosh pit, right? Who's missing? No, we're all here. And shit, these kids are pushing hard, okay, now Kazim and Jake said to push harder, let's get these kids. And that's it, we're pushing back, and wow, shit, we're actually pushing these kids, haha, good fun, what song is this, can't hear it, shit, that vodka was strong, okay, yeah, what the…, it's Carl's ashes, and this is funny, hilarious, but disrespectful, shit, so random, and now Kazim gives us some of Carl's ashes to spread around the place, to spread Carl's seed, as Kazim calls it and share him with everyone. They're waiting for Carl, they're waiting for him, and here he is. It's all about the waiting and only Kazim could come up with this. Well, I know Carl loved this place. And where to put my bits of ash? Oh, yeah, I know, in that corner by the dancing pole. The only bit of action Carl got in Birmingham was there. He actually liked that girl, and it happened, and he didn't expect it would happen, he was waiting to see what might happen, it's all about the waiting, and it happened, and she got close to him, and it happened there. And there it is, and that's his spot, and I'm leaving a part of Carl there, well, he left a part of himself there, or well, that chick took a part of him, he really liked her, but he was too shy to get her number. And she took a spiritual part of him away, so here it is. I'll leave a physical part of Carl here. I can't believe I won't see him anymore and yeah, maybe there on the leather sofa cos it was there where he started groping her and she said that it was too fast, and that she didn't want him to think badly of her or to judge her and Carl did his Carl thing, with his usual sweet awkwardness replied, *I don't judge people*, and she melted and she loved that and it was genuine and lovely to see and she was all over him. And here we go, these bits of ashes are gonna stay here, and you stay there, and stay everywhere, and everywhere will stay with you, and screw the waiting for the right moment and we're all waiting and I loved waiting for things with you and your waiting will be no more as you rest, as you rest in peace. Rest in peace, man. You'll be missed and I'll miss the waiting.'

## Alessandro

'Random as usual, what the fuck am I gonna do with it? He always calls me the boring Shitalian, but he's gonna see, top this, bastard! Shit, so what I, bollocks, I've just dropped a bit of the ashes, shit, shit, what am I gonna do with this? Oh, yeah, that's right. Haha, that'll be quite funny. Yeah, of course you wanted a threesome, you never said it, Carl, but so does every single guy, it's all that porn we watch, it screws with our heads. Oh, and yes, happy birthday, *amigo*. Okay, yeah, well, you're gonna have one. This is a bit harsh, but I have to do it for you, Carl, man, I guess I'll have to do it for you but I hope they don't mind. Those cool lesbian chicks from work are here. Wow, this is bad, they're lovely girls and so sweet, I remember how they stuck up for that new intern when he was being bullied, but they're cool, they'll be fine. Where are they? They were here, they were in the sixties room somewhere, oh, yeah, sorted, they're holding hands in the corner, and that's it, and that's it, man, you're in, a bit of drunk talk with them, a *see you later* hug and then that's it, sorted, just let your ashes fall onto their legs, that's it, man, you're in, you're having a proper make out with two girls in Ritzy and then some action at home. They're hot and they're really nice girls, you lucky man. Shit, can't believe I've done that. Shit, but I had to do it for you, Carl, man, I had to do it for you, anything for you, man anything for you, many things for you, for you many, any, all my love.'

# Jake

'Oh, buddy, I can't believe you're not here, you'd love it. Everyone's here tonight, of course, it's your birthday. Happy birthday, buddy. You kept it quiet. It'd be like the good old days. You'd love this, I remember how you used to say you wanted to live life, that you didn't want to be like a dead man's ice cream, well, you weren't. You lived life and you lived it well, and it's our lucky day cos they're selling ice cream here tonight, so you won't be a dead man's ice cream, man, I'll sprinkle your ashes in the fridge. The people in here are pretty alive. I hope you appreciate the symbolism, man. I went to school with the chick behind the bar handing out the ice creams. A good way of finishing the year after uni exams, some ice cream and a bit of Carl for everyone, this should have been advertised. Carl is the essence of life, and a bit of Carl will brighten your life and help with the waiting. This'll be done in no time. Time's gone and gone's here, and no more waiting for it. Hi, yes, no, long time, sure thing, give me your number, and this and that and this whole dialogue is nice and easy and yes, now I ask her to check what ice creams they have, and sorted, I knew it, she lets me in there, I open the fridge and sorted, sprinkled a bit of Carl magic over these bad boys and I'll get that ice cream there. I could have chosen my ice cream before pouring the ashes over the fridge, but I guess that'd make me a hypocrite. If it's good for others, then it's good for me and Carl's good, and necessary, and a necessary good to enjoy and appreciate life, and I miss your energy and how much life was into you. I miss you, buddy, and your waiting is gone but your energy's here.'

# Zain

'Well, this is a tricky one, so Fanny and I have agreed on the same thing, on spreading the ashes over some hot chicks, that's a challenge, good idea, Fanny, though. Come out for a smoke as we always do, pretend we bump into each other and scatter the ashes over some hotties. It is simple, straight to the point, disrespectful towards religious and non-religious people who consider someone else's ashes as part of the body, so many things are wrong with it. So many. Wrong on so many levels, but we'll do it for you, mate, bloody Mr Bright Side, and it's your birthday, happy birthday, dude. We have to do this for you, man. And I'm not even listening to Fanny, I'm nodding, and nodding, and waiting, everything's about waiting, and waiting to wait, and waiting till sorted. All done, seen, victims chosen. Those over there. Well, sign, sign given, Fanny acknowledged it, okay, sorted, wow, we have to go for it, shit, my hands are sweaty and all the ashes are getting stuck to them, bollocks to that. Fuck, he's going, he's going for it, shit, shit, shit, wait, mate, just wait, bollocks, just wait, it's all about the waiting and wow, that was awkward, the blonde one didn't take it well, haha, how moody! With good reason though, shit, good work, Fanny, the ashes are all over the girls' tits, he got some chunky bits down her cleavage, good work, unfortunately for her, she was sitting down. Well, that was okay, we both apologised to the girls, one of them took it well, the other one didn't, wow. That was all we could do, say we were sorry, tell them we just bumped into each other and dropped our cigarette ashes over them, asked them if they were burnt from our cigarettes, and they didn't even reply and I'd have done the same, but the blonde was fuming, oh, man, glad we don't have to do this every weekend, but of course, we'd do it for you, Carl, good work, mate, you'd love it. We got you right in there, mate. Okay, just apologise once more, and sorted, and okay, Fanny, let's just go back in there.'

# Myles

'Tee tee tee TEE tee, tee tee tee TEE tee…, shit this is this is it, *Mr. Brightside*, by The Killers. This is it, it's the song, shit, Carl's song, shit, and it's your birthday, happy birthday, Carl, and where's everyone, all cool and I am… not in a cage, who's missing? Who's missing? Shit, we're all here, and… I've been fine and we're all fucking here, man, this is it, Carl, man, this is it, your fucking song and I, I… don't want everything I just want you here and we're all here, man, and you're here with us, and this is a proper Friday Club night out, man, and we're in Ritzy and… the good nights didn't start here but so many good nights finished here, and yes, we're in Ritzy, and this is a big mosh pit, man, and we're all pushing and pushing each other and I can see your urn, Kazim has it and… how have we ended up with your urn here? And it's cool, pushing though, a really cool vibe and jumping and life got messed up. And we miss you, and… I'd give you a kiss if you were here, and you'd love it here and it's such a cool vibe and now that you're gone and… it's like falling asleep forever, and you loved this song, and it was your song, and you were it, you were Mr and chicks come and go… and we've shared many taxis together, and you loved this place and you wanted to live your life and do good things and I… remember you smoking a cigarette, and you said it better than anyone else did, you just nailed it when you said it, and didn't care about anything else and you're… in an eternal bed, and you didn't want to be a dead man's ice cream and you wanted to do something, and you did, you overcame your fears and your limitations and had a normal life, despite the odds and you and now you're gone and I… am sick, cos I miss you, and you, you, you did something for us, and for everyone you met, you were nice to people, and friendly and had no fucking bullshit, and now that you're gone and… my head will always remember you, and your head was different to other people's, and we loved you for this and you were nice to everyone and you never wished any bad on anyone, and you were not worried when things turned sour… or touched sour, touched sour? And that's a lot more than a lot of people can say, and you were free of jealousy and… your chest was free of jealousy, and we miss you here, and this is it, the pre-chorus kinda thing, and it slows down as we wait to jump and… we take off as we jump for a bit now, and people wait, and… we won't let you go, and it's all about the waiting, and Ritzy is getting ready and … I look around and I can see you here and yep, mate, it's all happening, and we're all here for you… and you took control of your life despite the challenges, and yes, we are waiting, and one more second and at times, we can all see… how you were free from jealousy, and people turn bitter as they get older and they get older and less pure and you were free from all that, and we're jumping, all of us are jumping now, everyone's jumping, and to have a good time we are… swimming in our dreams with you and everyone in Ritzy is jumping, and even those creepy faces on the wall are… choking with happiness, jumping and choking, and choking and jumping, and this is the song, and this is the song, and loving and parting with a loved one is just… the price everyone pays for loving others, for everyone in this place, this is song for this place and you're gone and me, I don't know… where destiny will take me but I'll do what you did, man, and I can't believe I'm crying, and we're all crying, crying for you, Carl and I will and do my best and open… my eyes as you taught me to do, and open them up to the world of possibilities through my darkest times… cos you were Mr Bright Side, and shit, we're jumping, and crying, but happy, but crying, and I miss you, and wish you were with us, but you're with us tonight and fucking doing it… your dreams were never in a cage, and we all should do it and what's Kazim doing? He's crying, but… he's been fine, and he's walking away, we're all in the mosh pit here and he… doesn't want to feel down and he won't, and what happened to you, and what happened to you, and things happen, even though… it started having a great time together and Kazim's looking around and we're devastated you're gone and…. I still don't know how things have ended up this way, and shit, and we're all dancing but Kazim's oh now, he's jumping with us for a bit more, and shit happens and… we send kisses your way, but we didn't spend enough time together and… we only spent a bit of time together, and a short kiss, and what's happening to us? To the world? To us? To our friends? And of course, I feel tired at times but… I won't fall asleep now, and we're all falling, waiting to fall, but you've fallen and… I won't get a taxi yet and he's gone, and you're gone, but Kazim's stopped jumping and things happen outside… while he smokes, and where is he going? And where and where and what and where, but the important stuff is what happens to us here and now and… we won't be going to bed, and where is Kazim going? And he's walking away and we miss you, and having to let someone go, it does that and… my stomach is full with sadness and, and Kazim's going towards the DJ and he's got your urn in his hand and is he gonna do it? And I know, I kind of know what will happen and… I don't think this is just in my head, he's going to do it, and is he gonna do it and not wait for it? Or no, he is and it doesn't matter what could possible kinda randomly happen to us and… he is touching your urn gently and yes, he's gonna do it, and he's getting closer and Kazim grabs the urn tight against his skin, and… rubs his chest, and he's getting closer to fucking doing the unthinkable and… he starts taking off the lid and not literary but shit, no fucking way, and no, haha, legend, it's gonna happen, when shit happens you gotta… let it happen and we won't let you go and I can't look, and I can't look, and loving and letting someone or somewhere go and… I can't look, but he's doing it and yes he's doing it, Kazim is doing it and as a happy person and … he is in control, and Kazim's doing it, he's by the DJ and now he's opened the urn wide open next to the fan which spreads cold air around the dancing room and good and bad things spread equally, unfortunately and… you flew over the sea to come to us and he's shaking the urn by the fan, and he's doing it, and Carl, your ashes are coming out, and your ashes are coming out and…. your ashes are swimming through the air and being blown by the fan, and it's getting cloudy, and it was right, they were right, the newspapers were right and everyone in this room is… choking on your ashes, well, not choking choking on them but everyone's breathing them in and coughing, and your ashes are general all over Ritzy, and just as you filled our lives, you filled the lives of all the living and the dead, and loving someone and missing someone it is, it is but… a fair price to pay for loving and that we all pay, and can't ignore, and we won't be a dead man's ice cream, because I can hear it, and we can hear it, and I can hear it that… you're calling us, and you want to tell us to be happy and you want for us to be happy, all those people that just breathed you in, they just have to do it, and they all wish you a very happy birthday. You showed us the secret is simple, stop waiting to wait and tell ourselves to… open our eyes, and I and everyone will be happy, and don't be a dead man's ice cream, just open up your eyes, and you did it, and we can all do it, everyone can do it, and I can do it and… you were Mr Bright Side and you taught us that, that we are all Mr Bright Side and we can do it, and I won't be a dead man's ice cream either and… I will never forget this image of your ashes flying through Ritzy and hitting everyone's lungs with your love and… I will never surrender to the sadness and believe that I am done and… I will never believe that destiny's a weighted stone hanging from our necks, cos we can do what we want with our lives and… I will never stop breathing this Birmingham air that you filled with hope for us, and everyone's missing you, and Kazim's crying, and all your friends here are covered in tears, and can't believe I'm also crying, and we miss you, and we really miss you, and you touched everyone in this room in a way that no one has done before, pretty much as your ashes have done, and the bouncers are going towards Kazim as he shakes the urn and the last bits of your ashes hit the fan, and the air in the room is turning black and falling softly into every part of this nightclub and turning everything black, but I can only see white because you told me, you told me how to see the light, because you told me how to do it, you told me how to be, you told me how to be Mr Bright Side, and it all started when you said, *yes*, you said *yes, I will, yes*, and you stepped into that plane to take you to your new life.'

Printed in Great Britain
by Amazon